APPLE TREE YARD

APPLE TREE YARD

LOUISE DOUGHTY

SARAH CRICHTON BOOKS

FARRAR, STRAUS AND GIROUX   NEW YORK

Sarah Crichton Books
Farrar, Straus and Giroux
18 West 18th Street, New York 10011

Printed in the United States of America
Originally published in 2013 in slightly different form by
Faber and Faber Limited, Great Britain
Published in the United States by Sarah Crichton Books / Farrar, Straus and Giroux
First American edition, 2014

Library of Congress Cataloging-in-Publication Data
Doughty, Louise, 1963–
   Apple Tree Yard / Louise Doughty. — First American edition.
      pages   cm
   "Originally published in 2013 in slightly different form by Faber and Faber
Limited, Great Britain"—Title page verso.
   ISBN 978-0-374-10567-9
   1. Women geneticists—Fiction.   2. Adultery—Fiction.   3. Deception—
Fiction.   4. Psychological fiction.   I. Title.

PR6054.O795 A86 2014
823'.914—dc23

                                                                    2013034170

Designed by Abby Kagan

Farrar, Straus and Giroux books may be purchased for educational, business, or
promotional use. For information on bulk purchases, please contact the
Macmillan Corporate and Premium Sales Department at 1-800-221-7945, extension 5442,
or write to specialmarkets@macmillan.com.

www.fsgbooks.com
www.twitter.com/fsgbooks • www.facebook.com/fsgbooks

1   3   5   7   9   10   8   6   4   2

To

Everyone who walks around,

Knowing the truth to be

Different

Like the eye, the ear and the elbow, the genome shows no element of design, but is instead filled with compromise, contingency and decay.

—Steve Jones

We go through life mishearing and mis-seeing and misunderstanding so that the stories we tell ourselves will add up.

—Janet Malcolm

CONTENTS

APPLE TREE
YARD

PROLOGUE

The moment builds; it swells and builds—the moment when I realize we have lost. The young barrister, Ms. Bonnard, is on her feet in front of me: a small woman, as you probably remember, auburn hair beneath the judicial wig. Her gaze is cool, her voice light. Her black robes look chic rather than sinister. She radiates calm, believability. I have been in the witness box two days now and I am tired, really tired. Later, I will understand that Ms. Bonnard chose this time of day deliberately. She wasted quite a lot of time earlier in the afternoon, asking about my education, my marriage, my hobbies. She has been down so many different avenues that at first I am not alert to the fact that this new line of questioning has significance. The moment builds but slowly; it swells to its climax.

The clock at the back of the court reads 3:50 p.m. The air is thick. Everyone is tired, including the judge. I like the judge. He takes careful notes, raising his hand politely when he needs a witness to slow down. He blows his nose frequently, which makes him seem vulnerable. He is stern with the barristers but kindly to the jury. One of them stumbled over the words of the oath as she was sworn in and the judge smiled and nodded his head to her and said, "Do please take as long as you like, Madam." I like the jury too. It seems like an acceptable cross section to me: a slight predominance of women, three black people and six Asian, ages ranging from around twenty to midsixties. Hard to believe such an innocuous group of people might send me to prison; even harder to believe it now, while they are slumped in their seats.

None of them are in the perky, upright pose they all adopted when the trial began, faces bright, filled with the adrenaline of their own significance. Like me, they were probably surprised at first that the courtroom hours are so short, ten in the morning at the earliest, until lunchtime, finishing no later than four. But we all understand now. It's the slowness of everything—that's what's so exhausting: we are well into the trial now and weighed down by detail. They are feeling smothered. They don't understand what this young woman is driving at any more than I do.

And then, in the wood-paneled dock, behind the thick sheets of toughened glass, there is you: my co-accused. Before I took the stand, we were sitting side by side, although separated by the two dock officers seated between us. I had been advised not to glance over at you while the other witnesses were being questioned—it would make me look more like your conspirator, I was told. While I have been on the witness stand myself, you have looked at me, simply and without emotion, and your calm, almost blank stare is a comfort, for I know you are willing me to remain strong. I know that seeing me here, raised up and isolated, stared at and judged, will be making you feel protective. Your stare may not look intent to those who don't know you, but I have seen that apparently casual glance of yours on many occasions. I know what you are thinking.

There is no natural light in Courtroom Number Eight and that bothers me. In the ceiling there is an arrangement of latticed fluorescent squares and there are white tubes on the walls. It's all so sanitized and modern and stark. The wood paneling, the drop-down seats with their green cloth covers, none of it fits: the life-changing drama of why we are here versus the deadening mundanity of the procedures.

I glance around the court. The clerk, sitting one row down in front of the judge, has sagging shoulders. Susannah is in the public gallery, next to a bunch of students who came in about an hour ago and a retired couple who have been there from the start but who are, as far as I know, unconnected with our case, just theater fans who can't afford a West End show. Even Susannah, who is watching me with her usual care, even she is glancing at her watch from time to time, waiting for the end of the day. No one is expecting any major developments at this stage.

"I would like to take you back a bit, in your career," Ms. Bonnard says, "I hope you will bear with me." Throughout my examination by her, she has been scrupulously polite. This does not alter the fact that she frightens me, her unnatural composure, her air of knowing something infinitely useful that the rest of us have yet to learn. I guess her to be nearly twenty years younger than me, midthirties at the most—not that much older than my son and daughter—she must have had a stellar rise through chambers.

One of the jury, a middle-aged black man wearing a pink shirt and sitting on the far right, yawns conspicuously. I glance at the judge, whose gaze is purposeful but heavy lidded. Only my own barrister, Robert, seems alert. He is wearing a slight frown, his thick white eyebrows lowered, and he is watching Ms. Bonnard intently. Later, I wonder if he registered something at that point, some clue in her apparent lightness of tone.

"Can you just remind the court," she continues, "when was it you first attended a committee hearing at the Houses of Parliament? How long ago now?"

I should not feel relief but cannot help myself—it is an easy question. The moment has not yet started.

"Four years ago," I reply confidently.

The young woman makes a show of glancing down at her notes. "That was a House of Commons Select Committee on—"

"No," I say, "actually, it was a Standing Committee at the House of Lords." I am on sure territory here. "Standing Committees don't exist anymore, but at the time the House of Lords had four of them, each covering a different area of public life. I was appearing before the Standing Committee on Science to give evidence on developments in computer sequencing in genome mapping."

She cuts across me. "But you used to work full-time at the Beaufort Institute, didn't you, before you went freelance, I mean? The, er, Beaufort Institute for Genomic Research is its full title I believe . . ."

This non sequitur baffles me for a moment. "Yes, yes, I worked there full-time for eight years before reducing my formal hours to two days a week, a kind of consultancy role where I—"

"It's one of the most prestigious research institutes in the country, isn't it?"

"Well, along with those in Cambridge and Glasgow, in my field, I suppose, yes, I was very . . ."

"Can you just tell the court where the Beaufort Institute is located?"

"It's in Charles II Street."

"That's parallel with Pall Mall, I believe. It runs down to St. James's Square Gardens?"

"Yes."

"There are quite a lot of institutes round there, aren't there? Institutes, private clubs, research libraries . . ." She glances at the jury and gives a small smile. "Corridors of power, that sort of stuff."

"I'm not . . . I . . ."

"Forgive me, how long was it you worked for the Beaufort Institute?"

I am unable to prevent a note of irritation creeping into my voice although that is something else I have been cautioned against. "I still do. But full-time, eight years."

"Ah, yes, I'm sorry, you've said that already. And during those eight years, you commuted every day, bus and Tube?"

"Tube mostly, yes."

"You walked from Piccadilly?"

"Piccadilly Tube, usually, yes."

"And lunch hours, coffee breaks, plenty of places to eat around there? Pubs after work, et cetera?"

At this, counsel for the prosecution, Mrs. Price, gives a small exhalation and begins to lift her hand. The judge looks over his glasses at the young woman barrister and she raises the flat of her hand in response. "Forgive me, My Lord, I'm getting there, yes . . ."

My Lord. My previous experience of criminal courtrooms was limited to television drama and I had been expecting Your Honor. But this is the Old Bailey. He's a Lord—or she's a Lady. You may find the wigs and the ceremonial ways that people refer to each other strange or intimidating, I was advised. But I don't find the wigs intimidating any more than the arcane forms of address; I find them comic. What intimidates me is the bureaucracy, the stenographer clickety-clicking away—the laptops, the microphones, the thought that files are accruing on me, more and more, with every passing word—the whole great grindingness of these procedures. That is what intimidates me. It makes me feel like a field mouse caught in the giant turning blades of a combine harvester. I feel this even though I must be as well prepared as any witness. My husband saw to that. He hired a top barrister, at four hundred pounds an hour, to prepare me. I have remembered, most of the time, to look over at the jury when I give my answers rather than turning instinctively toward counsel. I have taken the advice that the easy way to remember this is to keep my feet placed so that my toes are pointing at the jury. I have kept my shoulders back, stayed calm, made good eye contact. I have, my team is all agreed, been doing very well.

The barrister has acknowledged the judge's authority and now looks back at me. "So in total, you've been working in or visiting the Borough of Westminster for, what, around twelve years? Longer?"

"Longer, probably," I say, and the moment starts building then, there, a profound sense of unease located somewhere inside me, identifiable as a slight clutching of my solar plexus. I diagnose it in myself even as I am baffled by it.

"So," she says, and her voice becomes slow, gentle, "it would be fair to say that with all that commuting and walking from the Tube and lunch hours and so on, that you are very familiar with the area?"

It is building. My breath begins to deepen. I can feel that my chest is rising and falling, imperceptibly at first, but the more I try to control myself, the more obvious it becomes. The atmosphere inside the court tightens, everyone can sense it. The judge is staring at me. Am I imagining it, or has the jury member in the pink shirt on the periphery of my vision sat up a little straighter, leaned forward in his seat? All at once, I dare not look at the jury directly. I dare not look at you, sitting in the dock.

I nod, suddenly unable to speak. I know that in a few seconds, I will start to hyperventilate. I know this even though I have never done it before.

The barrister's voice is low and sinuous. "You're familiar with the shops, the cafés . . ." Sweat prickles the nape of my neck. My scalp is shrinking. She pauses. She has noted my distress and wants me to know that I have guessed correctly: I know where she is going with this line of questioning, and she knows I know. "The small side streets . . ." She pauses again. "The back alleyways . . ."

And that is the moment. That is the moment when it all comes crashing down, and I know, and you in the dock know too, for you put your head in your hands. We both know we are about to lose everything—our marriages are over, our careers are finished, I have lost my son's and daughter's good regard, and more than that, our freedom is at stake. Everything we have worked for, everything we have tried to protect—it is all about to tumble.

I am hyperventilating openly now, breathing in great deep gulps. My defense barrister—poor Robert—is staring at me, puzzled and alarmed. The prosecution disclosed its line of attack before the trial and there was nothing unexpected in its opening statement or from the witnesses it put on the stand. But I am facing your barrister now, part of the defense team, and your defense and my defense had an agreement. What is going on? I can see Robert thinking. He looks at me and I see it in his face: there is something she hasn't told me. He has no idea what is coming, knows only that he doesn't know. It must be every barrister's nightmare, something that finds him or her unprepared.

Below the witness stand, sitting behind the tables nearest to me, the prosecution team is staring at me too, treasury counsel and the junior next to her, the woman from the Crown Prosecution Service on the table behind them, and on yet another row of tables behind that, the senior investigating officer from the Metropolitan Police, the case officer, the exhibits officer. Then over by the door there is the victim's father in his wheelchair and the family liaison officer assigned to look after him. I am as familiar with the cast of this drama as I am with my own family. Everyone is fixed on me—everyone, my love, apart from you. You are not looking at me anymore.

"You are familiar, aren't you," says Ms. Bonnard in her satin, sinuous voice, "with a small back alleyway called Apple Tree Yard?"

I close my eyes, very slowly, as if I am bringing the shutters down on the whole of my life until this moment. There is not a sound from the court, then someone from the benches in front of me shuffles his feet. The barrister is pausing for effect. She knows that I will keep my eyes closed for a moment or two: to absorb all this, to attempt to calm my ragged breathing and buy myself a few more seconds, but time has slipped from us like water through our fingers and there is none of it left, not one moment. It's over.

PART ONE

X AND Y

1

To begin where it began—really, it began twice. It began that cold March day in the Chapel of St. Mary Undercroft in the Palace of Westminster, beneath the drowned saints and the roasted saints and saints in every state of torture. It began that night, when I rose from my bed at four o'clock in the morning. I'm not a true insomniac. I have never tossed and turned night after night or spent weeks in a dreary fug of exhaustion, gray faced and careful. Once in a while I find myself suddenly and inexplicably awake—and so it was that night. My eyes sprang open, my mind sprang into consciousness. *My God*, I thought, *it happened* . . . I went over what happened, and each time I went over it, it seemed more preposterous. I rolled beneath the duvet, the motion heavy, closed my eyes, then opened them immediately, knowing that sleep would not come again for at least an hour. Self-awareness: it is one of the chief bonuses of advancing age. It is our consolation prize.

There is no clarity or insight at that hour. There is only the endless turning and churning of our thoughts, each one more confused and circuitous than the last. And so I rose.

My husband was sleeping soundly, his breathing rasping, harsh. "Men can achieve a persistent vegetative state during the night," Susannah once said to me. "It's a well-known medical condition."

And so I rose and slipped from the bed, the cold of the room frosting my skin, and took my thick fleece dressing gown from the hook on the back of the door, remembered that my slippers were in the bathroom, and pulled the door to behind me, gently, because I didn't want to wake my husband, the man I love.

There may be no clarity or insight at that hour, but there is the computer. Mine is in an attic room, with sloping ceilings at one end and glass doors leading onto a tiny ornamental balcony at the other, overlooking the garden. My husband and I have a study each. We're one of those couples. My study has a poster of the double helix on the wall and a Moroccan rug and a clay bowl for paper clips that our son made for me when he was six. In the corner is a stack of *Science* magazines as high as the top of my desk. I keep it in the corner so it won't collapse. My husband's study has a desk with a glass top and white built-in shelving and a single black-and-white photograph of a San Francisco trolley car, circa 1936, framed in beech and hung on the wall behind the computer. His work has nothing to do with trolley cars—he's an expert on genetic anomalies in mice—but he would no more have a picture of a mouse on his wall than he would have a fluffy toy on his easy chair. His computer is a blank, cordless rectangle. His pens and stationery are all kept in a small gray drawer unit beneath the desk. His reference books are in alphabetical order.

There is something satisfying about turning on a computer in the middle of the night: the low hum, the small blue light that glows in the dark, the action and atmosphere both replete with the sensation that other people are not doing this right now and that I shouldn't be doing it either. After I turned the computer on, I went over to the oil-filled radiator that stands against a wall—I'm usually the only one in the house during working hours and have my own radiator up here. I clicked the switch to low and the radiator made a clicking and pipping sound as the oil inside began to heat up. I went back to my desk and sat down on the black leather chair and opened a new document.

Dear X,

It is three o'clock in the morning, my husband is asleep downstairs, and I am in the attic room writing a letter to you—a man I have met only once and will almost certainly never meet again. I appreciate that it is a little strange to be writing a letter that will never be read, but the only person I will ever be able to talk to about you, is you.

X. It pleases me that it's actually a genetic reversal—the X chromosome, as I'm sure you know, is what denotes the female. The Y is what gives you increased hair growth around the ears as you age and you may also have a tendency toward red-green color blindness as many men do. There's something in that that is pleasing too, considering where we were earlier today. Tonight, right now, synergy is everywhere. Everything pleases me.

My field is protein sequencing, which is a habit hard to break. It spreads through the rest of your life—science is close to religion in that respect. When I began my postdoc, I saw chromosomes everywhere, in the streaks of rain down a window, paired and drifting in the disintegrating vapor trails behind an airplane.

X has so many uses, my dear X—from a triple X film to the most innocent of kisses, the mark a child makes on a birthday card. When my son was six or so, he would cover cards with X's for me, making them smaller and smaller toward the edge of the card, to squeeze them on, as if to show there could never be enough X's on a card to represent how many X's there were in the world.

You don't know my name and I have no plans to tell you, but it begins with a Y—which is another reason why I like denoting you X. I can't help feeling it would be disappointing to discover your name. Graham, perhaps? Kevin? Jim? X is better. That way, we can do anything.

At this point in the letter, I decided I needed the loo, so I stopped, left the room, returned two minutes later.

I had to break off there. I thought I heard something downstairs. My husband often gets up to use the toilet in the night—what man in his fifties doesn't? But my caution was unnecessary. If he woke and found me missing, it would not surprise him to discover me up here, at the computer. I have always been a poor sleeper. It is how I have managed to achieve so much. Some of my best papers were written at three in the morning.

He is a kindly man, my husband, large, balding. Our son and daughter are both in their late twenties. Our daughter lives in Leeds and is a scientist too, although not in my field, her speciality is hematology. My son lives in Manchester at the moment, for the music scene, he says. He writes his own songs. I think he's quite gifted—of course, I'm his mother—but he hasn't quite found his métier yet, perhaps. It's possibly a little difficult for him having a very academic sister—she's younger than him, although not by much. I managed to conceive her when he was only six months old.

But I suspect you are not interested in my domestic life, any more than I am interested in yours. I noticed the thick gold wedding ring on your finger, of course, and you noticed me noticing, and at that point we exchanged a brief look in which the rules of what we were about to do were understood. I imagine you in a comfortable suburban home like mine, your wife one of those slender, attractive women who look younger than their age, neat and efficient, probably blond. Three children, at a guess, two boys and one girl, the apple of your eye? It's all speculation, but I'm a scientist, as I've explained, it's my job to speculate. From my empirical knowledge of you I know one thing and one thing only. Sex with you is like being eaten by a wolf.

Although the heater was on low, the room had warmed up quickly and I was becoming drowsy in my padded leather chair. I had been typing for nearly an hour, editing as I went, and was heavy headed, tired of sitting upright and tired of my sardonic tone. I scanned through the letter, tightening the odd phrase here and there, noting that there were two places when I had been less than frank. The first was a minor untruth, one of those small acts of self-mythologizing where you diminish or exaggerate some detail as a form of shorthand, in order to explain yourself to someone—the aim concision rather than deceit. It was the bit where I had claimed that I write my best papers at three in the morning. I don't. It's true that I sometimes get up and work in the night, but I have never done my best work then. My best work is done at around 10:00 a.m., just after my breakfast of bitter marmalade on toast and a very large black coffee. The other place where I had been less than truthful was more serious, of course. It was where I referred to my son.

I closed the letter, titling the file *VATquery3*. Then I hid it in a folder called *LettAcc*. I spared a moment to observe myself in this act of artifice—as I had when I reapplied my lipstick in the chapel. I slumped in my chair and shut my eyes. Although it was still dark outside, I could hear a light chirrup and tweeting—the optimistic overture of the birds that stretch and flutter in the trees as dawn breaks. It was one of the reasons we moved to the suburbs, that peeping little chorus, although within a few weeks I found it irritated as much as it had once pleased me.

A one-off, that's all. No harm done. An episode. In science, we accept aberrations. It's only when aberrations keep happening that we stop and try to look for a pattern. But science is all about uncertainty, accepting anomalies. Anomalies are what create us, viz. the axiom *the exception that proves the rule.* If there was no rule, there couldn't be an exception. That's what I was trying to explain to the Select Committee earlier that day.

There was snow in the air, that's what I remember about that day, although it had yet to fall. That dense and particular chill the air seems to have just before—*the promise of snow,* I thought as I walked toward the Houses of Parliament. It was a pleasing thought because I had new boots, half boots, patent leather but with a small heel, the sort of boots a middle-aged woman wears because they make her feel less like a middle-aged woman. What else? What was it that caught your eye? I was wearing a gray jersey dress, pale and soft, with a collar. I had a fitted wool jacket on top of the dress, black with large silver buttons. My hair was freshly washed: maybe that helped. I had recently had a layered cut and put a few burnt-almond highlights in my otherwise unimpressive brown. I was feeling happy with myself, I suppose, in an ordinary kind of way.

If my description of myself at that time sounds a little smug, that's because I am—I was, I mean, until I met you and all that followed. A few weeks before, I had been propositioned by a boy half my age—more of that later—and it had done my self-confidence no end of good. I had said no, but the fantasies I had for some while afterward were still keeping me cheerful.

17

It was the third time I had appeared before a government committee and I knew the routine by then—I had been presenting to them the previous afternoon, in fact. At the entrance to Portcullis House, I pushed through the revolving doors and slung my bag onto the conveyor belt of the X-ray machine with a nod and a smile at the security man, remarking that I had worn my chunky silver bracelet on my second day to make sure I would get the free massage. I turned to be photographed for my *Unescorted Day Pass.* As the previous day, I made the arch go *beep-beep* and raised my arms so that the large woman guard could come and pat me down. As a pathologically law-abiding woman, I'm thrilled by the idea that I need to be searched: either here or at an airport, I'm always disappointed if I don't set off the alarm. The guard felt along each arm, brusquely, then turned her hands and placed them in a praying position so that she could pass the edges of them between my breasts. The male guards stood and watched, which for me made the body search more ambiguous than if they were doing it themselves.

"I like your boots," the woman guard said as she squeezed them lightly with both hands. "Bet they'll be useful." She stood, turned, and handed me my pass on its string. I slipped it over my neck, then had to bend slightly to press it against the pass reader that made the second set of glass doors swing open.

I wasn't up before the committee for another half hour—I had arrived early enough to buy a large cappuccino and seat myself beneath the fig trees in the atrium at a small round table. I scattered a crust of brown sugar across the top of my coffee, then, while I read through the notes I had taken the previous day, ate the remaining crystals by licking my forefinger and sticking it in the small paper packet. On the tables around me were MPs and their guests, civil servants, catering staff on a break, journalists, researchers, secretarial and support staff . . . Here was the day-to-day business of government, the routines, the detail, the glue that holds it all together. I was there to help a committee pronounce on recommended limitations to cloning technology—most people still think that's what genetics is, as if there is nothing more to it than breeding experiments, how many identical sheep we can make, or identical mice, or plants. Endless wheat crops; square tomatoes; pigs that will never get sick or make us sick either—it's the same unsubtle debates we've been having for years. It was three years since my first presentation to a committee, but I knew when I was asked to appear again this time I would be rehearsing exactly the same arguments.

What I'm trying to say is, I was in a good mood that day, but other than that, it was really ordinary.

But it wasn't ordinary, was it? I sat there, sipping my coffee, tucking my hair behind my ear when I looked down at my notes, and all that time, I was unaware that I was being watched by you.

Later, you described this moment in great detail, from your point of view. At one point, apparently, I looked up and gazed around, as if someone had spoken my name, before returning to my notes. You wondered why I did that. A few minutes later, I scratched my right leg. Then I rubbed at the underside of my nose with the backs of my fingers, before picking up the paper napkin on the table next to my coffee and blowing my nose. All this you observed from your table a few feet away, safe in the knowledge that I wouldn't recognize you if I looked your way, because I didn't know you.

At 10:48 a.m., I closed my folder but didn't bother putting it back in my bag, so you knew I was on my way to a committee or meeting room nearby. Before I stood up, I folded my paper napkin and put it and the spoon into my coffee cup, a neat sort of person, you thought. I rose from my chair and smoothed my dress down, back and front, with a swift brushing sort of gesture. I ran my fingers through my hair, either side of my face. I shouldered my bag and picked up the file. As I walked away from the table, I glanced back, just to check I hadn't left anything behind. Later, you tell me that this is how you guessed I had children. Children are always leaving things behind, and once you have developed the habit of checking a table before you walk away, it's hard to break, even when yours have grown up and left home. You didn't guess how old my children were, though, you got that wrong. You assumed I had had them late, once my career was established, as opposed to early, before it got under way.

I strode away from the café table confidently, according to you, a woman who was on her way somewhere. You had the opportunity to watch me as I walked all the way across the wide, airy atrium and up the open staircase to the committee rooms. My stride was purposeful, my head up, I didn't look about me as I walked. I seemed to have no sense I might be being observed, and you found this attractive, you said, because it made me seem both confident and a little naïve.

Was there any inkling, for me, that day, as I sipped my coffee? You wanted to know that later, egged me on to say that I had sensed your presence, wanting me to have been aware of you. No, not in the café, I said, not a clue on my part. I was thinking about the easiest way to explain to a committee of laypeople why so many of our genes are non-functioning as opposed to protein coding. I was thinking about the best way to explain how little we know.

Not a hint? None at all? You were a little hurt, or pretended to be. How could I not have sensed you? No, not there, I would say, but perhaps, maybe, I wasn't sure, I felt something in the committee room.

My presentation had gone according to plan and it was close to the end of my morning. I had just completed an answer to a question about the rapidity of developments in cloning technology—they are public, and reported, these inquiry committees, so they have to ask the questions that represent the public's concerns. There was a brief hiatus while Madam Chair asked to check her papers to make sure she had got the question order right. One of the MPs to her right—his name was Christopher something, the plastic plaque in front of him said—had been gesturing in frustration. I waited patiently. I poured a little more water into my glass from the jug in front of me, took a sip. And as I did, I became aware of an odd sensation, a prickle of tension in my shoulders and neck. I felt as though there was someone extra in the room, behind me—as if, all at once, the air was full. When Madam Chair looked up at me again, I saw her glance past me, at the row of chairs behind me. Then she returned to her papers, looking up again to say, "I beg your pardon, Professor, I'll be right with you." She leaned over to the clerk sitting on her left. I've never had a professorship in a British university—the only time I have ever had that title was when I was teaching in America for a year while my husband was part of the USC Research Exchange Plan in Boston. She should have called me "Doctor."

I turned. In the seats behind me, in two rows, were the MPs' researchers with their notebooks and clipboards, the helpers, those there to learn something that might help them up the career ladder. Then, out of the periphery of my vision, I saw that the entrance door in the corner of the room was—softly, noiselessly—closing. Someone had just left the room.

"Thank you for your patience, everyone," said Madam Chair, and I turned back to face the committee. "Christopher, I beg your pardon, you *were* listed number six, but I have a hand-annotated early draft and misread my writing."

Christopher whoever-he-was sniffed, hunched forward in his chair, and began to ask his question in a voice loud enough to betray his ignorance of basic genetics.

The committee broke for lunch about twenty minutes later. I had been asked to attend after the break, although we had covered the bulk of my territory. They were only playing it safe so they didn't run the risk of recalling me later in the week and paying for another day of my expenses. The clerks and researchers headed out of the door as I stood and put my papers away. Several of the MPs had made for the Members' exit and the rest of the committee was conferring softly. The sole reporter on the press bench was making a few notes on her notepad.

The corridor outside was busy—all the committees seemed to have broken early for lunch—and I stood for a moment wondering whether to go down to the atrium café or to leave the building altogether. *Fresh air would be good*, I thought. Eating in the same café as members and their guests had long since lost its novelty value. While I hesitated, the corridor cleared a little, and on one of the benches opposite, there was a man. He was seated and talking quietly into a mobile phone but looking at me. When he saw I had noticed him, he spoke briefly into the phone, then slipped it into his pocket. He kept looking at me as he rose to his feet. If we had met before, the look might have said, *Oh, it's you.* But we hadn't met before and so it said something entirely other—but still with an element of recognition. I looked right back, and all was decided in that instant, although I didn't understand that for a very long time.

21

I half smiled, turned to walk down the corridor, and the man fell in step beside me, saying, "You were very articulate in there. You're good at explaining complex subjects. A lot of scientists can't do that."

"I've done a lot of lecturing," I replied, "and I've had to give quite a few representations to funding bodies over the years. You can't risk making them feel stupid."

"No, I daresay that wouldn't be a good idea . . ."

I don't know it yet, but the man is you.

We were walking alongside each other, as if we were friends or colleagues, and the conversation between us was so easy, so natural—a passerby would have assumed we had known each other for years—and at the same time, my breath was slightly short and I felt as if I had shed a layer of skin, as if something, simply the years perhaps, or normal reserve, had dropped away. *Good Lord*, I thought, *this hasn't happened to me in years.*

"Do you get nervous before giving evidence?" You continued to talk to me quite normally, and I followed your direction.

We descended the stairs to the ground level and, without either of us particularly leading the way, or so I thought, we walked across the atrium to the top of the escalator going down to the tunnel through to the main building of the Houses of Parliament. It was a narrow escalator, too narrow to allow us to stand side by side, and you gestured for me to step onto it first. I had the opportunity to look at you, to observe your large brown eyes and direct gaze, steel-rimmed glasses, retro-ish or perhaps just old-fashioned, I couldn't decide which, wiry brown hair with a slight wave, a little gray. I guessed you to be a few years younger than me but not much. You were a head taller than me, but then most people are. As I was on the step below you on the escalator, you were a lot taller at that point. You smiled down at me as if you were acknowledging the essential silliness of this. When we reached the bottom, you fell into step next to me with one sure stride. You weren't notably good-looking, but there was something about the way you moved, a sleekness and confidence. You were wearing a dark suit that looked, to my inexpert eye, expensive. Yes, it was something about the way you held yourself that was attractive, a kind of male grace. Your movements were relaxed, you seemed at ease with yourself—I could imagine you holding your own on a tennis court. I was pretty sure you weren't an MP.

"So do you? Get nervous, I mean?"

It was only as you repeated the question that I realized there had been a silence between us as we descended. "No," I said. "Not with this lot. I know a lot more than they do."

"Yes, I expect you do." You acknowledged my expertise with a slight nod.

We walked in silence along the tunnel, past the stone lion and unicorn on either side, until we reached the colonnade. It was the strangest thing. We were walking, people were passing, we were relaxed together in a quite familiar manner—still we had not introduced ourselves. No names, no normality—this was the way you knew, I see now. We were skipping stages, establishing that the usual rules did not and would not apply to us. All this I realized only in retrospect, of course.

As we entered the part of the colonnade that is exposed to the open air of New Palace Yard, I shuddered and crossed my arms. It seemed natural to turn left and step through the Great North Door into the Great Hall. It was full, this lunch hour—school parties, students, milling tourists. We were in the public part of the Parliamentary Estate. To our left as we walked across the vast stone hall were the queues of visitors behind ropes, waiting for access to the galleries of the Houses: a group of elderly women, two men in plastic macs, a young couple standing very close together facing each other with their hands tucked into the back pockets of each other's jeans.

At the far end of the hall, we stopped. I looked behind, at the doorway that led back outside, the white air framed like a picture. How many times in a life does a person get to feel an instant attraction for someone one has just met, the eyes locking, the sudden and overwhelming conviction that this is someone he or she is meant to know? Three, four times, maybe? For many people, it happens only as they go up the ascending escalator at a railway station or in a department store while someone else goes down the descending escalator on the other side. Some people never get to experience it at all.

I turned back to you and you looked at me again. That's all.

You paused briefly, then said, "Have you seen the chapel in the crypt?" Your tone was light, conversational.

I gave a small shake of the head.

"Would you like to?"

I was on the edge of a cliff. I know that now.

"Sure," I said conversationally, mimicking your tone. Mirroring, it's called. We do it all the time.

You bent your head slightly toward me. "Come with me," you said. As you turned, you placed one hand on my elbow, the most delicate of touches through my jacket, steering me, while hardly making contact. Even after you took your hand away, I felt the imprint of your fingers there. Together, we mounted the wide stone steps at the far end of the Hall. At the top of them, beneath the stained-glass glory of the Memorial Window, was a security guard, a stout woman with curly hair and glasses. I hung back as you approached her. You stooped to speak to her. I couldn't hear what you said, but it was clear that you were joking with her, knew her quite well.

As you walked back to me, you held up a key attached to a black plastic rectangle. "Remind me to give it back to Martha or I will be in a lot of trouble," you said.

We turned. I followed you down a smaller set of stone steps and through some black iron railings to a heavy wooden door. You opened it with the key. We stepped inside. It closed behind us with a solid *thunk*. We were at the top of another set of stone steps, quite narrow this time, which led down a twisting stairwell. You went first. At the bottom of the stairwell was another heavy door.

The Crypt Chapel is small and ornate, its arches bending over like low-hanging tree branches, its ceiling covered with golden tracery. There are wrought-iron railings in intricate patterns in front of the altar and a decorated baptistery with a font—members are allowed to baptize their children here, you tell me, or get married. You are not sure about funerals. The walls and floor of the chapel are tiled, the columns marbled, it seems like a heavily decorated but secret place—perhaps because it is a church underground: hidden worship.

I walk down the aisle and, as I do, the emptiness of the place dispels any sense of consecration. There are no pews, just rows of stackable chairs. It feels disused. My footsteps echo. The whole point of a church is that anyone can wander in at any time—this is kept locked and opened up for members only. You follow me down the aisle, slowly, at a distance, the soles of your shoes a soft tread. I hear the contrast with my own sharp heels. Although I have my back to you, you carry on talking to me about the chapel, how its real name is the Chapel of St. Mary Undercroft but everyone calls it the Crypt Chapel. Its walls were plastered over for many centuries but in the fire of 1834, the plaster fell off and the riches of the chapel's decoration were revealed, not least the large, carved bosses showing scenes of martyrdom. And there, above us—I still have my back to you but you invite me to look up— one saint roasted, another drowned . . . St. Stephen, St. Margaret, you say. You point out the pagan gargoyles. *Barbarism*, I think, *medieval barbarism.* I remember the holiday my husband and I once took to northern Spain, where every small town seemed to remember the Inquisition with its own, often graphic, museum of torture. Marble, stonework, elaborate tiles, Latin inscriptions, all that High Church ritual—no, I don't feel any shred of spiritual contemplation here, just a mild intellectual curiosity and—what *is* that, I wonder, as I spin slowly round on one heel . . . I realize, as I turn, that I am doing it because there is silence. I am turning because you are not talking anymore; there are no more shuffling sounds on the flagstones. I cannot even hear you breathe.

You have not evaporated. You have not disappeared, or secreted yourself behind a pillar or in the baptistery. You are standing still, and you are looking at me.

I look back at you and I know, without either of us saying anything, that this is the point where the moment will slide.

Your shoes, the sound of the soles of your shoes, moves, echoes, approaches me. As you reach me, you lift one hand slightly and it is completely natural to lift my hand in return. You take my hand in yours.

Your grip claims me. You lead me back down the aisle, to the back of the chapel. "There's something I want to show you."

We step behind a screen and there is another heavy wooden door, narrow and very tall this time, in an arch shape.

"Go in first, it's a bit tight in there," you say.

I open the door—with some effort, it's very heavy. Behind it is a tiny room with a very high ceiling. Immediately in front of me is a bright blue metal cabinet, like a filing cabinet but with a variety of electrical buttons and lights. Next to it, leaning against the wall, is a dirty mop standing on its handle and a set of metal stepladders. To the left, the thick ropes of dozens of rubber-coated electrical supply cables stretch above, disappearing into the ceiling. "It used to be a broom cupboard," you say as you step in behind me.

The room is so small, you have to press against me so that we can close the door.

"There," you say.

On the back of the door, there is a small black-and-white photograph of a woman, and beneath it, a brass plaque. Emily Wilding Davison. I am standing facing the plaque, looking at it with my back to you. You are directly behind me, very close, so close that I feel you even though you are not touching me—what I mean is, I can feel that you are only just not touching me. You bring one hand over my shoulder and point at the plaque. Your breath stirs my hair as you speak.

"She hid here on the night of the census, 1911," you say, and without turning I say quickly, "Yes I know this story," even though I can't remember the details. It's a suffragette story; it belongs to me, not you. Emily Wilding Davison threw herself beneath the hooves of the king's horse during the Epsom Derby. She died so that women like me, who live in this country in the early part of the twenty-first century, could take things for granted: that we vote, we work, expect our husbands to unload the dishwasher. We don't have to give our husbands everything we own when we marry them. We don't even have to marry them if we don't want to. We can sleep with whomever we like—within the limits of our own personal morality, of course—just like men do. No one takes us to the village square and stones us anymore, or places metal torture devices in our mouths for talking too much, or drowns us in a pond because a man we rejected has accused us of being a witch. We are safe, surely, now, in this time, in this country, we are safe.

As I turn toward you, your hands go to either side of my head, your fingers in my hair, and I lift my hands and place them lightly on your upper arms as you tip my head back gently, closing my eyes.

We kiss—your mouth soft, full, all the things that mouths should be—and I realize I knew this would happen from the minute I set eyes on you in the corridor outside the committee room, it was just a question of how and when. You step forward and lean against me so that I am pressed against the back of the door. The slow compression of my body by yours: it squeezes the breath from me and I am returned, for the first time since my twenties, to the wild dizziness you feel when a kiss is tender yet so inexorable that you can hardly breathe. *I can't believe I am kissing a total stranger,* I think, and know that my disbelief is half the thrill. It won't be me who breaks it off—I will keep on doing it until you stop, because it's completely absorbing, this sensation: silent, eyes closed, all my senses concentrated on the grazing of our tongues. I am nothing but mouth.

Then, after a long while, you do something that will endear you to me when I think about it later. You pause. You stop kissing me, withdraw your face, and as I open my eyes I see you are looking into mine. You still have one hand in my hair, your fingers entwined. The other hand is resting on my waist, and you are smiling. Neither of us speaks but I know what you are doing. You are looking into my face as a way of checking that this is all right. I smile back.

I still don't know who was responsible for what happened next. Was it you, me, or both of us at the same time? My hands move down—or did you push them down?—to where the thick leather of your belt is held by its buckle. I try to extract the belt, but my fingers tremble and the leather is stiff and unyielding, refusing to budge from its clasp. You have to help me. There is another clumsy moment when you tug at my neckline. I am still wearing my jacket and you haven't realized that underneath it is not a skirt and blouse but a dress. You stop and remove your glasses, dropping them into your jacket pocket, and as you do, I bend and unzip one of my boots and slip it off. Then, bending again, awkwardly because I am still wearing the other boot with its small

27

heel, I slip one leg out of my tights and knickers. When you enter me, the feel of skin against skin is delicate electricity, like the static you get from freshly laundered clothes. The only naked part of us, the only point where my flesh is in contact with yours, is inside me. We say nothing.

Even now, the memory of this moment has the power to freeze me, midtask, whatever that task may be, and make me stare into the middle distance, still astonished at how easy, how natural it was, how something that had always seemed so freighted with taboo or convention could happen at the mere slipping of the physical impediments from our bodies. One minute we are kissing, and that in itself seems extraordinary, the next we are having sex.

I don't come. I am too bewildered. I suppose I enjoy it, but "enjoy" isn't the right word. What I feel is the same breathless excitement I imagine people feel when they are on fairground rides, where it is possible to take pleasure in the fear because the danger is illusory; however scared you are, you are safe. I go with you. I follow you. I am scared as hell but I feel completely safe. It has never been like this before.

Afterward, we stand for a while. You are still pressed against me. I become aware that we are both listening. How many keys are there to the chapel, I wonder? We are listening for the sound of footsteps on a tiled floor, or voices. It is silent. Simultaneously, we both give a brief exhalation, somewhere between a cough and a snort of amusement. It expels you from me. You stand back, pressing yourself backward in the tiny space, put one hand in your pocket and recover your glasses, then hand me a cotton handkerchief. You smile at me and I smile back in acknowledgment, put the handkerchief between my legs as you button yourself up.

You have to leave the tiny room first. I pick up my boot and follow you. I make my way across the chapel floor, disheveled and hobbling, my tights and knickers round one ankle, one boot in my hand, a cotton handkerchief jammed between my legs. You fetch one of the chairs for me and sit me down, like a paramedic seating a road crash victim. You step back, regarding me with amusement, your eyebrows raised, and I half stand, dropping the boot to the floor so that I can use both hands to pull my knickers and tights back up, scrabbling a little because the leg of my tights that came off was pulled inside out, and now, of course, I feel ridiculous and am reminded how in all first encounters, the undressing is heated and enticing but the getting dressed again after is usually an embarrassment. It's so many years since I've had a first encounter, I had completely forgotten this.

When I have sat back down again, you kneel at my feet, on one knee, and pick up the boot from the floor—I have a flushed and momentary thought that the tights I am wearing that day are not new—then you slip the boot over my foot, zip it up for me, look up at me with a smile, still clutching my calf in both hands, and say, "It fits!"

I smile back, place one hand on your cheek. I love the fact that you are taking charge because I am trembling now. You have noticed this and I can see from the smile on your face that you like it. You reach up with one hand and place it on the back of my head and pull my face down toward you for a long kiss. It makes my neck ache after a moment but I like it because you are kissing me as though you still mean it and we both know that is unnecessary now.

Afterward, you pull back and say, "We'd better get that key back to Martha."

I look around for my handbag and realize it must still be in the room—I don't even remember putting it down. "My bag," I say, gesturing. You fetch it for me, then stand over me watching as I fumble in it. "Wait a minute," I say.

I am looking for my makeup bag. I don't have a powder compact but the very old eye shadow in there, which I never use, has a tiny mirror in the lid. I hold it up in front of me, examine my face in minute circles, as if I am looking for a clue as to what sort of person I am. I find my lipstick and apply it lightly, rubbing my lips together. *To emerge from the crypt with lipstick reapplied too heavily would be a bit obvious,* I think, and am surprised at this insight. Anyone would think I do this all the time.

When I stand up, my legs are still shaking. All the while, you have been watching me with that wry expression on your face, as if it amuses you to have so discomfited me, to observe how effortful it is for me to recompose myself into the self that feels able to face the outside world.

You check your watch. "Time for a quick coffee?" you ask, but the tone in which you say this suggests to me that you are saying it to be polite. I have the presence of mind—and later I congratulate myself on this—to say, "Actually I have a couple of errands to do outside the building and then I'm giving evidence again this afternoon," and you pull a face of mock disappointment, but then something buzzes in your pocket and you extract a phone, turn away from me, check the screen, press a few buttons . . . When you turn back, I can tell that for you this encounter is over. The message you just received has made you think of the next thing to be done.

As we walk toward the door, our footsteps loud and purposeful now, the sounds of two people exiting, I say, "Hold on a second." You are slightly ahead of me, and I can see that the back of your jacket is creased. I brush it down sharply with one hand, two deft, swift strokes. You glance over your shoulder as I do this, give a half smile. "Thanks," you say, but it is a distracted thanks. You hold the door open as you leave. I walk through it but then step back, to allow you to go up the stairs ahead of me. I need you to emerge into the world first, so I can copy your nonchalance, watch you as you return the key to Martha, then bid you goodbye and turn on my heel. As we climb the stairs, I note that your jacket is still crumpled and think how next time I see a man with a slightly crumpled suit jacket I will be reminded of today and wonder what he has been up to. As it is, the next time I see that same expensive gray suit is in the dock of Courtroom Number Eight at the Central Criminal Court, Old Bailey, EC4.

2

The next morning, I am sitting at the kitchen table, reading the free local newspaper that comes through our door once a week, when my husband lumbers in. He is also a slow starter in the morning; neither of us likes to talk. These are the commonalities that glue a long marriage—it isn't whether you are each other's soul mate or intellectual equal: it's whether you are both happy with no more than an exchange of grunts over breakfast.

He is already dressed. It's an early start for him that morning, and I am grateful for that because my head is still full of the Crypt Chapel and the sleepless night that followed and I want to be alone to do a little gentle musing, convince myself how normal I still am. My husband blunders gently to the kettle and makes himself a mug of tea, murmuring, "Want a refill?" I shake my head. He takes his tea upstairs. The floorboards creak on our first floor and I hear him walking around his study, directly above the kitchen. Then I hear him using the electric toothbrush in the bathroom next door to the study. I know that when I go upstairs I will find the cup of tea on his desk or by the soap dish on the sink, cooling and untouched. Ten minutes later, he walks down the stairs, comes back into the kitchen, walks over to me, bends his head. I lift mine in return and he gives me an absent, dry-lipped kiss goodbye. He goes out into the hall, comes back in again. "Did I give you the car keys?"

I look at him and say, "Brown coat."

"Ah," he says, reminded of what he was wearing when he came

home the previous day. My husband isn't as absentminded as this makes him sound: contrary to popular mythology, scientists are rarely scatterbrained individuals with wild eyes and sticky-up hair. The reason he ambles into the kitchen and asks for his car keys is not that he is incapable of locating them himself; it is to remind me that after many years of marriage, he still loves me. And I tell him where they are in order to remind him that I still love him back.

One of the nicest things about being self-employed is the silence in the house that follows the echo of the front-door slam.

I give an unwarranted sigh and take my phone out of my dressing-gown pocket—putting clothes on will be an optional extra this morning. I google "sexual health clinic private." I have no intention of going to my local clinic, wherever it is, and sitting in a waiting room for two hours with a dozen sobbing teenagers.

I make the appointment. In my head I run through the list of everything I should get checked, beginning with thrush, through syphilis, gonorrhea, etc., and ending with HIV, although the HIV test will tell me only whether I was HIV positive before yesterday and if I want to be sure I will have to be tested again in twelve weeks' time. I know I won't get myself tested again. In twelve weeks, it will be forgotten, done with. Chances are, even this first appointment is unnecessary. The only reason I am getting myself checked is so that I can congratulate myself on how rational I am. At least I don't have to worry about pregnancy— three years ago I slid through the menopause, no hot flashes, no drama, my periods just got gradually lighter, then stopped. I don't have to worry about my husband's sexual health either. He and I have not had sex for nearly three years. I have made the appointment for ten days' time in order to see if I have any symptoms developing before I go. There is every possibility I will cancel it.

I pour away the dregs of tea, put the mug in the dishwasher, get a cup and the small cafetière out of the cupboard, and go to the fridge for the coffee. While the kettle grumbles, I lean against the kitchen countertop and send my husband a text reminding him to check the tax disc on his car, as I'm going to get a new one for my car this morning anyway. We worry about each other's cars since the children left home. At least we haven't resorted to cats.

It takes me three days to feel used. *Not bad*, I think. *Not bad at all.* A certain degree of plaintiveness kicks in only because I have to go up to Westminster on the Friday, not to the Houses of Parliament but to meet a colleague from the Beaufort Institute for breakfast. I normally do only Mondays and Tuesdays in the office—I'm what's called an honorary associate principal, which, strange to think it, means they believe it improves the status of the institute to have my name and photograph on the front inside page of their brochure. I have asked my colleague, a dull man called Marc, to meet me outside the premises. If I go into the office, I won't get out for the rest of the day.

Going back to the Westminster area reminds me that I have not been summoned back—by you, I mean, not wanted or bidden, not even inquired after.

Marc is a human resources manager, which means he has had his sense of humor surgically removed. He wants to discuss the possibility of my covering a colleague's maternity leave. I gave up working for the Beaufort full-time because I couldn't stand the daily commute anymore. The thought of doing it again for six months makes me want to thump my forehead on the edge of the restaurant table while he talks me through the terms and conditions.

Emerging from my breakfast meeting, I think I should go straight home and tackle the slithering pile of invoicing on the side of my desk. Instead, I decide that as there is a little weak late-winter sun and it's a Friday, I may as well wander up to the Houses of Parliament. When I get there, I skirt Parliament Square and take a walk over Westminster Bridge and pause to lean back against the stone balustrade and watch the tourists holding their iPads up to Big Ben. A man at the far end of the bridge is playing the bagpipes. Seagulls shriek accompaniment. When I am bored of watching the tourists, I turn my back on them and stare down at the river. I think of you kneeling at my feet, slipping my boot on. I remember placing my hand on your cheek and your smile at the tenderness of the gesture. I want it to happen again, even though I'm still not sure what it was, and I realize that all my rationales, my clinic appointment, my grown-upness about the whole thing, is a sham. I can't stop thinking about you, about the pressure of your body against me, slowly squeezing the breath from me as we kissed against the back of that door. My head has been spinning all week.

Fool, I think. You will never see him again, get used to the idea. Process it. If you had turned him down in the chapel, he would have demanded your name and phone number and be pursuing you like a heat-seeking missile all week, but you didn't, did you? You went along with it. He will have hardly given you a passing thought.

I'm only guessing, of course. I don't know anything about casual sex. All my life, sex has been the start of something. Animals don't have casual sex because they understand only the biological imperative— although arguably, this makes all their sex casual, if you're going to be anthropomorphic about it. The human desire for casual sex is an interesting experiment in the collision between gratification and genetic self-interest. You think too much, my first boyfriend was fond of saying to me, that's your problem. He was a sexist bastard—probably still is.

I watch the gray water of the Thames slip below Westminster Bridge, flowing soundlessly, endlessly, to the sea. Animals no more think about the rationale behind mating than water does about its desire to flow downstream. A group of tourists next to me are shouting, gleefully, in Spanish. *Daft git*, speaks a small, amused voice in my head. You've been used, what did you expect? A bunch of flowers afterward? Chalk it up to experience.

I am being so grown-up about it, handling it so well, so rationally, that I leave the river to the tourists, cross Bridge Street, and walk to the entrance of Portcullis House, even though I have no business there that day, and push through the first set of revolving glass doors and linger until I see a security guard I recognize—the large woman who frisked me on Tuesday. I am wearing the same boots. She smiles at me and I shake my head. "I'm not due in today. I'm just wondering, did anyone hand in a scarf on Tuesday?"

She leans on the X-ray machine. She's bored, there's no queue, she's happy to make conversation. "What does it look like?"

I think of my new wool scarf, the one sitting neatly folded on the top shelf in our cloakroom. "It's gray, with a white thread running through it." While I say this, I look through the glass screens at the atrium café and the curved staircase leading up to the committee rooms, as if there was the remotest chance you might be wandering past at that moment.

She scratches her ear and wrinkles her nose. "If you'd left it here it would have gone to the office anyway, but I don't remember it. You can send them an e-mail. I'd do a note but it would take about ten days to get through the internal system anyway."

"Okay, thanks,"

I go back out into the cold. The weak sun is no match for the icy breeze blowing off the river, but I stand on the steps for several minutes, looking around as if I might be waiting for someone. *God, you're pathetic*, I think.

It's Friday. No self-employed person gets any work done on a Friday, although we pretend that we do. I decide to walk up to Piccadilly. Maybe I'll go to a bookshop, or the Royal Academy. Maybe I will just go home to the suburbs, where I belong.

I turn into Parliament Square from Bridge Street and walk past the front of the Houses of Parliament, where more tourists take it in turns to pose beside the unsmiling armed policemen at the Members' Entrance and the antiwar protesters stand in front of their tents on the other side of the road. A few steps from here is where I exited on Tuesday, my legs still trembling, to walk around for a few minutes in the cold air before going back to the Portcullis House entrance for the afternoon's session. I am reliving the aftermath. I walk up past the ugly block of the Queen Elizabeth II Conference Centre and up Storey's Gate. I decide to cross Birdcage Walk and skirt the edge of St. James's Park, a park that always looks different to me each time I walk through it. This time I notice the swans, the Hansel & Gretel house, the tumescent fountain—Lord, how obvious. I try not to feel wistful—I don't deserve to, after all. I try to enjoy being a tourist in my own town. I think how seldom I do this, wander a bit: my life is normally a cacophony of deadlines. After crossing the Mall, I mount the steps up to Carlton House Terrace and turn left down Pall Mall to cut through St. James's Square. I could sit in the square for a while, but it's cold, and too close to my office. I walk up Duke of York Street, looking for a café—I'm quite close to Piccadilly. Now I am away from the immediate environs of the Houses of Parliament, I can stop for a coffee without feeling as though

I am stalking you, lingering somewhere close to where you might be. I will sit somewhere and pretend I am checking my e-mails on my phone while I watch other people and assess their levels of purposefulness relevant to mine. I will do that until I can't kid myself anymore, then I will go home.

Halfway up on the left, there is a small Italian place with waitress service and a round table in a bay window, perfect for my purposes. An old-fashioned bell gives a clunky ring as I push the door open. It is warm inside. There is no music playing. Someone has even left a folded newspaper on the table for me.

I sit and wonder what I would do if I saw you stride past the window. I could hardly run out of the café and call your name. I don't know your name.

Why me? That is what I really want to know. Why me?

While I am lost in this internal and enjoyably pointless dialogue—an undistressed dialogue, I must say, I'm still being very rational about the whole thing—a woman outside the café window has paused to have an altercation with the driver of a green van that is parked by the curb. The woman is saying something sharp and the van driver is sitting back in his seat with his large, heavy arm hanging out of the window. He is smoking and looking straight ahead and, from the movement of his lips, swearing viciously at the woman.

He must do this all the time, I think, and by him I mean you, of course, not the van driver. I am thinking of your quiet confidence, the slow prowl of your movements, the lack of anxiety or haste on your part. You knew exactly what you were doing. I wonder how often you do it. I wonder if it's a game—do you try and nail one a week, perhaps? I think of all those MPs' offices, the endless corridors, cloakrooms, toilets, cubbyholes. Perhaps—and this one, for all my attempts to be grown up, makes me shudder—you are a member of some sort of website club, where you all compete to see who can lay claim to the most absurd or unlikely encounter: the middle of the day in the heart of the oldest democracy in the world, that must score quite highly. The thing is, and this is only vanity—or optimism—on my part, I do have a feeling that you operate with a certain degree of discrimination. I don't think you go dogging in supermarket car parks in Essex. The slow grace, the politeness with which you operated, even as you opened up a woman you had never met before: there was nothing rough or sordid about what you did. You looked into my eyes, you kissed me afterward, you knelt at my feet as you slipped on my boot. You are a promiscuous man who likes risky sex with strange women in unusual places—but you do have very good manners.

I'm not suggesting that, morally, there is any difference between what we did and the actions of people who *do* go dogging in supermarket car parks in Essex. You couldn't slip a paper between us. The stonework, the mosaics and marble—we just had a classier backdrop than a scrubby hedge and a row of large recycling bins, that's all.

As I am thinking all this, I notice that the woman pedestrian has gone and the green van is pulling away from the curb, the driver still mouthing swearwords. As the van moves away, I see that across the road, on the opposite pavement, there is a man in a navy pin-striped suit standing facing me, looking at me through the café window. The man is you.

Six months later, after the car crash and our subsequent breakup, when we are reunited briefly and lying on the bed in the empty flat in Vauxhall, you will tell me about this encounter, that you saw me on the security cameras at the entrance to Portcullis House, that you came down to the entrance while I was standing outside and decided to follow me. You noticed as soon as I descended the steps that I was walking with a lack of purpose. You were no more than a few meters behind me as I crossed Parliament Square. At one point, as I wandered through St. James's Park, I turned and looked round and you thought I might have spotted you, so you hung back a bit. When it was clear I hadn't, you neared me again and took the risk of walking very close to me as I ambled up Duke of York Street. I didn't turn again. You watched me go into the café and sit down, then decided to wait for a bit to see if I was meeting anyone. You stood on the other side of the street, in a shop doorway, and although I looked out the window—gazed out of it—for most of the time I was seated there, I didn't notice you. *People see what they expect to see*, you say. You enjoyed watching me, you tell me. It aroused you to observe me when I didn't know that you were there. And I told you that the main reason I didn't see you was that I was lost in my thoughts of you. This pleased you immensely. You had guessed as much. You could tell, you said, by the way my eyes stared, the thoughtful set of my mouth, that I was thinking about what we had done in the chapel in the crypt. The arrogance of this assumption annoyed me then and I rolled on my back on the bed, away from you, and tried to backtrack, claiming I wasn't thinking about you that day in the café after all, that I was thinking about the introduction I had to write to a new university textbook, a collection of essays taking a wide-ranging approach to molecular biology. You knew I was lying. You rolled on top of me, pinned my arms above my head with one hand and dug your fingers into the soft part of my waist with the other until I admitted I had been thinking about you, you, you . . .

When I had conceded this, shrieking and begging for mercy, we embraced for a long while, until I lifted a finger and traced the curve of your shoulder and asked, "But how *did* you know I would be in Westminster that day?"

"I just had a feeling, that's all," you said, shrugging lightly. "Just had a feeling it might be worth turning up." I looked at you. "Or maybe," you added, turning, propping your head up with one hand, elbow bent and staring at me with studied casualness, "or maybe I had been watching the security cameras at that entrance every morning since Tuesday, hoping to bump into you . . ." As I carried on looking at you, your face became hard. "Or maybe I got some friends of mine to alert me if you came through the security checks." I looked at you, and your eyes were still hard and held mine until you observed a shadow of genuine doubt cross my face, and then you broke into a smile and said, "I'm only joking! It was a coincidence . . ."

We are seminaked when this conversation takes place. It is six months and a whole world of happenings after the encounter we are discussing, when I see you standing on the other side of the street after the green van pulls away.

I see you standing across the street, and all at once can feel the biggest, broadest smile coming to my features, and I see it mirrored in the smile you are giving me, even though the traffic crisscrosses between us. You break the smile only to check from side to side before you step into the road.

And then you are there, in the café with me, relaxed in your navy blue pinstripe (I have a moment to reflect that it doesn't look as smart as the gray). You fill the small café, in fact. Your smile alone could fill it; teeth and eyes, this is what I notice about you today. "Well, well," you say, as you pull out the chair and sit down opposite me at the small round table. "So, you are going to buy me a coffee after all."

I turn to summon the waitress.

It will be during this meeting that I ask, the first of several occasions, "So, what is it you do, exactly?"

On this occasion, you will shrug. "Civil service, all very boring, looking after the Parliamentary Estate, oiling the wheels for the people in charge . . ."

It is a question to which I never get the same answer twice.

We are in the small café for an hour and a half. We have a second coffee after the first, which would be enough to make me feel speedy and strange even without your company. You pester me with questions about myself. Where do I live? Do I like my job? How long have I been married? Have I ever been unfaithful before? You seem particularly interested in that one. When I say, *not exactly*, you accuse me of being evasive. Most people embarking on an affair meet, introduce themselves, find out a bit about each other, and then proceed to wild sex. We appear to be doing it the other way around.

I throw a pointed look at the broad gold ring on your wedding finger. "And what about you . . . ?" I parry. I don't see why this should all be one-sided. We have already established that we have two children each, although mine are grown up and yours aren't, but I'm asking something a little more specific here.

You smile. "Do you mean am I about to say my wife doesn't understand me?" You give a tight-lipped grimace. "No, I'm not. She understands me all too well."

I realize we are agreeing terms.

"My husband and I probably married a bit young," I say, "but I don't regret it, just when we did it maybe. When I married, not who I married."

We are, of course, establishing that neither of us is looking for a parachute. Inexperienced as I am, I recognize the importance of this negotiation and the significance of the fact that we both think it important.

"What's your wife like?" I ask, and know immediately that I have overstepped the mark. How fine is the line between making conversation and prying.

You adopt a slightly distant look. "Tell me something you've never told your husband, just one thing." I hesitate and you say, "Something innocuous if you like."

"I hate his haircut," I say, "always have. The thing is, he's not vain at all, and I like that about him. He doesn't need petting and praising all the time, he just gets on with it, he's quite unaware of himself in lots of ways. And although I think that's sort of admirable, I do look at him and wish he'd get a proper haircut, but he's always had it the same way, his hair is very straight and a bit too long so it just sort of flops. It seems a bit late to tell him after thirty years."

You beam unself-consciously and run a hand through your own wiry, brownish hair, revealing some gray beneath, and it occurs to me that you probably are quite vain, maybe even dye your hair on top, and if my husband were vain I would dislike this but as he is not, your vanity is, if anything, just another one of your endearing qualities. That is why I have tried to ask about your wife—it has not escaped my notice that you deflected that question. It is not that I want to pry. On the contrary, I would really prefer it if we just pretended neither of our marriages existed. I am trying to find out what your wife is like because I need ammunition. I want to arm myself with counterqualities. Whatever she is, I want to be the opposite. Tell me she likes blue and I will never wear blue again.

I do find out what your wife looks like eventually but in what I think we can call somewhat unfortunate circumstances. Even if I had been inclined to be reasonable about her at the beginning of our affair, what came later put paid to rationality on either side. As it was, my first sight of her came when I was standing in the witness box at the Old Bailey, giving evidence at our joint trial.

It is later on, after I have broken down and told the truth to the court. I am midsentence, but speaking hesitantly, answering a question about the flat in Vauxhall, explaining how innocuous our discussions were on the only occasion we were able to spend a few hours together there.

When the interruption comes, it is so unexpected, it electrifies the court.

"You bitch . . . filthy fucking *bitch*!" At first, the exclamation seems to come from nowhere, from the heavens perhaps, and as I register the shock on the faces of the jury in front of me and the judge's indignant alarm, I look around. The shout has come from the public gallery, which is to my right but behind me, raised up in the ceiling. I turn to see that, at the front of the gallery, there is a blond woman in large glasses who is sitting in the front row, not far from Susannah. The woman's face is a mask of hatred. She is staring at me with the palpable venom of someone who has been restraining herself for far too long.

"You filthy, filthy, fucking, *fucking* . . ." It is as though she thinks she is muttering to herself but can't help vocalizing.

The judge leans forward and speaks sharply to the clerk of the court, who already has a phone to his ear and is nodding. The door to the public gallery opens, and two security guards, an attractive young black woman with a ponytail and a thickset white man, enter. While the man waits at the top of the short flight of stairs that leads down to the front row, the young woman descends, leans across Susannah, and hisses, "Madam! Madam!" gesturing at the blond woman, who says nothing, rises, clomps heavily up the steps, and is ushered out.

And that, as you know, will be the first and only encounter I ever have with your wife.

We are still in conversation in the café on Duke of York Street, deep into our mutual exchange of confidences, when you sit back in your chair and say, abruptly, "I have to go now."

If you have checked your watch, you have done it surreptitiously. I feel deflated because I have had no warning, or perhaps because I sense this is the way it will always be.

You extract a phone from your pocket. "Give me your number."

You punch it in as I say it out loud, then you press Dial. Inside my jacket pocket, my phone shudders twice.

"Now you have mine too," you say efficiently, job done.

You slip your phone back into your pocket and look at me. It is a long look, a look that asks a question and gets the answer it wants.

I look back at you and say softly, seriously, "Is this really going to happen?"

"Oh, yes," you say immediately, looking down at me as you stand. "I'll call you later," you add. You bend slightly, glancing outside the café window as you do, grab the hair at the back of my neck, and tip my head back in a quick, possessive gesture that makes some part of my insides melt, swiftly and sweetly, raspberry sorbet, I think. You plant a firm, damp kiss on my lips, turn, leave.

You are taking the phone out of your pocket to make a call before you are even out of my sight down the street. While I am still looking out the window, the waitress approaches silently, as though she has been waiting, and places the bill in a saucer on the table in front of me. I glance around and see that the café has filled up with people ordering lunch and that a couple is queuing by the door. I have outstayed my welcome.

Even as I rise, placing the money for our coffees on the saucer and reflexively pocketing the receipt, lifting my coat from the back of the chair, even as I button the coat, tie the belt, shake out my hair, I am writing another letter to you in my head.

3

Dear X,

You asked me if I have ever been unfaithful to my husband before and the honest answer, in the terms in which you meant the question, was no, but when I said, "Not exactly . . ." I wasn't being evasive. Although the brief incident I am thinking of came nowhere near sex, it did have significance for me. Its significance came in relation to you.

It is not the middle of the night. It is the middle of the day, the following Monday, to be precise. It is the Monday after our Friday coffee but the first opportunity I have had to write down my thoughts. We have met only twice, but apparently we are having an affair. I am working from home today—I'll be in the office Tuesday and Wednesday this week. I have a thousand things to do but instead I am writing another letter to you. We have just talked on the phone for over half an hour. And the minute we stopped talking on the phone—you actually asked me what I was wearing—I came upstairs, opened up *VATquery3*, and began another letter, but letters are long, and writing is slower than talking and talking slower than thinking, and I've stopped writing almost immediately. I sit back in my chair. Through my study window, fat clouds are moving with improbable speed across a pale sky, like clouds in a time-lapse film. There is a flutter against the window and a bird, a starling, comes to land on the sill, sees me looking out, and freezes for an instant, its head turned and one round eye regarding me with what seems like skepticism. It bats itself away. I have a feeling that all my letters to you are destined to remain unfinished, but I still need to articulate the things in my head and so I am thinking the rest of this, and I know that later I will be confused; have I thought it, or told you, or written it down? They are becoming one and the same, all blending in my head.

Until I met you, I was not the sort of woman to throw caution to the wind, on the basis that things thrown into the wind have a habit of blowing back in your face, as anyone who has ever tried to scatter a parent's ashes on a cliff top has probably discovered (as I found out at the age of eight, but that's a whole other story). So no, I had not had an affair before I met you, but there was a small incident, about three months ago. Why do I need to tell you this story? I need you to know that when I said, "Well, not exactly . . ." I wasn't being evasive, although you read it as such. I need you to know about it for reasons of ego. It is worrying me, how easy you found it to have sex with me. I could have said, how easy you found it to seduce me . . . but seduction suggests a process of persuasion over the passage of time. You just went right ahead and I went right along with it—there wasn't any persuading necessary. I need you to know this was not normal for me, and that if you had tried a year before or a year later, or simply when I was in a different mood, it would never have happened. You caught me at the precise moment I was ripe for it. On another occasion, it wasn't so much that I might have said no. I wouldn't even have realized you were asking the question.

And I need you to know the beginning of the other story, of course, and how Ms. Bonnard was able to make me look so bad in court. Was it the beginning, that day? I don't know—the sharp focus of hindsight, the endless questions, was what happened to me later inevitable, back then? When you are a rational human being, with free will and agency, is there any such thing as a point of no return?

I am fifty-two. I have status and gravitas—when I don't have my tights around my ankles in a secluded chapel beneath the Houses of Parliament, that is. I have reached the stage of my career where my opinion is valued, paid for, and so it was that, on a rainy December day, three months before you and I met, I was running along a slick street lined by large square buildings, slightly late, on my way to sit in on a three-hour presentation seminar by MSc students at City University. It was my second year as an external examiner on two of their postgraduate programs, which in this case meant that at the end of the winter term I had to observe as a group of prospective scientists presented live abstracts of their dissertations in progress. This particular morning, a Monday, was the first occasion I had met this group and the first time I had been to the department's new premises, although I knew the two lecturers who were looking after me from the previous year, George Craddock and Sandra Doyle. They met me in the foyer of the new main building. I was late but had nearly made myself later by stopping for a takeaway coffee on the way—I had a vague memory from the previous year that I hadn't been offered coffee. This is always one of the tricky issues of being asked to a morning event. Will you get offered coffee, or do you arrive Styrofoam cup in hand, having forked out £2.60 unnecessarily, to be greeted with a disappointed look from a host or hostess who has the cafetière and biscuits all ready, neatly arranged? It is an implicit criticism to turn up with a Styrofoam cup, after all.

On this occasion, I ran up the steps wet and flustered and hadn't stopped for a coffee after all and knew as soon as I entered the new building that was a mistake. Straight ahead of me was a vending machine. It's never a good sign when there's a vending machine in the foyer. George and Sandra were both sitting on a bench just inside the door, talking quietly. "Don't worry," said Sandra, as they rose to their feet. "This lot are party people, they'll all be late."

"Hi, sorry, nice to see you both again . . ." I shook their hands.

"Want to risk it?" said George, apologetically, indicating the machine with one hand.

I pulled a face. I meant it as no but he took it as yes, thrust his hand into his trouser pocket, and began to jangle it up and down among the loose change in its depths.

"I'll get it," said Sandra, moving over to the machine, money already in her hand. She didn't ask if I wanted milk or sugar.

While she got my drink, George turned to his left and pressed the lift button. Sandra brought the coffee over in a plastic cup so thin it was hard to believe the hot liquid didn't melt it. I took a sip and winced.

"Sorry about the coffee!" George declared, as if he had cracked a tremendous joke. "Bet you're a latte girl, eh?"

"It's okay," I said, glancing down at the cup, "I like to pretend I'm classy but in fact I'm really easy." Sandra and George smiled in the way that people do when someone with seniority makes a joke about herself. "Cheap and easy, that's me."

The door to the lift opened and we stepped inside—it was tiny and mirror paneled from waist-level up. It seemed an inappropriate lift to be carting gaggles of students, but maybe they just bounded up the stairs. I was sweating in my business suit, with a mac on top, unable to lift my plastic coffee because Sandra and George had to stand so close to me, close enough for me to observe that George had nicked himself shaving his neck that morning, just beneath the border of his artfully scrubby beard. In eighteen months' time, I would discover that his blood type was O positive.

I wanted to ask them what the students were like, but they weren't supposed to influence me before I heard the abstracts. In any case, Sandra was wrong about them all being late. As we entered the lecture room, twenty-five expectant faces turned toward us. They watched us as we walked toward the desks laid out for us to one side, three chairs, three bottles of water on the table. George took the chair on the left and gestured for me to sit next to him, in the middle, a position that confirmed my status. Sandra broke the tension by raising her hand to the students and saying, "Heavens, everyone here on time for once, just because we have a rock star with us today."

A good-humored murmur went around the room and I threw Sandra a smile. I remained standing for a moment, so they could all get a good look at me. I put the coffee down on the desk next to my bottle of water and removed my mac, all slowly—George leapt to his feet to take the coat from me and hang it from a hook on the back of the door. I looked at the students.

There were fewer women than the other MSc program I examined. The other one was called Genetics of Human Disease and the majority of the students on it were female—because it was about saving the human race, I suppose. When it came to this one, Bioinformatics, the gender proportion was reversed. The young men due to present that morning sat in a row at the front. Two of them were looking down at their papers. The other three—and I knew instinctively that they were all friends—were staring at me. Directly behind them was a group of young men in a cluster, lounging back in their chairs, relaxed. It wasn't their morning. They hadn't got the short straws. They were here to watch their buddies and gather material for the piss-taking session that would take place, loudly, in the corridor afterward. The seven women on the course were all grouped together at the back of the room.

The young man nearest to me was sitting at the very end of the tables with nothing in front of him and one hand resting casually on the edge of the table, leaning back in his chair, legs splayed and crotch on full display, in a gesture so obvious it made me want to laugh. I met his gaze briefly, in order to demonstrate that I wasn't intimidated by him, and he met my gaze right back. He had thick dark hair, solid wrists, hands that were large and meaty. I had encountered this scenario or similar several times before, but as I sat down, smoothing my skirt, and took my folder from my bag, I realized I was particularly alive to it that morning. These young men, so full of testosterone they bounced with it, they were like puppies. They couldn't help themselves. What amused me, as I put down my notepad and wrote the place, time, and date at the top of it, was the thought that if anyone, let alone me, suggested to these young males that they were responding to me on a sexual level, they would be horrified—I was old enough to be their mother, after all. But even so, they could not stop themselves from rising to the challenge. Here I was, an unknown female in their midst, in a situation in which they were potentially on show. Perhaps some of them, on top of that, were nursing a lurking Mrs. Robinson fantasy, or maybe some of them were intimidated by young women of their own age and preferred the idea of someone more motherly—but even if neither of these factors came into play, there was something in them that responded to me on a very elemental level, even if all they wanted was the thought of being able to brag about it afterward: *That examiner, thinks she's going to fuck me over with her marking pen, well, I'll fuck her.* It was simple aggression on their part—that's all really, chimpanzee behavior. It amused me. I was safe, after all, and in a position of power.

The large boy stared me out for the whole of the morning, so obviously that I began to wonder if Sandra or George would take him to one side afterward and reprimand him. Once in a while, he leaned to one side and whispered something to the boy sitting next to him, a smaller lad with sandy hair and keen gray eyes. Listen, Junior, I felt like saying, I'm far too old to be offended by this stuff. Have you any idea how used to it you are by my age? Those boys thought I was unsettled by their big firm bodies—but when push came to shove, so to speak, I would be reading their papers and marking them on the basis of whether they had a firm grasp of sequence analysis. Lads, lads, I wanted to say, technique is more important than stamina.

The presentations began. First up was a very short boy who coughed his way to the lectern. He took several nervous sips from a water bottle before he began, fiddling anxiously with the mouse pad on the laptop. Eventually, the title of his PowerPoint presentation was displayed on the board behind him: "Combined Use of Restriction Enzymes in Isolating Cosmids and Plasmids: A New Approach?"

After the third presentation, there was a break. Most of the students stayed in their seats. Two of the girls went out and came back with Diet Cokes. I excused myself and went to the ladies' so that I wouldn't have to make small talk with Sandra and George—there would be enough of that by the end of the week. In the chilly, gray toilet, after I had washed my hands, I leaned forward into the speckled mirror and passed the tip of my forefinger under each eye, where there was the barely detectable smudge of eyeliner after my walk in the rain. I reapplied my lipstick. It was pathetic and I laughed at myself while I did it, but I could not resist these small acts of vanity. *How obvious and silly we all are, us humans,* I thought. *Even me. Especially me.*

Back in the room, as I approached our table, George smiled at me and patted my chair for me to sit down. Sandra said, "Hey ho, another day, another dollar."

"Not yet," muttered George.

We wrapped up just before one o'clock. George and Sandra would take me out for lunch on Friday so I knew I could escape without causing offense. As it happened, it was a busy week, that week. My VAT return was due and it was my first year of annual accounting. Filling in the nonsensical form made me want chew the arm of my office chair. And I had some dry cleaning to pick up on the way home.

As I came down the steps outside the building, having said goodbye to Sandra and George in the foyer, I saw that the sandy-haired boy was waiting for me, leaning against the railings to the right of the steps with his arms folded and a cycle helmet looped over one finger. I slowed down my pace and he gazed at me with his gray eyes. He made no pretense that the encounter was accidental, giving me a half smile of acknowledgment and propelling himself away from the railings without using his hands, just the momentum of his body. He had sunglasses on his head, even though it was December, on the pretext that a little thin winter sun was shining. I wondered if he would remember that before he put his cycle helmet on.

I nodded in acknowledgment as I passed him and walked off down the street. He followed me, doing a quickstep to catch up.

"So what did you make of the presentations?"

I gave him a look that was meant to be stern but I suspect seemed merely ironic. "You wouldn't really expect me to say, would you?"

"I think they all did pretty well," the sandy-haired boy said, "although I thought Sundeep didn't really get to the heart of why high throughput data analysis has transformed the way we sequence. It's not just about speed, is it?"

I maintained a diplomatic silence.

"We googled you, of course," he said casually, "they made such a big deal about you being our external examiner, Sandra and George, honestly, you would have thought we were having the queen. So we all looked you up, and I have to say your CV really is impressive."

"Thank you," I said, and I thought my voice was dripping with sarcasm, but if he noticed, it didn't alter his tone.

"Basically, you have my ideal job," he continued. "In fact, I was wondering if I could pick your brain sometime, about the Beaufort Institute." We passed a group of his friends and he raised his hand to them. Two girls in the front of the group giggled. After the group had gone past, he said in a low voice, almost a murmur, "I would be *extremely* grateful . . ."

We had reached the main road. The roar of taxis and buses was immediately apparent. I turned to him firmly and said, "I'm going this way," indicating down the street. It was a clear dismissal. The world of science is, like many others, all about patronage, about your professor giving you that sparkling reference to the right funding body at the right time, about your head of lab allocating you your own corner for research at just the point you need it. But, morally suspect as patronage is, there is still a convention that it is earned.

He held my gaze. "I would really appreciate it," he said, "and I promise not to ask any more questions about what you think about everyone else's work, or mine either. You'll find I'm quite . . ." He trailed off, but the way he said it rendered his meaning quite unmistakable.

He paused, still staring at me with his open, gray, hungry eyes.

"I'm very discreet," he added.

Oh, the arrogance of youth, I thought. Let's presume for a minute I *was* up for an affair—no, I mean a quick shag—with a boy half my age, what made him think I would choose him? I could easily have the meaty dark-haired one if I wanted; he was much closer to fantasy boy-toy material than his bold friend here. I thought of saying as much to this fair man-child in front of me, but there was something about him, the innocence in his direct, priapic gaze, that made me feel touched rather than offended. Not flattered, though. I am far too much of a realist to be flattered.

"I have a card," he said suddenly, as if he had only just remembered. Then the card was in his hand, and he held it out, and it was a plain white card with his name, Jamie something, and his e-mail address and mobile phone number, and in case I didn't get the message, he stared at me hard again as I took it from him. That's all we need, us humans, just a stare. Peacocks spread their tails. Orangutans hoot. But *Homo sapiens* has evolved to the extent that we can propagate the species with one long, lingering look.

I returned the stare briefly in what I hoped was a blank, noncommittal fashion, then looked at his card before I slipped it into my pocket and turned away. He gave me a smile—no, it was a half smile. A full grin combined with that stare would have been creepy, so this was a careful half. I turned away but couldn't resist glancing back as I walked off. He was standing there quite shamelessly on the street corner, staring after me with that half smile on his face, and, vain creature that I am, I gave him a half smile in return.

I know what you're thinking. Is that it? Is that what she calls nearly having an affair? Doesn't sound like much, in your terms, does it? You can have full coitus in the Houses of Parliament and it is still touch and go whether you would think of it as an affair. One lingering look from a boy on the street, is that it?

Well, that wasn't quite it. I didn't call Jamie-something, but I want you to know that I thought very seriously about doing so, planned it, envisaged it, rehearsed it even. I showered for him that night. I dressed for him the next morning. I am not sure what reflects more badly on me—my reasons for contemplating calling him, or my reasons for not doing so. Reasons for: it would be an interesting and appropriate revenge against my husband (more of that another time). It would be an uncomplicated fuck, or series of fucks—Jamie would lose interest fairly quickly, I was sure of that. He wasn't attracted to me as an individual, after all—he just hadn't nailed an old one yet. And I would learn something I had been curious about for some time. As a young woman, an important part of arousal for me had been the contemplation of my own body. I had loved long baths, sunbathing, keeping my skin nice. I wasn't a beauty but I had still been a narcissist in the way that all young women are taught to be narcissists, every time they turn the page of a magazine or watch TV. Since I had had children, put on weight, aged, I had had sex only with my husband and so was still able to see my body through his eyes, as he remembered it, not as it really was. If I had sex with this boy, I would be stripped of that delusion. I would see myself through his eyes—that was if I even let him look. I would probably want to do it in the dark or, better still, stay fully dressed. Maybe both.

This was what interested me: would the contemplation of *his* body, which was no doubt beautiful, would that be enough to arouse me, or did I still need to feel lovely myself to achieve any sort of abandonment? Could I reverse the equation? Could I become a voyeur?

I thought all of this sitting on the Tube going home, and I have to tell you that by the time the train had pulled into my stop, I had committed infidelity many times in my head and was already wondering what to wear the next day in order to excite Jamie's older-woman fantasy a little further. None of this reflects well on me, but I suspect that my reasons for eventually not calling, for keeping Jamie-something's card on my desk but never using it, reflect even more badly. Cowardice, of course, the simple fear that I had read the signals wrong, that I was just an old lady too easily flattered by the attention of such an eager puppy—that was the first reason. There was also the issue that it could end my days as an external examiner—even be worth a paragraph in a tabloid, I thought: a breach of trust. But ultimately, what made me hold off was the thought that I would have to make the first move. I had his contact details but he didn't have mine. I have never made the first move in my life. I just couldn't bring myself to do it.

The next day, I was back in the same building. Jamie did his presentation and it was solid rather than sparkling. The large brown boy continued to stare at me and his mates clustered round him, impressed by his bravado, and by the end of the week I was weary of their games and thought, *Oh, leave me alone and let me do my job.* I was even weary of Jamie's doggedly friendly gaze. At lunch with George and Sandra on the Friday, we went through the students in alphabetical order and we all thought the same. The two obvious stars were a boy called Pradesh and one of the girls, Emmanuella, both of whom had chosen original subject matter but had not relied on its originality to score them points all on its own, a common failing in postgraduate students. They had been thorough and methodical, and presented calmly and well. There was a prestigious work placement at stake at the end of the year, and either Pradesh or Emmanuella would get it, that is if one or both of them were not poached by a PhD program first, which often happened with the most talented MSc students. I wondered whether that was what made the boys at the front of the room so obvious. Perhaps they already knew, in their heart of hearts, that they were not star material; that for all their ambition and cleverness, they were destined for a teaching or technician's job in a sixth-form college or a low-grade university at best. I doubted very much whether a prestigious research institution like the Beaufort would touch a boy like Jamie. Maybe he wanted to fuck me because he knew that I had indeed—simply by being who I was—already fucked him.

At the time of my writing that second letter to you, I had no idea how that morning at the university and you would become linked in court, how a line would be drawn, as thin and tenuous as the strand that links a spider's web to a gatepost. The strands that a spider spins are made of protein, of proteinaceous spider silk, to be precise. The stickiness of them is due to droplets along the length of each strand, and the interesting thing about those droplets is how they are sensitive to the force any object may apply in an attempt to pull away from them. So, if a droplet touches an inanimate surface, for instance, it will merely adhere. But when this same droplet is touched by something that attempts to escape, it becomes rubberized, expanding after the retreating object in order to hang on to it, almost as if it was chasing after it, you might say. There was no relevance, but it would all be made to be relevant, as would almost everything else I have ever done, all woven together in a narrative, to glue us, the flies in the web.

4

The next time you and I have sex, as you may or may not remember, is in a disabled toilet down a corridor at the back of the House of Commons staff canteen. We have tea and cake in the canteen first, which is at ground level and has a view over the river but smells, as all staff canteens do, of green vegetables overboiled. It is late afternoon and outside, already, the light is fading. The sky is gray; the Thames slips and slides in an oily fashion. At the far end of the canteen, a group of catering staff lounge around a table in their white jackets and navy aprons, taking a break after the lunchtime rush. We sit close to the window and you divide a piece of carrot cake in two, meticulously, with a plastic fork. When I leave half of my half, you polish it off without comment. Underneath the table, one of your knees has found my two, demurely pressed together to one side, and pushed between them. As foreplay goes, it is simple but effective.

After half an hour, we leave our table and walk to the back of the canteen, past the screen-covered Members Only area, and take a wooden door that has embossed gold letters reading NO EXIT. It leads to the left down a plush corridor. We pass a room with the door open and you pause to peer inside. It is the sort of room that could be a study or office but is being used as a temporary storeroom. There are box files on the shelves that cover one wall. On a table just inside the door, there is a row of desk lamps, brass ones with green glass shades, about twenty of them. You step back into the corridor. For some reason, the room won't do. The disabled toilet is round another corner, at the bottom of a corridor that is a dead end, and for a toilet, it is quite classy, with wood paneling and carpet. The many rails at different heights are useful for leverage, I discover. During it, during the silent period of mutual absorption right in the middle, you take my chin in your hand, cup it, and turn my face gently toward the large mirror. "Look in the mirror," you say. And at first I try to turn away but you hold my face more firmly then and say, "Look," and I look, and I see us, both partially dressed, disheveled and abandoned, the firm muscle of your thigh, my own soft white one raised, my eyes wide and my gaze still touched with disbelief, and you press the side of your face against mine, still holding my chin, and whisper in my ear, "Isn't it beautiful? You're *beautiful* . . ."

The following day, I forget my phone when I go out to have lunch with Susannah in Harrow-on-the-Hill, and when I get home I find six missed calls from you and four text messages, starting with, *Good morning . . .* and ending with, *So it's the silent treatment is it? What have I done to deserve this, pray?* When I call you, charmed and laughing, to explain, you demand to know who Susannah is (my oldest friend), where we went for lunch (the new Malaysian), whether she is good-looking or not (emphatically yes), and would she fancy a threesome? (Funnily enough, I've never thought to ask.)

All day, our texts continue. Have I ever had a threesome? (No, I haven't.) If I did, would I like it with another man or woman? (I haven't a clue.) What's the weirdest place I've ever done it? (How staid my life has been.)

The next day, I text you while I am waiting on the platform at my local Tube station. I am on my way to a presentation at the Combat Cancer Development Fund about proposed changes to funding legislation. I am high on our conversations of the previous day, high on what we are doing. My text is cheery: *Hey you. In town today, Charing Cross. Lunch?* You don't reply, but after a while, my train goes underground. I emerge at Leicester Square rather than change to the Northern Line, with plenty of time to walk to the Development Fund's headquarters on the Strand, fully expecting a reply from you to pop up on my phone. There is nothing. I turn my phone off and on again. Still nothing. I pretend to myself that I don't find this annoying, as I stride along. You're a busy man. That's fine. I'm busy too. I'm still not exactly clear what it is you do that keeps you so busy, but so what? You don't know anything about what I do either. It nags at me, though. Why are you so evasive about your job? Civil servant? You're not like any other civil servant I've met, and I've met quite a few.

When I go into the presentation, I leave my phone on the table in front of me, on silent, and look at it from time to time. Nothing. The talk is being given by a young woman from the Department of Health, who is standing waiting for us as we filter into the room. When she thinks it is time to start, she coughs, looks at us, then taps her Biro against the water glass on the lectern in front of her. "Jolly good," she says brightly.

She stands at the board and talks us through impending changes in NHS funding policy due to the forthcoming new act, which is making its slow progression through Parliament at the moment. Afterward, we will have a chance to question her, and some of the questions will be hostile, as scientists are as resistant to change as any other breed of person. There are around thirty-five scientists in the room, some representing institutions, like me, some from universities, all of whom may be affected by the new legislation. I know about half of the people in the room, although I have chosen to sit on my own, this particular morning. I don't feel like making small talk.

In the coffee break, I text you again. *Hey busy man, let me know either way. Have something else on later.* I have no plans after the presentation and am not particularly busy that day, but you don't know that. I am irked. Maybe I got it wrong when I suggested lunch. Maybe I should have texted, *Fancy a quick fuck . . .* That would have got a response.

After the coffee break, the question-and-answer session begins, but I am so irritated by your silence, I cannot listen to what is being said, and with my distraction comes a degree of insecurity that makes me look at the efficient young woman before me and, as an experiment, try to imagine how you would see her. Before what happened between us, I would have observed that she was attractive and thought no more of it. When you have a grown-up daughter as lovely as mine, you can never bring yourself to resent young, pretty women. You know what they are in for, after all. You know how insecure they feel about their loveliness, how vulnerable inside. You feel protective toward them, even though they would be horrified to think they need protecting. But this morning, I look at this young woman through your eyes—through the eyes of a man with an irrepressible sex drive. (Tell me, my dear, is it difficult being such a man? The world is full of lovely young women, after all, and everywhere you turn you are bombarded with images of female availability. Isn't life a perpetual torment?) I observe her as you might observe her, and as some of the men in the room are probably observing her too. She is dressed in the uniform of the young, up-and-coming civil servant—the new breed, that is: black trousers, matching fitted jacket, low-cut pastel-colored shirt that reveals the hint of a plump curve—the outfit of a woman who is, for the moment, having it all, and sees no reason why she should ever stop having it. Her hair is honey-brown, layered, well cut. It swings as she moves her head. She seems unself-conscious to me, confident that her intelligence and diligence are enough to see her through the routine task of presenting facts to a room full of scientists—several of whom are twice her age or more—confident she is our intellectual equal. She seems like a young woman who would never simper when she announced her achievements, as women of my generation are still—to our shame—prone to do, a young woman who feels, quite justifiably, that she has nothing to prove. When she concludes her talk and asks for questions, half of me wants to cheer and half of me wants to weep.

I look at her and imagine being you. I imagine ignoring the work she put into her presentation, or being able to see it only through a mist of sexual desire. (Is that what it is like to be a man? I am genuinely curious.) I imagine you wanting her as badly as—far more badly than—you wanted me. It comes to me that you would never ask a lovely young woman such as her into a disabled toilet, or take her by the hand into the Crypt Chapel, or lead her into a storage cupboard. What would she think of a middle-aged man who made such a move? The thought fills me with unease, but then the man next to me raises his hand and says, "I'm not sure I agree with that last point. I think we should have a show of hands on who in the room would make a decision like that without referral." The young woman raises her eyebrows at us and her questioning gaze invites us to vote. My colleagues all glance at each other. I frown as if I'm not sure either way. Effortfully, I push you to the back of my mind.

I walk slowly back to Leicester Square Tube, my phone in my hand. I check it for one last time before I descend the steps. I could text again, or call, but instead I am going home in order to punish you. You will text me when I'm underground, really wanting to have lunch, only to get no response. You will call my phone only for it to go straight to voice mail. You will curse that you have missed an opportunity. Maybe you will wonder what I am doing, who I am with.

The carriage I get into is less crowded than usual and I get a seat, plumping myself down with a sigh. Opposite me are three teenage girls, chewing gum, all messy ponytails and hoop earrings and teeth, shouting and pushing at each other, and I observe how loudmouthed and beautiful they are and think of my daughter and her friends at that age, full of noise and light and loyalty toward each other, and the young civil servant and how, yes, the world is indeed full to the brim of young women such as these, who probably drive men such as you half-demented with the fact that you can never have them.

I remind myself that you called me beautiful. In the disabled toilet, you told me to look in the mirror, and I smiled at our mutual dishevelment and how we looked, half-dressed and glued at the groin, sexy and ridiculous at the same time, and I turned my head away shyly and you held my face and turned my head back, gently, and whispered, "Isn't it beautiful? You're *beautiful* . . ." Sitting on the Tube, I remind myself of that with an edge of desperation. I try to be calm and positive, to think of my good points—my hair is still thick, my neck unlined. Beautiful? I am fifty-two years old. *You fool*, I think then. You have two chief qualities in his eyes: your availability and your willingness.

I walk home from the station, heavily: still no call or message from you. The house is empty, thank God. I avoid the mirror as I hang up my coat and kick my shoes into a corner. *You fool.* Your abdomen is soft and full, your breasts shrunken—you have a figure like a jelly baby. Do you think any man in his right mind, of any age, would actually *choose* you? Don't be an idiot. He sees something in your eyes, that's all, and it isn't beauty. It's acquiescence.

I walk into the kitchen and graze the cupboards and fridge—a rice cake, a bit of hummus past its sell-by date, a few grapes, and a yogurt. I eat standing up, leaning against the granite countertop. I put my phone on the kitchen table to stop my looking at it four times a minute. Eventually, I go to the cupboard we call the larder and find an old can of beer, room temperature, with dust around the rim. I pour it into a tumbler and add ice cubes, which make the contents of the glass foam like a lab experiment—still, a better idea than opening a bottle of wine that early in the day, I think. I take my warm, foamy beer, ice cubes clinking, and wander into the sitting room, still in my work suit, and slump on the sofa. I channel-hop from one rubbish daytime television program to the next, something I never normally do.

Eventually, I go upstairs and open up another letter to you, but get only as far as one line.

Dear X,
    I don't think I can do this anymore.

I am cool with you the next day, when you call. You offer no explanation for your silence the previous day and I am determined not to ask. From the way you speak to me, lightheartedly, I can tell that yesterday was yesterday, you had been busy and you saw no reason to offer explanation or apology. What about today? you want to know. Where am I? I admit that I will be in town later and you say, great, we can meet for a coffee around three o'clock, in that patisserie on the corner of Piccadilly, just past Fortnum's. If I am good, you say, you will let me buy you a cake.

You are late. You come in, distracted, still clearly running through something in your head, sighing, smiling at me, saying, as you sit, "Hang on just a minute, I'll be right with you." Then you get three phones out and check each in turn before slipping them, one by one, back into their pockets. I have never known anyone who seems to own as many electronic devices as you do. What *is* it you do, exactly, and why are you always so evasive?

You stop and look at me. This is a habit of yours I find both exciting and disturbing. Just at the point where you seem distracted and I feel free to observe you, you will stop whatever you are doing and look back at me, catching me in the act, reversing our interaction. All at once, I am not watching you—it is you watching me watching you, which is a different matter altogether.

"I was just thinking," I say, before you can ask, "that I've never known anyone who has as many mobile communication devices as you. What are they all for? What is it you do, exactly?"

You give me a keen look. "You know what, it's really quite strange you should ask me that right at this very minute."

"Why?"

"Because," you say, "I have something for you." You raise a finger in a give-me-a-minute gesture, bend, and pick up your briefcase. You flick the clips open with a twin gesture of both thumbs, and despite my resolution to be cool, I feel a thrill of excitement thinking where else those thumbs have been recently, where else they have been flicking. You open the briefcase but the hinged side is toward me, so I can't see inside. You lift something out, slam the lid shut, and put the briefcase back on the floor.

You put it on the table between us: a small, cheap mobile phone. I look at it and you push it across the table. "I got the same brand you have already so you don't need a different charger."

I stare at it.

"It's for you," you say, "a present. I realize it's not quite pearl earrings or a compilation CD of romantic hits of the eighties, but it's all yours."

I pick it up. "What's it for?" I say stupidly.

"I believe it's traditional to use them for making phone calls and sending texts, but I suppose you could juggle with it, if you like, or use it to prop up a wobbly table leg or . . ."

"Yeah, all right, smart-arse . . ." I note, with delight, that we are at the stage of taking the mickey out of each other.

"Seriously, though," you say, staring at me, "can you keep it safe?"

I raise my eyebrows at him.

"You're a bit slow on the uptake today, aren't you?" you remark. "Look, it's a pay-as-you-go phone. It works like any other phone, except this phone is for one purpose and one purpose only."

I pick up the phone and turn it over, as if it might suddenly turn into a small handgun.

"It's for calling me," you say, leaning forward in your seat. Your voice drops and you glance from side to side. I am in no doubt that the conversation has become serious. "You'll find a number in the contacts list, a new number. I've got one just the same. From now on, you call me on that number and that number only, okay?"

I look at you. "Okay," I say softly.

"There's some money on it already, but you'll need to top it up sooner or later, when you do, go to a shop in town, nowhere near your home or where you work. Never go to the same shop twice."

I want to make a joke, to return to the banter, but it is clear from your expression that would be inappropriate. You want me to understand you are in earnest.

The phones were never discovered by the prosecution. You took mine back from me in the car, the day it happened, and you disposed of them both, I never found out where, down a drain somewhere, perhaps, in a rubbish bin. Perhaps you buried them. Perhaps even now, those phones lie nestling together beneath the earth in a garden or park somewhere. That's what I would have done, if their disposal had been up to me.

"What's your e-mail address?" I ask. It seems an odd question, when you have just given me a pay-as-you-go phone, but the letters I write to you come to mind and I think how much human contact is via e-mail these days and how odd it is we don't do that. You must have a work e-mail address, after all.

You shake your head. "E-mail leaves a trail," you say.

"Why would anyone bother?" I ask, with a small scoff of skepticism. I'm enjoying the subterfuge but really, I am thinking, isn't this all a little self-important? It's flattering to our sense of ourselves, I suppose; it adds to the adrenaline of what we are doing, but it's hardly necessary, is it?

You lean back a little in your seat, glance around, lean forward again. You regard me seriously, then say, "Is your husband a suspicious man?"

A sudden image of my husband comes to mind, as I found him last Sunday evening around nine o'clock, in his study, head bent over his desk. On the far corner of the desk was the salad I had brought up to him two hours previously. I had come into his study silently to collect the plate. He indicated with a wave of his hand that I could take it for him, giving me a quick thumbs-up gesture to say, *it was good, thanks*, without noticing that he hadn't actually eaten what was on it. Suspicious? My husband? If he was working on a new paper, I could invite a rugby team round for group sex in the hallway and he wouldn't notice.

"No, he's not suspicious," I say.

"What if he finds this in your handbag, what would your cover story be?"

I give a small snort. "He would never go through my handbag! Never in a million years!"

"What would your cover story be?" you insist.

"Look," I say, smiling, "we just don't have that kind of marriage, thank God. We don't look in each other's bags. We don't go through each other's credit card bills. We never have done. Even when—well, under any circumstances. I just wouldn't do it and neither would he. It's . . . it's . . ." I search for the right word. "Well, it's undignified. If he found that phone in my handbag, the conversation would go, 'What the hell were you doing looking in my bag?'"

"Look," you say, with a small sigh of impatience. "The point of the question is not, how likely is it that this phone will be discovered. The point is, in the unlikely event of it being discovered, what's your story? Your story has to trip off your tongue, immediately. If you make it up on the spot, there will be a pause, however momentary, and uncertainty in your voice, and in that pause your husband will be able to tell you are lying."

"You don't know my husband."

You look at me much as a weary math teacher might look at a bright but stubborn pupil who is willfully refusing to understand calculus.

"Okay, okay." I raise my hands. "I'll say that one of my colleagues at work left it on my desk during a meeting and that I've been walking around with it in my handbag for ages and must remember to give it back to her."

"That's good," you say, "because it would explain why you've had it in your bag for a while. Months ago would be even better. Tuck it in a compartment, a zipped compartment. Then say that you had the meeting months ago. Your colleague thought she had lost the phone and canceled it, so that's why you haven't rushed to return it. It must have been in your handbag for months. You just haven't thought about it. That way, if he checks your bag regularly and has found it more than once, you're covered."

I can't help but smile at the idiocy of this—the idea of my husband checking my bag even once, let alone repeatedly, but I am distracted by the infinitely pleasing thought of . . . *months*. He said months. He's thinking this may go on for months and months.

At that point, appropriately enough, my phone rings, my normal phone, that is. I was checking e-mails while I waited for you and it is on the table in front of us. The screen lights up and I glance down and, superimposed over a picture of my children standing next to each other at my daughter's graduation is the word BLOCKED.

I ignore it, take a sip of my coffee, and you look at me and say, with a tight smile, "Why don't you answer it?"

I shrug. "It's a blocked call; it will be a work call, or spam."

My phone stops ringing. I glance down at it. BLOCKED MISSED CALL. After a second or two, the screen goes black.

You lean back in your seat again, regarding me. "Don't you want to know who it was?"

I give a small laugh. "No, I'm talking to you. If it's important, they will have left a message."

You pick up my phone and look at it. "No message as yet."

"Well, maybe it will come through in a minute. If it doesn't, then it wasn't important. I get them all the time, don't you?"

"What?"

"Blocked missed calls." This is true. I've had a lot more in the last few months, for some reason. If I answer, there is no one there, just the empty space of a failed connection. My phone number must have ended up on some sort of spam list, like e-mail addresses do from time to time.

You are frowning slightly. "How often do you get them?"

I shrug again. "Several times a week. Sometimes a message from work pops up later, the next day sometimes, which is really annoying. Sometimes it's just nothing. Couple of times there were five or six in a row then nothing for a fortnight. Why? It's not that unusual, is it?" You listen to this intently, more intently than I mean you to, for it wasn't something that had been bothering me. Like everyone, I get spam texts from insurance companies offering to help me win compensation for accidents I haven't had, phone calls from people wanting to upgrade my phone just after I've upgraded, e-mails from U.S. army generals who want to deposit hundreds of thousands of dollars in my account or medical foundations offering me a penis extension. Clothing catalogs pour through my door, three leaflets a day from pizza parlors. How many pizza parlors can there be in west London? We are all of us stalked, every day, stalked by junk mail and e-mail, stalked by nonspecific, scattershot requests. The odd blocked missed call doesn't seem a cause for alarm.

You sit and listen to me with an expression of unwarranted seriousness, I think. "When was the first call?" you ask.

"The first where there wasn't a message, you mean, when I wondered if it was spam?" I shrug. "After Christmas, I think, the New Year . . . Look, it's not a—"

"Wasn't me, then," you say, with an unamused smile. "Must be a secret lover who predates me."

Oh, I see . . . I think, suddenly understanding, and I give you a warm smile and shake my head a little and even though you don't smile back I am happy right then because it is two-nil to me this afternoon. I am feeling the same glow of unexpected pleasure I felt when you said *months*. You are jealous. Because a blocked missed call is the kind of thing you would do, you are assuming that the blocked missed calls I am getting must be from someone like you. *I love men*, I think. I'm no biological determinist—but men, I love them. You give me an open-faced, slightly frowning look, and in the face of your patent annoyance the insecurities I felt the previous day evaporate. Am I going to have to play games to keep you interested? It isn't my style. But then, this whole thing isn't my style.

I pick up the pay-as-you-go phone and turn it over in my hand. It is much smaller than my usual phone. It will slip into a pocket without any difficulty at all.

5

For six weeks, it goes on, you and I, in a heady blur. We meet for sex. We meet for coffee. We never meet for lunch because you are too busy for lunch and we never meet for dinner because we can't meet in the evenings. I have no idea what you like to eat. Perhaps you don't eat anything. I don't know what films you like or books you read or whether you have ever played a musical instrument. We have sex; we drink coffee; we talk. We don't really talk about our home lives; we never use names for my husband or your wife. Occasionally, we talk about relationships in general or past lovers, but mostly we have one topic of conversation and one only: us, ourselves, what we are doing, what we are thinking and feeling about each other.

In between meetings, I am crazed with desire and I write letter after letter to you on my computer, and I am grateful that you have banned e-mail contact between us because within hours of writing them I feel sick with embarrassment at what I reveal about myself, at my paltry attempts to sound cool and analytical while revealing I am the opposite.

I don't always manage things well in my head.

One day, we arrange to meet outside Portcullis House, a building I now feel a certain affection for. It is past the end of the day—you are working late for some reason—but you still keep me waiting for half an hour and when you arrive you do so without apology, as normal, and I can tell that whatever has delayed you is still on your mind. You smile your half smile and don't speak. *Fine*, I think. Well, I won't make conversation either. Maybe I have things on my mind too.

Descending the steps, we turn right, toward Westminster Tube station. There is a tiny coffee bar there that we have used before, with two stools in the window. It is dusk, chilly for the time of year—groups of shivering tourists dressed too optimistically are huddling together, blocking the pavement. We weave our way between them. The silver cube of the Tube entrance swallows and disgorges suits. We have nearly reached it when you take my arm and wheel me round to go back the way we have come. "Let's walk along the river," you say. It is the first thing you have said to me.

We go round the corner, back past the entrance to Portcullis House. Across the river, the London Eye is lit at intervals by bright blue lights, a slowly turning fairy circle in the gray and purple sky. Still in silence, we walk down Embankment, unhurrying, past the rows of tourist coaches parked and empty. Beyond them, the crowds of visitors thin and the street becomes easier to negotiate. We walk past the back entrance of the squat, redbrick building that is the Territorial Policing Headquarters, with the lampposts outside that always make me smile—the old-fashioned police lamppost, *Dixon of Dock Green, Z-Cars* . . . Crime never paid back then, not when you had to fiddle with a dial to clear the fuzz from your mahogany-encased television screen, not in black and white. It's all wafer thin and brightly colored now and unforgivably instant in its clarity—you can see the news presenters' pores beneath their orange makeup. There is a lot more ambiguity around nowadays as well, I've noticed recently. Crime pays now, all right. Well, right now at this minute, walking next to a man I shouldn't be with, I feel like it pays.

We walk slowly past the rear entrance of the Savoy and beyond, out of touristland and into the land of government buildings. After a few minutes—we still have not spoken—we reach Victoria Embankment Gardens, set back from the road and the river, a thin strip of park with a single path that snakes through it, lined with benches. In the gathering dark, we have it to ourselves. On the road, still visible through shrubbery on which the spring growth seems decidedly bare, black cabs, lorries, cars thunder by in a haze of inner-city pollutants, and beyond the traffic, the river rushes to keep up. We pass a rectangular lily pond on our right. A sign behind it reads DANGER: DEEP WATER. *Bit late for that,* I think.

A few yards farther on, there is the statue of the weeping woman. I have passed it before: it's a noticeable sort of statue. There is an ordinary stone plinth with a bronze bust on top: Arthur Sullivan, 1842–1900, the kind of thing you see in parks all over London, the forgotten philanthropists or composers or writers, the generals and explorers and educationalists, those Victorians who built us. But this one is different, for leaning against the stone is the life-size form of a young woman, also cast in bronze. She is turned away from passersby, weeping against the pillar, one arm above her head, stretching upward, and the other bent so that she can bury her face in it. Her perfect, lithe body is resting in an attitude of utter despair.

I pause. You pause too and, still without speaking, we look at the young bronze woman, the curve of her firm, high breasts—she is topless in the classical mode, of course—the robes gathered around her hips, the half-dressed hair that flows in tendrils down her back. *Her despair is the despair of youth,* I think. She is every first-year student who has woken on a Sunday morning and remembered that last night, at that party, the young man she loved left with his arm round someone else. She is someone who thinks that despair is a country she has entered, like a desert where she will die of thirst. I remember heartbreak at that age, how all-consuming it was. Is heartbreak even possible now, I wonder? I'm fifty-two. Anyone my age knows that all things pass. If the transitory nature of our feelings means that true heartbreak is impossible, then where does that leave happiness?

Something about her has made us stop and look. We still have barely spoken to each other. You take a few steps round the side of the plinth and read the inscription. I come and stand by you and look at it while you read aloud.

IS LIFE A BOON?
IF SO, IT MVST BEFAL
THAT DEATH WHENE'ER HE CALL
MVST CALL TOO SOON

Through the middle of the poem, running from the top of the plinth to almost halfway down, there is a long streak of green mold.

"It's death she's upset about," I murmur. "I always thought it was love."

"It's a bit of a no-win situation, really, according to the poem," you say. "Either life is a boon, in which case we should all be weeping because death is going to come and spoil everything, and soon. Or else, well, or else life isn't a boon after all, just a grim old business."

I look at you. "Which side of the argument do you fall on?" I try not to sound too serious when I ask this question.

You look at me, unfooled by my facetiousness. Then you reach out a hand and touch a heavy lock of hair that hangs to one side of my chin, twisting it between your fingers. "Me?" you say, staring at me. "Me? I think life is a boon."

We move toward each other. Your hands go to either side of my face, your warm rough palms against my cold soft cheeks. I tip my face up to you and close my eyes.

Without speaking, we leave the weeping girl behind and within a moment have reached the edge of the gardens. Temple Tube station is brightly lit, the coffee and flower stalls outside are not particularly busy— it is past the peak of the rush hour, almost dark. Just past the Tube, we turn left down a narrow road called Temple Place that leads away from the river. Temple Place narrows further and becomes Milford Lane, which ends in a tiny yard with a brick entrance through which I can just see a row of stone steps.

"Can you get up to the Strand through there?" I ask. I haven't been this way before.

"Yes," you say, "it comes out just below the Royal Courts of Justice."

But it isn't justice or the bright lights of the Strand you have in mind. You turn on me. One hand goes behind my head, fingers entwined in my hair, the other to my shoulder. You pull my mouth toward yours. At the same time, you press forward, forcing me to stumble backward against the wall, just to the right of the entranceway to the steps. I let out an involuntary gasp.

You stop and look around, with the intent glance I now know means you are doing what you have previously referred to as *a risk assessment.*

To your right—my left—there is a building but no windows look down on us. On the other side—I follow your gaze upward—there is a CCTV camera but it is turned away from us, pointing up another alleyway. You kiss me, briefly, firmly, then move your head back a little so you can continue to glance from side to side while slipping your hand inside my coat, pushing my thighs apart. "*Oh . . . ,*" I say, but this time it is more a groan than a gasp, deeper, more resonant, within.

At that point, there comes the scrape of shoes on stone, a hasty approach. We spring apart, my coat falls back, I let out a snort of amused alarm, and a young man in a business suit rushes down the stone steps and out into the yard, hurrying past us without a glance, heading for the Tube. You are facing away from me now and the yard is unlit so it is only as you turn back, a smile on your face, that I see you are holding a cigarette between two fingers.

"I didn't know you smoked!" My voice is breathy from our near discovery.

"I don't," you say, dropping the cigarette back into your pocket. "I keep one in my left pocket—explains all sorts of things, why you're outside, why you're loitering, and you can approach people for a light if you need to. Newspapers are good too. No one ever looks at someone reading the *Evening Standard* on the street and wonders why he is standing there. He is just someone reading the paper."

More footsteps on the stone, heels this time, two young women in smart skirts and jackets come down the steps together, talking to each other. One of them gives me a look as she passes, a dismissive sort of look, as though she might think ill of me if she could be bothered to think of me at all.

You take my arm. "Come on," you say. "I was planning on coming inside you but it's still too busy round here."

Back at the Tube, you turn to me and say, "Right, then," and I realize you are planning on leaving me here to get the Underground while you go on elsewhere. I experience a moment of confusion—suddenly, you seem to be in a hurry to depart. But if we had achieved solitude in the little yard back there, you wouldn't have been thinking about rushing off at this particular moment. You would be focused on me.

"Yeah, sure," I say, "I'll get it from here. See you, then, talk tomorrow," and turn quickly. I am determined to be the one walking away.

I am no more than a step or two away before you catch up with me and take my arm. "Hey . . . ," you say.

We stop, facing each other. I look down at your shoes. What sort of stupid game are we playing, anyway? We're both middle-aged. It's ridiculous. We are ridiculous.

"You've been there before, haven't you?" I mumble, and it is only as I say it that I realize that that is what is bothering me. I had thought we were ambling along Victoria Embankment but you knew exactly where we were going. You had a plan. Perhaps you were even deliberately late to meet me because you thought there was a better chance of us using that alleyway the darker it got.

You sigh. It is a sigh that makes me feel childish. "Look . . . ," you say, and I wait. I am not going to help you out this time by pretending I am as casual about this as you are. All at once, I refuse to let you off the hook. "You know, you know me by now . . . ," you say. You lift a hand and run it through your hair. Your expression is a little pleading. Around us, people hurry to and fro, people who are late getting home. No one looks at us as they rush past.

"Is it, is it what you do?" I ask, and I keep my tone deliberately light. I don't want to panic you into lying to me.

"Well, yes," you say. "It's what I do, it's what I've always . . ."

"What, kind of, your thing?"

"Yes, that's it, it's my thing. It's just what turns me on, I suppose. Car parks, toilets, out-of-doors, I don't know. I suppose . . ." You lift your hands helplessly.

There are a million questions in my head, starting with, *Does your wife know? Do you do this with her, or have you ever done?* And continuing with, *So just how many affairs have you had before me?*

You shrug boyishly, look at me, and grimace. "I just find it, I don't know, it's the naughtiness of it, I suppose, the risk factor, I don't know. Look, I guess it's a sort of addiction, a kind of adrenaline. Loads of people do it or other things like it. Everybody wants to take risks some-times, don't they? I look at the people I work with and it's just a question of what form their risk taking takes. One of my colleagues goes paragliding on the weekends. He breaks his collarbone every time he lands. He has four children. At least I don't jump off cliffs."

No, I think, a little bitterly, *you just ask other people to.* We are standing outside Temple Tube in the midevening dark and it's colder than it should be this time of year. It occurs to me that I am not turned on by the possibility of discovery—the opposite, in fact. What turns me on is the thought of a hotel room, crisp white sheets and plump soft furnishings, low lighting, mirrors only we can see, anonymity and privacy, being somewhere where no one can find me, but all I say is, "Well, I guess this is a conversation we will have to have another time."

"Let's have it now," you say, and I smile inwardly, for the one thing I am sure of is that there is nothing more likely to keep you with me than the thought that I might be withholding information. I am reminded of what Susannah said to me once: *There's a certain sort of man whose very charm lies in his predictability.* I would repeat this remark to you but suspect you would find it offensive.

"Go on." You lean in toward me.

I shake my head a little, but smilingly.

You lift a finger and give a gentle but decisive stab at my forehead. "What's going on in there, then? Right now, what's going on in there?"

I look around. "We're pretty close." I mean to the area where you work, and that there's a chance someone who knows you might go past. But I'm prevaricating. I wasn't worried about that when we kissed in Victoria Embankment Gardens, and we were closer then.

You fold your arms and glower at me, playing interrogator. "Well, you'd better tell me what's on your mind, then, or we could be here awhile."

"What does it *mean*?" I ask, and even to my own ears, it sounds like a feeble question. "The risky sex, what does it mean?"

To your credit, you take the question seriously. You shrug. "It doesn't mean anything, I don't think. It's just what I like, like some people like it in the mornings and some people want to dress up and others like it best in the shower. Some people like chocolate sauce, I don't know. It doesn't mean anything." A group of women in high heels, tripping out somewhere, shove past us so close that you have to take my elbow and pull me gently to the side, but still no one looks at us. We are just a man and a woman having a conversation before they part.

I am in something of a fix. What I really want to know is, *Have you taken another woman down that little lane, like you did with me just now, and I'm guessing the answer is yes and that last time it was more successful because it was later in the evening.* But I can't ask that without sounding insecure, and in a minute you're going to guess I'm feeling insecure anyway and suddenly I can't stand the humiliation of that and there is only one way to deflect your attention, so I say, "Want to know what I fantasize about?"

"Of course."

"Alien abduction."

Your stare turns into *What?*

I smile and nod. "I do, I fantasize that I've been kidnapped by aliens, and I'm on a round white bed, completely naked of course, and there's a sort of balcony around the bed, all the way round, and on the balcony are aliens, and they are all looking down at me, at me being naked— small men with pointy heads."

"You're making this up."

I laugh at him. "Er, yes, it's a fantasy."

"No, I mean you're making this up on the spot. You're taking the mickey."

I shake my head. "I'm not, I promise. Honestly, it's what I think about quite often, in the middle, you know, I'm on the round white bed, and it's warm."

"*Pointy heads?*"

"I know, pretty obvious, eh?"

You raise a hand and scratch the back of your head. "I don't know, for some reason I thought the sexual fantasy of one of the nation's top analytical scientists would be something a little more sophisticated."

"Sophisticated as in doing it down back alleys during rush hour?"

A brief pause. "One-nil." We are smiling at each other, the tension broken. I have convinced you I am your equal in this sort of banter. I have managed to swerve away from a moment of humiliation.

Pride is a terrible thing. It is what makes me turn away from you at that point, when all I really want to do is walk along the river hand in hand, then go down to the South Bank and sit in the bar at the Royal Festival Hall and listen to some jazz if someone is playing, then have dinner in a restaurant somewhere, our knees brushing against each other beneath the table. Pride is what makes me leave you without even asking if such a scenario is possible. I want to do it so much I can't stand the thought of being turned down. My husband is at a concert tonight. I could be out all night, if I wanted. Maybe you could too. Maybe you headed toward the Tube because you were just assuming I had to be home. Maybe we are about to miss out on the rare opportunity of a whole evening together because neither of us will raise it as an option, neither of us wanting to be the one who is available.

"I'd better go," I say as I turn.

You don't even try to give me a chaste, public embrace but raise your hand in farewell, let me go. I pause in the Tube hall to renew my Oyster card in the hope you might follow me in, but you don't, of course. It's all I can do to steel myself not to run down the road after you even though I don't even know which direction you were going in, whether you were going home or back to your office, to a late meeting elsewhere, or a leaving do or an evening with friends or . . . to meet another woman, perhaps, now darkness has fallen and the alleyways are emptying. I have no idea, and no right to ask.

As I go through the barrier, the phone you gave me buzzes in my pocket and I lift it out. You have texted: *When you get home, send me pic of what you do when you think about the men with pointy heads. Please!* And despite myself I smile, for I know I have to take this for what it is and to try to feel that life is a boon—confusing sometimes, and frustrating often, but a boon.

That night, I wake up about an hour after my husband and I have gone to sleep. He is turned away from me, on his side, snoring softly. I can just see his form from the green glow given out by the clock that throws the time in large digits on our ceiling. We both like a little electric light while we sleep, the legacy of all those years we left a landing light on and our door open in case one of the children woke in the night. The duvet has slipped down and his large, speckled back is exposed. The thinning patch of hair on the back of his head makes me feel protective toward him. I smile to myself as I think of how hard he is to stir sometimes, particularly in the first hour of sleep. My husband goes down into unconsciousness as surely and as swiftly as a deep-sea diver goes into the sea.

I'm fucking a spook.

That explains everything: the ease with which you move around the Palace of Westminster; the way you are mostly the master of your own timetable but then are suddenly called away on urgent business; your periods of silence. It explains why you are an adrenaline junkie, why when you want me you are capable of pestering me with calls or texts and want me absolutely *now* but at other times you seem almost indifferent. It explains your extreme secretiveness, the intensity of which has always struck me as beyond that required by simple adultery—the business with the pay-as-you-go phone, your banning e-mail contact, the melodrama of our arrangements. Maybe that's just how one conducts an affair when you are used to being involved with matters of national security.

Now I know why you want to know so much about me but reveal so little about yourself, why you often seem convinced to the point of arrogance that you can persuade me to do anything you want, in the nicest possible way, of course, why you know so much about CCTV cameras and camouflaging yourself on the street. With all these thoughts comes a thrill—is it excitement or fear or some weird combination of the two? If you are a spook, then what happens if you think I am holding out on you? Can you trace the location of that phone you gave me? Have you banned any written contact between us to protect me because your association with me could put me at risk? What happens if—and this thought feels new, fresh, damp from the egg—*what happens if I want out?*

My husband murmurs in his sleep, turns over to face me, murmurs again, turns back. I think of the seriousness of the expression on your face when you gave me the pay-as-you-go phone. Have I completely misjudged you, what we are doing, I mean, who or what you are? Is there any chance you could be vengeful or dangerous, that my husband could be at risk, maybe even my children? This thought makes my heart pound and I have to breathe deeply and say to myself, *Don't be stupid . . . no one is at risk . . .* It's the middle of the night. Everything is disproportionate in the middle of the night. It's a well-known fact.

Rationalize this, I think then. It's just sex. It will peter out once this man loses interest and, once you've worked through his repertoire of favorite locations, he almost certainly will. That's the kind of man he is. It will last three months at most. Your pride will be wounded and you'll get your heart a little bit broken and you'll think you deserve it, and you'll moon around for a bit, then shake yourself down and everything will get back to normal. That's all that's going to happen.

Should I feel more guilty or less because you work for the security services? I ask myself. But then I realize that guilt is not something that needs to be talked away in my head, not really; it is simply absent. The truth is—and it is not something I am proud of—I feel I am owed this. I am owed you. For twenty-eight years, I have done everything asked of me, worked hard and supported my family, loved my husband, raised my children. I have made my contribution to society. I recycle the newspapers every week. Doesn't that buy me something? *I am rationalizing like a man,* I think. This is exactly what a man would say to himself the night after he has seduced his secretary. No one will ever know; no one will get hurt. But I have not seduced my secretary. I have chosen carefully, even though I didn't know I was choosing at the time. I am doing this with a man who has the means and motivation to ensure we will never be exposed. I have not pursued a young and vulnerable woman over whom I have authority of some sort. I have not taken advantage of my position and allowed myself to become involved with someone who adores me, or fallen in love and had a wretched two-year love affair involving comprehensive deceit of the person I live with. I have made my bargain. I'm fucking a spook. He's a risk taker. He likes pursuit and novelty. It may sound dangerous, but actually, it couldn't be safer.

Outside, in the garden, comes the short, harsh yelp of one of the urban foxes that live around here, then silence.

6

It's difficult for me to talk about what happened next, my love. That won't surprise you, I know. At this point in my story, I am pausing, in my head, my heart too—I feel myself slow and shudder, tense, the way that someone who is terrified of spiders would as she hovers at the threshold of a room she knows might contain them. There are places I don't want to go—or, to be accurate, one place I don't want to go—but I am trying to be honest, however painful it is. I am trying to say to myself that if I can face this, if I can tell it, as if it were just a car crash that once happened to me, it will be okay. Yes, that's it, tell it like it was a car crash, tell how I was driving along the middle lane of a motorway and looking in my right-hand rearview mirror because there was some scary silver car approaching fast in the overtaking lane and I thought it might be dangerous. I was scared that, as it overtook me, it would stray into my lane, and just as I had my eye on the scary silver car wondering how dangerous it could be, some innocuous-seeming family saloon came at me from the left, from the slow lane, and slammed into me.

Car accidents happen all the time, everyone knows that, common as muck, so common we take them for granted. Yet however frequent car accidents may be, nobody believes it will ever happen to them. If you've been driving safely for years, you have the illusion that car accidents are other people's tragedies, perhaps even that it's more likely to happen to some people than others, that somehow they must have been just that little bit careless or incompetent, if not downright stupid. It won't happen to you, though. You just can't imagine yourself being a victim.

I go up in the air, spinning helplessly in the lump of metal in which I am trapped, and don't even have the time to acknowledge that the likely outcome, when my somersaulting car hits the ground, is that it, and I, and everything, will burst into flames.

As soon as you came into the café that night—the night it happened—I saw that you were in a dangerous mood.

The light in the café is brown and dim, but even before you see me, I recognize the expression on your face. Your moods are always endearingly obvious, I think. I watch you approach the table where I wait. As usual, you are late. You glance around as you walk into the center of the café. You see me but your look is unseeing: you are annoyed with someone else, not me, but you can't help it spilling over. This has happened before and I know our conversation will be tinged with aggression on your part and a kind of defensive banter on mine. I am determined to hold my own on these occasions. Sometimes you make a derogatory remark, brief and offhand, about your wife. It is the only time you are disloyal toward her. "I had better not be long," you might say, "or I'll be in trouble *again* . . ." On such occasions, I am torn. It would be wrong of me to encourage this disloyalty—and given the long hours you work, I am sure you deserve every ounce of trouble you are in. You have said very little about her, but I am quite certain she is not an unreasonable woman. At such moments, even though I am crazy about you and have never met her, a certain degree of female solidarity kicks in. At the same time, there is a small, mean part of me that is glad, that wants to say to you, *Confide in me, be disloyal with me, I won't betray your trust and it will bind us.* That would be a short-term strategy, though; I know that instinctively, new as I may be to the infidelity game. Whatever minor advantage I might gain by encouraging you to be disloyal to your wife will come to rebound on me eventually. It's a bit late for me to try to claim the moral high ground, given what we are doing, but I feel I should at least do my best not to compound my status as . . . as what? The easy one? The cheap date? How does it work in your head, my sweet? Are you really that traditional? Are there wife-type women and mistress-type women, in your head? If so, aren't you a little confused? I couldn't be more traditional or wife-type, in so many ways. If we had met and married when we were young, I would be at home now, and when you were back two hours later than you said you would be, I have no doubt that with me, too, you would have been *in trouble*.

We are meeting in a café behind St. James's Church, one of those cafés that like to masquerade as sitting rooms. You slump down in the armchair opposite mine, take one of your phones out of the pocket of your bulky wool coat and check it, put it back. You look at me and smile, but I can tell you're not with me. *It's a work thing, then,* I think, *not the wife at home this time.* You've left the office to meet me with something important unresolved.

I am on my way to a faculty party at the university. The head of sciences is retiring and is throwing a huge bash, all his staff, selected external examiners like me, and various scientists from private institutions and funding bodies. The head of sciences is married to a French wine merchant and caterer, and expectations of this party are unusually high for a faculty do. I haven't been to a party for a while and am looking forward to it. I have suggested this coffee because you haven't yet seen me dressed up, only in my work clothes. I was hoping to impress you with my glamour but even though I had warned you by text that I was in party gear, you have yet to notice.

"Shall I get you a coffee?" I say, in a voice I mean to be kindly and understanding but to my ears sounds patronizing.

You don't seem to notice that you're being patronized, or if you do, you're too distracted to care. "White americano," you reply, no thanks or acknowledgment, and you get one of the phones out of your pocket again and immediately start checking e-mails. It's hard to know what to do at such moments. It is human nature, faced with such behavior, to become annoyed and demanding, but of the many roles I would like in your life, petulant mistress is the last, so I rise and go to the counter. When I have ordered, I look back at you—you are tapping something into the phone. I pay for the coffee and glance back again, still standing waiting at the counter. You are tucking the phone into an inside pocket—and then, that done, all at once you look at me and see me watching you from where I stand, and there it is: that coruscating smile. And I know that whatever was bothering you has been resolved and that for the next few minutes or however long we have, you are mine.

I turn back to the counter as the barista places the coffee in front of me, pick it up, and then make my way back to you, weaving between the crowded tables. I do not look at you, but know that you are looking at me. Now, I have your attention. I ease my way through the tight spaces between chairs with a sideways sway of my hips. I know that the dress I am wearing flatters me, the fine black material gathered and ruched in the right places. I know it makes me seem voluptuous rather than plump, and that this is something you are observing. It is an odd and arbitrary business, getting you to notice me. I was wearing exactly the same dress when you entered the café but your mind was elsewhere. Now, suddenly, I am receiving the full beam of your attention, and the more you stare the more I sway and the more I sway the more you stare, and by the time I reach our table, I am wet already, just from being observed by you, and your lips are parted slightly as I place the coffee down in front of you.

"You know it's really quite demure . . . ," you say, nodding toward the dress. Still no *thank you*.

"Think so?" I smile.

"Well, your text said *party* frock. It's longer than I expected, long sleeves, but that bit . . ." Your gaze lingers on the wide space above my cleavage. This part of me has not aged, for some reason. I have yet to grow the brown spots and lizard lines that some women do, although I am sure it won't be long.

I raise my own coffee to my lips and take a sip, looking at you over the cup as I do. You watch me carefully. I put down my cup and wait for you to speak.

You lean forward in your chair. "Go to the ladies' and take your knickers off."

I stare at you. You move your head in a small gesture: *go on*.

I rise from the chair again with the same disbelieving mixture of irritation and compliance I felt when I got you your coffee while you checked your e-mails. *What am I? What do you think I am?*

In the ladies' toilet, I pee, then do as I am bid.

What am I? I look in the mirror as I wash my hands afterward. My knickers are balled up in my handbag.

As I emerge from the ladies', you are watching me, and you continue to watch me as I make my way through the tables. You glance at the length of my body and raise your eyebrows. I sit and open my handbag. You peer in, then without even looking round to see if we are being observed, reach in for the balled-up pair of knickers and enclose them in your fist. You lift your hand and look at the knickers briefly before tucking them into your coat pocket. "A thong. Easy access, eh? Demure dress but a thong underneath. Nice."

I affect outrage, although I knew that was what you would do. "Give them back," I hiss, looking around. The other tables are close to ours but we are slightly lower because we are sitting on the easy chairs and the murmur of conversation is loud enough for us not to be overheard.

"No," you say, staring into my eyes.

"Give them back," I repeat, achieving an easy mix of laughter and insistence.

"You're wearing hold-ups, aren't you?"

"It's warm tonight . . ." I laugh, but awkwardly because the truth is, I wore hold-ups for you in anticipation of exactly this scenario.

"Go to the party with no knickers on. Wander around and only you and I will know. But the men will all be like dogs. They will be able to tell even though they don't know what it is about you."

"You won't even be there."

"I'll still know."

"Give them back."

"Okay, in a bit. I'm just keeping them hostage for a while . . . Okay?"

You reach into a pocket for your phone, and for a minute I think you are going to check your e-mails again but you press a few buttons then hold it out to me. "This is what I did in my lunch hour this morning, thinking of you."

My sweet, I never owned up to you then because I didn't want to deflate you, but the videos never did it for me. They say men are turned on by images, women by words. I don't know if that's true. I liked some of the visuals. I liked the photo of you that you sent me once where you rested your phone on the dashboard of your car and took a picture of yourself, cross looking, stuck in a traffic jam. I don't know why I liked that one so much, but I did. It was the combination of you looking cross and sexy with the fact that you wanted to share this with me, that you were annoyed about being stuck in a traffic jam. Extraordinary what can be arousing. Your simpleness, that was what turned me on that evening in the café. It wasn't the video—it was your plain belief that what did it for you did it for me and that that was all we needed. Your straightforward and profound arousal: your bossiness combined with your need; you were like a toddler sometimes. You wanted it when you wanted it, right there and then. Did I desire you so much that day because I was enjoying being wanton or enjoying indulging your desires? Truly, there are some things that scientific research has yet to explain.

About half an hour later, I say to you, "I should go. I should be there for the speeches."

"Are you going to have a good time?" you ask, suddenly sulky.

"You bet," I say. I'm in an upbeat mood and it shows, drunk on your desire for me even before I get to the party and have any alcohol. I haven't quite worked out how to get my knickers back.

"Come on," you say, and rise from your chair. "Let's go for a walk."

We leave the café and I turn toward Piccadilly, but you turn in the opposite direction, heading south, and begin to walk down Duke of York Street. I catch up with you and look at you but you seem distracted again. Halfway down, you stop, quite close to the café where we had our first coffee, and I wonder if you are about to remark on it. Then you start walking again, striding off without even looking to see if I am behind. I catch up with you, a little out of breath. You glance around, then stand on the curb for a moment, leaning forward, about to cross the road. A taxi comes swinging round the corner and you put out a hand to bar my way. As it sweeps past, you step out and I follow.

On the other side of the street, you walk down a small street that forms a dead end. Although this is a busy area, with early evening drinkers carousing behind the leaded windows of a pub on the corner, there is nothing down this side street—no pedestrians and no cars as it is restricted parking. There are no entrances to the buildings either— both sets of buildings show us their backs, their blank double doors for loading and unloading. There are no handles to the doors. People open them from the inside to receive goods, that's all.

I know what you want—it was obvious as soon as we turned into this small dead end. There is a doorway halfway down on the left. You hustle me into it, with my back against the door, tucking yourself in against me so that we are sheltered from sight of anyone walking down the main road. We are overlooked only by the back of the building behind you, which you assess for a moment and decide is safe, before turning to press your mouth down on mine. As you do, you raise the skirt of my dress and your hand is hard and warm and, well, how can I put this? You always did know which button to press.

And then you are inside me, and I don't believe we are doing it, in Piccadilly, in the rush hour, with a thousand people hurrying by a few meters away.

Afterward, you press your mouth against mine again, briefly, and return my knickers to me, then step back, scanning from left to right as you do, as I pull them on over my hold-ups and boots. No one has walked down the street during that time, but we have been only a matter of minutes. Before we step out of the doorway, you look at me, smile, then lift your forefinger and stroke it down the length of my nose. "Okay?" you ask softly. I nod.

We walk back down the street together, toward the bright lights and the bustle of commuters, me a little unsteady in my heeled boots. As we reach the end of the alley, I glance up and see its name on a high plaque: APPLE TREE YARD.

PART TWO

A, T, G, AND C

7

Being in the dock at the Old Bailey is like being a member of the royal family—or a president or pope, perhaps. Sitting there, surrounded by guards and bulletproof glass, is probably the closest an ordinary mortal can get to replicating the state of constant protection that such people live under. People are not horrible to you when you are a defendant in a criminal trial: people are kind, in an infantilizing kind of way. You are the center of everyone's concern. It is all about you.

Although the dock is at the back of the court, the court is shallow and wide, so you can see everything before you. The only person whose view is as good as yours is the judge, directly opposite. You and the judge are the North and South Pole of the judicial process. You are escorted to and from the court; so is he. You are fed, catered for; so is he. You and he both have the power to stop proceedings, object to jurors, challenge witnesses—although you must do it via your advocate. There is only one difference between you. He is North and you are South—you are each other's inverse but there is no doubt who sits on high. He might send you to prison for the rest of your life. You have to try not to think about that bit, though, because if you do, you will go insane.

The best way of not thinking about that bit is to think about your rights. Your rights matter here, and part of the judge's job is to have due regard for your rights. Robert, my barrister, told me the only thing a crown court judge fears is a successful appeal. They don't even like unsuccessful ones. It is the only time their judgment is called into question. For that reason alone, the judge, however powerful, must be vigilant. Your rights and needs must not be traduced or ignored in any way. This gives you a sense of power—fragile, illusory, perhaps, but power nonetheless. And so, for the duration of the trial, you and the judge feel not so much opposites as partners locked in a kind of arranged marriage. You spend a lot of time staring at him, wondering who the hell you have been landed with. He spends a lot of time staring back, no doubt wondering the same.

During the opening days of the trial, I followed the evidence closely, of course; every remark from the prosecution barrister, the demeanor of each witness. There was a sharp difference between the professional witnesses—the forensic experts, the police officers, Witness G—and the amateurs, the bystanders: the young man from the grocer's shop who saw you getting into my car, the landlady, the taxi driver. The professionals often remained on their feet in the witness box, addressing the judge with sharp deference, reading the oath clearly and loudly. The amateurs gave a little bow of gratitude when the judge said to them, "Behind you, you will see a drop-down seat, please feel free to use it . . ." and then sat with alacrity, eager not so much to get off their feet as to do anything the judge suggested might be a good idea. They looked frightened but brave, determined to do their duty.

At first, as the witnesses were speaking, I stared at them, as if I could read in their faces my eventual fate, as if each statement, no matter how insignificant or banal, might be the turning point in my ordeal. If anyone said anything I disagreed with, I made a note of it and raised it with Robert at the end of the day.

Later on, I came to realize that none of these witnesses would prove crucial to the way our trial would go—there was only one witness who would do that: me. But I did not have to take the stand during the prosecution case—the prosecution had no right to oblige me to do so. No defendant can be compelled to speak as part of the case against him or her.

Even during the prosecution case, when I expected to be concentrating carefully, knowing I would later take the stand, there were so many longueurs and legal arguments when the jury was not allowed to be present that my attention would sometimes shift momentarily from the professionals and my gaze would flick up to the public gallery. It remained empty for some of the trial—there were parts of my evidence when the public gallery was emptied, and it was closed for Witness G, of course. Sometimes the security guard was slow about admitting people in the morning or after the lunch break, and the door opened only well after proceedings were under way. Susannah told me later that there was a lot of waiting around on a concrete stairwell. The first day she arrived she was caught out, as many are, by the ruling that mobile phones are not allowed in the gallery and there is no locker or cubby-hole in which to leave them. A security guard told her that if she went over the road to the café, the owner there would look after her phone if she paid him a pound.

Susannah was in the gallery nearly every day—she used up half her annual leave in order to support me. She, too, had a notebook. The jury must have noticed her and probably assumed she was my sister, or a cousin, and as she is the nearest I have ever had to one, that was fine by me. My mother died many years ago and I've hardly seen my father since he moved to Scotland with his new wife, just once every few years. He and I spoke on the phone a grand total of three times while I was on bail. My brother lives in New Zealand. So it was just Susannah up there, among the students and retired people and the occasional gawper whose role I couldn't identify.

No one came for you, my love, as far as I know—with the exception of your wife on that one day when she caused a disturbance and found herself banned thereafter. It made me wonder about your life, even more than I had already, that is. Many of the questions I had were answered during our trial, including many things I had chosen to find mysterious for my own purposes. You became named and concrete during our trial: that was one of its many ironies.

Sometimes, I would look up at Susannah and notice the empty seats beside her. I imagined my family there: my husband, my son, my daughter—Guy, Adam, Carrie. I missed them so much; I was hollow with missing them. The fact that I had pleaded with them to stay away from the trial did not make me miss them less, rather more. They are not the viscera of this story, those three—they are not the drama, the life or death business of it, but they are its beating heart. They are my day-in day-out people; I inhale and exhale them with each breath. When the hours are added up at the end of it, they will win.

You asked me once how Guy and I met, and I said with a shrug, "At university," as if that explained everything. Later, I felt guilty about that shrug. It's an easy line, after all. The university boyfriend and girlfriend, sometimes they stay together and get married, sometimes they don't—it makes it sound as though they have no daring or imagination.

It was only two weeks into my fresher term at university when I first set eyes on Guy, in the café in the science block. There was a group of ten of us crammed around one small table, nursing instant coffee in plastic cups. Girls were unusual on science courses back then and there were only three around the table that day. The other two had become firm friends already, sensing a shared enjoyment in their minority status.

"So, who are you?" one of the confident girls said to me, across the table, in front of everyone. We had met before but my name hadn't registered. The boys were all lounging in their seats, some swinging their chairs back, arms wide. Opposite me around the table was a broad-shouldered, rangy boy with long straight hair and a slight frown, flicking through his folder of notes. I had noticed him as soon as we sat down and felt, without knowing why, that the other girls had noticed him too. It was partly his size but mostly his indifference. The other boys were all showing off slightly for our benefit, talking in that loud, shouty-boy way, popping biscuits in their mouths whole, picking their noses.

"Yvonne," I said to the confident girls, who were sitting next to each other, to the right of the large silent boy. "Yvonne Carmichael."

"Yvonne." The girl who had asked the question tipped her head on one side. She lifted her left hand and pulled a thick strand of shiny dark hair over her shoulder, twizzled it round one finger, then tossed it back. "I've got an aunty called Yvonne."

Two of the boys grinned oafishly.

"Yvonne Carmichael?" The large boy had looked up from his notes. I nodded.

"You're the one who got the Jennifer Tyrell Prize."

90

I nodded again.

"What's that?" said the other girl, loudly, leaning forward in her seat and looking hard at the large boy.

The large boy looked at me and raised his eyebrows, inviting me to answer.

"It's a science essay prize for sixth-formers. Her parents set it up." Jennifer Tyrell had been a particularly brilliant science undergraduate in Glasgow who had been killed in a road accident in her first year. Her parents had set up a nationwide essay prize in her name in order to encourage girls to go into science. It was a fairly obscure prize, run by some educational institute in London, and known only to the heads of sciences for sixth-formers around the country. When I won it, for an essay titled, "Of Mice and Molecules," I got two paragraphs in the *Surrey and Sutton Advertiser*.

"Gets hundreds of entries," the large boy said. "Open only to girls. Yvonne Carmichael."

"That's just so sexist," said one of the confident girls.

The boys around the table were nodding enthusiastically, but I wasn't paying them any attention. I was looking at the large boy and noting the emphasis he put on my name.

By the end of that first term I found myself in an established position within our social group: implausibly, I was Alpha Male's Girlfriend. Guy was hardly Alpha in the traditional sense—he was bulky but utterly uninterested in most forms of sport—and yet his absorption in his work and air of genuine indifference affected the other boys as much as it affected me. They were all much in his thrall. Often, I would be the only girl at their shared house over a weekend, and one of them would get me on my own and confide in me about which girl he fancied and ask my advice. When Guy and I split up for two terms during the second year, no fewer than three of them propositioned me, but that was all to do with Guy's status, I knew that: they didn't want to fuck me, they wanted to fuck him. It's one of the things that women find hard to grasp—the role of male competitiveness in sexual attraction toward them. It's hard for us to think of ourselves as a prize: just as hard, in its own way, as it is for us to think of ourselves as prey.

Guy and I married the summer after we graduated and I was

pregnant by the autumn. Most people assumed the pregnancy was an accident, or even our reason for getting married in the first place, but Adam was a very planned baby, as was Carrie shortly after. We had discussed it at some length. The best thing, we decided, was to have our two children in quick succession while we were both working on our PhDs. That way, we could combine writing our theses with the full-on bit of child rearing and they would both be in school during our postdocs.

Guy completed his PhD in three years and mine took seven. Funny that.

I remember the day he rang me, all excited, thrilled to bits in fact, unable to keep the news to himself until he got home. He had something to tell me: he had just been made head of lab.

Adam and Carrie were nine and eight at the time. I had picked them up from school a couple of hours before but then taken them to the shops, so we had only just got in. Carrie was in floods of tears because her best friend had told her she wasn't anymore. This seemed to be an existential question: "I'm *not* anymore . . ." she was crying. Adam was hunched over a saucepan on the floor of the kitchen, slopping eggs around with a wooden spoon—I had told him he could beat them for me while I talked to Dad on the phone. We were having scrambled egg on toast. That's what we did for supper when Guy wouldn't be home in time—reprised breakfast.

I looked down at the floor. Well, we were having however much scrambled egg would be left in the pan after Adam had spread half of it over the linoleum. We were living in a two-bedroom first-floor flat with no carpet in the hallway. The couple in the flat above us were newlyweds who rowed incessantly, the screeching of a couple whose mutual loathing spilled outside their arguments and into every aspect of their lives. Sometimes, lying awake at night listening to them tramping around and sniping at each other, I felt as though the unhappiness in their flat was seeping down through the ceiling into ours, like damp.

Carrie was sitting on a chair, still wailing with a catlike rise and fall, well past the stage of acute distress but wanting my attention nonetheless. Adam was trying to scoop up an egg yolk from the floor with the wooden spoon, to get it back in the pan. He had the temper of a much younger child. I knew he was seconds away from hurling the spoon across the room, where it would somersault in the air before crashing against the wall above his sister's head. I was watching this about to occur with the phone to my ear, as Guy told me that he had just been offered his dream job. Principal investigator: the grant had come through that morning. He had funding to hire a postdoc and two PhDs, all working to his direction. He was captain of his own ship. The lab was his. I inhaled silently and told him that was brilliant news and amazing and so exactly what he deserved.

The weekend after, I threw a fit as screechy as the couple in the flat above us and told Guy that I would never be able to finish the project proposal I was working on unless he took the kids out for the afternoon on the Sunday, and he did, without demur. This was the thing he never understood: yes, he would give me time to work when I demanded it, but my time was considered to belong to our family unit unless I signaled that I wanted out. His time was considered to belong to himself and his work unless I demanded that he opt in.

Even the nice ones don't understand what this is like. *What's the problem?* They say it sadly, trying to do the right thing. *All you have to do is ask . . .*

Guy's jollity at that time, that's what I remember—and what an effort it was to hide my sourness. He had everything he had ever wanted. Head of lab and access to the Mouse Library at the most prestigious cancer research institute in the country. "You wouldn't believe how well they are stocked," he said. "They have every single strain, every combination. You should see the index." The mouse librarian had taken him through it with pride—cancer research was always the most well funded area for bioinformaticians, still is. "The mice are on tap."

And he had me and two beautiful children, and was away enough to think my concerns about Adam's behavior were down to maternal anxiety. Guy was an optimist, in those days, and the seriousness of his enthusiasm infused our everyday life. It was only after we had named Adam and Carrie that he put their initials together with his and nicknamed me Timmy—the name of a cat he had had as a child. "The nucleotides are reunited!" he would declare as he came home. The first time he said it, I thought it was quite witty.

But here is what you can never quite grasp about children at that age—even though you know it to be true, you are so absorbed with them that you can't get your tired head around it: they grow up. They stop throwing eggy spoons across the kitchen or wailing about their best friends. They start hiding themselves from you, getting ready to sneak out of the house without you noticing, sneak out permanently, I mean, when they—and only they—deem the moment is right. One day, you are sobbing with self-pity as you scramble eggs and pretending to the children that you have a fly in your eye. The next, you find yourself standing in your son's bedroom holding the swimming towel he was so fond of when he was four, which you have just dug out from a cupboard, and you press your face into it and weep because he and his sister are grown up and have left home and you can't believe you weren't more patient, more kind, more prescient in realizing how quickly this moment would come.

Guy and I were on our own again a lot younger than our peer group. You would think that we would have used that time to get reacquainted as a couple, the way some retired people do, but of course we were far from retired. Our careers were at their peak. This is possibly why the first I knew of my husband's lover was when she came round to our family home in the middle of the night and trashed my car. She probably wanted to trash his car, but his was in the garage, mine parked in our short gravel drive, right outside the bay window to our sitting room. She let herself in through the little wrought-iron gates, ripped off the aerial and the windscreen wipers, and smashed two side windows—I think she was too timid, despite her wrath, to go for the windscreen, or maybe she was afraid of the noise it would make. As it was, we heard nothing—our bedroom looks out over the back garden—although some of the neighbors must have been disturbed; it would have been nice if one of them had called the police.

The first I knew about it was at breakfast time. I was in the bedroom. I was still working full-time at the Beaufort and that day was interviewing for a research assistant. I was ironing a shirt that I thought made me look crisp and authoritative. Guy had dressed already and gone downstairs to make us tea. He came back upstairs carrying nothing, gray faced. He stood in our bedroom doorway. I looked at him and our gazes locked in the way that gazes do when there is some important information to be exchanged. My first thought was, *Adam.*

He saw my eyes widen in alarm and shook his head, *no, not that.* Then he raised both hands, as if to ward off blows, although all I was doing was standing with the ironing board between us, in my underwear and tights and skirt.

"Look," he said, patting the air gently, "look, just stay upstairs, okay?"

I could not imagine what he was on about.

"Look," he repeated, "you're going to have to trust me. Just . . . stay upstairs."

He turned and left, closing the door very softly.

I was still holding the iron. I glanced at the clock beside the bed as if it might be displaying answers but all it said was 7:10 a.m. *I have to leave the house in twenty minutes,* I thought. For want of imagination, I continued ironing my shirt.

I had just clicked off the switch at the power point when I heard voices downstairs. I went to the bedroom door and opened it a crack. The first voice was Guy's, low, placatory, the second was female, high, distressed. Our front door slammed.

I left the bedroom and stepped softly out onto the landing; the landing stretches to the front of the house and has a small square window overlooking the drive—I was still obeying the injunction to stay upstairs, after all. Guy was standing next to my car, waving his arms. In front of him was a young woman in a red coat and jeans. Her form was slight. She had a lot of dark hair that fell in front of her face, and from the movement of her shoulders she appeared to be crying.

Guy disappeared from sight, toward the house. I heard the front door open again, the jangle of keys, the door slam. Back outside, he opened the little gates and gestured toward the pavement. The young woman went meekly and stood there, watching while he got into my car, slamming the driver's door behind him, reversing it out and onto the street. Once it was parked on the road, he strode back across the gravel and opened the door to our garage.

It was still early in the morning, full light but with a heavy dew on the grass. I remember thinking that I wouldn't have time for breakfast, not even a cup of tea. All this time, the young woman had stood on the pavement. I couldn't see her face and she didn't appear to have a handbag of any sort. Her hands were shoved in her pockets, her shoulders turned inward as if she was cold. I guessed she was around the same age as our children.

My husband reversed his own car out of our garage. Once in the road, he opened the passenger door and the young woman, head still bent, leaned as if to climb in, then appeared to change her mind and stood up straight, shaking her head. She pointed back toward our house and said something in a small, high voice, although I couldn't make out her words. At that, Guy opened his door and jumped from the car, the engine still running, and as he stormed around the front of the car I saw, to my astonishment, that his face was enraged. Taking the woman by the upper arm, he pushed her unceremoniously into the passenger seat, slamming the door behind her, storming back round to his side. This pantomime shocked me more than anything. Guy has never had a temper.

The young woman sitting in the passenger seat still had her head bent and, I guessed, was still sobbing. Guy didn't speak to her as he put the car in gear and reversed briefly before pulling sharply into the road. Leaving my car parked on the road and the garage door and gateway wide open, my husband and the young woman drove off.

Had this sequence of events been less extraordinary, I might have jumped to conclusions more quickly, but it all seemed so odd that my normal thought processes were not quite functioning. The strongest emotion I felt as I stared after the car was concern for this young stranger who had turned up at our house so early, and clearly in some sort of distress. It was only when my gaze fell back to my own car that I saw the broken side window. It was the front window, on the passenger side. There was broken glass on the passenger seat—I could see that from where I stood, although I discovered the other broken window on the driver's side only when I went down to investigate. Broken glass. I woke a little from my surprise and began to form a hypothesis.

This may sound strange to anyone who is not dedicated to her work, who is not used to being half of a couple equally dedicated to their work, but before I went downstairs, I put on my freshly ironed shirt and suit jacket and picked up my briefcase. Downstairs, all was normal as far as I could tell, apart from the fact that my car keys were missing from the hook beneath the mirror in the hallway. I slipped my feet into my black shoes. I found an umbrella from the wicker box in the cupboard where we keep umbrellas. I double-locked the door behind me. I closed the garage door and slipped the key in the gap at the bottom where one of the wooden planks is damaged, where we always keep it. I closed our little iron gates behind me. I looked at my damaged car. Guy had gone off in his own car but with my keys in his pocket. I had no idea where the spare set was and in any case did not have the time to wait for a mechanic to come and fix the window. I had only enough time to walk to the station. I really couldn't afford to be late that day.

While I waited for my train at our local station, I looked at my mobile phone, as if staring at it would produce an explanatory phone call from Guy. A picture came to me in my head, my husband driving, furious and silent. Silent is his default mode when he is angry, which was why I had been so surprised to watch him shoving the young woman into the passenger seat. Then I thought about that slight young woman in her red coat, sobbing as she sat in Guy's car, and as my train pulled in and I joined the other commuters on the platform edging forward, my hypothesis took shape, using what little evidence I had from what I had observed, was tested by a counterhypothesis, then became firm. I guessed everything.

Later, that evening, when we were both home, Guy told me the full story and I discovered that my guesses had been pleasingly accurate—I took refuge in that. I had been interviewing all day, so although he and I had exchanged a couple of texts while I was at work, we had not had a chance to speak and I think, in retrospect, that is what saved me from hysteria and possibly saved our marriage. I had time to think of a strategy.

This much I knew. I was capable of forgiving my husband an affair.

I considered it beneath my powers of logic, my intelligence, to be vengeful or clinging. But I would not forgive him if he lied to me after the events of that morning. I would not forgive being treated like a fool.

One of his texts had said that he would be home by 6:00 p.m. and that we would "talk." My interviews were finished by 3:30 p.m. and I should have stayed to discuss the candidates with my colleagues, but I told them I had something to sort out urgently, and left. I was the senior assessor that day and they relented without questioning me.

So I was able to ensure I was home first. I half expected my car to have been towed away or to have a POLICE AWARE sticker on the windscreen, but it was just as I had left it that morning. Inside the house, I changed out of my suit immediately and then—bizarrely—did some housework. I would rather not think about the logic behind this. Perhaps there was part of me feeling more threatened than I was prepared to admit, part of me that wanted to make our home as tidy and welcoming as possible. Or maybe it was a simple desire to restore order, to have the walnut floor in the kitchen swept, the shoes tidied away, the stainless-steel stove gleaming clean. Whatever it was, by the time I heard my husband's key in the door, I was ready, seated at the kitchen table dressed in leggings and a long stripy top, my hair piled on top of my head in a clip and my mouth brightened with a little lip gloss, nothing too obvious. There was a bowl of olives, an open bottle of red wine, and two glasses all waiting on the table. I hadn't cooked, I would like to point out. I hadn't gone that far.

When he came into the kitchen, he looked like a man who needed to sleep more than he needed to talk. Unshaven, his features heavy and downward drawn, his coat hanging unbuttoned. He stopped in the doorway and took in the scene—the open bottle of wine, me waiting, casually dressed and trying hard not to look expectant. He dropped the two sets of car keys down on the countertop next to him and sighed, but I knew that my strategy had been the right one.

"Take your coat off," I said, as I lifted the bottle and poured.

He went back out into the hallway, returned, sat down, and lifted his wineglass, trying not to seem too grateful for it, I thought.

I said, gently, "I think you had better tell me the whole story."

"Don't patronize me," he replied as he lowered his glass.

I allowed a little iron to enter my voice. "Given that my car is sitting outside our house with two windows smashed in, now may not the best time for you to attempt the moral high ground."

He looked at me for no more than a moment, then said, "She's a PhD at the lab next to mine."

The rest of it was very close to what I had guessed, bar the length of his affair. It had been going on for two years. That hurt, I have to admit. Two years during which I had not had one inkling, not one iota of suspicion. Things between them had been going badly for a while, though. She had become clingy, questioning him about his friendships with other PhDs and researchers. *Of course she had*, I thought when he mentioned this. The partners of the unfaithful, they are most suspicious and insecure of all, for they know their lovers to be capable of deceit of the most comprehensive sort. Why would she trust his assurances?

She had taken to ringing his mobile phone during the night and leaving messages on it while it was turned off, sometimes twenty or thirty messages at a time. Sometimes she would speak, sometimes she would play loud music down the phone. Sometimes she would be in a club and there would be shouting and laughter in the background. He told me this bit with some bemusement, but it was obvious to me she was trying to make him jealous. Then, last night, she had left a message at 3:00 a.m. saying, "I'm coming. I can't stand it anymore. I'm coming to you now." She had got a night bus part of the way from her flat share in Stroud Green, then trekked several miles through swathes of suburbs to get to us.

"It must have taken her hours . . . ," I said.

He was picking up the message on his phone in the morning as he walked toward the front door to collect the milk—yes, unbelievably we still get deliveries in this backwater of ours—we have a pint a day. He opened the front door to see her curled up, a ball of wet-eyed misery, in our front porch. She had walked all that way and trashed my car in the driveway but been too scared to ring the bell.

That was the point at which he had come upstairs and told me to stay where I was. When he went back downstairs, she had stepped into the hall. They argued. He took her outside and extracted his car from the garage, then drove her home in total silence. Outside her flat, she had wept copiously while he had told her, quite coldly I imagine, that if she ever pulled a stunt like that again, he would never speak to her for as long as he lived.

At one point, some time after we had opened a second bottle, he looked at me and said, "Is there any point in me saying I'm sorry?"

"I know you're sorry," I said, and I did.

We achieved a kind of intimacy that night, a joint euphoria at having coped with the drama of his admission—but what followed, the weeks and months that followed, was far from euphoric. I knew he would end the affair but I also knew it would take a while. He was too nice a person to be brutal to a distraught young woman who cared for him and whom he had allowed himself to fall for, despite her vulnerability and youth. He was close friends with her supervisor—she could have made a case against him had she chosen to take it that way. But she was in love with him. She didn't want his head on a plate, she wanted his heart. I am sure she had it, in the early days, but his affection for her would have waned as she became clinging, needy, childlike. After a while, he would have felt not passion but a strong and burdensome sense of responsibility. Even though he told me it was over, and I believed him, I knew there would have to be that painful, wretched period at the end of any relationship, where you stay together longer than you should in order to be horrible to each other, to make you both feel relieved when it's finally over. And I knew this bit would be hard on all of us but particularly hard for me because there was nothing I could do but sit on the sidelines working on my saintly, understanding act and waiting for him to realize how saintly and understanding I was. Back off, that was all I could do.

There was one thing I did during that period that I shouldn't have done. I told Carrie, our daughter. I didn't plan it, but she happened to phone when I was at a low point. Guy was out, staying late at the department marking papers, he said, but I knew he was seeing *her,* and it was three months after the incident with my car windows and I was still waiting for it to burn itself out. Carrie rang to confirm that she was coming home that weekend, and as I said, "It will be so nice . . ." my voice cracked and she said, "Mum, what is it?" There was a pause while I gulped on the line, and she added, "Is Dad there?"

"No . . . ," I said, before adding feebly, "He's out."

"Have you been arguing again?"

"Again?" I said, a smile in my voice despite the fact that tears were flowing down my cheeks. My Carrie, so young, so wise. She was cohabiting and sort of engaged to another young scientist called Sathnam. We adored him and wanted them to marry, but they said they couldn't until his devout grandmother had died. Guy and I just wanted them to get on with it, to give us grandchildren. We thought Carrie would come back to us then.

"Ye-es . . . ," she said slowly. "When Sath and I came for the bank holiday, you bickered from Friday evening until Monday afternoon."

"Did we? Is that why you haven't been back in a while?"

"No," she said, "we've just been busy, but I was worried."

"You didn't say anything to Adam, did you?"

"Mum, I'm not stupid."

We have a silent agreement, Guy, Carrie, and I. Adam must be protected at all costs.

I was surprised to hear my daughter thought her father and I had not been getting on well lately. I hadn't noticed. It occurred to me that maybe that was the problem, that somehow Guy and I had slid into being not nice to each other without even noticing.

We saw so little of our adult children at that time—Adam in Manchester, Carrie in Leeds. They are in their twenties, we used to say to each other, comforting ourselves with the recollection of how little attention we paid our own respective parents at that age. They will come round, we would say, when they have families of their own and realize the value of grandparents, or when they move back down south, or when we retire . . . But we missed them both, Guy and I. We had to make an effort not to call them too often, not to ask them every phone call when they were coming home.

And so I told Carrie that her father had been seeing someone else. Guy was furious with me later, and rightly so, and suddenly it was as if the wrong I had done in involving our daughter almost balanced out the wrong he had done in having an affair.

We confided in Carrie jointly, on her next visit home. She came without Sathnam. We sat at the kitchen table and held hands across it and explained to her that we had worked through it, that we wanted her to know it was okay, that she mustn't feel she had to protect us by not telling us what she really thought, or about any problems she might be having of her own.

Then we asked her, as we always ended up asking her, if she had been in touch with Adam lately. Only on Facebook, she said. Then, unexpectedly, she added, "Do you remember what he used to do when you two argued, when we were little?"

"Every couple argues," Guy said. "We're only human."

I placed my other hand on his arm, to quiet him.

Carrie glanced from him to me. "He used to go behind the sofa and crouch down and put his hands over his ears and scream . . ."

"I know," I said. "I remember."

"He used to do it much older than was normal, I mean, not when he was a toddler but ten or twelve, didn't he?"

Guy and I looked at each other. We all fell silent.

"Older than that," I admitted eventually. "Quite a lot older."

It took us a reprehensible amount of time to acknowledge that something was wrong with Adam. Teenagers. All the literature tells you one thing and one thing only—that whatever they are doing, give them a break, cut them some slack, it's normal. And of course, it started slowly, his inability to get out of bed in the mornings, refusing to do homework, cutting classes at school . . . There was the time he shaved his head in strange diagonals and then locked himself in the bathroom and shouted at the mirror and kicked the back of the door. There was another time he came home from a visit to the high street and threw his headphones across the hallway at me and told me that people had been listening to the music he was listening to when they walked past him and smiling at him because they thought it was such stupid music. There was no point when we admitted to ourselves just how worried we were. It all began in dribs and drabs, and with each new drib and drab we convinced ourselves it was par for the course, and of course, it was. When he started spending all day in bed, refusing to leave his room or open the curtains, our first thought was, *It's drugs, he's taking drugs.* I remember the day Guy and I searched his bedroom. It was a summer evening and, unusually, he had made the effort to go out with friends. We almost tiptoed in, glancing at each other. It was like any teenage boy's bedroom: T-shirts scattered over the floor, a mixture of clean and dirty; two drawers on the chest of drawers hanging open to reveal a tangle of socks and boxers that appeared to have been balled before they had been shoved in there and from which rose a smell familiar to any parent. The space above his bed was plastered with photographs of friends or pictures of young women he had cut out of lad mags, a couple of them with corners hanging loose where the Blu Tack had failed to adhere. His old guitar, the one with the broken string, was on one side against a wall. I thought it was too close to the radiator and moved it, then remembered we were doing a secret search of his room and put it back where it had been.

He had taken his current guitar out with him for the evening. We knew he smoked roll-ups, of course, and he would have taken his tobacco tin and packet of papers out with him as well. His dressing gown was hanging on the back of his bedroom door. We had allowed him to graffiti the door with seductive-smelling spray paint, congratulating ourselves on the idea that if it was something we allowed him to do at home, this would reduce the possibility of him doing it on a railway arch while a friend dopey on ketamine held him dangling from the bridge by his ankles. We were not the only parents at his school whose child had come home with his jeans smeared with the chalky-gray giveaway of anticlimb paint. We lifted the dressing gown down and pulled the pockets inside out and found another packet of papers there and a few shreds of tobacco, along with some shredded tissue, that was it. I pulled one of the pockets inside out. Its interior was coated with a fine white fur, where the tissue inside had dissolved during the wash. I bent and lifted the pocket to my nose, sniffed. Nothing. I pushed the pocket right way out again, turned to Guy, shrugged and smiled.

I look back to that evening now and how relieved we were when our search proved fruitless, how we argued lightly, still in hushed tones, about whether his jeans had been left in a crumpled heap on the floor or on the bed, because after we had searched them we couldn't remember exactly where they had been and wanted to leave everything as it was. We talked, snickeringly, of how the best thing would be to tidy the room up, then act all indignant with him when he got home. *We just couldn't stand it any longer!* We went downstairs and cracked open a bottle of wine and sank it with alacrity while we discussed how great it was that our son probably wasn't a dope fiend after all. The bitter irony of that evening: if we had known what was coming instead, we would have been overwhelmed with joy to discover a few dark crumbs of skunk in a matchbox in a pocket of those worn, favorite jeans or that saggy blue dressing gown hanging from the back of his graffitied door.

So I sit in the dock in Courtroom Number Eight at the Old Bailey, and I stare at the empty seats in the public gallery and feel both grateful for and despondent about the absences there. I persuaded Carrie and Guy to take Adam to Morocco for a fortnight in case any reporters try to track them down. I sold it to them as a protective measure for Adam, rather than for all of them. Guy won't stay the whole fortnight, I know that much. A, T, C, and G; the double helix. No one has ever called me Timmy except for Guy, and he hasn't done it for a long while.

I am always there, in that dock, each morning, as are you, before the public gallery opens. We are there before the jury is admitted too, before the judge arrives. We have to be in place for the business of the court to get under way, nothing can happen without us, and so we get to sit and watch as the barristers come in, as they flick through their papers, sighing, wander over to each other's stations and rest their elbows on their opponents' box files and say things like, "I booked Val d'Isère, in the end." We get to sit and watch while the clerks come in to check that everyone is in place before they go and tell the judge we are all ready and waiting. And we get to stare up at the empty public gallery and wonder who will come into it today, because anybody can, of course, as long as they leave their mobile phone at home.

Why did you have no one for you, my love? I never had the chance to ask. Why no brother or sister or loyal friend? Had you ordered them to stay away, as I had my family? There are so many questions I will never get the chance to ask.

About a year after my husband and I had survived his affair, we had a row one night, in the kitchen. I thought we were safe then and past the stage of recrimination. We had looked over the cliff edge, taken each other by the hand, and stepped back. We had closed ranks, pulled up the barricades, the drawbridge, flooded the moat, whatever. Maybe we had. Maybe our argument that night happened because we were secure again, finally, and we could allow ourselves a little nastiness, a few halfhearted forays into the blame game.

I can't even remember what set off the argument that evening, some minor domestic matter, but whatever it was, in the midst of an otherwise innocuous debate I rounded on him, as we cleared up after a meal, suddenly finding myself with my hands clenched into fists, pressing my knuckles down on the countertop, saying, brokenly, "You haven't even told me her name!"

Guy stopped where he was, halfway across the kitchen with a cheese grater in his hand, and looked at me, his expression one of astonishment followed swiftly by resignation. He turned and sat down at the table with a sigh. "Look . . . ," he said, putting the grater on the table in front of him.

My voice, when it came, was weak and tremulous, almost a whisper. "You haven't even told me her name . . . ," I repeated.

"Rosa," he said, and the prettiness of the word lodged like a small piece of glass in my heart.

After that, there was a long silence between us while he remained seated and I moved around the kitchen distractedly. Although we did not speak, we were both continuing the argument in our heads, and that became apparent the minute we opened our mouths.

"Look, Yvonne . . ."

"Yes, yes! Look!"

"I haven't . . ."

"Haven't what?"

Silenced again, he pressed his lips together, evidently deciding that if I was going to be unreasonable, so was he. He pushed at the cheese grater with one finger and it tipped over with a clatter. "Well, you can either keep this up indefinitely or you can forgive me and move on."

"Oh, come on, you got off pretty bloody lightly, wouldn't you say?"

"Saint Yvonne." He sighed, rolling his eyes.

"Would you?" I snorted derisively.

"Yes," he said, indignantly, "yes, of course I would."

"You wouldn't!" I huffed, turning and opening the dishwasher, which I had loaded and set going only minutes before. Unprepared for my attentions, it billowed steam, gushed hot water. I slammed the door shut, turned on my husband. "If it had been me, I would never have heard the last of it. You would have held it against me for years."

"That's not true," my husband said, his voice suddenly calm and conciliatory. He was right, it wasn't true. I had said it only because it was the first thing in my head to throw at him. "I would have forgiven you; we would have talked it through. I love you, you love me, we would have put Adam and Carrie first like we always do, like we're do-ing now. I would not have—"

"Cared . . . ?" I mutter. That was closer to the mark, closer to what I really felt. Guy was rowing back from a full-blown row but I was not quite ready to, not just yet. I had a bit more energy left.

"No that's not it, of course I would have cared. I just would have been able to bear it, in the interests of keeping us together. I'm not pos-sessive in that way, you know that. I never have been."

This was true, and admirable, but it didn't make me feel good. I stopped bustling around the kitchen and leaned back against the coun-tertop, crossing my arms and staring at him through narrowed eyes. "So, in other words, you wouldn't care." I hated myself when I argued like this.

"I wouldn't care so much about physical infidelity that I would let it ruin what we have together, no."

"What if I fell in love? What if I fell in love with someone else, like you did?"

"I'm sorry. You know I am, you know how sorry I am . . ."

And for the first time in this discussion, my voice became a little softer too. "I'm not asking for another apology . . ." I go to the table, sit opposite him, reach out and take his hand. "I'm interested, seriously, do you think you would, forgive me? If I fell in love with someone else, really?" My motive for this was not entirely intellectual. It wouldn't do him any harm, I thought, to contemplate the possibility. He looked over at me. "I'm not planning on doing it." I laughed a little. "I'm just interested."

This was always the way to pique my husband's interest, to appeal to his analytical side.

He took the question seriously, thought for a bit. "You could have sex with someone else," he said, "and I wouldn't like it, not at all, would much rather you didn't, for the record. But I would deal with it by not thinking about it. If I imagined it I would hate it but I would manage not to imagine it, in the interests of preserving what we have, what we value, which we both know is something worth preserving."

"But what about love?"

He paused again, thinking it through, trying to be honest, and I always did, still do, love this about my husband, that he doesn't try to patronize me by saying what he thinks I want to hear. "Yes, I would forgive you if you fell in love with someone else," he said evenly. "It would be very painful for me, of course, because I'm used to the idea that you love me and only me, but I know"—he hesitated only for a second—"I do know now, that it is genuinely possible to love two people at the same time. Even at the height of . . . of what I was doing, I never stopped loving you, not for one second. In fact, in some ways I was more in love with you than ever because I knew I was jeopardizing what we had. I know that sounds like an excuse, but it's true."

We sat for some time after that long speech. Like many men, emotional articulacy had not been my husband's strong point in the past, for all his capacity for analysis, so I was impressed by the length of this speech and by the plain truth of what he said, touched by his capacity to be honest with himself, and me. I no longer wanted to score points off him or make him feel guilty. And then, just as I was beginning to feel warm toward him, he said something that reminded me that he was, after all, a man, and one with flaws, just as I was a woman with flaws.

"There's really only one thing I would find hard to forgive." I looked at him but he was looking down at our clasped hands, passing his thumb gently over my fingers, stroking them.

"What?" I asked.

"Public humiliation."

He looked at me then, and his gaze was cold.

8

We walk out of Apple Tree Yard and into Duke of York Street. You have left me before you have gone—this often happens—but I don't feel wounded this time, more smug than anything: I am getting the hang of this. It is as if, at the age of fifty-two, I have discovered an unexpected ability to play the piccolo, or tap dance, something that was always latent within me that I had simply failed to explore. I am walking a step or two behind you and I reach inside my coat and brush down my dress. Then, hastening after you, I button the coat up to the top, push a hand through my hair—the small gestures that arrange me to be public again.

We part at Piccadilly Circus Tube, you giving me a brusque hug, the sort I have come to expect, where you reach an arm around my back and give me a short, firm pull inward, your forearm clutching me and releasing me the instant my body makes contact with yours. It is the sort of hug you could safely give me if your in-laws were passing by. I turn and walk back down Piccadilly itself, cross at the pedestrian lights, and cut up Air Street. It will take me twenty minutes to get to the faculty party, walking harder than I would like to in my heels, and a light rain has started to fall, April rain, fine and drenching. I don't mind—at that particular moment, I don't mind anything.

I am strutting, just a little, in my high-heeled boots—they are my stiletto ones, not the lower-heeled patent boots I was wearing when we first met: party boots, show-off boots. I look at the people rushing past me as I walk up Regent Street. How many of them are really in a hurry?

I wonder. How many of them are on their way home? How many are running to something or away from something else? I know the rush-hour commute so well, it's in my muscles. The hectic pace of those around me is infectious: it feels impossible, at this time of day, to walk down the street slowly, to avoid shoving and pushing if you get on a crowded bus or Tube. How many of the people rushing past me are happy? I wonder. I am happy. A double life, and I'm good at it. Maybe it's me who should be the spook.

I have crossed Oxford Street and am zigzagging north and east through the backstreets when something unusual happens. A woman is walking toward me, a small woman, even shorter than myself, Japanese, expensively dressed in a green silk dress and short leather jacket. She is answering a call on her phone, opening the conversation quite happily. She has several large shopping bags on the other shoulder. After a couple of sentences, while she is still a few feet away from me, she stops dead in the street. Her face becomes a mask. The shopping bags drop from her shoulder. Her knees buckle and she collapses onto the pavement, letting out a cry as she falls but still clutching the phone to her ear.

I stop where I am for a moment, then approach. She is sobbing and shouting into the phone in Japanese. Clearly she has just been given some terrible news. One minute she was walking along with her shopping, the next, she gets a phone call and she is on her knees, in the rain, crying and shouting.

I hesitate in front of her. After a minute I say, "I'm sorry, can I help you?"

She looks up at me, her expression both bewildered and dismissive, as if she can't understand why I am standing in front of her or what I might be saying, baffled and angry through her mist of tears. Then she returns to shouting and crying into the phone.

It seems prurient to stand there, so I step past her and continue up the street. When I glance back, she is still on her knees, still crying.

The party is in full swing by the time I reach the group of buildings known as the Dawson Complex, the main hub of the university's administrative offices and the home of several lecture theaters. The head of science made it very clear in the invitation e-mail that although the university is providing the venue, the food and wine are on him. A gang of students has been pressed into service as catering staff and as I stride into the foyer, my heels clicking sharply, I am greeted by a line of undergraduates with clipboards waiting to tick off guests' names. This is not typical of university parties, which don't normally involve anything as fancy as a guest list—usually it's plastic cups and white wine at room temperature—but this party is different, a bit of a show. The head of science has dedicated three decades to education and is now heading inexorably into the private sector. A tall man with large glasses, he is standing in the foyer next to the students with clipboards, waiting to greet people, a humorless grin on his face.

"*Yvonne,*" he says as I enter and steps forward to kiss me on both cheeks.

After a few pleasantries with the head of science, I walk down the corridor that leads to the events hall, the center of the Dawson Complex. On the left, there is a row of newly assembled metal racks for people to hang up their coats. The racks are already full, just a few metal hangers left, squeezed together at the end with raffle tickets Sellotaped to them. I am standing on the edge of a group of people, waiting to hang up my coat, when a tall woman student dressed in a black shirt and black jeans comes along, holding a tray of wineglasses. "Dr. Carmichael . . . ," she says, pausing to offer me the tray. I don't recognize her and haven't put on my name badge yet but she must be a former examinee of mine so I smile, take a glass, and say, "Oh, thanks, how are you doing?"

"Great. I'm starting at the Vicenzi Center in the fall."

Now I remember, a clever American, her PhD was on distinguishable personality traits resulting from conditional susceptibility due to the SERT gene variant. "That's great, good luck."

"Thank you. I can't wait."

Behind her, walking down the corridor, I see two bald men, one tall, one short. "Is that Professor Rochester?" I ask, staring at the short one. The question is rhetorical as I'm sure it is. I take a sip of wine. It hits my empty stomach. Eli Rochester runs Glasgow. In my field, he is God. I glance at her. "*Rochester* is here."

The student leans in, raising an immaculately shaped eyebrow. I still can't remember her name but recall now that I liked her a great deal, her sardonic intelligence. "*Everyone* is here, Dr. Carmichael," she murmurs as she turns away.

I edge toward the coatrack, unbuttoning my coat with my free hand as I do, and the man in front of me says in a familiar manner, as he turns, "Here, you'd better let me take that."

For a moment, I'm not sure what he means, then see he is looking at my wineglass. "Thanks," I say.

"Yvonne," he says, a note of admonition in his voice as he takes my glass from me and stands waiting while I shrug off my coat and find a free wire hanger. "I edited your essay." Oh, yes, he's a science publisher. I've actually done quite a lot of work with him but it's been mostly by e-mail.

"Harry!" I say. "How are you?"

"Good, good . . ."

As Harry and I walk down the corridor together, I realize that something in me is alight this evening. It is strange the way this sort of narcissism attracts people. I wonder if it is down to the wineglass in my hand, or the number of people who have greeted me enthusiastically before I'm even in the door, or the presence of so many illustrious colleagues in my field—which, of course, flatters my decision to attend the party myself—yes, it is all those things. But it is also you. I have just done something that most people at this party would never dream of doing, that I myself would never have dreamt of doing before I met you. And I have done it without being caught, I have pulled it off. Later, I will be going home to the nice house I share with my husband and here I am at a party full of high achievers in my field and, guess what, *I'm one of them*. This is my life. Five minutes ago, it seems to me, I was one of the students with a trayful of wineglasses, eager to exchange a few words with a professor in my field. And now here I am, as if by magic, and people are coming up to me and it's taking me a minute or two to recall their names.

I have finished my first glass of wine by the time I have got to the end of the corridor. I detach myself from Harry as I reach the events hall, which is heaving. It's early but already there is an edgy feel to the event, people on their second or third glass, the laughter and chatter reaching to the high ceiling. Maybe it is the combination of the mundane setting with the volume of alcohol and attendees—it's like an office Christmas party, everyone drunk or getting drunk, everyone networking. Scientists may not let their hair down often, but when they do, they do it to the power of n.

I spot a group of people I know, researchers from Guy's old institute, but I hang back for a minute, surveying the room. They will ask why Guy isn't here—he's giving a talk in Newcastle—and then they will ask how my job is going. I don't want to get stuck with people I know too early.

I edge my way around the room, depositing my empty glass and picking up a full one as I go, and suddenly find myself beside the illustrious Professor Rochester, but he is surrounded by acolytes and looks deep in conversation with one of them. I move away, raising my glass to safety above people's elbows, sliding sideways through bodies as I negotiate the room.

"Yvonne!" It's Frances, a technician I've worked with at the Beaufort. I like her a lot. She's in her sixties and there's nothing she hasn't seen.

We embrace briefly. She leans in to hiss loudly in my ear, *"How much do you reckon this has cost him?"*

I shout back in hers. *"Thousands!"* In the current climate, the head of science would not have dared used a penny of university money.

"C'mon," she says. "Let's do a circuit of the room. Let's see if we can track down the lesser-spotted canapé . . ."

Two more glasses of wine go down my throat while we hunt. Surely there should be hordes of students with snacks? None are in sight, although occasionally, frustratingly, we glimpse people with something pinched between their fingers, raising it to their mouths. I have had nothing to eat since a sandwich at lunchtime and am already fuzzy headed but, what the hell, everyone else in the room is clearly going that way too. It's that kind of party. If necessary, I'll drop forty quid on a cab to get home. I don't have anything urgent tomorrow morning and I don't mind paying for an expensive black cab if it's been a free night out.

"Have you heard, there's *dancing* later . . . ?" shouts Frances above the hubbub as we ease past a cluster of bacteriologists from Sweden. I know they are bacteriologists because they are shouting to each other furiously about the Meselson and Stahl experiments. Those experiments took place in 1958 and bacteriologists still argue about them. I think one of them might be someone I had a short-lived feud with on the letters page of *Nature* magazine a couple of years ago.

"You have to be kidding . . . ," I murmur, but Frances doesn't hear me as my words are drowned by the shrieking of a sound system from the side of the room. We grimace and turn. Then there is a *phup-phup* as someone on the raised dais at the end taps a microphone. *God, the speeches*, I think, tossing back my glass and looking around for a refill before they begin. The head of science rarely uses one word when twenty-eight will do.

Sometime around 10:00 p.m., the evening becomes hazy. I look at my watch and think I should call Guy and tell him I am going to be later than I said, then I remember he is in Newcastle. The party invitation said until midnight, but I hadn't imagined I would stay for the duration—now it's looking as though I will be here till the bitter end. I feel bewildered with drink, sick and unsure, too drunk to drink but too drunk to stop. It's ages since I've been this drunk. Years. I have fraternized with the research scientists and lost Frances somewhere along the way and even said a brief hello to Eli Rochester, who, to my astonishment, remembered meeting me at the Advanced Bioinformatics symposium in Chicago six years ago—and it comes to me with a sticky kind of suddenness as I stand there that my heels are higher than I am used to and I should really take my glass of wine outside, right now.

I peer through the long windows at the courtyard at the back of the main hall, which is full of smokers. As I stand, looking at them, thinking about joining them, my elbow is nudged from behind, and I turn to see George Craddock beaming at me.

"Oh, hello," I say brightly, relieved to see a friendly face. "Is Sandra here?" I don't know why I assume they always come as a pair, just because they work together.

"She left awhile back," he says. He lifts his glass toward the court-yard. "I saw you earlier but I couldn't get to you, going outside?"

I really, really need to sit down. "Good idea," I say, and lead the way.

George and I get outside and sit down on a low brick wall. He is wearing a long-sleeved shirt with a pattern of tiny flowers—a designer-type shirt. It suits him. He has a packet of cigarettes in his hand. He takes one out and gives it to me and, stupidly, drunkenly, I put it to my lips and then lean forward into the lighter that he holds up to my face. It's something of a flamethrower and I inhale deeply then sit up straight before I singe my eyebrows. I break into a fit of coughing.

"I knew you'd be a secret smoker!" he says.

I shake my head, laughing a little. "I'm not, I promise!"

"Yes you are," he says. "You're one of these people who think it isn't smoking that gives you cancer, it's going into the newsagent and buy-ing them."

George is definitely more witty when he's had a drink or two, I think.

"God weren't the speeches awful . . . ," he says.

We launch into a tirade against the university authorities and those who fund them, starting with the dean and ending with our current minister for education. George has always struck me as somewhat con-servative and I'm surprised to find out he agrees with me about the current problems in higher education funding. Much as lecturers like him moan, though, our field remains well funded in comparison to the arts—I think of how much easier my daughter's career path has been than my son's—and we discuss how the head of science probably has some fairly romantic delusions about the private sector. Yes, there's a lot more money sloshing around, but it's a lot more brutal as well. Those paymasters expect results.

We are outside for a long time. Even without my coat, I don't feel cold. At one point, a group of people join us and they talk for a bit, then melt away. The wine servers don't bring the bottles around the courtyard, but George goes in and refills our glasses a couple of times. Inside the building, the lights are dimmed and music begins to boom. Unfortunately, the lights are not dim enough for me to avoid seeing the Swedish bacteriologists letting their hair down. Frances comes over to me while George is getting me another drink and says, "I've got to go, darling, I'm completely plastered."

"Me too," I say. "I'm going soon too."

"See you next week," she says. "Don't end up dancing, will you?"

"No chance."

George returns from refilling my glass, and as he hands it down to me, I stand, staggering a little, and say, "You know, I really shouldn't drink any more of this, I don't think."

"You're probably right," he says. "Shall we go? I'll walk to the Tube with you."

"Yeah, definitely," I say, opening my handbag and realizing that my chances of locating the ticket I had torn from the metal coat hanger as I hung up my coat are zero.

There are blank bits, then. I remember being in the corridor. I remember struggling to get the coat from the hanger. I remember George holding my bag as I put my coat on, shrugging it onto my shoulders but not bothering to do it up. I remember the sound of my heels as we crossed the foyer and I remember George saying, "I've just got to get my briefcase from my office."

I remember leaning back against the wall of the lift and closing my eyes.

Then, George and I are walking along a darkened corridor. The Dawson Complex was built in the sixties and above the main, high-ceilinged ground-floor rooms is a warren of offices, ill-lit. At one point, my shoulder scrapes along the breeze-block wall. George catches hold of my arm. "Come along," he says, in a friendly, amused kind of way. "You need to sit down for a bit."

Inside George's office, he closes the door behind us with one foot and goes over to his desk. There is a small two-seater sofa along the opposite wall and I drop down onto it, my coat askew. *Oh, crumbs*, I think, *I haven't been this drunk in years.* I should have eaten something in the café with you, and as I think this, the memory of you and what we did earlier comes into my head and I give a small smile to myself, thinking of all the illustrious scientists downstairs and how I walked around the party with my job and my degrees and *if only they knew* . . .

George turns on a small lamp on his desk and busies himself with some papers, putting them into a battered brown briefcase. Then he clicks the switch on the electric kettle that sits on a corner of the desk. He turns and I'm aware of him looking at me but I let my head flop back against the sofa. When I sit up again, he has walked over to the light switch by the door and turned off the overhead light. The light on his desk is dim. The kettle is making a bubbling sound. "What are you smiling about?" he says, and something about the tone in which he says it makes me a little uneasy, but before I have time to really register this thought, he has knelt down in front of me, on the floor in front of the sofa, and put his mouth on mine.

Oh, shit, I think, *oh dear* . . . I put both hands against his chest and push him away, very gently. I feel mortified for him.

"Look, I'm sorry, no," I say, giving a half laugh. How stupid of me to have given him that impression. God, what an idiot I am. "I'm really sorry—my life's quite complicated enough as it is."

He sits back slightly on his heels. I too am sitting up by then and his face is quite close to mine. He puts his head on one side. "How's Guy?" he says then. He knows my husband's name—well, of course, I suppose he would, we're all in the same field, but as far as I know, they have never met.

"Fine . . . ," I say.

"Does he know you're fucking someone else?"

I look at him, the trim beard, the thin-rimmed glasses—similar to the ones you wear—his friendly smile. I am bemused, far too bemused, and too drunk, to pull off the ridicule that this question warrants if I am to give a convincing denial.

His smile broadens, his face still close to mine. "Why else would you describe your life as complicated . . . ?"

I shake my head, still baffled by the turn this encounter has taken. I don't say anything, I just shake my head.

"I've always thought you were greedy," he says, and his voice is low and dark, but he's still smiling, and I'm still confused, and then he hits me.

There is an explosion inside my head—it feels as though the blow has happened inside my head—then a moment of stunned unreality, followed by a split second of unconsciousness. I give a yelp of pain and disbelief as I fly sideways off the sofa. My left ear is singing. And then I am on the floor, with my head against the back of the sofa, and he is fucking me.

His weight is pinning me down and he is grunting with exertion. I feel a pain in my ankle and realize it is pressed against the square metal leg of the desk opposite the sofa. I do not believe it is happening.

George Craddock looks at me as he fucks me. He still has his glasses on. "If you lift your head off that sofa, I'll hit you again," he says.

He pushes into me hard and my head moves upward but it is a short, involuntary movement, not a serious attempt to get up or resist.

He hits me again, a good, hard, open-handed slap across the face. My head snaps back. I get the message. I use my neck muscles to press my head against the sofa. I close my eyes and put my hands over my face.

It feels as though it goes on for a very long time, but in truth, it can only be a matter of minutes. After a while, still at it, he says, "Why have you got your hands over your face?"

I don't answer. I keep my hands over my face, tensing all my muscles to remain as still as possible despite what he is doing. I want to protect my face.

"Take your hands away from your face," he says. When I don't move, he repeats, his voice low with threat, "I said, take your hands away from your face." I still don't move. I am like a tortoise that has withdrawn into his shell, or a hedgehog in a ball.

He pulls my hands away from my face and holds them to one side with one hand encircling my wrists. With the other hand, he slaps me again.

After this, I begin to plead with him. "Please . . . ," I say. When he doesn't stop, I try using his name. "George, please . . . please . . . ," I say.

"Please what?" he says. My eyes are open now and I am looking up into his face. He is smiling down at me. "Please *what*?"

When I don't answer, his face darkens and he draws back his hand, high in the air. I cower down, as much as I am able. "Please don't hit me," I beg.

It is the right answer. He smiles at me again, and lowers his hand.

His exertions increase then, he lowers his head until it is beside mine, his face pressed into the edge of the sofa cushion next to where the back of my head is pressed. I see the white oval of light on the desk opposite, staring down at me. I see the swivel chair in front of the desk and his battered leather briefcase sitting, still open, on the chair, the normal objects in the room. He is muttering into the sofa cushion, "Fuck, *fuck . . .*" and pushing into me with desperate vigor. After a while, he lies still. He is wearing his name badge from the party and the metal clip on it is pressing painfully into my chest.

"*Shit,*" he says then, and slips out of me, small and limp. The feel of him brushing my thighs makes me shudder. As he raises himself, I manage to lever up a little on my elbows. He kneels for a bit, between my thighs, his trousers hanging down, his shirt and jacket loose, his face shiny with sweat. He plays with himself slowly as he smiles at me. Then he says, in a chummy tone of voice, "Too much wine, I think . . . sorry . . ."

"You *hit* me," I say.

He is still grinning as he gets to his feet. He picks up his briefcase from the swivel chair and drops it to the floor, where it falls sideways. "Thought you'd like that," he says, pleased with himself, then adds, "I liked hearing you beg."

I haul myself up to the sofa, where I sit for a moment or two. I am shaking from head to foot. My teeth are chattering.

He is still looking at me. "Better not go down just yet, eh?" he says. "Too many people still about." As he watches me, he begins to touch himself again, holding himself between his thumb and forefinger. "Those boys . . . ," he says. The stroking is working. *Dear God,* I think, *we're going round again.* He gets off the chair and approaches me. "Give me your mouth."

It is gone 1:00 a.m. before he falls asleep, briefly, his forearm resting across my neck. I lie very still for a long time before I attempt to move and when I do, he wakes immediately. I am careful to smile. "I'd better go . . . ," I say lightly. I am taking the risk that his falling asleep means the adrenaline has drained away. He will be tired.

I have judged accurately. "Yes, I suppose so," he says sleepily. "Going to have a bit of trouble explaining this one at home, aren't you?" His tone of voice is openly nasty now, which is less threatening than that smile. It's going to be okay, I keep repeating inwardly, as long as you're really careful now, he won't hit you again.

He stands up and rearranges his clothing, then bends and picks up his briefcase, righting it, lifting it onto the desk, opening it and peering in.

I am fairly certain it is over but I can't be sure, so I am very calm, almost casual, when I say, "Well, I'll see you soon, then," standing as I speak, smoothing down my dress and pulling my coat together, shaking my hair. My knees are knocking.

"I'll walk down with you," he says.

He locks the office door behind him and I wait in the corridor while he does. It all has an air of unreality now. I want to be home: the best way to get home is to be as normal as possible. I stand next to him while we wait for the lift. In the lift, I lean back against the wall and close my eyes. When I open them, he is looking at me and smiling. The lift doors open and we walk swiftly out into the deserted foyer. Along the corridor, there are a few stragglers talking but the double doors to the events hall are open and I can see that it is brightly lit and empty but for the students moving around with black plastic dustbin liners. I pray we will not see anyone I know. As we cross the foyer, George Craddock takes hold of my arm, holding it by the elbow. "We'll have missed the Tube by now," he says. "We'll share a cab."

Outside, the light rain has started again, fine and cool. I stand, swaying with shock, on the pavement. After a few minutes, a black cab with its yellow light on draws to a halt before us. George Craddock speaks to the driver and I hear the driver reply, "I'm only going south." The cab pulls off and George turns to me and says, "It's against the law for them to refuse, you know. We could report him. He had his light on." As if by magic, another cab pulls up, and George opens the back door and ushers me in. I obey. He speaks to the driver, then gets in next to me.

In the cab, I huddle as far away from him as I can get, pressed into the corner, my face turned away. We don't speak as the cab speeds through nighttime London. I am beyond speech. The roads are empty of traffic; the rain has stopped; it is a clear black night. Buildings loom and rush by. Streetlights flash at me. After a while, I close my eyes.

It is only as we are driving through Wembley that it comes to me that he must not discover where I live. I open my eyes, turn to him, give a small grimace. "My husband will still be up, waiting for me, I expect," I say.

"It's okay," he says, "I'm getting out first, anyway."

We drive for a few minutes more.

"Lucky we live in the same direction," he says. Then, "I'm not that far from you as the crow flies."

I feel sick.

"You didn't know that, did you?" he adds. Then he leans forward and taps on the glass divide. The driver slides it back.

"You can let me out at this intersection here," George says.

The cab pulls up just before a light that is flashing amber. A lone dog trots across the road ahead of us, thin and loping, its head down. George has undone his seat belt and raised his backside from the seat in order to be able to root in his pockets. While the cab's engine idles, he fiddles around, then drops a ten-pound note and some pound coins onto the seat behind me. "There," he says. "It won't be half but you're going farther than me."

Then he is gone.

The cab moves off again. I exhale, very slowly, closing my eyes again.

I still have my eyes closed when the cab halts outside my house. The driver must have asked me which road at some point but I have no memory of it. My head is full of blanks: the blanks are filling it so full that there is room for no more than the demand of the present moment, and that is that I pay the cabdriver and get into my home and lock the door behind me and go upstairs and get under my duvet and hide. I scoop up George Craddock's money from the seat next to me, get out of the cab, slam the door. The driver has lowered his window. I hand in George's money and then say, "Just a minute . . ." and lift up my handbag, scrabbling in it for my purse. The driver watches me all the while. My hands are shaking. After a moment he drawls, "Want a receipt, love?"

"Yes, please," I say. Be normal, then it will be normal.

I give him some more money, he gives me change and the receipt, looks at me as he does, and then says thoughtfully, "All right, love, good night, then."

"Thank you, you too," I say, turning away.

My house is in darkness. I let myself in the front door and, even though Guy is away, stop and stand in the hallway, listening. I do not put on the light, but there is a little streetlight shining through the glass panels above the front door, weakly illuminating the familiar objects there, the stand in which we put umbrellas, the side table with the glass bowl we bought in Sicily. I know that if I stand there any longer, my knees will give way, so I walk into the house. Then I remember I haven't put the chain on the front door, so I go back and do it. Then I go into the sitting room and put the light on and check that the windows are securely fastened and close the curtains. I go from room to room throughout the house, doing this in each one, checking the windows again and again. *Go to bed*, I think. *Just get under the duvet, go to bed.*

In the bathroom, I tip the toothbrushes out of the toothbrush holder and fill it with water. I fill it and drink three times. I do not look at myself in the mirror above the sink.

In the bedroom, I shed my clothes, leaving them on the floor beside the bed. Thank God Guy is in Newcastle. I get into bed, then get out again and take the chair from in front of the vanity unit in the corner and put it up against the back of the bedroom door, even though it doesn't reach the handle. Then I get back into bed, turn off the bedside light, pull the duvet up to my shoulder as I am shivering from head to foot. My last thought, before I tumble into unconsciousness, is, *How could I have been so stupid?*

After five hours, I snap awake and know instantly what happened to me the night before. I fall into the shower. I turn the water on full, very hot, and feel the fine needles of it pierce my skin, scrub myself over and over until I am red and raw. When I am soft, clean at last, I stand beneath the scorching water for a long time, letting it run down my back while I lean my forehead against the smooth white tiles. *If I don't tell anyone*, I think, clearly and calmly, *I can make it go away.*

It is only when I am downstairs, wrapped in a toweling robe, with coffee brewing, that I check my phone. My handbag is on the kitchen table. I don't remember leaving it there the night before, but then I can remember very little about what I did when I got into the house.

There is a text from Guy. It arrived at 11:58 p.m. the previous night. *Talk went well. Hope the big party good. Text me you're home OK. Will be back around 6 p.m.* The kitchen clock says 7:20 a.m. I text back. *Sorry just saw your text. Party heaving, bit boring. Glad talk went well. See you later.*

Afterward, I sit for a moment with the phone in my hand. I imagine calling my husband. He will probably still be asleep in his hotel room in Newcastle. My call would wake him. I imagine the slight frown he would give as he picked up his phone, wondering what it was that I could be calling about this early. I imagine telling him. I imagine him calling the police. I imagine them coming to this house, two officers in uniform, radios crackling fiercely on their chests. I imagine them taking me somewhere. I imagine me in a room at the back of a police station, lying on my back, naked from the waist down, my knees raised. Perhaps my feet would be in stirrups. There would be chilly metal objects and a man, or maybe woman, who doesn't smile because his or her sole objective is to hunt around, probing for evidence. And what would that person find there, my love, my dear X, when he delved and scraped with the tools of his profession? What would be found among the traces of my assailant, the DNA ducking and diving but unable to hide? You: he would find you. Apple Tree Yard, that's what he would find. I put my mobile phone back in my handbag.

9

I stay in my kitchen for two hours, wrapped in my fluffy dressing gown, sitting with my legs up on the neighboring chair, one laid there as if it is broken, the other bent, drinking coffee and staring at the wall, shuddering and sore, unable to move. Every now and then I have to shift a little because I am getting stiff. It makes me wince.

At 9:30 a.m., my phone rings: I lift it from my bag, see it is Guy, and screen the call. He leaves a cheery message repeating the information from his text the night before. The talk went really well. He hopes the party was good. He looks forward to hearing all about it. He thinks he might have to go straight to the office and get some work done when he gets back, will I mind? He might as well, because he had forgotten he was due to meet Paul for a drink at eight. I leave it twenty minutes and then text him, *Sorry was in shower. No problem. Think have virus, so at home today, don't worry about this evening, might get early night.*

After I have sent this, I remember that I am supposed to be meeting Susannah that afternoon. Susannah will be sure to ask me about the party. Susannah knows me better than any person on earth. I can't see her without telling, so I can't see her. I send her a text too.

After I have sent this text, I sit with my phone in my hand for a few minutes, staring at it, as if I expect that, stared at for long enough, it will transform itself into another object—a pearl, perhaps, or a mouse that will jump from my palm. Once you have not-told, you have to keep on not-telling. *That's how easy it is*, I think. That's how easy it is for your life to become a lie.

Around midmorning, I go upstairs, slowly, like an invalid, taking the stairs one at a time, grimacing as I do, gripping the banister and noticing the whiteness of my fingers, the veins on the back of my hand. I take my handbag with me and I drop it onto the bed. Beside the bed is the crumpled heap of party clothing that I was wearing the night before, my best dress, the hold-ups, the thong knickers—easy access— and matching bra. I go to the wardrobe and pull out a plastic bag and push all the items into it. I tie the handles tightly, then hide the bag at the back of my wardrobe. Later, some weeks later, I will secrete the bag into another bag and then deposit it into a rubbish bin on a shopping trip to Harrow. It will disappear into the bin; my favorite dress, the best underwear I hardly ever wore, my party persona, gone for good.

I lie down on the bed, on top of the duvet. I curl myself into a ball. I lie there for a very long time watching the still, silent room—the lamp on the bedside table with the crust of dust on the rim of the shade; the rug, which is new; the heavy chest of drawers Guy keeps his underwear and T-shirts in—it's slightly too large for the space between the two windows where we keep it. This is the fabric of my life, these objects. I take them for granted. I am shivering as if I have the flu. It won't be permanent, I think, a few days, that is all. I don't mean the shivering. I want to fall asleep but can't.

Sometime around noon, I haul myself up, raise some pillows behind me, and lean back against the headboard. My stomach is empty and hollow and I feel sick, but I know there is no point in trying to eat. I pull my handbag toward me and check both of my phones this time—I keep the pay-as-you-go one in a zip pocket inside the bag. There are four work messages on my usual phone. On the pay-as-you-go one, there is a missed call from you but no voice mail message—there is also a text.

Hungover? Had a good night? Missing me?

I am so raw and needy, tears spring to my eyes at the sight of your words—to know you are thinking of me, wondering how my party went, a little jealous, perhaps, because I have not rung you yet this morning to give you an account of my evening.

I text back. *Hungover. Had a bad night. Missing you loads.*

After I have pressed Send I sit for some time with the phone in my hand, staring at it, willing it to ring. If you suspect something has happened, you will be on the phone immediately, pressing me. I pray, weakly, childishly, that you will call. "What do you mean, a bad night?" you will ask.

You don't call. You have taken the word "bad" to mean no more than the opposite of "good": "bad" in the sense of boring, tiring, too drunken . . . I am disappointed. I was hoping for more from you. You are an expert interpreter, after all, and it's not usual for me to report something was bad. We are still exhilarated by each other—we are normally on a high every time we speak. But maybe there is something nagging at you now, as you get on with whatever you need to be doing, some small sense that all is not well with me? I think about this, try to imagine where you may be, who you are with, what you are doing. I think of you in some sort of strategy meeting, discussing agent deployment (this is how little I know of what you do) around a square table with some mugs of instant coffee and a half-eaten plate of biscuits. No, I conclude, you haven't guessed that anything is wrong. I know you well enough by now to know that any hint of withheld information on my part would have you on the phone at once. My text has been sufficiently humorous to deflect you and I am disappointed beyond belief at the success of my strategy.

I put both phones back in my handbag, lie down, and curl on my side again.

It begins inside as a dry sobbing, like a series of tiny depth charges that jolt my stomach. After a few moments the tears start to flow and they do not stop.

I manage to doze a little. I go downstairs, wandering from room to room. I check that the chain is still on the front door. *Not that far, as the crow flies.* I can't face eating but I have a cup of tea.

It is midafternoon when you call. I stare at the phone in my hand as it rings, and my heart is in pieces, for I want you so badly that I think I will die, literally, lie down and die, if I don't speak to you. But I know that as soon as I answer the phone and have a normal, flirty conversation with you, then we will be acres apart, as far apart as I am from Guy or you from your wife. I am weak, though, and wounded, so instead of doing what I should do—screen your call and send a cheery text like I did before—I answer. It's the middle of the working day. You'll be busy. If I keep it short and chirpy and pretend I am busy too, you'll never know. Then I'll have the weekend to recover myself, to summon my strength.

Do you remember this conversation, my love? It is burned into my memory as if it had been branded there with a soldering iron.

"Hey, Hangover," you say brightly, "how are you feeling?"

"Fine." That's all I say, one word, devoid of intonation.

There is a second's pause on the line, then you say, your voice low and serious. "What's wrong?"

When I have finished telling you, there is another pause on the line, then you say, "Do you have any marks on your face?"

"No," I say. "He used the flat of his hand."

"Anywhere else?"

"There's some bruises on my thighs, finger bruises." I pause. "And I'm bruised inside, internally I think . . . and I think I have an anal tear."

You do not pause or draw breath. "The bruising on the thighs is good, anal tears are very common with consensual anal sex. Any restraint injuries, any bruising on the wrists?"

I wonder how you know to ask all this. "No," I say. "He didn't restrain me. He didn't need to. He hit me instead. I didn't fight back I didn't . . ." I break down.

"Yvonne . . . ," you say then, and your voice has a depth, a softness I've never heard before. "Yvonne . . . you're doing so well . . . You've done really well, now listen. Do you want me to send some people round, to take a statement? I can have them with you in an hour."

"People?"

"Police officers. There'll be two of them, either a man and woman or two women. They have specialist units now. It's not like it used to be."

"No," I say.

You pause. "Are you sure?"

For the first time since what happened, I feel capable of thinking. "You know as well as I do, this can't go to court."

There is a long silence between us then, while we wordlessly acknowledge the truth of this, the consequences for both of us. The silence is so long it is like a warm bath. I feel so close to you.

Eventually you say, simply, truthfully, "Oh, dear . . ."

"It's okay," I say, sniffing bravely. "I'm okay."

"No," you say, "it's not okay, and you're not okay, either."

"I will be."

"Where's your husband?"

"Guy's on his way back from Newcastle. He'll be late tonight. He's meeting an old friend. I've told him I'm ill. I'll probably sleep in the guest room, that will be fine, we do that when one of us is ill."

"Will you be able to be normal for him tomorrow morning?"

"Yes, I'll just be ill."

We actually have a busy weekend, busier than usual, socially: the theater with friends on Saturday, a Sunday lunch with Guy's sister who lives in Pinner. I can't imagine how I am going to get through it, but it will keep me distracted, or maybe I'll be ill enough to just stay in bed.

"You know that if I could come to you now, I would," you say.

"Yes, I know." I can tell by your tone that you are preparing to end the conversation. I try to think what might delay you. "What are you doing this weekend?" This is breaking one of our unspoken rules. You and I have never asked each other about what we do when we are at home with our spouses, as though that drawing of a line, that loyalty, somehow makes what we are doing acceptable, as if all we have to do to justify ourselves to ourselves is to compartmentalize.

"We've got some people coming round for dinner tonight." It's the first time I've heard you use the plural pronoun: "we" as in, *me and my wife*. "The kids have drama club on Saturday morning, maybe take them to see a film later. It will be all right, I suppose, but I'll just want to talk to you."

That was enough. There is another pause, then I manage a small, ironic sound, to tell you I am smiling a little. "This isn't exactly what you signed up for, is it?" What I mean is, things are suddenly serious now and that was never in the plan. I can't imagine having sex with you at the moment. I can't imagine ever having sex again. Will it have occurred to you yet, the consequences of this for us?

"I signed up for you."

10

On Monday, you and I meet for a walk near King's Cross. We meet there because you have something you have to do nearby, you don't say exactly where, or what. You only have a half-hour window, you tell me. I am waiting by the newsstand in front of the main station and I see you first, emerging from the crowds on the concourse. In front of me, a teenage boy is doing a strange whirling dance, wheeling his arms slowly like an airplane. Through the wheeling arms, our gazes meet. We give each other a long look as you approach. You take hold of my upper arm, gently, and draw me toward you, then kiss the top of my head.

We turn and walk in front of the station, heading away from it with no discussion of our direction, cross the busy intersection, and begin to walk slowly up Caledonian Road. For a few minutes, there is a comfortable silence between us as we walk. I wish we were able to hold hands, then, at the very moment I am wishing this, you take my arm and tuck it around yours, drawing me close, and we walk like that for a hundred yards or so. We are away from the main business of the station, but this stretch of the road is still unmistakably the King's Cross area—cafés, bars, porn shops. We pass the Bangladeshi Centre and, on the other side of the road, a large hostel with youngsters smoking outside and bunk beds backed up against the windows, their bundled duvets pressed against the windowpanes like clouds on the wrong side of the glass. A few yards down, a brown-skinned young man in a gray hoodie sits on the step of a terraced house with crumbling pink paintwork. He is smoking and has a baby on his lap, sitting perched on one knee, with a mop of thick dark hair and a gold earring. As we pass, the baby gives me a beautiful gummy smile and I smile back. The young father sees his baby smiling, then looks at me, beaming with pride.

We are promenading, like a couple in a costume drama, Jane Eyre and Rochester perhaps, or Elizabeth Bennet and Mr. Darcy. Didn't they disagree a lot? You and I have never had a disagreement. We haven't had the chance. I feel a perverse sorrow that we have never had a row. That happens, presumably, with any affair that lasts for any length of time. There must be a point where you allow yourselves to be irritated with each other occasionally, in the same way you do with your spouses, a point where any affair stops being adultery and becomes bigamy. It is a point we will never reach.

We turn left as the street bends and end up walking along Wharf-dale Road and then, still without any discussion about our direction, up York Way, until we reach the canal. We pause and look down over it. The water is black but the wind ruffles it into wavelets that are crested by tiny flashes of neon blue. Among the reeds that line the bank, a thin, solitary duck is pecking hopefully. Three narrow boats are moored in a row just beyond the reeds. One of them has an armchair screwed to the top, facing the weak sun.

You indicate an empty bench on the towpath and we descend the steps, slowly, still arm in arm. As we sit, I let my hand fall from your arm, and you do not reclaim it although we sit close enough for our hips to touch through our coats.

"What time's your meeting?" I say, pointlessly. It just seems odd not to be making conversation when there is so much we won't have time to say.

"Soon," you reply. A cyclist idles by along the towpath, ringing his bell as he disappears into the blackness beneath the bridge.

We talk a little bit about our weekends, and our schedules for the week ahead. We don't discuss what has happened—I thought we might, would have liked to, in fact, as you are the only person I can talk to about it, but I'm also frightened of where such a discussion might lead, so I don't raise it. Half an hour is nothing, and because it isn't time to discuss anything in depth, we don't seem to be discussing anything at all. Thirty minutes. We must have used up half of those minutes already, just meeting and walking a bit and finding a place to stop. I'm afraid of the time, this afternoon. A lorry thunders down York Way, its roar a sudden blare, and I flinch. I'm afraid of everything.

It is good to see you, but later, for reasons I won't be able to be precise about, I will feel that this meeting was not a success. You seem distracted—maybe it is just how little time we have. You have an intriguing habit when you are thinking hard. It makes me smile, sometimes. Your look becomes concentrated but somehow vacant—I can almost see the cogs turning in your brain. It reminds me of how, when my children were three or four, they often talked to themselves when they were thinking something through, whispering their thoughts out loud. I am not claiming you are that transparent, of course—the opposite, in fact, as that vacancy in your eyes makes you quite opaque—simply that, although I cannot tell what is happening in your thoughts, I know that something is. Something is going on.

It is quite hard, this look of yours. It is not affectionate or knowing. You are not thinking of me.

You lean forward on the bench and rest your elbows on your knees, staring thoughtfully ahead, then you turn and stare at me for a bit, and then say, "Have you told anyone about us?"

"No!" There is indignation in my exclamation. Is that what you have been thinking about?

You continue to stare. "No one? You sure? Not a late-night confidence with your friend Susannah, a talk over a bottle of wine?"

"I haven't told a soul." The only blurting I have done is to my computer—it's all there, disguised, buried, and nobody uses that computer but me. And I realize that is why I started writing that account, to prevent myself from telling Susannah. What has happened between you and me has been so extraordinary, so out of character for me, that I would have burst with it if I had not written it down.

I want to parry this line of questioning. I don't like it. "Have you?" I ask, and you give me a glance.

"No, I haven't."

"Who would you tell if you were going to tell, just if?" The slight note of merriment in my voice is edged with desperation. I know there is no chance you have a confidant. I am asking because it has come to me that I have no idea who your friends are or even if you have any. Is someone like you allowed friends, or do you merely have associates? If you compartmentalize, then that means that I am, and will always be, trapped in my own compartment in your head. I will never be general or ubiquitous. I will never be truly present for you.

My question has been so daft that you don't even answer—that's an irritating trait of yours, ignoring what you consider to be insignificant or foolish in my curiosity about you.

The cogs are still turning. "We need to have an agreement," you say, and you reach out and take my hand in yours, holding it between both of yours in your lap. You squeeze, lightly, the slightest of pressure from your fingers as we both stare straight ahead. On the bank opposite, there is a gleaming office building. A collection of white plastic bags drifts by on the surface of the canal, blown by the wind. "I need to know that if you are ever asked about me, you will say this. We met in the House of Commons. We've talked a few times. We've become friends. I've been asking your advice because my nephew is doing his A levels and is interested in a career in science. We're acquaintances, friends if you like, but nothing more. If you are ever questioned in detail, then stick to the truth of the meetings, precisely, time, place, what sort of coffee, et cetera, but leave out the sex. We've met infrequently enough for it to be innocuous, without the sex, I mean. Can you do that?"

"Of course," I say, but my voice is small and sad. I want your focus to remain on me, on what has happened to me, but you are, naturally enough I suppose, thinking ahead to what might happen if I change my mind and report the assault to the police, to how you might be exposed in court if anyone looks into my life. You are thinking about your marriage, your career. I don't blame you for this—it is one of the things I have loved about you, that you are discreet and want to protect your family life, for I want to do the same and would be horrified if you felt otherwise, but the weak part of me feels disillusioned. That part of me wants you to put me first, right here, right now, wants you to tell me that you are going to track George Craddock down and beat him to a pulp, regardless of the consequences.

His face is in my face. I see it all the time. I see the students glimpsed at the far end of the corridor as we left the building, moving around the events hall with their black plastic dustbin liners. Why should that picture come into my head, time and time again? I don't understand why that image is stuck in my head. It comes to me how much I want George Craddock to be on the receiving end of physical harm. This is a new thought. I have never wanted that for anyone. But what I want is for him to feel hurt and afraid. I want someone to do to him what he did to me—befriend him, in a pub, maybe, spend the evening drinking and chatting, then, in a car park, in the dark, beat him and bugger him, and afterward pretend that nothing was wrong and that he liked it. I am not fantasizing about Craddock being arrested or humiliated in court or slopping out in prison—I am not (and as it turns out, never will be) fantasizing about the due process of law taking its course. I am fantasizing about him on his hands and knees in a car park with his trousers round his ankles, sobbing with fear and pain, scrabbling for his broken glasses on the rough tarmac.

Be careful what you wish for, my aunt used to say, darkly. Aunt Gerry had a pessimistic view of life, but then she had ended up raising me and my brother when she hadn't expected to, so maybe she felt entitled. Be careful. You were thinking ahead, but much further than I could have imagined. I should have given you more credit.

You leave first, of course, striding from the bench to your meeting, or whatever it is, and I sit there for a while, pointless pride ensuring that I don't watch you mount the steps to the road—but then I crack and look up, just in time to see you striding down York Way, on the pavement above me, already on your phone. I check my watch and tell myself that I will sit for another fifteen minutes, no more. After that, I don't know what I will do. Throw myself into the black water of the canal, perhaps, along with the solitary duck and the floating green algae and the puffing plastic bags.

I never did tell Susannah about you, you know. Guy and I met Susannah when we were students. She was his friend first, then mine, then best woman at our wedding—I refused point-blank to call her a bridesmaid. She wore a satin suit with flared trousers and a fitted jacket: it accentuated her height, her slenderness—everything about her I have ever envied was apparent that day: the cheekbones, the short dark hair, the light brown skin. She used to laugh at me when I told her I wanted to be elegant like her. "When you're as tall as me, it's really easy to get an undeserved reputation for elegance, all you have to do is stand still." Once, when we were both drunk together, she confessed she had always wanted to be "short and cute" like me. *Cute?*

For some years after our wedding, despite or perhaps because of her beauty, Susannah remained single, often coming over to our place on a Friday night. I would get Guy to put the kids to bed so she and I could sit and eat pretzels with our wine while dinner cooked and often she would sigh and talk about some man. Guy and I loved these stories but felt guilty about loving them, living vicariously through her romances, as if she was our own personal soap opera. We met a procession of them, over the years. Each relationship would last a year or two. There was the tall one who called her "wifey" and pinched her cheek and, to my horror, made her simper in return. There was the older Jewish one who played the piano and was crazy about her. She dumped him—inexplicably in my view—just as I was wondering where I would buy the hat. Then there was the sullen Dutch one who scarcely spoke a word—she assured me he was the best lover ever, really athletic, she said. Then, when we were all twenty-eight, she met a fellow doctor at a conference, Nicholas Colman he was called, two years younger than her but charming and mature, good with our kids when he came round.

It all seemed so obvious. I started thinking how, if they got a move on and had their children quickly, we would all be able to go on holidays together. And Susannah and Nicholas Colman did marry, had a son immediately: Freddie, my godson, as close as a cousin to my two. Then, when Freddie was three, just after Susannah had been made a consultant, Nicholas Colman fractured her left cheekbone. Even now, when she turns her head in a certain light, you can see, if you look closely, a small asymmetry in her features. When she smiles, a barely detectable shadow crosses her face. You have to know her face really well to see it.

It took her another three years to leave Nicholas Colman after the cheekbone incident. We are taught we can redeem them, she said to me once. We are taught it as soon as we can read. We can turn the beast into a prince, if only we love him enough. And, she said, you know instinctively how bad it's going to get when you leave, so you keep putting it off. You think that while you are with them you might be able to control it a bit, but you know that once you leave, you will be in real danger.

In the end, it was Guy and I who called in the police, after an incident where Nicholas Colman turned up at our house and banged on the door for an hour and a half while the three children were upstairs. Guy was out when it started. Susannah and I sat cowering in the kitchen saying things like, "He'll stop soon." But he stopped only when Guy came home. Guy told us later that as he walked up our short drive, Nicholas Colman turned and smiled and held out his hand and said, "All right, mate?"

For a couple of years after that, Susannah and her son Freddie holidayed with the four of us. Nicholas Colman dropped out of the picture after the court case and the injunction, thank God. Freddie has turned out handsomely. He studied law at Bristol and is now doing some sort of accountancy training on top of it, something to do with corporate finance, and although he will finish the process of his extended education with massive debts, it is already clear that within a few years he will be able to buy us all out three times over. Sometimes, I have to try hard not to wish my own son was more like Freddie. I have never admitted this to anyone.

Susannah has always been soft on Guy. They flirt with each other outrageously. It's a standing joke between us. She thinks I am lucky to have him. I do too, of course, but it annoys me how easy it is for a man to look good to those who observe him from outside a relationship. He doesn't hit you, he's not an alcoholic, he's good with the kids—all these things are told to women, even by other women, by way of emphasizing just how lucky they are. Guy scores points just for not beating me up. I wonder if anyone has ever said to Guy, "Let's face it, she doesn't hit you, she's not an alcoholic, and she is really good with those kids. You should be grateful."

So no, I haven't confided in Susannah, but that's not to protect you or me or even Guy. It's to protect her.

I rise from the bench and walk slowly back to King's Cross station. I have to walk slowly as it still hurts—that's because it's healing, which is drawing the skin tight. I go into the main station because I know somewhere in there will be a branch of Boots and I think it might be a good idea if I buy a bottle of water and something to eat, and some Vaseline.

It takes about ten days for the initial period of shock and denial to wear off—ten days to a fortnight. During that period I don't eat, I don't sleep. I shower often. The two pictures remain in my head: his face in mine, the students drifting about the hall like ghosts, far off in the distance, not seeing me as I pass. Guy is busy at work, and that's good. Susannah sends me a couple of e-mails asking when we are going to meet and I put her off. At work, I am on automatic pilot. Luckily for me, I have enough seniority to appear busy and not have to explain to anyone why. All I have to do is be a little brusque with the people around me and they leave me alone. On the two days I go into the Beaufort, I ask my personal assistant—the one I share with two other associates, that is—to hold my calls while I'm working. She doesn't query this. She becomes protective of me. I hear her saying to someone on the phone, "Dr. Carmichael has to prioritize, you know . . ." She's the kind of PA who enjoys fielding calls. If she were a different gender and three stone heavier, she would have made a terrific nightclub doorman.

I am at my desk at the Beaufort when I get the e-mail. It is ten days after the assault. Later, I think it was lucky I was at work. Although I have my own office at the institute, the walls are made of glass from waist-height upward and I am visible to anyone in the open-plan office outside, so I am forced to pretend.

My in-box is already open and I am going through it, when it pings up, there at the top, with a tiny yellow envelope next to the name: George Craddock. In the subject line it says: *Lecture next month.*

I am frozen in my chair, motionless but for the breath quickening harshly in my throat.

*Yvonne—just to confirm our lecture date in Swansea next month.
It's on Thursday 28th. I suggest we meet at Paddington and travel
down together. If we meet at 14:00 hrs that should give us plenty of
time. I'll confirm train times soon. The fee is £300 plus expenses.
Possible to get there and back in a day but maybe we should book
a hotel.*

The Swansea lecture, him introducing me then chairing a discussion on examining processes, was a possibility we had discussed last time I did the external examining for him and Sandra, but we hadn't agreed on a date or confirmed it; it was just something he had asked me if I was interested in. My heart is thumping, my hand shaking. My scalp feels as if it has tightened on my skull.

If I had been at home I would have stood up and run away from the computer, run downstairs to my kitchen, or left the house altogether, or locked myself in the bathroom perhaps and sat on the toilet with the lid down, as I used to do at school during playtimes rather than face the rough-and-tumble of the playground. But I am at work, at an institute where I am an associate, well regarded, competent. I know I must act swiftly but unequivocally. I have to let him know that although I did not send police officers with handcuffs to his door, I am not going to pretend it didn't happen. I will never be rid of him otherwise. I hit Reply. I type very quickly.

I won't be coming to Swansea. Please don't contact me again.

Before I hit Send, I look at those two sentences for a long time. I shouldn't be saying "please." I should be telling him, not pleading with him. "Please" was what I said, repeatedly, during the attack, and much good it did me. But if I leave it out, it's an imperative, a command, and that might anger him. It comes to me with great force, and it is a sober and simple thought, that I am very afraid of him, viscerally afraid— afraid in the way I was afraid of dogs as a little girl, when I would take a mile-long detour home from school rather than go past a neighbor's house that I knew contained one.

He knows about you. He has something on me. We are not safe.

Fear fought with my education, my achievements, my politics: fear won. "Please" stayed in.

I hit Send, then block his e-mail address.

I call you straightaway. You pick up the phone and I say quickly, in a low voice, "It's me, I've had an e-mail." There is a pause on the line, then you say, "I'm going to have to call you back. Where are you?"

"In the office."

"Okay, I'll call you right back."

Right back turns out to mean two hours. I have already deleted the e-mail but I relate its wording to you, and my reply. You say, "Good."

"Where are you?" I ask. A drink after work would be good, really good—an alcoholic drink, a very large, very cold, very dry glass of wine. I haven't drunk a thing since that party, the thought has made me feel nauseous, but suddenly I want one, with you. Maybe I could even flirt with you. I am beginning to feel it is important I do that soon. I need to try to get back to how I was before.

There is a microscopic pause, then you say, "Leytonstone," and I don't believe you. I think you have told me you are on the outskirts of town so that I won't ask you if we can meet after work.

"You did really well," you say. "If he contacts you again, let me know."

"Okay," I say, deflated.

"I'll call you later," you say, and hang up.

I don't hear from you for two days. When you contact me, it is by text. *Any more e-mails?* I leave it an hour before I text back. At first I just type, *No.* Then I look at it for a bit and change it to *Nope.* You text back immediately. *Good x.*

That isn't enough, I think. *That won't do.*

The next day, I get a missed call from you. I ignore it. I am at a one-day conference called "Metabolic Pathways and the Commercial Imperative." Scientific conferences are not known for their snappy titles, although the Beaufort Institute's lecture program achieved a short-lived notoriety thanks to me when, having failed to attract enough takers for a series titled "Women in Science," it changed the title, at my urging, to "Sex in Science" and found the students turned up in droves. The first thing I do, when I arrive at "Metabolic Pathways," is scan the lecture theater for George Craddock, even though commercial medicine isn't his field and the chances of him being there are tiny. I scan the room as thoroughly as someone afraid of bombs or fire might check out the emergency exits. Only when I am sure he is not there do I sit on one of the bench seats and open the cardboard folder they have given me, bowing my head over it.

There is a buffet lunch in a crowded corridor. There are sandwiches on oval foil platters, small triangles of alternate white and brown bread with a variety of fillings, all of which exude mayonnaise. There are some chicken drumsticks covered in a very sticky maroon-colored paste. The man I am talking to, a principal from Hull, has six of the drumsticks heaped on his paper plate in a pile. He notices me noticing his plate. "Off the carbs . . . ," he says apologetically, nodding at the pile.

"Hey, Yvonne . . ."

I turn and see that Frances is at my elbow. She looks at the man with the drumsticks.

"We're colleagues," she says, by way of explanation. "We work together at the Beaufort. Frances Reason."

"Oh," he says, mouth full, raising the half-eaten drumstick, signaling as an alternative to conversation, and turns away.

"I've been trying to get hold of you. Rupa is in rottweiler mode." She means my PA. "How was the rest of the party? Wasn't it awful? It was just so awful I felt I had no choice but to get completely plastered. I felt terrible the next day. How about you?"

At that point, someone nudges me from behind in an attempt to get past and I use this opportunity to tip orange juice over myself—easy enough to do—my cup is held awkwardly because I have an empty paper plate in the same hand.

"Shit," I say to Frances. "Excuse me." I turn and dump my plate and cup on the table.

I get to the stairwell. The ladies' toilet is on a half landing one flight up, but three people are queuing outside it. I keep going up the stairs.

I keep going up and up and up, almost running now, out of breath, until I reach the top floor of the building, floor five, which is deserted. I push through a wooden door with a round porthole window and behind it there is a short, wide corridor with a disabled toilet next to a lift. I go into the toilet, which is cold and tiled, and I flip the handle lock and then I bend double and, holding my sides, say out loud to myself, "I can't do this on my own."

By the time I have composed myself, the two o'clock talk is well under way. As I leave the disabled toilet, the door bumps shut behind me. No one is around up here. At the end of the corridor is a floor-to-ceiling window, but it is made of frosted glass so I can't see out. I walk along the moist brown carpet until I reach it and then I lay my forehead against the glass. I need the anesthetic of its cold, hard surface.

I lift out my pay-as-you-go phone and call your number. Because I need you, I don't expect you to answer, but you do.

"Hi," I say.

"Hi," you reply. "You okay?"

"No," I say, but without drama. It's not as if there is anything you can do, and it comes to me like a thick blanket being placed gently over my head, the knowledge that there is nothing you can do.

"Oh, dear," you say. "Oh, dear . . ."

11

I am in a minisupermarket close to my house when you call. It is a week after the e-mail incident and my collapse at the one-day conference. Since then, I have canceled as much as I can and stayed at home. So here I am, handbag on one shoulder and wire shopping basket in the other hand, standing in front of the newspaper rack and staring at a tabloid newspaper. It has a picture of a famous footballer on the front, a family man, a role model for the youth of today. He has been arrested. The four-letter word is huge. It sells newspapers, after all.

It is everywhere. It is in every television drama, news item, casual conversation. It is waiting for me when I pop into my local Costcutter for a pint of milk and a head of lettuce. At the moment that you decide to ring me, I am rooted in the aisle and I have just decided that I can't stand it anymore. I am about to rip the newspapers from their stands and throw them to the floor. I will punch the poor shop assistant who will rush to stop me.

"Hi," I say to you. I now understand the origins of the phrase "my heart was in my mouth." It's more in my throat, I think, not just my heart, all my internal organs, it's like everything is shoved up beneath my chin. I can't breathe.

"Listen," you say, your voice brisk. "There's someone I want you to talk to."

"Okay . . . ," I say slowly.

"He's a police officer," you say. "Specially trained, one of the ones I've told you about—"

I cut across you. "I've told you I can't, you know I can't . . ." I am standing in my local supermarket, in the newspaper aisle, hissing into my phone at my lover. "You know why I can't. We just can't, that's it."

"Just meet this man," you say. "He's happy to give us some informal advice. I've briefed him. He can help talk you through the options."

I press the phone to my ear. I think how tired I am of telephone conversations with you—not tired of them, I suppose, tired of their limitations. Telephone calls, cafés—that's all we are and it's no longer enough. A woman with a wheelchair shoves past me, banging the back of my heel with one of the wheels rather than saying "Excuse me." I shoot her a venomous look. She shoots it right back. The world is full of aggression and unpleasantness, and I am about to add to it by losing it, badly, in Costcutter.

"What would happen if she found out?" I ask. "Your wife. What would happen, if you were a witness in court and everything about us came out, not just the sex, the type of sex, where and when?"

"She would throw me out," you say simply.

"You would lose everything."

And then you say, without flourish or emphasis, "If you want to go to court, I will stand in the dock and tell them what you told me. It's called early reporting. It doesn't mean reporting it to the police, necessarily, you can report a crime to anyone and it counts. You reported it to me. I'll stand in the dock and say so."

"Everything about us will come out."

"Not necessarily. No one knows about us, after all." *Yes, they do*, I think. George Craddock knows about us. He doesn't know your identity but he knows of your existence and you can be sure it will be the first thing he will mention when they question him. I haven't told you about what I said to him. I'm too ashamed. To have betrayed you in that manner, stupidly, drunkenly, and with such consequences— how can I admit to that? It is the only thing I have ever withheld from you.

"You would lose everything," I say. "Your marriage, your home, your job maybe . . ." *I love you*, I think, but I don't say it. I say, "It's not just about protecting you, it's about protecting myself, my family, my home, my job too."

"And now you're saying that so I don't feel bad about the fact you can't go to court because of me."

And despite it all, I smile, as I wander away from the newspapers to the fruit and veg aisle. I have to put the phone in the crook of my neck while I reach out for an iceberg lettuce with one hand and toss it into the basket I am holding with the other.

"Let's just meet my friend for a coffee," you say. "It can't do any harm."

It did do us some degree of harm, later.

We meet in a chain coffee store in the West End. You and I meet first. For once, you are waiting for me when I arrive. You are already seated at a small round table with three chairs, two coffees in Styrofoam cups on the table, and a piece of carrot cake. I look at you and you give me a soft, warm look. "Carrot cake," I say. You smile.

We don't talk about the discussion we are about to have. I had imagined we would lay down a few rules, what we can or can't say—it is still vital that nobody knows about us, after all. But it is as though we both feel the need to be a bit normal. We talk about what we watched on television the previous night.

When the friend comes in, I am somehow surprised, even though I didn't know what to expect. He holds out a hand and introduces himself as Kevin. He is a small, wiry man in a navy blue suit. He is young, but has thinning hair and a dark mustache. He strikes me as the kind of man who is normally very mild mannered but who could, if the situation demanded it, be a right hard bastard.

He and you nod at each other, and I have the feeling that you are more respectful acquaintances than friends. I wonder if, perhaps, you have done him a favor of some sort in the past and now he is returning it.

"Would you like me to get you a coffee?" I say, looking round as he seats himself.

He shakes his head. "Thanks, sorry, I don't have very long."

"Thanks for coming, Kev," you say, soberly. There will be no small talk, I gather, no chumming up. This will be a businesslike discussion. I feel grateful.

"Do you want to tell me the circumstances?" Kevin says, looking at me. I appreciate his use of euphemism, and knowing that I will not be able to get through this discussion unless I make extensive use of it myself. I leave out the bit about us, of course, everything about us, and our encounter in Apple Tree Yard. You have told Kevin that I am someone you have met through your work at the Houses of Parliament, someone who has come to you for advice, that's all. I wonder, though, if Kevin has guessed at anything else between us—he's a detective sergeant, after all. If he has, he gives no sign of it.

The euphemisms. How mild they seem. "He turned me over," I say at one point, and Kevin lowers his gaze discreetly.

I stay calm, articulate, dry-eyed. It occurs to me, briefly, how my calmness, the lack of tears, would count against me if I was making an official complaint. I disassociate during this. I watch myself giving an account, presenting information in the same way I would present a re-search paper at a conference or symposium. At the end of it, I fall si-lent. There is a long pause while you both wait for a bit, to be sure I have finished. I draw a deep breath, then I look at Kevin and say, "I need you to be completely honest, about what will happen, if I go to court, I mean. I need all the facts before I can make a decision." I sur-prise myself in using this phrase as, up until now, I have been con-vinced that the decision was already made. "I'm not the sort of person who would want you to be tactful, please just tell me."

There is a pause, then you say to Kevin, as if to ameliorate my de-mand for honesty, "She had injuries."

Kevin cocks his head on one side, frowns. "Any restraint injuries?" he asks. "Bruising to the wrists?" It's the same question you asked.

"He didn't restrain me," I say. "He didn't need to. I was drunk. He slapped me. It happened too fast."

"Well, injuries don't mean anything unless there's a record of them anyway," Kevin says. "Unless you've been examined by a profes-sional and they are recorded. And even when we have injuries, if the man claims it was consensual S&M, it's quite hard to prove other-wise."

"But if he had beaten me to a pulp, then we would be in with a chance?"

Kevin takes the question seriously. "Yes, but the fact that you were drunk would still count against you. Alcohol is a gift to the defense."

I don't reply because I want Kevin to continue—I need to hear this, all of it.

Kevin leans forward in his seat. "The first thing his solicitor will do, as soon as he's charged, will be to hire a private detective. Any secrets in your past?" I keep my gaze on Kevin. I do not look at you. He continues. "Internet searches, questioning friends and family and work colleagues, starts with that. If there's nothing in your present life, they will get to work on your past, starting with tracking down your sexual history, all your old boyfriends. They will be looking for anyone who says you like being hit or you like it rough. Any sex videos, topless photos, that kind of thing."

"I didn't think they could do that anymore."

Kevin gives a small, unamused snort. "They can do anything. If they are challenged, all they have to do is give a reason to the judge why it's relevant to the defense. So any ex-boyfriends who say you like it rough—"

"They won't find any. I don't."

"Your husband . . ." Kevin glances at my wedding ring.

"They will go after my husband?"

"Possibly. They might put a private detective on him too. Let's say, for instance, that your injuries had been recorded by a medical professional, then in that instance they might try to claim they were caused not by their client but by your husband—jealous rage, that kind of thing."

I have a brief vision of Guy on a witness stand in court.

"Any mental illness in the family?"

I look at him.

"You have a history of any sort?"

You are both looking at me.

"No."

Kevin glances at you, then back at me. "No mental illness, or depression?"

"Family members, not me." There is another pause while you and he wait for me to elaborate. "My mother committed suicide when I was eight years old. She had a long history of depression, probably exacer-

146

bated by having children." I don't look at you but I can feel you watching me carefully. "And when he was sixteen, my son was diagnosed with bipolar disorder, his manic episodes were quite severe. Since then, he's had three spells in institutions. He's living in a hostel in Manchester now, he is taking medication, I believe, doing quite well. We're not really in regular contact, though, which is a worry . . ." Once I start talking about Adam, I don't want to stop. This is why I try not to talk about him in daily, ordinary conversation, because I cannot bring myself to discuss my son using generalizations. Anyone who knows about him has to know the whole story, how awful it has been for all of us, how close it has come to destroying our family, how I would give up my work, sell our home, and live in a ditch if it would make Adam well. I can say none of this in front of you and this young detective, so I dry to a halt.

Kevin glances at you as if looking for a clue as to how direct or challenging he can be, then says gently, "Manic depression's hereditary, isn't it? Your mother, your son . . ."

"Actually," I say, "the genetic link isn't proven, it's no more than a tendency. Environmental factors can often . . . often it's, well, nobody really knows."

"So you yourself have never fallen ill?"

I allow myself a wry smile. "Well, I had therapy for a few months in my twenties, doesn't everybody?" I look from you to Kevin, but neither of you smiles back. "I was young, the children were small, my postgraduate work wasn't going well, it was just the usual . . ." You are both silent. "I had a brief spell of postnatal depression after my daughter was born but it was . . . it was, well it just cleared up after about six months, I didn't even . . ."

Kevin presses his lips together.

"The investigating officers are obliged to tell the defense anything they discover during the course of their investigations that might assist the defense. It's called disclosure." Disclosure is something that will later become crucial to our eventual fate but not in the way we are discussing it here.

"And what about him?"

Kevin shrugs again. "It doesn't work the other way around. The defense doesn't have to disclose anything they know about their client. The defense's only obligation is to get their client off."

I pause. "My husband can't know," I say. "Nor my children. They can't know either. My son is fragile. We can't have our lives exposed in court."

"Ah," says Kevin. At this point, a woman with a child in a stroller pauses close to our table. She is hunting for something in a plastic bag slung over one of the stroller handles. "Here you go," she says to the air above the stroller, then bends down and puts a blue plastic rabbit on the lap of the infant strapped into the stroller. We wait until they have moved on before continuing.

"You fall into a category my unit calls too-much-to-lose victims," Kevin says lightly, in a nonjudgmental kind of way. "The younger victims, they are often easier to persuade to go to court. To be frank, they don't know what's coming and don't ask. But older ones, professional women, you know, they do ask. Although there's a whole argument within the service that we shouldn't say. Some people even think we should be serving victims with witness summons, forcing them to go to court—never going to get conviction rates up otherwise."

He sees the alarm on my face. "We would never do that, not with someone like you, anyway; we do with domestic abuse sometimes, when we know that next time he's going to kill her."

"They will set the dogs on me." I say this without self-pity. "And my family."

For this whole discussion you have remained silent, but now you lean forward and say, quietly but earnestly, "You *are* entitled to anonymity."

"Well, strangers won't read your name in the newspaper, it's true," Kevin says, "but any family members who are relevant to the defense can be put on the stand, and all your work colleagues at that party, of course."

I think how, at that party, there was almost everybody I admired from my professional life, everyone from Frances at the Beaufort Institute to Professor Rochester—and a lot of people who know Guy as well. I think how, if this goes to court, no one will ever talk again about how I was the first person to qualify the Wedekind experiment. Mine is the generation that moved from hand sequencing verbally, in pairs, sitting on stools in labs for hours on end, to placing samples directly into million-dollar computers the size of industrial washing machines. We are the pioneers of protein sequencing—I worked with a team that named genes as they were discovered, names that will last as long as science itself. But if I take this to court, there is only one thing about me that will be remembered. No matter what I have hypothesized or discovered, no matter what I achieve, I will spend the rest of my professional life being defined not by what I have done but by what has been done to me. I will be the woman in the George Craddock rape case. I will never be anything more.

"Why are they still allowed to do this?" A note of despair enters my voice, even though it's a self-indulgence that should be beneath me.

"If the issue is consent, then you could argue the defense has no choice. Helps that you're a person of good standing. Girls on housing estates . . ." He shakes his head. "Young girls like that, been out drinking . . ."

I am nauseated. "The people who defend these cases . . . ," I say quietly.

Kevin shrugs. "There's no shortage of them."

A long silence follows. You and Kevin both watch me, carefully, waiting. I feel a great wave of hopelessness washing over me. In order to make one last attempt to stop myself from drowning in it, I say, "What do you think our chances would be?"

Kevin purses his lips again. "In court?" He glances at you, then back at me, as if, for the first time, wondering just how honest he should be. "Well, these cases are notoriously difficult to prove . . ." *These cases*, I think bitterly. I am one of *these cases*. "And this one would be very difficult. You were drunk. You spent the evening with him. So most people would call it a date rape." At the sound of that phrase, I flinch visibly. Kevin pauses briefly, then continues. "The injuries might be helpful if there was a record, but without one they are meaningless. And if there's anything in your past, any evidence of dishonesty or lying, or worst of all any previous allegations of this sort—if it's happened to you before—your chances are zero."

It comes to me that you may have told Kevin to be honest as well. I am grateful.

There is another long silence. Then I say, "Thank you for being so frank with me. Thank you for coming." I want to lighten the atmosphere a little before he goes. "Do you get asked to do this often, give informal advice, I mean?"

He grimaces in reply. "More often than you could imagine." He picks up his briefcase from the floor next to him and puts it on his lap. He is preparing to leave. He glances at you and hesitates for a fraction of a second, then asks you quietly, "Want me to log this conversation?"

You look at him and, almost imperceptibly, shake your head.

My gratitude toward Kevin makes me want to detain him. And I feel a sudden need to impress upon him that I am a person of agency, not just a victim. I look at him. He is midthirties, I guess. Probably living with his girlfriend. I imagine her as a nurse, perhaps, or a teacher, maybe a childhood sweetheart. No kids yet, talking about it. They both like a takeaway on a Friday night, a film on DVD. They hold barbecues at the weekend. They go to Homebase on Sundays to buy shelving and talk about whether they should go to Cyprus in the summer. In their own, understated, way, they love each other very much.

"How do you do this?" I ask. It's a genuine question. "This sort of work, I mean." I imagine there are a lot more glamorous areas of policing he could be involved in. Murder squads, drugs, undercover work—and instead, he spends his time with this, with people like me.

He looks surprised, as if this question has never occurred to him before. "I joined the police in order to catch criminals," he says simply.

"Don't you get depressed?" I ask.

He takes the question seriously. "Not when I'm doing the job, not when I'm out there, or interviewing. In court, though, sometimes. You do all that work, and you go in thinking it's solid, and then . . . well, then."

"You know," I sigh, thinking out loud. "I just find it hard to believe that anyone could go for me, does that sound ridiculous? It's just, I know what happened, I know I'm telling the truth, and after what happened, how could anyone want to go for me? I just can't imagine someone setting out to make me look bad, to treat me like that, after what's happened." *How privileged my life has been thus far,* I think, *for me to feel that way.* To him, I must sound naïve to the point of stupidity.

Kevin looks at me. "Last year," he says, "I had a case, one of those girls I was talking about earlier, fourteen years old, council estate, sweet kid but been in a bit of trouble at school. It was a gang rape, in a park, there were five of them, men from the estate where she lived. She'd been drinking beer with them, a summer's evening. They'd given her that superstrength lager, and I don't think this kid had any idea how strong that stuff is. She wasn't all that bright, to be honest, shoplifting and so on. There were five of them, and they each had a go, in the bushes. Lots of people walking past on the path a few yards away but she was too scared to call out, petrified someone would see them and word would get out she was a slag, she said. Five of them, so that means in court there are five defense barristers. She's fifteen years old by then, and she's in the witness stand for five days in a row, and these five defense barristers stand up, one after the other, and call her a liar, five days in a row." He stops and looks at me, a quick glance that takes in my expensive suede jacket, my scarf. "And that's what we do to children."

I look at you, helplessly.

You say softly, "Thanks, Kev. Thanks for your time."

Kevin stands, holds out his hand. Shaking his hand seems absurd but I do it anyway. You do the same.

"Good luck," Kevin says, nods goodbye to me, to you. Then he turns and leaves the café, and I watch him walk off down the street, the small man in the neat navy suit, for all the world like an estate agent, or a man who sells broadband connections.

You give me a look that makes me think you are wondering if I am about to cry. I don't cry. I put my hand on the table and you take the hint and cover my hand with yours, pressing lightly. We sit like that, in silence, for some time.

After a while you say, "You didn't tell me your mother killed herself."

I give a small shrug. "She'd been ill more or less on and off since I was born. I was raised by my dad and my aunt who lived next door. Mum was in and out of hospital. I always thought of her as ill."

"Tough call," you say.

"It's a long time ago." It was a long time ago. I think of my aunt, who was kindly and brisk and there every day to make me and my brother oven chips and baked beans after school until my father got home from work. She was a good mother to me and lived to see my children when they were small. I think of how the way to get my father's attention was to show him an A in a circle at the bottom of an essay, of how he would demonstrate physical affection only when I was asleep, tiptoeing into my room at night to stroke my hair in the dark, and how I would struggle to stay awake after lights-out in order to catch him at it. He remarried when I was seventeen and moved to Scotland as soon as I left home to go to university—my brother was five years older than me and had already left home to work on a sheep farm in New Zealand. I always knew he would leave as soon as he could. Crawley had never been quite outdoorsy enough for him and Gatwick Airport was temptingly close. My upbringing was not particularly hard, under the circumstances, and I refuse to be defined by it. I felt loved as a child, cared for. I have married the right man and raised two children. I have made a good life for myself. I am nobody's victim.

The weight of your hand resting on mine—I like that. I turn my hand beneath yours, palm upward, so that our fingers can intertwine and clutch. *How little we know of each other,* I think. Nothing, in fact: only this, only now. The lives we have led before we met, the children born and brought up, the jobs held, the traumas and upsets and joys, extended families, friends, acquaintances—the webs of our lives: we know nothing. I don't even know if your parents are alive or dead. You and I have the opposite of what Guy and I have. Guy and I have acres of knowledge but no intimacy—you and I have an intense relationship that exists in a vacuum.

I move my thumb against yours; the friction is comforting. Your nails are always neatly filed and clean—that touch of vanity again. Clean, how clean and simple are our desires, how straightforward, yet how open to misinterpretation by others.

Eventually, I say softly, "Apple Tree Yard."

You lean in slightly, tightening your grip around my hand. "There was no CCTV. I'm sure, I checked. If you don't tell them they don't have to disclose it to the defense. Don't tell them about Apple Tree Yard, don't tell them about us. No one has any way of knowing. Nothing is written down anywhere. There's no paper trail and I can dispose of the phones. Nobody can prove anything between us other than an acquaintance."

"I'd have to lie in court," I say, "when they go through my movements earlier that day, I'd have to describe my whereabouts. If I told the truth about what you and I were doing, nobody would ever believe me about the other thing. Or even if they did, they would think I was a slut who deserved everything she got."

Opposite where we are sitting is a large wooden-framed mirror, hung in order to make the café appear larger, I suppose. Reflected in it is the side of the counter with its rows of cakes. In front of the cakes, there is us, seated at our small round table, a middle-aged man and woman, not looking at each other, clutching hands. We are framed perfectly by the mirror, the row of cakes behind us, the soft lighting above that matches the soft music playing and the gentle talk of the other customers. Our demeanors are unmistakably somber despite our physical affection. We look like a couple that has just agreed to divorce.

I think that if I could climb into that mirror, experience the whole world the wrong way round, from the wrong side of the glass, everything in opposite, it would seem no stranger to me than what is happening now.

12

For the rest of that week, I am very low, I don't know why. I should be feeling better, relieved. It's not going to go anywhere so now all I have to do is get over it. It wasn't as if Kevin told me anything I didn't already know. I wake a lot in the night. I stare at the ceiling for a couple of hours before falling back to sleep. In the mornings, I feel drugged and have to push myself up into a sitting position, and even then remain for a long time on the edge of the bed before I can stand. I sit slumped with my elbows on my knees, my head in my hands. I have to be careful not to let Guy catch me doing this.

Guy is busy at work. You are busy too. You call occasionally, doing your best, but sometimes, in your voice, I hear the strain of you doing the right thing, hear it in the way you ask how I am. I am different now. I start screening your calls until I feel strong enough to pretend. On the occasions where I sound all right, I can hear the relief in your voice. I am careful to end the call first, and after we hang up, I cry. I cancel all the work appointments I can. I take a few days' leave from the Beaufort, which I am due, staying in e-mail contact, making a phone call now and then. But even phone calls are effortful. I don't want to talk to anyone.

That weekend, Guy and I go to a dinner. Guy and I are not really dinner party people—he hates chitchat and will sit there with his head hanging until someone says something interesting. When they do, he will perk up, like a Labrador about to be taken on a walk. Dinner is the last thing I feel like, but I'm working at being normal.

As we are getting ready to go, Guy says to me, "Aren't you showering?"

I am pulling a stretchy blue dress over my head, made of a synthetic fabric that gives an electric crackle as I work it down my body. "Trying to tell me something?" I murmur, going over to my vanity unit and picking up the expensive perfume he bought me last birthday. *Mist . . . mist . . .* it goes as I press the gold button and draw lines of vapor across my wrists.

"No, it's just you're showering all the time these days."

We arrive at our friends' house in Harrow-on-the-Hill. Harry and Marcia's house is huge: one of them has family money. People we don't know will be at this party, and as we approach their door I hope there will be no barristers or lawyers. Since meeting Kevin, I've been looking at the people sitting opposite me on the Tube, the smartly dressed ones who might work in the legal profession, and wondering if they are the sort who would be happy to try to get a not-guilty verdict for George Craddock.

It's a big dinner party, twelve people around a long oval table in a yellow kitchen with a conservatory extension and a glass roof. We get to the pudding without incident, although Guy tells me later I was quiet all evening. Then it happens. The big news story that week is of a politician who has been accused of sexual assault by a hotel maid in New York.

"It's the wife I feel sorry for," says our friend Harry, who owns the house we are sitting in, whose teenage children trail in and out of the kitchen, going to the double fridge and extracting two liter-bottles of fizzy drinks, then trailing out again. They have friends upstairs. There's a small child too, a late baby, but she's asleep somewhere.

Next to Harry is a man with a fine white goatee beard, a line like an upward-pointing arrow on his chin. "Well, I saw the maid on television . . . ," he says dismissively, as if that settles it. He trails off, then when he sees we are looking at him, he adds, "She lied to the grand jury."

I don't know you, I think, staring at him.

The wife of the man with the goatee beard, whom I also don't know, bristles. She is sitting directly opposite her husband. "She lied about her immigration status. Don't you think most people would do the same if they were desperate for a job in New York?"

Goatee beard is drunk. He reaches for the wine bottle in the middle of the table and upends it over his glass. "My wife knows what she's talking about," he says to the glass. "She's an immigration lawyer. If we get a minicab home, she'll have another client by the end of the journey."

"Whereas my husband . . . ," the wife begins, looking around at us and smiling—but before she can get any further, our hostess Marcia cuts in. She doesn't want the evening to sour and I don't blame her. There's nothing worse than a married couple sniping at each other across the table as the evening wears on, not when you've put all that effort into dinner. I like Harry and Marcia. They threw large dinner parties even when their children were small, at the stage when most of us could scarcely be bothered to boil an egg for guests. The food is always good, the wine good—they like mixing up their friends, people who don't know each other, they are innately hospitable, generous people.

"The thing I think is so ridiculous," says Marcia, keen to lighten the atmosphere, "is, honestly, how could anyone *force* anyone else to have oral sex? Wouldn't you just bite it off!" She slaps the table lightly as she says this and looks round at us all, inviting us to laugh. She has blond hair that flips upward at the ends, gravity-defying little flips. She is wearing a plain black dress, the knot of a silver necklace at her throat. Her husband adores her.

I feel my breath hot inside me. Why is this kitchen so hot? And something very odd begins to happen. In my head, I turn on her and give her the speech I would like to give, about how stupid and ignorant a comment it is, about how unless you have experienced fear, you have no idea how paralyzing fear can be, about how depressing and infuriating it is—unbearable, in fact—that women peddle this ignorant crap as well as men. And, in my head, I rattle through this argument at great speed and with great articulacy, culminating with . . . but I say this last bit out loud: it pops out, not as an angry climax to an angry speech, oh, no, it comes out cool and clean.

"Well, I suppose you would, wouldn't you, Marcia, with your perfect home and your perfect husband and your perfect fucking kids? You'd probably enjoy it."

There is an ugly and baffled silence. Everyone looks at me.

I am holding my desert spoon. I fiddle with it. Marcia served a lemon pudding of some sort, my favorite. What a yellowish evening this is: sunflower-colored walls, my blond hostess, the lemon pudding.

"Well . . . ," Marcia says, still smiling, looking around, a little helplessly. "Well, I didn't . . ."

I sit back in my chair, affecting casualness, and toss the spoon onto the dining table, where it lands with a metallic clatter. "You know what the really scary thing is, as far as I'm concerned. What it is, is, you're a perfectly intelligent woman but nothing really bad has happened to you, and despite your intelligence, you simply don't have the imagination to understand what it's like when bad things happen to other people. But the scariest thing of all . . ." I lean across the table toward her and the venom in my voice is unmistakable. She is looking down now, her perfect complexion going pink. "They let people like you sit on juries."

The silence that follows is thick, in the yellow room. We are all staring at Marcia, until she is released by one of the teenagers calling down from the stairwell, "Mum! Mu-um!"

In the car going home, there is a long silence, then Guy says, "Was it really necessary to go in that hard?"

"Oh, for Pete's sake . . . ," I mutter. I think of reminding him of the number of times he has offended people at parties.

"She's a nice woman," Guy says, sighing gently. "We like her, remember? She's not stupid, she just said a stupid thing. She's a nice woman."

"That makes it worse, not better."

He has the sense to give up.

We arrive back at our house. Our little gate is open and he reverses carefully into our drive, the familiar crunch of gravel. He lets the engine idle for a bit, then turns it off. We sit in silence, in the dark. Neither of us moves.

Guy is staring straight ahead. *Please, please don't ask me what is wrong*, I think.

"Yvonne . . . ," he says.

I open my door, clamber out with some haste, slam it behind me. When I get to our front door, I remember that he has the house key, not me. I have to stand waiting for him while he gets out of the car, slowly, locks it carefully, checks that it is locked.

It takes me another two weeks to work out what I have to do and there are some dark moments along the way. I can't get hold of you, and I begin to suspect you are screening my calls. I don't blame you. You are screening until you have time for a long conversation because you don't feel able to have brief ones with me anymore. I am avoiding everyone else in my life. You are all I have. I am sorry.

On Radio 4 one morning, a Home Office official taking part in a debate about sexual assault says that of course he believes sentencing should be toughened up when it's a *serious* assault. At such moments, it is hard to find my way around my own kitchen.

The inevitable happens. I haven't seen you for a week, we have spoken once, briefly. You are scared, I think, and why wouldn't you be? I'm scared too. I wait until Guy is out of the house one afternoon and even take a glass of wine up to my study in the hope that it might help.

I open the familiar document. My heart is like lead. I know that I still can't send a letter or e-mail to you, now more than ever, and that if I am to do this in writing, it will have to be in the ridiculously condensed form of a text, but if I am ever to work out what to say in that condensed form, then first I have to try to communicate it to myself.

Dear X,

Before I began this letter, I attempted to reread the early ones I wrote, the ones where I was so sure of myself. I had to stop. It was painful for me to see the full stretch of my delusions laid out in words, the way I was so certain I could handle whatever you, or anyone, threw at me. None of what I have previously believed about myself is true.

How can I ever begin to list the many ironies of my situation now? Chief among them is that if I had described your behavior to a friend, she might have been concerned for me. The unpredictability, the risky sex, the possessiveness—all these would have rung alarm bells to anyone who cared for me, as I would have been alarmed if a friend of mine had detailed her involvement with a man like you. And yet all the time, while I was wondering if you might, possibly, be dangerous, while I was wondering if my excitement over you was merely thrilling or downright foolhardy—all that time, someone as seemingly harmless as him was waiting for me, waiting for his opportunity.

When I was younger, I would have been scared of a man like you. I would have run a mile. But you came to me at an age when I believed I didn't need to be scared anymore. Which men to be scared of—it's something any girl or young woman learns, instinctively, as soon as she is old enough to leave the house on her own: the man in a suit who stands too close to you at the bus stop; the wet-lipped old guy who waits in the middle of the pavement, staring as you approach; the loud, drunken lads in the pub who will shout obscenities at chucking-out time.

But now I know how wrong those instincts can be. Now I know it can come from any direction, even one you believe to be so innocuous that there is no harm in getting drunk, in being alone with him in a room, because this one doesn't seem at all dangerous, does he? And, hey, even if he does make a pass at you, you can handle it, can't you? You're a mature woman. You have degrees to prove it. One good hard slap, that's all it took.

I'm not afraid of dangerous men anymore. I'm afraid of friendly, ordinary men. I'm not afraid of burglars or strangers after dark. I'm afraid of men I know.

At that point I stop and stare at the screen for a long time. I read through what I have written, close the letter, feel grateful that no one but me will ever read it, then send you a text.

Dear You. What we have been doing was a game but something has happened that was all too real. I know how difficult this has been for you. I stop at this point, begin to cry. *So, probably best if we are not in touch for a while.* I stop again. I have to be unequivocal. *It's really better that way, so don't call or text. I'll be in touch when things look up. I'm sorry.* I sob a little, salty tears of self-pity flowing down my cheeks. I am aching to sign off with affection, to tell you how much I want you and need you now, but instead I write: *I'm going to press Send now before I lose my nerve. My husband is home so that's it for now. Yx.*

I press Send. Then I put the phone down on my desk, cover my face with my hands, and cry a solid, loud, hearty cry. Guy won't be back for another two hours. I can cry as loudly as I want.

After a while, I stop crying. I wipe at my eyes with the sleeve of my top and see immediately that, as it is light green, I have smeared mascara over it. *I liked that top*, I think. Oh, well. Silly cow. Serves you right. What did you expect? I imagine myself telling someone—a police officer, or a jury, perhaps?—the whole story. The vast majority of people would think I deserved everything I got. Maybe they'd be right too. I think of young women whom this happens to, how they must feel defined by it. I am fifty-two years old. I have lived a lot and done a lot and, with luck, will live a lot and do a lot more. I feel the strange wash of weary calm that always comes after a long cry.

I pick up the phone and look at it, turn it over once in my hand. I know there has been no immediate response from you because there has been no buzz or vibration but I still look at the messages folder, just in case. Then, on an intake breath, I turn off the phone.

―――

The first day without you is painful in a way that is almost exquisite. I imagine quitting smokers must feel like this, or crash dieters—the early determination, where the loss of what you have given up is replaced with the adrenaline of denial. Then there is the fine business of tormenting oneself, of picking at the loss. I had a friend in the first office I worked in, Siobhan, who was prone to ear infections. When she got one, the itching would drive her crazy. She used to try to clean the inside of her ear with cotton buds but that only made it worse, pushed the irritation farther in. So she would sit at her desk sometimes while I watched in appalled fascination, and screw a tissue up into a point, dampening it slightly with her tongue, twisting it round and round until it formed a long, fine conical shape. She was a small woman, with pale skin and gamine features. She would concentrate very hard as she rolled the tissue, the tip of her tongue protruding from her mouth. Then, with an expression of intense concentration, she would insert the spear of tissue into her ear and prod inside, deep in her ear, at the source of irritation and itching and pain. She would tell me that it would make a tiny *doink doink doink* sound inside her head, this action. It had no lasting effect, she knew that before she did it. It was just that, for the few seconds of that small motion, as the itch was temporarily satisfied, she would have the illusion of rapture.

In the same way, that first day, I turn my phone on and check it every hour, as if to prod at my pain, to prove to myself you will not reply. And when I see that you have not replied, I feel a piercing combination of vindication and dread—I have poked at my grief for a few seconds. *Doink doink.*

The first day turns out to be the easy bit. Even on the second day, I still feel a perverse satisfaction in my ability to make myself suffer. I tell myself the lack of response from you vindicates my decision. Perhaps you really did want out but didn't feel able to say so under the circumstances. Very probably, you are relieved.

On the Thursday morning, I return to my desk at home after going to the loo, and see that on my regular phone, my normal one, there are three blocked missed calls. I pick up the phone and look at it. It could be you, or it could be the spam calls I was getting a month or so ago. I turn on the pay-as-you-go phone to see if you have left a message there, but there is nothing. I turn off both phones.

For a few days more, I have the illusion that I have done the right thing and that doing the right thing means I am getting better. I am kind to myself. I bathe often. I am nice to Guy. I try to think as much as possible about Guy. I go for walks in the park. I tell myself the worst is over. It is time to put it all behind me now.

I go into the Beaufort Institute again, returning to my regular work schedule. There is one loose end to be tidied up. I send an e-mail to Sandra. *Hi Sandra, Just to give you a heads-up, I thought I should let you know I won't be returning to the external examining position next academic year—I thought the more notice I gave you the better. It looks like I might be doing a full-time maternity cover here and so my diary is going to be stuffed. I'm sure you've got a list, but let me know if you want me to suggest some names for you. I hear Mahmoud Labaki is very good, a hard marker. Guy has worked with him a lot and really rates him—let me know if you need his contact details. See you soon I hope, Yvonne.*

After this, I send an e-mail to Marc in Human Resources. The person he found for the maternity cover has just pulled out on him, so I know he will be pleased when I tell him I can take it on after all. He e-mails me back immediately, delighted. *It's working,* I think. *That's all I can do for now, keep busy.*

A week after my mother's cremation, while her ashes were still in a pot-bellied urn on a shelf in the kitchen, my father came home one day with a present for me—a new kit. It was the February half term; I was off school. I think my aunt must have told him I needed something to take my mind off what had happened. It was a resin kit, for making paperweights and keepsakes and jewelry. It came with metal bottles of liquid that needed mixing together with spatulas, then pouring into molds. I spent the whole of that half term making things. I had to spread newspaper over the kitchen table, at my aunt's insistence, and then pour liquid from the large bottle into the mold. When I had done that, I mixed in a few drops from a much smaller bottle of hardener. It fascinated me—that something that was liquid could be made solid by the simple addition of a few drops of a different liquid. What caused that? How did it work? The little molds came in different shapes: circles, ovals, squares. You could sink things in the liquid—flower petals (but they turned brown), strands of hair, beads. My most successful object was an oval, into which I sunk a tiny plastic ballerina that I think was once a cake decoration. The objects hardened overnight. By the end of the week, I had quite a collection of them. I went round the house and hid them in as many different sorts of places as I could find—in the bathroom cabinet, in my father's wardrobe, on a window-sill on the half landing. I had the idea that I, and other members of my family, would, in future, stumble across the objects accidentally and be pleased. No one ever commented on them, though, and eventually I forgot them myself, finding one or other of them many months later, in a box or cupboard or on a shelf, undiscovered, covered in dust.

13

The quality of blue that the sky has in May is quite unlike the quality it has at other times of the year. Summer throws everything it's got at us then, as if to remind us what it's all about: dense blue, impenetrable. June is more confused: muddled skies, showers. In June we are reminded, yes, the British summer, this is what it's like. It's rubbish, really. Why do we live on this damp island? July is unpredictable: it does it on purpose. It likes to let us know it could go either way, depending on its mood. Most of the time we are philosophical, but every now and then, the odd blasting hot day arrives to give us a bit of false hope. In August, a kind of collective stalwartness sets in. Rain lashes down on the bank holiday but we are British, we can handle it. We never expected any different. The false hopes of July, the muddled skies of June, even the blank blue of May—none of it had us fooled, not for one minute.

It was a long summer, my love.

I try to get out of the house. I go to the Beaufort more often than I need to, considering my full-time post doesn't start until September. The woman I am doing the maternity cover for, Claire, is huge with twins. When she walks down the corridors at work, people give her wide berth, as if they are worried about bumping into her and setting her off like a car alarm.

London is a city of over eight million inhabitants; it is heaving, this summer, but it is empty without you. Guy and I moved out to the very edge of London to get away from it but all our journeys are back in, as if we are iron filings drawn to a magnet. Living on the edge of a city means you get to see a lot more of it than if you live right in the middle. You get to traverse it every day.

Our local station is a terminus. "There's only one problem with the end of the line," Susannah said when we moved there. "It's the end of the line." When I get the Tube into town, I travel overground for half an hour, watching the dense expanse of suburbs passing by, relentlessly, the houses that back onto the railway line, the washing hanging out, the children and dogs in the small square back gardens. All these millions of people: what's the point of any of them, when none of them is you? It is a relief when the train goes underground at Finchley Road. The population shrinks to the inhabitants of my carriage and I know that none of them is you already.

What is it I am pining for, exactly? We had so little time together and I'm too traumatized to miss the sex. I am missing the way that you concentrated on me. I am missing how the beam of your attention seemed to create a protective barrier around me that nothing else could penetrate. I am missing who I was when I was with you. Maybe I'm just missing myself.

Maybe this is all it is: the price we pay for what we do is proportionate. Maybe all that endless summer amounted to was the inverse of the heady spring you and I had spent together: the secrecy and excitement of what we did, the exhilaration—and yes, the joy, the joy of doing something that wasn't wise or logical, merely desired. Then I had to pay. You go into a shop for an ice cream, you have to give the man behind the counter some money. It's really not difficult.

When I am at work, I cannot permit myself to imagine you only a few streets away, that would be too painful—so the way I deal with it is to imagine you gone, vaporized. It's easier when the school holidays start, because I know your children are still school-age, so you are probably in France or Spain or Italy—somewhere. I imagine you on a windy beach, playing cricket with them, bowling at them with long, easy overarm strokes, your T-shirt billowing away from your back in the sea breeze, the children jumping and shrieking, your wife lying on a towel a few feet away, reading a book. In September, it will get harder again, but in September I will start my maternity cover and that, along with my freelance work, will mean the next six months will be very full.

Throughout the summer, I set myself false deadlines. *By the end of May, I will start to be better*—okay then, by the time Guy and I take that long weekend in Rome in June, or when I come back from it, I will start to forget everything that has happened, him and you. Rome is good. In Rome, I can walk down a street and not bump into anyone I desire or dread. But my loneliness returns with renewed force the minute we step off the plane at Heathrow, the minute I am back on the same island as you. Absurdly, I scan the people waiting at the barriers in the arrivals hall, the minicab drivers with their signs, the anxious parents, families. Do I really think you would have somehow found out I was away, checked the inbound manifests, and disguised yourself as a driver just so that you could wait at the barrier to catch a glimpse of me? At such times, I feel a fleeting fear for my own sanity.

At the end of August, Adam comes home. It is the first time we have seen him for nearly two years. We have spoken to him seven times during that period, only two of them at any length. The first we know about his visit is when he sends Guy a text, the Thursday after the bank holiday. *Might come by tomorrow for couple of days, OK?*

My son did not text me. My son knew that if he texted me, I would text back asking what time he would arrive, if he would be hungry, how long he would be staying . . .

So Guy texts back. *Great. See you then.* Then he sits me down and gives me a long list of things I must not ask our son about. I must not ask him where he is living at the moment. I must not ask him if he has a girlfriend. I must not ask if he is taking medication or rehearsing with a band or looking for a job. I must not say, in that significant way that I do, "And . . . how are you?"

I stay at home all day on the Friday, cooking a casserole and cleaning the house. At ten o'clock that night, with no sign of our son, Guy insists we eat the casserole rather than saving it until the next day, then go to bed.

On the Saturday, at around three o'clock, the doorbell goes and I stay upstairs and let Guy answer. He will do it much better than me.

My son. I hear him downstairs, in my house—my son, the voice I know so well I could imitate it, the *yeahs* and *sures*, the deep scratchiness of it. I force myself to walk downstairs slowly. "Hi," I say as I wander down to greet him.

He fills the hall, my boy. He has inherited his father's height and bulk, the slightly turned-in curve of his shoulders. He is wearing jeans and trainers and a green jacket with some faux-military trimmings. At the sight of him I am awash with love, and reminded, with a pain like a shaft of light, just how many young women would love him too, if he were open to being loved. "You know nothing," he said to me once, on a visit a few years ago when I tried to talk about it, about how much love was out there. "Nothing." Later, Guy says there was a girl, after all, who had told Adam that she had aborted his baby but Adam didn't know if the story was true.

He has stubble on his face—it suits him—and his thick brown hair looks untrimmed but in a trendy, deliberately disheveled kind of way. He hates it when I stare at him so I am careful to glance at him briefly, enough to take him in, then look at my feet as I descend the stairs. Has he lost weight, or put it on? Does his gaze have that dull, off-center look that it did when he was taking Carbatrol? It's hard for me to look at him without making a diagnosis, or without the emotion showing on my face, how much I miss him, how desperate I am. So despite the fact that I haven't set eyes on my own son for nearly two years, I am careful to avoid his gaze as I wander down the stairs toward him.

"Hi Mum," he says, and I can hear from the drift of his voice that he has turned toward the kitchen.

Adam is home for four days. He sleeps a lot. At night, in our bedroom, Guy and I have whispered conversations where he hissingly demands that I do not ask Adam a *single* question, not one. I think he's overreacting.

Adam seems pretty good to me, good in comparison with what we have faced before: I think he could manage a little light discussion, but I bow to Guy's insistence.

The smell of my son in my house, the shape and shade of him moving from room to room: that is enough. I don't work while he is here, although I pretend to, up at my computer in my study. I cannot bear the thought of leaving the house while he is around, but after four days, I relax a little and decide to go to the supermarket, leaving Guy and Adam sitting on the back doorstep in some damp sunlight drinking tea in companionable silence while Adam smokes a roll-up. I think, as I drive there, how it is a good idea to give them some time alone together. Maybe Guy will be able to glean some information that Adam wouldn't divulge if I was in the house.

I push my trolley up and down the aisles, filling it with food that Adam might like, not the stuff he liked as a child but the stuff I am guessing he might like now, seeing as I'm not allowed to ask; veggie burgers and chorizo, fresh pasta and oven chips—my choices are eclectic. I buy a huge amount even though we still have a stack of food in the house from the shopping I did before he came. Queuing to pay, I throw in a bumper family pack of Liquorice Allsorts.

I am out of the house for only an hour, but I know as soon as I step in the front door that Adam has gone. There is an Adam absence in the air, in the quality of the light, the not-quite silence as Guy's footsteps shuffle across the hall to greet me, to take the plastic bags from my grasp. Adam was waiting for me to be out of the house so he could leave. He wanted to avoid the conversation that might happen when he bid me goodbye.

I stare at Guy accusingly. The plastic bags are overfilled, heavy, the handles stretched into wires that cut my fingers. Guy has to ease them from my grasp. "I tried," he says gently.

My son's visit and departure make everything worse again. I stay busy, and the following week, I begin the maternity cover. This would help if it weren't for the commuting, when I am forced to think. I think about my son, about how I might not see him again for another two years, how I have failed at the only relationship with a man that really matters. I think about Guy, about how self-contained he is, how it is probably my fault, that I have allowed that to happen because it suited me too. I think about you, and gradually, inevitably, my thoughts turn bitter. Why have you given me up so easily? Why did you take my text at face value? I might be wrong, of course. You might be missing me desperately, holding yourself back from calling because you think it is best for me. You could be thinking about me all the time. Or you could be completely careless of how I am. You could be absorbed in a new love by now. I imagine the many different sorts of women you could be involved with. I imagine them one by one.

Then, finally, it happens, and when it happens the worst thing about it is its inevitability, as if I had been waiting for it, not wondering if but merely how and when.

Ten minutes' walk from where we live, just before the main shopping precinct, there is a hairdressing salon run by a very small, very beautiful Italian man. It is more of a street-style salon than you would expect a woman of my age to patronize but that, of course, is why I go. I have my highlights, lowlights, whatever they are, redone about once every two or three months. The Italian, Bernardo, talks to me about Italy while he gives me a scalp massage. He tells me how in Italy, all the women want to look the same. That's why he came to London, because every woman is different. He employs Japanese and Polish and Korean stylists, and another Italian man who makes eyes at every customer, male or female, whose open gaze demands to be loved. I think he might be going out with one of the Korean women but I'm not sure. I enjoy the soap opera of this place; I like observing the intricacies of the relationships the staff have with their customers and with each other. I like listening in on other haircuts. I look at my fellow customers' reflections as I sit with folded foil in my hair—their reflections in the mirrors in front of them reflected in the mirror in front of me. I am never sure whether they can see me watching them or not.

I am sitting in the chair being finished off. Bernardo has done the blow-dry—he is snipping at the odd millimeter, here and there, taking

his time, just to make me feel a bit more special than his other customers. He is asking me whether or not he should have a coffee machine
in his shop and I am telling him not to bother. He has just stood back
to admire his work and I am turning my head slightly, with a little
shake to see how the layers fall, when I glance out of the window of the
salon and I see that, standing in the street on the other side of the glass
panel, looking in, is George Craddock. He is watching me through the
glass panel. He smiles.

I hide in the toilet of the hairdressing salon for nearly fifteen minutes.
Outside, Bernardo must be wondering if something is wrong. Maybe I
don't like the cut after all, or I am ill. I could call Guy and ask him to
come and get me, but I would have to pretend I *was* ill, and then keep
that pretense up, and my behavior recently has been odd enough as it
is. And if I call Guy and he comes and George Craddock is still out
there, then he will see Guy, know what he looks like, if he doesn't
already, be close to him, close enough to say, perhaps, "Hello there,
George Craddock, I work with Yvonne. I don't believe we've met."

I can't call you. It's a Saturday. And anyway, I can't call you.

Eventually, I know that my only option is to leave, to hold my head
up, however sick I feel inside, and walk out of the salon.

When I get outside, I glance up and down the road, but there is no sign
of Craddock. He could be watching me, of course, but somehow I
feel that if he was still around, he would have approached me
immediately—*it's an ugly coincidence,* I say to myself, *that is all.* The
chain stores are close by: he could just be out shopping. I will have to
use a different hairdressing salon from now on. Bernardo will wonder
when I don't come back.

I turn left and stride down the street, away from home, toward the
big shops, vigorously, not looking around. If he is following me, then I
need to know for sure. As I pass the entrance to Marks & Spencer, I
turn suddenly and stride through the automatic door. Without looking
behind me, I go straight to the escalator up to the first floor—it's one of
those escalators that speed up when you step on it, which is something
I normally find disconcerting but at this particular moment feels

helpful. On the first floor, I weave among the Saturday shoppers through to the ladies' lingerie department. He can't follow me in here without it being obvious. Partially hidden behind a row of sports underwear and minimizing bras, I turn to watch the top of the escalator. For several minutes, my heart crashes against my chest as I wait for the top of his head, then his face—the face that was in my face—to sail upward into view.

It doesn't happen. After ten minutes or so, I turn away, and begin a slow trail around the department, picking things up, putting them down. I will browse for a bit before I leave, I think, just to be sure. I have just turned to go when I feel the phone in my pocket buzz. I consider ignoring it but still extract it from the inside pocket of my jacket. There is a text from a number I don't recognize. It says, *Great haircut.* I delete it.

After that, there is a flurry of incidents. I begin to get blocked missed calls on my regular phone almost every day—sometimes a dozen in a row, sometimes at intervals, sometimes nothing for hours. Then it all goes quiet for a week. Then it starts again. At work, I get another e-mail from him, a casual one copied to five other people, including Sandra, suggesting we all meet for a night in the pub to brainstorm about the future of the MA program. At first, I am baffled because I have blocked Craddock's work e-mail address, but then I check and see that he has sent it from a home account. Everyone hits Reply to All and two out of the five people think it's a great idea, two will come if they can. Sandra's reply reminds George and everyone else that I'm not doing the external examining anymore but says she hopes I'll come anyway to give everyone the benefit of my wisdom. I don't respond. I block his home e-mail too.

A week later, I get a text while I'm walking back to my house from the Tube. It's from my cousin Marion, who lives in Bournemouth. I'm in touch with her only occasionally. The text says, *You'd better check your e-mail, you're spamming everyone! Hope you're well. Love Marion x.* I get home and find that I am locked out of the Hotmail account I set up when I first went freelance, because it has been hacked and is sending everyone in my address book links to pornographic websites. My Google account is more recent, and there are several e-mails in it from people who have both addresses, letting me know it is happening. Some of them are understanding, some indignant, as if I have deliberately, stupidly, sent everyone a corrupt link. It takes me three days to clear up the mess.

Then it stops.

The maternity cover post keeps me busy: not the work itself, which I know well, but reacquainting myself with the processes of being full-time, the different rhythm of my week, the different sort of tiredness I feel—this all provides distraction. A month into the post, Sandra sends me a confirmation of the time and date of the pub get-together. I imagine George Craddock standing in her office and saying, "By the way, why don't you give Yvonne a nudge about the pub? Even if she's not examining for us it would be great to have her input." I send her a quick one back. *Sorry, up to my eyeballs! Talk soon. Yx.* Under normal circumstances, I would have added, *Say hi to everyone from me.* I imagine how guilelessly George Craddock might say to Sandra, "That's a shame, we'll have to get her out for a drink another time." There are a hundred different innocent ways he might try to make contact with me. I must have a strategy prepared for each.

How I feel, during this time, swings wildly from rank fear and paranoia to a kind of determined pragmatism. Sometimes I think I am in danger—he knows by now that I'm not going to the police, for reasons of my own, and if I'm not prepared to report one attack, what's to prevent him from assuming I won't report another? At other times, I say to myself, *He's a functioning member of society, with things to lose, presumably, a home, a family.* He isn't interested in me. He is just trying to prove to himself that he didn't do anything really wrong, that he can contact me and I will go along with it and then that will reinforce his conviction that his behavior was acceptable. Perhaps he said to himself the next day, *Might have gone a bit far last night but she was up for it.* Perhaps he thought, when he e-mailed or texted me, that it was a bit of a joke. *This will give her a shock!* He's a university lecturer. He holds down a job, operates on a day-to-day basis, presumably doesn't have a criminal record. He would never dream of following a woman down a dark alley at night and dragging her into the bushes—well, he might dream of it, fantasize about it, but he would never actually do it. I think about his students. I wonder if they are at risk, but somehow I doubt it. Harassing students gets picked up on pretty quickly these days, in most institutions, at least. He's not stupid. And anyway, I think what he likes best is humiliating a woman who regards herself as above him. It comes to me, this thought, as I am at my desk—that I did regard myself as above him, that that was probably obvious to him.

But surely, if I just give it a bit more time, he will give up, lose interest. It's a game to him. If I don't respond, just carry on going about my normal life, it will stop. It hasn't been consistent, or immediate—some bits of it, like the hacking of my Hotmail account, I'm not even sure was him.

It happens on a Sunday. Guy is away at a weekend conference in Northampton but has just called me to say he is finishing early. I decide to go out to the deli that I know stays open till four on a Sunday and buy some bits to eat, welcome-home bits, olives and fresh anchovies in oil and overpriced focaccia. I want to greet him, my husband. I have missed him over the weekend. I'm not feeling particularly anxious or low that day. I think I am doing quite well.

It might have happened quite differently, if Guy hadn't called when he did, if I hadn't gone out to the shops. It was thanks to that trip to the deli that I saw him but he didn't see me.

I am on my way back, and as I turn the corner into our road, a thin film of September drizzle begins to fall. It is the end of the month and today, although it has been sunny, the curve toward October has begun, a change in the air quality. The weather people are predicting an Indian summer next month, October will be hot and glorious, according to them, but it certainly doesn't feel like that today. I stop, put down my shopping bag, and lift the hood of my raincoat over my head, smoothing my hair away from my face and tucking it into the hood. And then, as I bring my head up, I see that walking toward our house, not more than a hundred yards ahead of me, is George Craddock. My stomach folds in upon itself, over and over—I can think of no other way of describing it. As I watch, he walks past our house and as he does, he slows his pace and glances at it, although he does not stop.

I turn immediately and stride back down the path. What will he do when he reaches the end of the cul-de-sac—do a circuit, or walk back the way he came? If he does a circuit, I will have time to reach the main road before he makes his way back and sees me. If he turns on his heel as soon as he passes our house, then he will see me, hurrying away.

I walk swiftly but do not run. When I reach the main road, I walk down it and go straight to the station, passing through the wide, high-ceilinged entrance hall, slapping my Oyster card down and moving through the barriers in one swift motion, my handbag bumping against my hip and my shopping swinging in my hand. A Piccadilly Line train is right there, waiting for me, doors open. The Piccadilly Line takes a lot longer than the Metropolitan Line to get into town and usually I take the purple one and change at King's Cross, but right now, the blue one will do just fine. As I step onto it, the beeping noise begins, the doors slide shut. Only when they are shut and the train is pulling out of the station do I turn in my seat to look back and see if he has followed me into the Tube station. I can't see him anywhere.

I take the train to Green Park. I get off and walk down into the park and, without even thinking about it, I unzip the compartment in my handbag where the pay-as-you-go phone that you gave me has been hiding all this time like a lucky charm and I turn it on and I dial the only number I have on it, your number. To my surprise, it rings. I would have expected it to go straight to voice mail. My heart leaps at the thought that you leave that phone on, although, of course, there could be any number of reasons why you do.

I am standing beneath a tree in Green Park, a large, spreading one, the leaves beginning, very faintly, to yellow, and when your phone eventually goes to voice mail I stand and listen to the silence that follows the beep and then say, stupidly, redundantly, "It's me." I hang up.

A couple of droplets of water fall from the tree, one neatly finding a small space of bare neck between my coat collar and my hair. I go and sit on a bench, the phone in my lap. Twenty minutes later, you call. It seems completely natural that you do. I have not doubted it.

"Hi," I say.

"Hi," you say back. "Has something happened?"

I am glad we are skipping the small talk, the how-are-yous and how-was-your-summers. I could not have tolerated those. "I'm not sure," I say. "I think so. I think I've got a problem. I'm sorry. Where are you?"

"I've come to get cigarettes for my wife's brother," you say. "Officially that is, I mean, that's officially what I'm doing. I was sitting trying to think of an excuse to leave the house but luckily my brother-in-law ran out of cigarettes just as we needed milk too so that's how come—otherwise it might have been an hour or two. Where are you?"

"Green Park."

"You're working today?"

"No," I say. "I had to leave home in a hurry. I mean, I was out any-way, but I had a visitor. I can't go home." And I tell you everything, everything that's been happening. I keep it to the facts. I don't need to tell you what it's been like, the last few weeks—you of all people don't need that explained. I suppose that if this had been an ordinary call, I might have berated you for the long silence on your end, but that seems immaterial right now. Now, I need you; and now, you are here. After I have finished, there is a long pause, and when your voice eventually comes, it is low and warm. "Are you okay?" you say.

"I will be. I'll give Guy a call in a bit. I'll make up some excuse why I came into town and then go and meet him off his train at St. Pancras. We can go home together then." I give a sniff. "All he did was walk past the house. It's perfectly legal, isn't it, walking past my house?"

You have not asked if I was sure it was him. I am grateful for that.

"Even the hairdresser's, it's the main road; he could have just been passing."

"Hmmm . . . ," you say. "Where are you tomorrow morning?"

"I don't know, work, I suppose. I don't want to be in work but then I can't be at home, I don't know. I'm easy to find."

"Okay," you say, "this is what you're going to do. Don't go home, like you said. Go somewhere nice now or shop or see a film, call your hus-band now and arrange to meet him at St. Pancras, but be really nor-mal, don't let him guess. It's important to act normally, when you meet him and when you go back home together, can you manage that?"

"Oh, God . . . ," I say, looking up at the sky. Act normally? What else have I been doing these last few weeks?

"You can do it. You're stronger than you think."

"I know, I know."

"Now listen, tomorrow morning, can you take the day off work, ring in sick or something, can you get to Vauxhall by noon?"

"Yes, of course. Well, I'll go in at the usual time and then when I get there I'll feel unwell and leave midmorning."

"Okay, take the Tube to Vauxhall, be there by noon, when you get off, check your phone. I'll call or text instructions."

"Am I going to see you?"

"Oh, Yvonne, of course, of course you are."

"Say my name again."

"Yvonne. You're going to see me tomorrow. We are going to be together tomorrow morning."

I exhale very slowly, as if I have been holding my breath for twelve weeks. There is a silence between us while we listen to each other breathe.

After a long time you say softly, "I have to go now. Take care today, just be out and about, and at home with your husband this evening, and tomorrow you're going to meet me, okay?"

"It's good to hear your voice," I say.

You pause briefly, then say, "It's good to hear your voice too." You hang up.

I sit on the bench, the phone still in my hand. After a while, I look up at the sky.

14

I am at Vauxhall well before noon, emerging from the Tube to the clamor of the inner-city motorway that leads up to Vauxhall Bridge. A vast shopping and office complex looms to one side, with a café with seats outside overlooking the wide intersection. I sit on one of the seats although I don't buy a coffee; I'm jumpy enough as it is. In front of me, lanes of traffic—cars, buses, lorries—branch in all directions. The blare of so many vehicles is somehow insulting; it's hard not to take it personally. At ten past twelve, you text me: *Where you?* I text back, *Vauxhall, by the bridge.* You reply, *Wrong side, go through arch, Kennington Lane.*

Across the vast intersection is the redbrick railway arch of the mainline station, fronted by the peculiar steel structure that houses the ticket office, which once won some sort of architectural award. I have to wait for three different sets of pedestrian lights to change in my favor, trotting from the safety of one traffic island to another, before I can reach the arch. When I've passed through it, I negotiate two more busy intersections before I reach the beginning of Kennington Lane. I take my phone out to text you for further directions, but you have already sent me a message. *New coat? Collar suits you.* I look around, and although I would never have imagined myself to be up for games, I can't help smiling as I do. I check across the street, up and down it, and am lifting my phone to text *Where are you?* when I turn and see you there, only a few feet away, in a doorway, watching me with a smile, and I feel a slight sense of anticlimax, surprisingly, for you are just a man, after all, a man standing in a shop doorway, in a suit and glasses: average height, wiry build, coarse brownish hair, and this is all so public, this reunion, and so unexpected, and I don't know what our relationship is now or how I feel after the long silence between us—and all of this adds up to me having no idea what to do.

For a moment, I see my uncertainty mirrored in your face, then you step toward me and say in a mock-conspiratorial voice, "Come with me . . ."

We walk down Kennington Lane together, then take a left turn. On the other side of a road is a park with, oddly, a small paddock and a young woman riding a horse, just five minutes from the roar of Vauxhall Station. A sign pinned on the fence, amid some tall nettles, says, DO NOT FEED THE HORSES THEY BITE. I stop and point at it.

"I've got something better than that," you say. "Look."

On our side of the road, there is the entrance to a city farm, and just beyond it, an animal enclosure with hay and sawdust and—sitting with its back to us, gazing around disdainfully, a white llama. Beyond the llama, a couple of unimpressed turkeys strut and peck and a goat is wrenching hay out of a stall.

"Vauxhall has llamas," I say. "I never knew that."

"I think it's just the one llama."

"I didn't even know there was a farm here."

"I'm full of surprises," you say, pleased, as if it's your farm, your animals.

We walk down the street a little farther, turn a corner, and before us are two narrow roads forking away and a short terrace of Victorian houses squeezed between them, shaped like a wedge of cheese—the rooms at the apex of the triangle must be tiny. We walk past it to the far end and you stop and extract a key. I look at you—I had assumed we were going to sit in the park or a café. There are three doorbells in the entranceway. The masonry has peeling paintwork. Someone has hung a duvet cover as a makeshift curtain in the window of the ground-floor flat.

You push the door open and a slew of envelopes and advertising leaflets crests behind it. As I step in behind you, you bend to pick up the post and sift through it before tossing it on a small shelf behind the door. I watch you do all this partly because I still can't quite believe it's you, but also because it seems quite natural that it is. The hallway is painted the same color of all hallways in all Victorian houses in London that have been chopped into rental flats: Landlord Magnolia, Guy used to call it. It reminds me of the flat Guy and I had when we were first married, the one with the couple upstairs, where I raised my children when they were tiny and Guy and I struggled to write our PhDs, and still, sometimes, in my roomy suburban house with its garden and two apple trees spaced wide enough apart for us to sling a hammock between them in the summer, I have to catch myself and remind myself that I don't live somewhere like here anymore.

You go ahead of me up the stairs, and I follow. It is like being a couple.

The flat is on the first floor, and before you open the door, you stop and check the cheap ply doorframe, which has some scratches on it, as if you are making sure of something. I am guessing this flat is somehow connected with your work, that you are familiar with it but don't normally have access to it—but I'm only guessing. We step inside, into a tiny square hall. You stand and listen for a minute. It is completely quiet. Then you walk into the sitting room and I follow; a low two-seater sofa, a drop-leaf table against the wall, net curtains through which the street below is mistily visible. I take a few paces inside and look around: cheapness, emptiness, anonymity. I want to stay here for the rest of my life.

I turn back to you and you are standing a few feet away, watching me. Your gaze is soft, apologetic. "It's the best I could do . . . ," you say quietly.

I lift both arms, then let them fall back. "I worked it out some time ago, what you do . . ."

You look at me.

"It's okay," I say. "I know you're not allowed to talk about it, that's why I haven't asked." I look around the sitting room. "I suppose this is what you call a safe house."

You come to me. You stand in front of me and, very gently, part my coat and push it from my shoulders. I let my arms drop to allow the coat to fall and you take it and toss it onto the sofa. Then you face me again and, still very gently, you run your hands down my upper arms, starting at my shoulders, ending at the elbows, stroking both arms at the same time, the lightest, softest of touches through my cotton shirt.

"It's safe enough," you say. "We're here now, you're safe with me."

And I do what I have been wanting to do for twelve long weeks. I dissolve into you.

Later, we lie next to each other on the small double bed in the bedroom. It's at the back of the house, with the same net curtains over the window and a view of the backs of other houses: windows and gutters and pipes. Even though the bed is nearer to being one and a half than a double, it fills the room. On one side, there is a small bedside cabinet made of wooden laminate. On the other, the wardrobe has slatted sliding doors—it wouldn't be possible to have one with doors that opened outward. The wood-chip wallpaper is painted Landlord Magnolia like the hallway. There is a bare lightbulb hanging from the ceiling and a single strand of cobweb hanging down from it.

The daylight in the room is light gray, harsh. We are lying in a tangle, semidressed, a duvet with no cover in a crumpled heap at our feet—we were too hot beneath it. We have had sex, and then talked. You have told me about watching me through the café window that day, the day our affair began with an exchange of phone numbers, even though we had already had sex by then. I work out that that café was almost directly opposite Apple Tree Yard, but we could never have known what we would do there a few weeks later and where it would lead. After a while, our talk becomes desultory and you fall asleep. I lie there, wrapped round you with my eyes open. One of my arms is trapped beneath you and it starts to tingle, go dead.

After a few minutes, I raise my head slightly and see that you are awake, after all, and looking at me, and I have the feeling you have been looking at me for some time. I shift my trapped arm, settle into a different position a few inches farther away, where we can stare at each other. You lift a hand and clear the hair away from my face. A reflexive vanity on my part makes me wince at how brutal the daylight is in this room, the white and gray light through the net curtains. I smile but you do not smile back. Your look is solemn.

"You know what we are going to have to do, don't you?" you say.

I return your look.

Then you say, without flourish or rhetoric, "We're going to have to warn Craddock off."

"How?" I ask.

You pull me into you, against your chest. "Leave it to me."

After a while, you fall asleep again, breathing deeply into my hair. We will talk when you wake but I'm in no hurry for that to happen. I need the loo, in fact, but I don't want to break this moment, I want to stretch it and stretch it, in the small gray room, stretch it until it is as thin as the net curtains over the window, or the strand of cobweb hanging from the bare lightbulb above us.

When we are dressed and drinking instant coffee—black, because there is no milk in the flat—on the sagging sofa in the sitting room, you tell me your plan. We will do it together, you say. If there is any come-back, then our story is that I confided in you because you had told me you worked in security at the Houses of Parliament, because I needed advice and didn't want to talk to anyone close to me. Kevin the cop will confirm that story if we need him to. You will find out Craddock's address. ("How will you do that?" I ask, and you give me an amused look. "That bit really isn't difficult.") I will pick you up at the nearest Tube station wherever that may be, this weekend, and drive you to Craddock's house. You will go in and speak to him. I will stay in the car.

You see the doubt in my face as I look at you over the cheap, cracked mug; you misinterpret it. You assume I am thinking that this won't be enough to solve the problem when in fact what I am doubtful about is the prospect of driving to wherever it is Craddock lives, the thought of going near him, even with you. Fear, I think, a particular sort of female fear: is it fair to expect you to understand that? You have your own fears, of course, but I know that what I am feeling now is very specific, the gut revulsion of being near to someone who has been inside me when I didn't want him to be. Once someone has done that, it is very hard to get him out.

You don't understand this, I know. You think my doubt is that Craddock won't be frightened enough by us turning up at his door.

"I could phone him, anonymously, but I'm not sure that would do it. Or I could just get someone else to sort him out," you say. "I know some dodgy people, wouldn't be hard."

I shake my head.

"Or we go back to the police, back to Kevin. Report him. We can add harassment as well now. At the very least his bail conditions would include not contacting you."

I shake my head even more ferociously, thinking about Adam and Carrie and Guy and my career—in that order. It comes to me how much I want you to confront him, how much I will enjoy imagining the fear and uncertainty on his face, faced with you. *That bastard will wet himself*, I think then, and it is a small, mean thought that has nothing to do with justice.

"You know," you say, a little carefully, "you could come in with me." When my eyes widen, you put down your coffee cup and lean toward me. "You're going to bump into this man professionally, sooner or later, you won't be able to avoid it. Don't you want to look him in the face while I frighten the living daylights out of him?"

"No . . . ," I say, shaking my head, "no, I don't." How different the rest of our lives would have been if I had said yes.

"Well, then." You move across the sofa toward me. You take my mug from my hands and put it down on the carpet. You put your mouth on mine. I taste the burnt taste of coffee as our tongues mingle briefly. You kiss my forehead, hold my head in your hands. "It's settled. This weekend. And after I've finished, he will never come near you again."

At the weekend, the hot October we have been promised arrives. We wake up on Saturday morning, open the curtains, and there it is. Guy and I have coffee in the sun on the brick patio at the back of the house, me in shorts, vest, sunglasses, him with his shirt off, smiling at each other occasionally over the newspaper and letting each other know when we've finished each section—the picture of middle-aged bliss.

When we go inside, the light has filled our house with dust. I am calm and relaxed with Guy that morning, deliberately so, for all I can think about is what you and I are planning to do.

I dress carefully, when the time comes. I've told Guy I'm going to take some old clothes to the recycling unit, and they are bagged up in the boot of the car. I am wearing a cotton skirt, knee length, with a splashy pattern in purples and blues, along with a short-sleeved white T-shirt and a denim jacket. I am bare legged, in flat pumps. It is a Saturday outfit. You have not seen me dressed like this before. I take it as a good sign that I have a shred of vanity left; I am recovering, I think. It is because I am doing something, rather than being a passive recipient of what has happened to me. I am nervous, slightly febrile even, but happier than I have been in weeks.

When I get into the car, late afternoon, Guy comes to the front step to wave me off. I give him a cheery smile.

You are already waiting outside South Harrow Tube by the time I get there, and you are dressed casually too: loose jogging bottoms and a tight gray T-shirt, trainers and sunglasses, a hooded jacket over one arm and large Nike sports bag in the other hand. This is you, I think, you in a casual but purposeful mode, relaxed but determined. You stand with your shoulders back, looking around. I feel a twist of desire.

"You're late," you say, as you open the passenger door to my car.

"Five minutes," I reply.

It is only a few minutes' drive, as it turns out, round a few corners, through a suburb that people generally have aspirations to leave; rows of low-rise pound shops and off-licenses, the occasional empty-looking café. You are completely silent, apart from telling me which way to drive, and I feel a little deflated. I guess you are concentrating on what you have to do, what you are going to say, but I was under the impression this was something we were doing together. After a few minutes you say, "Right turn here," at the beginning of a dead-end road. "Drive to the end, turn around, park back there." You indicate a space. I execute a clumsy three-point turn, park where you tell me to.

I was hoping we would sit and talk in the car for a bit, but you bend to pick up your sports bag. "Maybe he won't be in," I say.

"He's in," you reply. "Wait here," you add, as if there is a chance I will do anything else. I turn to you, hoping for a brief kiss, but you are already getting out of the car. I watch in the rearview mirror as you walk back down toward the end of the dead end. Halfway down there is a small grocery store and then a low block of cheap square houses. You stop by a black door. You step up close to it and I see you lean into the doorway—are you ringing a bell, or letting yourself in by other means? I can't see. The door opens and you disappear inside. I peer through the windscreen at the iron post just ahead of where I am parked to check the parking restrictions—I'm okay after 1:00 p.m. on a Saturday. I don't want to draw attention to my car by being illegally parked. I look up and down the street for CCTV cameras but can't see any. It occurs to me that I am excited—I am beginning to understand the adrenaline of what you do.

You are gone for so long, dear God, why didn't I guess that something was wrong? Why didn't I do something? Much would be made of this in court later, as you know—the way I just sat in the car, waiting. Why did I make no attempt to call you on your phone? the prosecution will ask me. Why did I not get out of the car and bang on the door I had watched you enter? What did I think was going on? I knew full well what was going on, the prosecution will say. That's why I sat tight. That's why I waited.

I waited because you told me to wait.

I don't know how long I wait. I turn on the radio. The news headlines come and go—there is a program on Radio 4 about freedom of speech in Southeast Asia. After a while, I pip the button and listen to music, first classical, then I try and get some jazz but it's all adverts. I turn it off. I text Guy that I'm stuck in traffic. The sun fades and the sky becomes duller blue, then blue-gray, then just gray, and the orange lampposts come on at the end of the street even though it is still a long time till dusk. I watch the people going past, a woman with two children, one in a buggy; two teenage boys. At one point, a very elderly woman in a sea-green sari turns into the street and makes her way slowly past my car. She is tiny, child-size, her skin very dark and her wrinkles deep, but I notice as she passes the car that she is smiling, despite her knotted hands and slow, arthritic gait, as if she is lost in some distant but infinitely pleasurable memory.

Then, eventually, I see you. I haven't been watching the door the whole time, but I happen to be looking in the rearview mirror because the man from the grocery store is bringing in the brown plastic boxes that are stacked outside, and I am watching him, intrigued by how many he can carry in one go—he stacks them higher than his head. I am wondering if it doesn't damage the produce, doing it that way. You emerge from the black door, closing it behind you gently. You glance down the street, then in the opposite direction, run a hand through your hair and glance both ways again. You are wearing the jacket over your T-shirt now, still carrying the sports bag. You walk swiftly but calmly over to the car, open the passenger door, and get in. You pull the door behind you and, as you pull your seat belt over your chest, you say one word.

"Drive."

As we approach the Tube station, you say, "Go round the corner, park round there." I drive round the corner and park in a side street. You sit for a minute, then look up and down the street. After a moment or two, I can stand it no longer and I say, "What happened?"

You do not answer. You sit staring straight ahead, and there is that look on your face again, the one I have seen before, the one that tells me you are far away from me, lost in whatever thought process is uppermost in your mind. *I'm here*, I want to say. I need you to tell me what has happened.

Still staring straight ahead, you reach out a hand and place it on my knee, gripping it firmly—it does not feel affectionate or reassuring.

"I need you to remember," you say, still staring straight ahead, "what we discussed before . . . we met at the House of Commons, friends, that's all, okay?"

I had no choice but to trust you, did I, my love?

You look at me at last. "Give me the phone."

I look back at you, then reach and lift my handbag from where it sits on a backseat. I unzip the inner compartment and hand the phone over. You take it, bend, and slip it into the canvas bag at your feet, and then you return your hand to my knee.

"How will I contact you?" I say it weakly, for I now know enough to know that I can't know anymore.

"You can't, not for a while."

I draw breath.

"It's going to be okay," you say, but I'm not sure you are talking to me. "Just go straight home, be normal, okay? Remember what I've said, if anyone asks."

That's the point at which I notice that you are wearing different jogging bottoms—very similar to the others, still navy but the white stripe along the seam isn't there anymore. I look down and see that you are also wearing different trainers.

You turn and plant that brief kiss on my lips, draw back, kiss me again, say that one savage phrase, "Remember, okay?" then get out of the car, and I watch as you stride off down the pavement without looking back, glancing from side to side, your head down slightly, your shoulders a little hunched, as if to ward off the gathering dusk.

It is dark when they come. We find out later, it's because of the land-lady that they come so soon, the landlady who turned up unexpect-edly, the grocery man who saw you emerge from the flat and get into a white Honda Civic, and the CCTV camera on the main road that identified the number plate on my car as we drove back to the Tube. It is dark. For once I am sound asleep, down, way down; it is as black as the floor of the ocean down there. *I was undreaming*, I think later. I was that far down.

I am woken by the banging on the front door. We have an old brass knocker, older than the house itself. It makes a resonant, metallic clang that echoes through the house. We also have an electric bell built into the doorframe by the previous owners, who must have been unduly worried about missing visitors. But it is the banging of the brass knocker, *bang-bang-bang*, three times in quick succession, hard and loud, that wakes me. There is a short pause, then three more bangs. Then there is the sound of the buzzer being pressed hard for several seconds.

I am half sitting in an instant, propped up on my elbows, my thoughts racing, panting in the blackness. I have been yanked up from sleep with dangerous haste and all at once, I know everything, and realize that I knew from the minute you emerged from the flat; I know what happened, I know who is banging on the door in the middle of the night, and I know why they are here.

The electric clock on the ceiling says 3:40 a.m. I can just make out from its dim light that Guy has roused himself onto one elbow and is turned away from me, reaching out a hand to his bedside lamp. When he turns back, his face is crumpled and questioning.

Bang-bang-bang, hard and loud again, hard enough to shake the timbers of the frame, I think. Guy rises and snatches up his cotton gown, which is flung over the wicker chair close to his side of the bed.

Bang-bang-bang, then the buzzer again. He strides around the bed to the bedroom door. It is only as he reaches the door and opens it that I think to warn him by saying, "It's the police."

My darling Guy. He glances at me, then leaves the room and runs down the stairs. I realize that when I said, "It's the police," he has thought of Adam, that something has happened to Adam. He actually runs. I sit on the edge of the bed with my head in my hands. I do not run anywhere because I know it is not about Adam: they have come for me.

Adam, Carrie, my children . . . What will Guy say to them? It will be in the papers, he won't be able to keep it hidden.

Downstairs, there is the rustle and clamor of people filling the house, Guy's indignant voice, raised in query. My house, I have brought it into my house, my home—everything will come out now. As the men's feet thump up the stairs toward the bedroom, I am frozen where I am, sitting on the edge of the bed. I do not even jump up to put on my dressing gown. I imagine Guy, on the phone to Carrie, later that morning. I imagine him saying, "Darling, you're not going to believe this but Mum's been arrested."

"What for?"

It's the first question anyone will ask.

PART THREE

DNA

15

DNA made me and DNA undid me. DNA is God.

When people think about DNA, they are usually thinking about their genetic inheritance. They are thinking of how they have their father's brown eyes. When geneticists think about it, we think about how little we know, how environmental factors often turn the most identifiable of genetic traits into no more than tendencies and how the inexplicable outweighs the provable by a ton. The genome is like a huge muddy lake, and we so-called scientists are like divers, but blind ones, swimming slowly beneath the water, picking up objects from the silt at the bottom, turning them over in our hands and trying to smooth the mud away with our clumsy gloved fingers, unsure if what we have picked up is a pebble or a pearl or a discarded button.

But there are some ways DNA is certain, forensics, for instance. DNA is one of the few discoveries of humankind that mean there's no point in being a liar.

The first mistake I make, although not the last, is to lie to the police who come to arrest me. You have to be really stupid to be a liar—or really arrogant: I am neither, but I panic. When I am taken into custody, shocked and nauseated, my blood sugar low, the first thing I am asked is, "Where were you yesterday afternoon, Mrs. Carmichael?"

"I took some clothes to the recycling depot."

As far as my relationship with the investigating officers is concerned, it's downhill all the way from there. They show me the CCTV footage of my car driving along Northolt Road and I say, "I went for a drive." My car has been impounded, so later they find your DNA and a small smear of George Craddock's blood, in the passenger footwell, where it transferred from one of your socks.

Later I tell the truth—or rather, I tell some of the truth. You are arrested immediately, but I stick to the story we have agreed: you are an acquaintance whom I confided in because I was desperate. There must be a reason why you have told me to say this. You knew what you were doing. You're a spook. You know about DNA too, after all—and you're not stupid or arrogant either.

I am not sure what it says about me but even when they tell me more about Craddock's death, I remain unafraid. It all seems so absurd—not that a man is dead, of course, there is nothing absurd in that, or even that they are saying you did it, but absurd that I am caught up in it. Surely when the facts are known, it will be over; it is that simple. Perhaps it is this, my desire for simplicity, that keeps me focused on one thing: your welfare. When the police question me, I am not seriously contemplating my own complicity—I know myself to be innocent of that and of course you will have told them I am innocent of that too. I am thinking, *How can I help him? Even if he is proved to be responsible for that man's death, I cannot believe he intended it—how can I help him?*

So I stick to the story. I do as you told me to, that day in the car. I tell them about what Craddock did, how I went to you for advice when I didn't know where else to turn, that we had the discussion with Kevin, that I picked you up at the Tube to drive you to Craddock's house that day so that you could have a word with him. When, during my interview, the woman detective in the gray suit looks at me and says, "And how would you describe your relationship?" I look back at her and say, "We were friends."

"Just friends?"

I even manage a shrug. "I'm very fond of him, he helped me, he gave me advice when I didn't know where else to turn." I look at the table when I say this.

Later, she comes back. She says that you have given a statement saying you and I are lovers, that we met when I gave evidence to a House of Commons Select Committee. It's a good try, but she can't give me any details. She doesn't say anything about sex in chapels or disabled toilets. That's how I know they are trying it on. She doesn't mention Apple Tree Yard.

They have nothing on us, no phone records because we used the pay-as-you-go phones that you will have disposed of by now, no e-mails— there are the letters on my computer, which they confiscated the day after my arrest, but if they had found those, they would have confronted me with them. Only one person other than you and I knew about our affair, and that person is dead.

I look the woman detective in the face this time. "I can't imagine why he would say that because it isn't true."

DI Cleveland is the one they bring in to break me: a bulky man, a rugby-playing type, straight brown hair and pale eyes, handsome, slightly crooked teeth, the kind of man who was popular at school, I would guess, uncomplicated and fair-minded. He drinks pints with his male colleagues and looks after his team well. He has an air of kindness that belies his bulk. He is the sort of detective that vulnerable women would want to please, believing he would look after them. He leans forward in his seat, crossing his arms on the table so that his suit jacket hunches up a little from his shoulders. He looks directly at me, his pale eyes gazing into mine, and asks me how I am holding up. Then he says he's sorry and presents me with the statement Kevin has made about the meeting we had, in which Kevin says that he did, at the time, speculate that there was something more than friendship between you and me. (The crucial word here, of course, is "speculate.") Kevin's recall is very good. They have a lot of detail about the assault, all written down. DI Cleveland takes me through it, politely, and asks me to confirm what happened, item by item. Very gently, DI Cleveland is disassembling me. They tell me Craddock was divorced with one child and that his wife once made a domestic abuse complaint against him but withdrew it later and immigrated to America with the child. They tell me about the pornography they found on his computer, about the sort of sites he accessed. They tell me about the content of those sites in a lot more detail than I need to know. Throughout this, DI Cleveland is apologetic. He doesn't want to distress me any further than I have already been distressed. He's just doing his job.

I want to please this man. I want to break down and tell him yes, he's quite right, I urged my lover to crack my assailant's skull, it was planned and wanted—that's what DI Cleveland would like to hear. I cry a little, when he gets to the point in Kevin's statement where he repeats what I told him about my son's illness. DI Cleveland says he knows how difficult this must be for me. He says he can only imagine how angry and frightened I must have been after what George Craddock did, and then the stalking, he could completely understand how I would have wanted someone to beat the shit out of him. After all, says DI Cleveland, if someone did that to his wife, that's what he would want to do.

I lift my head, blow my nose with the damp tissue I've been wrapping round my fingers, and say, "I didn't suggest that and neither did he. We're just friends."

DI Cleveland gives me a disappointed look and leaves the room.

My solicitor is called Jaspreet Dhillon, of Dhillon, Johnson & Waterford. He isn't the duty solicitor I was given at Harrow Police Station, he comes recommended by a legal friend that Guy spoke to, the morning of my arrest, the morning he spent on the phone, ringing everyone he knew to find out what to do. Jas, as he invites us to call him, is in his midforties, bespectacled, immaculate. He's the best, we've been told, and we like him immediately. Jas's first victory is to get me bail—he's on board straightaway, at the magistrate's hearing, and we are up at the crown court for a bail hearing within two days. Everything happens a bit quickly for me, but it is thanks to this speed that I do not find myself splattered all over the press or the Internet: once I've been charged, it's all sub judice, no one can report anything lest it prejudices the trial. You are not there for either of these hearings—you will be charged later. Bail is unusual with such a serious charge, but my previous good character swings it. The conditions are strict. I am to reside at my normal address. No one else is to reside there during this time other than my husband. I am to report to my local police station three times a week and wear an electronic tag at all times. I must surrender my passport and a bond of one hundred thousand pounds—we sell our premium bonds, cash in savings, and borrow from friends to raise this while we wait for the remortgage on the house to come through. Above all, I am to have no communication whatsoever with you or any of your associates. The thought of you having associates is a slightly baffling one, and how would I have any contact with you anyway when you are locked up in Pentonville Prison? You do not get bail, of course. You are remanded in custody.

Guy and I take Jaspreet for a pizza after the bail hearing. Neither Guy nor I particularly likes pizza, and we have no idea whether Jas does either, but we feel grateful to him and after several days in custody, I want to be in a restaurant on principle. I also want a long shower—but I will be spending a lot of time at home in the coming months. Home will be my prison.

The three of us are seated at a round table that is slightly too small, hunched together. We have ordered, and I am really only making conversation when I say to Jas, "So when they've investigated more, at what point—I'm just wondering—at what point do the charges get reduced to manslaughter?" I have never thought of you being guilty of any more than that, and I am guilty of no more than driving the car to the venue where you got into a fight that was not of your own making. This is what has happened and this is surely what everyone will see once we go to court.

Jas looks at me and actually freezes. His glass of sparkling water is raised in his hand, halfway to his mouth, the bubbles in it fizzling and the slice of lemon swooshing to and fro.

I look from him to Guy. "But it will end up as manslaughter, and some sort of deal, won't it?" I say. "They won't waste a lot of public money if he says he killed that man but didn't mean to, surely?"

Jas gives one of his tight little smiles. "I'm sorry to tell you," he says, putting his glass down without drinking from it and looking at me, "that it's quite common for the prosecution to refuse to accept a plea of manslaughter and to insist upon a murder trial. Then of course the burden of proof is different, they don't have to prove who was responsible for the death, just whether or not they intended to commit murder, *or*"—he pauses for emphasis—"grievous bodily harm. That's enough for a murder charge to stick."

Guy frowns. "How does that affect Yvonne?"

The waitress appears holding a steak knife. "Who's having the calzone?" she asks.

"Thank you," says Jas, and she puts the sharp knife down in front of him, turns away. Jas takes a small, inward breath. He looks a little pale. I wonder if he is an asthmatic. "It affects Yvonne because if they are saying it was a joint enterprise, then that means she will be charged with whatever he is charged with. If they accept a plea of manslaughter from him, then that's the most she can be charged with too. But they quite often press for murder; I mean, people who know they have to admit to the actual act of killing will commonly try and get away with manslaughter. The minimum tariffs for murder are, well, twenty, twenty-five if it's a knife, thirty if there's proof of financial gain. With manslaughter you might get away with fifteen or even ten, depending on the circumstances of course. So you can see how, if you were charged with murder, you might try and get away with a manslaughter plea."

The numbers make my head spin. They are no more real than the five-hundred-pound notes in Monopoly.

"So if he's charged with murder and presuming he pleads not guilty, what will he say, what will his defense be?" asks Guy quietly. He is absorbing information more efficiently than me.

Jas shrugs. He's my solicitor, after all, not yours. "Well, it's impossible to say at this stage, all he has to say at this stage is not guilty and the grounds, and they could change as things progress, depends on the advice he gets. Dim rep, perhaps."

"Dim rep?"

"Diminished responsibility. It's grounds for a reduction in the charge, but the burden of proof shifts. It's the defense that has to prove diminished responsibility. Under the circumstances, if I was advising him, I would be going for loss of control, but there would need to be what's known as a qualifying trigger."

I can't help a note of indignation entering my voice, even though my husband is sitting right in front of me. "But it was self-defense, wasn't it? He's not guilty, not guilty of murder, or manslaughter, if they got into a fight and it was self-defense?"

Guy and Jas exchange looks. Then Jas says quietly, "His plea, his defense, Yvonne, I have to warn you, is a matter for him and his defense team. My job is to defend you." He lifts his left hand, turns it, looks at his palm as if there might be answers there, then back at me. "Yvonne, even though you will be charged with a joint enterprise crime, I need you to understand that it is time to think of yourself, for your sake and for your family's sake."

Guy goes quiet; we all go quiet. This lunch has taken an unexpected turn. We came in here to celebrate my bail—we shouldn't be discussing the case at all, not here, not like this. I think of the months ahead, the acres of time there will be to have these discussions, to worry about what might happen. I shake my head slightly. At that point, Guy rises from the table and tosses his napkin down. "I'm just going to use the bathroom before our pizzas arrive," he says, although normally he wouldn't feel the need to explain that. As he turns, he pats his jacket pocket, checking his phone is there.

Jas and I are both silent for a while. We are sitting in an alcove with some plastic greenery woven around a trellis divide. Plastic grapes hang from the plastic greenery. He looks at me, and his pressed-together lips form a small grimace. He removes his glasses, squints a little, puts them back on again, then says in a quiet voice, "I know you're a scientist but I'm not quite clear what branch."

"I'm a geneticist," I say. "I worked on the human genome project in the developmental stages, then I went to work for a private institute called the Beaufort. It advises governments and industry. Got paid quite well but missed my own research and the freedom. For the last few years I've been an associate, two days a week in the office, but I'm basi-cally freelance. Then I went back full-time for a bit, to do some mater-nity cover."

A small smile, then, "You must be very high-powered."

I shrug. "You reach a certain level where, well, I don't know, you've acquired a body of experience, I suppose. You get awarded points just for having done your job for a long time."

"I think, in your case, Yvonne, it's a little more than that." Jas is gaz-ing at me and I realize he thinks me guilty of false modesty. No, no, I want to say, you're quite wrong. My modesty is 100 percent sincere.

"As you're a scientist," he says, "maybe there's something you can help me with. There have been lots of experiments with chimps, haven't there?"

"Thousands," I say. "They are our nearest genetic cousins, ninety-eight percent of our DNA." I take a sip of water, and Jas does the same. "Mind you," I add, "we share seventy percent with fruit flies."

Jas doesn't smile. "Almost human, some people say. I suppose that's why people get so upset about experiments on them."

I realize he's driving at something that will turn out to be relevant to the matter in hand, my criminal defense, that is, and that this some-thing has been prompted by Guy's leaving the table.

"You might know about this particular experiment I'm thinking of," Jas continues. "I read about it in the papers, years ago, and it has always stuck in my mind because it's a particularly cruel one. Quite upset me. My wife and I, we'd just had our first child, our son, and of course you have children yourself, so you know that feeling, the feeling we all have, that we would die for them. You look at this baby and know you would walk into a pit of flames."

Who would have thought my solicitor could be so confiding? On our brief acquaintance so far, he has struck me as a likable but chilly, organized sort of person, but I know there is a point coming. With legal people, there is always a point. I glance toward the back of the restaurant but there is no sign of Guy.

"It's love, isn't it?" he says thoughtfully. "Pure altruism. Am I right in thinking that scientists have never really been able to explain altruism?"

I shrug. "A lot of scientists will tell you that altruism is very easily explained by the survival of the species. You're genetically programmed to feel you would walk into a pit of flames to protect your son."

"Yes but I'm not really sure that explains romantic love between adults—" he says.

I cut across him, "The propagation of the species requires—"

He cuts back, "But simple lust would do that, yet adult love does often involve self-sacrifice, even parents whose children have long since grown and fled the nest still feel profound and self-sacrificing love for each other." He pauses, a telltale pause. "And even couples, quite unlikely couples, can fall in love. And even when they don't have children together, and can never have children together because of their ages or because . . . because they are both married to other people, even people like that can come to feel a deep and profound love, a desire to protect one another, a capacity to sacrifice themselves in order to protect the other."

Now I understand why this conversation is possible only because Guy has left the table. *How clever and tactful you must be to be a solicitor working in criminal law,* I think.

"The thing is," Jas continues, "what this particular experiment, the one I have never forgotten because it really did quite upset me, what it demonstrated is that even the most altruistic or self-sacrificing love has its limits. It implies that there comes a point when everyone puts themselves first."

Jas glances at the back of the restaurant as well. We are both wondering why Guy is taking so long, I think. Jas speaks softly and slowly, without looking at me as he does. "It was a real experiment, this one I'm thinking of. Some scientists took a chimp, a female chimp, along with her newborn baby chimp, and they put them both in a specially prepared cage. The floor of the cage was made of metal, and it had filaments in it, and gradually, they turned a dial and the floor of the cage became hotter and hotter. At first, the chimp and her baby leap about a bit from foot to foot, then of course after a short while, the baby chimp leaps into its mother's arms, to be protected from the hot floor, and for a bit longer, the mother chimp continues leaping around the cage, trying to get away from the hot floor, trying to climb the bars that can't be climbed, but eventually, and they did it several times and found it was always true, eventually, every mother chimp does the same thing."

He looks at me, and all at once I wish he wouldn't.

"Eventually, the mother chimp puts the baby chimp down on the hot metal floor, and stands on her baby."

"The marinara?" The waitress has appeared in front of our small table, two pizzas in her hand and a third balanced improbably on her forearm. She puts them down, one by one. I look down at my choice, the name of which I have already forgotten. It has an egg congealed in the middle, surrounded by a limp drape of spinach leaves and white lumps of cheese that I know will make my teeth squeak when I chew them.

The arrest was difficult, the hearings were difficult, the endless legalities and meetings and discussions that followed over the months I was on bail were difficult too. But nothing was as difficult as the visit from my daughter that weekend.

Carrie: how to describe her? The straight brown hair cut in a neat bob, the immaculate handwriting—she was the kind of child who emptied the shavings out of her pencil sharpener—that was Guy in her. From me she inherited her short, square physique and large eyes. She baffled me, then and now. What happened to the door slamming, the screaming, the teenage irrationality and eye rolling? It was only later, as we lifted our heads from the slow tidal wave of Adam's illness that we realized—she had always had to be the good one.

So my daughter comes to visit the weekend after I have been arrested and bailed and she and I end up watching television together and discussing the extent to which female newscasters have their appearances sculpted and molded. She sits there on the sofa perpendicular to mine, her legs tucked underneath her, poised and careful as a cat. I don't think I have ever seen my daughter slump or lounge.

During the weather report, I pluck up the courage to say, "Dad's told you about what's going on." Guy is not in the room because he is spending all his time fielding phone calls and e-mails from friends and relatives. I'm not allowed to discuss the case with anyone, of course. Guy has become the wall between the outside world and me.

Carrie is holding a mug of green tea, a very large mug in the shape of the traditional American diner coffee mug, but huge. She bought it as a present for me when she and Sathnam went to New York, from a famous deli, but I never use it—it's too chunky for me. I save it for her when she comes home. My daughter takes a sip and then looks at me with her large eyes as she lowers the mug and says, "Yes, he's told me." And then she slowly removes her gaze from mine, peeling it away with all the care she might use to peel a plaster off a patient's arm. She looks back at the television, raises the mug again.

All mothers feel judged by their daughters: it is unavoidable. As they are coming into sexual maturity, emerging from the chrysalis of childhood, we are at the other end of the reproductive cycle, sagging and desiccating. What teenage girl would want to turn into her middle-aged mother? Everything we do or say, every dress we wear or new nail varnish we apply is disgusting to them. We are what they will become when it's all over.

I have had many failings as a mother—but in my favor I would point out that the one discussion I have never had with my daughter is the one that goes, *Have you any idea how much harder it was for my generation? Have you any idea how derided and undermined we were for even thinking we could enter the world of science?* I have never said that to my beautiful, high-achieving daughter. I have never presumed to know her inner life, or accused her of taking the freedoms she has for granted. I love her so much, and I'm so proud of her. I know she loves me too, but there is something about family emotion that she can't bear after everything we went through over Adam. I lift my legs onto a footrest in front of me and my trouser leg slides up and I see her glance over and notice the electronic tag on my ankle, a hard plastic manacle that I will never get used to. She looks quickly away.

Later Guy says he thinks she and Sathnam were considering marrying next summer but because of our crisis have put their plans on hold, but when I ask him for evidence of this, he changes the subject and I go and lock myself in the bathroom and brush my teeth furiously and glare at my reflection in the mirror and spit in the sink. I decide we won't ask her and Sathnam for Christmas, as we usually do—we won't have friends over either, well, maybe just Susannah, who has been phoning twice a day, but even her—maybe even to her we will say, *We would rather it was a quiet one this year, just us, it's difficult.*

In the New Year comes the news that the trial date is set for March. Then there is the inevitable delay, and another date set, June this time. Four weeks before the trial, Guy arranges for me to have three sessions with a barrister in order to prepare me for what I might face in court. This isn't my defense barrister, Robert, but someone who specializes in coaching witnesses. He does a lot of work with the police and public officials too, we are told. I am sitting in the bay window of the sitting room when he arrives. I have spent a lot of time on that window seat of late. I have piled it with cushions. As I have scarcely left the house for months on end, staring out the window is an important activity for me.

The barrister whizzes past in his car. I guess it is him because the car is a sleek black convertible, its bodywork glossy, the soft top matte. I don't know the make; I'm not good with cars. The car is going too fast for me to see who is driving but I am in no doubt. It has to be him. He must have gone round the block because a few minutes later, he comes back from the same direction as the first time, but more slowly, as if he is casing the joint. He pulls up at the curb, parks, and from my vantage point I can see him bend sideways, open the dashboard, and extract a small dark bag. I lean back slightly against the edge of the window, so that he won't see me if he looks toward the house. From the small bag, he takes out a compact mirror, an old-fashioned one like my aunt used to have, with a gilt lid. He checks his reflection, smooths his hair.

This first session will take place in my own home, I have been told, the next two at his chambers. He hasn't said as much, but I am guessing that he wanted to come and see me in my natural habitat. It will be the next two sessions when he gets rough with me, puts me through my paces, tries to prepare me for intimidation.

I stand in the sitting room for a bit, until I hear the doorbell, then go out into the hall. Guy emerges from the kitchen at the same time and as he does he gives me a steady look, as if to say, *We're paying a lot for this.* He knows my tendency to become competitive with professionals in other fields, to behave as though I'm thinking, I could have done your job if I had wanted to, I just chose mine. I look back at him. *I know, I know.*

The barrister is young, toothy, with sleek dark hair and glasses. He has his smile all ready as we open the door.

We sit at the kitchen table, the barrister and I, while my husband boils the kettle and fills the cafetière and I try not to think that I am about to drink what is, without doubt, the most expensive cup of coffee of my life.

The barrister continues smiling as he stirs the sugar he has added to his coffee with our thin, silver coffee spoons, then looks up from his cup and says to me, lightly, "So Yvonne, are you guilty?"

I resent him beginning with a trick but I have promised my husband I will be cooperative. I look right at him and say in a voice both mild and firm, "No, Laurence, I am not."

Laurence the barrister smiles at me, glances at my husband, looks back at me, and says, "Well, that's a good start, isn't it?" He taps the spoon on the edge of the cup, puts it down. "I want that in court. Firm but polite and without a hint of doubt, okay? That's a very good start."

We talk in general terms about court procedures and he gives us some depressing statistics. Research done at Harvard shows that people receive messages about other people in different ways. They have done pie charts. When you are talking to people, you receive messages in the following proportion: 60 percent through how they look, 30 percent through how they sound, and only 10 percent through what they actually say. As a scientist I am skeptical about statistics and the small, chippy part of me thinks of you and wants to say, *But what about how someone feels and smells?* I allow myself to think this only briefly. I cannot afford to think of you. While I am drinking cafetière coffee—my favorite Guatemalan blend—in my kitchen, sitting at my own table with my husband and a sympathetic barrister, you are in a cell in Pentonville. I permit myself a brief image of you in prison garb, lying on your back on a thin mattress, hands behind your head, staring at the ceiling.

"What should she wear to court?" My husband cuts to the chase. He knows that we are not paying this clever, callow boy four hundred pounds an hour to drink our coffee and suck up my sarcasm.

"Smart but not too businesslike," Laurence replies. "We do want the jury to see her feminine side."

"*Oh, Jesus . . . ,*" I whisper under my breath. If he hears it, Laurence shows no sign. Guy sends me another look.

"A blouse with a bit of embellishment, say?" Laurence smiles at me again, all teeth.

No one will be advising *you* to wear a blouse with a bit of embellishment, my sweet. What is the male equivalent? Perhaps there is no equivalent. Perhaps there is only male.

"I'm not sure whether the prosecuting counsel will be a man or a woman," Laurence says, "but if it's a man then it's likely that the junior assigned to him will be a personable young woman and that she will be in charge of questioning you."

"Why do you say that?" Guy asks.

Laurence shrugs. "Same reason they always use female defense barristers in rape cases—so the jury thinks, well, if that pretty young woman is defending the bloke in the box, then he can't be all bad, otherwise she wouldn't be doing it." He takes a sip of coffee. "It's a remarkably successful strategy, I have to say."

I am unable to keep the ice out of my voice. "And if you know this, and everyone in chambers knows it, then presumably the young pretty barristers also know it when they are assigned to defend rape cases?" I take my own sip. "That doesn't bother anyone?"

Laurence stretches an apologetic smile over his toothiness—he is not here to fall out with me. He speaks carefully. "Well, even rapists deserve a defense . . ."

"Even if it depends on—"

Guy cuts across me. "So the jury is more likely to think Yvonne is guilty if she's being cross-examined by a woman?"

"Yes."

I let out a short exhalation and look to one side. My husband and Laurence fall silent and I know they are both looking at me. Why have they sent me this boy? Later, I will be told sternly, *He's the brightest advocate of his intake, razor sharp.*

After a short pause, the brightest advocate of his intake says, "Shall we take a break? I'm sure this isn't easy."

"No, it's all right," I say, lifting my head from my hands. "You two carry on, I'll be back in five minutes."

I rise from the table. Laurence smooths back his hair. Guy watches me as I leave the room. As I mount the stairs, gripping the wooden rail, I hear him get up and go to close the kitchen door. Their voices are muffled but I imagine my husband is saying something like, *She's under a huge amount of stress at the moment.* Laurence will be nodding in sympathy.

In the bedroom, I go to the bed and lie down, flat on my back. After a moment, I put my hands behind my head, staring up at the ceiling.

I go back down after ten minutes or so. Guy is grim faced when I enter the room. I look from him to Laurence. Laurence is sitting very still and looking at the table. As I sit down again, he looks up. "Your husband has, ah, Yvonne, he has given me a few more details."

"I told him a bit more about what that man did," Guy says, without looking at me.

Laurence looks at me sympathetically. "I hadn't quite realized it was such a violent, er, such a . . . well . . ."

"You thought it was just . . . ?" I stare at Laurence, and then I decide to let the point go. "In your view, does that make my situation better or worse?"

Laurence glances at Guy. "I was just explaining to your husband that legally speaking it makes it rather worse. It gives you motive. Of course, it doesn't really explain why your codefendant behaved the way he did, given you were just friends. You hadn't known each other for that long, had you?"

"No," I say. The number of things that don't add up is so huge that the air is thick with them. The things not being said are like giant bats flying around the room—we all know it, but no one is going to say.

Even Guy, my own husband, has not questioned me about the nature of the relationship between me and you. He has taken me at my word.

"And of course, it's hard to know how the prosecution will play it at this stage," Laurence adds. "They could go hard on how brutal Mr. Craddock was in order to increase your motive or they could try and claim that you were lying about the whole thing, that you had consensual sex with Mr. Craddock and lied about it in order to get him into trouble."

I stare at Laurence, knowing that he will not recognize the dangerous quiet in my voice. "Why would I do that?"

Laurence shrugs. "Who knows, you were annoyed with Craddock because he didn't call you afterward, or something. That one comes up quite often." It is his lightness of tone that I find so offensive, his familiarity with all this, his easy and constant generalizing of what happens in *these cases*. I am not general, I want to say. I am particular.

At this point, even this unintuitive boy recognizes the look on my face. He tries to row back a little. "I'm only playing devil's advocate, trying to talk through all the possibilities. If we're going to prepare you, then you need to be ready for everything that could be thrown at you, and who knows, that's one angle they might take. The big problem in prosecuting sexual assault cases is the women never seem to fight back." Unforgivably, a note of genuine bafflement enters his voice. "It does make our job rather difficult."

I am staring at Laurence so fiercely that it is only from the corner of my eye that I see Guy rise and turn. Then I see he has plucked a knife from the magnetic strip behind our stove and is holding the knife against Laurence's throat. Laurence has frozen with his chin tilted upward. He has both hands raised slightly from the table. His gaze bulges—pleadingly—at me. I stare at Guy in shock but say nothing.

Guy's voice is very calm. "What are you thinking now, Mr. Walton?" he says.

There is a silence. Laurence has clearly decided it would be a good idea not to respond.

"Shall I tell you what you are thinking?" Guy says helpfully. "Would you like to know what is going on, right now, inside your head, biologically, I mean?" Laurence remains silent and completely frozen—he doesn't even gulp. Guy continues. "Here is how your brain functions in a situation of threat. I'll give you the simplified version. In your medial temporal lobes, you have a group of nuclei known collectively as the amygdala. It's part of the limbic system, but let's not concern ourselves with that now. In a situation of threat, the amygdala's function is to tell you, as quickly as possible, to act in the way that will ensure one thing and one thing only: your survival. You also have a cortex, of course, that controls logic, but that doesn't work as fast as the amygdala, as you are now finding out. Let me explain." Guy doesn't even draw breath. It's how he lectures, I've seen it, point by point without pause. "The logical part of your head knows there is not the remotest possibility that I am about to cut your throat," he continues. "A: lots of people know where you are. B: we are in my home and there would be blood everywhere. C: how would Yvonne and I dispose of your body? D: isn't she in enough trouble as it is? The logical part of your head knows that I am doing this only to make a point. But your amygdala, the instinctive part of you, is saying, screaming in fact: freeze, just in case, do the instinctive thing that will save your skin. As I said, the amygdala works faster than the cortex, that's how we've evolved. In a situation of threat, particularly a situation in which we are taken by surprise and there is no time to logically assess our chances of living or being killed, we are programmed to do whatever will ensure our survival. All we want to do is live, bottom line. In any situation where the level of threat is unknown, the amygdala will trump the cortex, every time."

Guy stops speaking but does not move, and after a moment or two, Laurence slowly lifts one hand and pushes Guy's arm away from his throat. "I think you've made your point," he says. Guy returns the knife to the right place on the magnetic strip and sits down.

Laurence the barrister looks at me.

I look back at him. I am damned if I'm going to apologize. Instead, I say, just gently enough, "You see, it's one thing discussing this professionally, the way you are, I mean, but for us there's a lot at stake, our whole lives." When he doesn't look mollified, I add, "It's been a very upsetting time, for both of us."

Laurence lifts his chin, as if he needs to stretch his still-intact neck. "Yes, I'm sure it has."

After Laurence has left, I lock the front door behind him, throw the bolts, put the chain on, even though it's only midevening. Neither of us will be going out again tonight, after all, and no one else will be visiting. I turn and see that Guy is standing behind me. Our gazes meet. He says, "Let's go up," and I understand from the softness of his voice and the expression on his face that, right at this moment, he can't take any more. I nod. He turns. I watch him climb the stairs ahead of me, and I know by the slump of his shoulders that he has truly had enough, enough of being the strong one, enough of not asking questions, and quite enough of standing by me.

I follow him into the bedroom. He sits on the edge of the bed, facing me, and puts his head in his hands. I go to him, kneel down before him on the carpet, between his knees. I take his hands away from his face, lower them, and look down at them. I hold his hands between mine, and all at once it comes to me that now I must ask him, beg him, for the one thing I truly need from him throughout what is about to fall upon us. I don't know whether asking him in his momentarily weakened state is a good or a terrible idea, but I know I must ask him now because it is so important and I may not get another chance. This, as it turns out, is prescient on my part. In two weeks' time, the police will come to rearrest me. I will be told that you attempted to send a note to me from prison—a quite innocuous note, apparently, but it's enough to count as potential contact between us, which is a breach of my bail conditions even though I didn't initiate it. A hearing will be held, without my knowledge, and my bail will be revoked. I will spend the remainder of it, and the duration of the trial, in Holloway Prison.

Even though I am looking down at Guy's hands, held in mine, I know he is looking at my face. In all our years together, I have never begged him for anything. We have argued, I have requested things from time to time; could he hoover the stairs because I hate hoovering, could he be more patient when he is driving, could he try and understand I get bad tempered when I have a deadline? Could he please, for both our sakes, finish it with his young lover, for once and for all . . . ?

208

But even then, I didn't beg. I have never had cause to beg as I am about to beg now.

"Guy . . . ," I say. We so rarely use our names to each other. What long-term couple does? Names are for acquaintances or strangers, signifiers for those who do not know us in the other more intimate ways there are to know someone.

"There's something I have to ask you." The tone of my voice is plain. He can be in no doubt of the seriousness of my request.

He doesn't say a word.

"I have to ask you, please, whatever else, please . . ." My voice does not crack or tremble. I look up at his face. He is staring at me. I still have hold of his hands. "Please stay away, from the trial I mean, please. Don't come to court." He stares at me, so I add, "There's nothing you can do."

At this, he pulls his hands free of mine in an angry gesture and rises, steps around me. I drop my head, thinking he is about to leave, walk from the house maybe, and my voice breaks. "Please talk to me about this, Guy, *please* . . ."

He goes over to the chest of drawers and rests his hands on it, lowering his head. "I wasn't about to leave the room. I don't walk out on you when you are in trouble, remember?"

I stay kneeling by the bed. I don't reply.

Eventually he says, "Jas said it's important I'm in the gallery. It will show everyone that I am standing by you. The jury will notice. *Her husband is standing by her.*"

"I know," I say, "I know that's what Jas said, maybe it's true." I take a deep breath, "but I can't do this if you are sitting there, listening. The things I will have to say, the things they are going to say about me, about what happened." My voice is almost a whisper. "How will I bear it? How will you? It will finish us."

I can't risk Guy feeling exposed and humiliated. If I had my way, I would send him to South America for the next few weeks. All the people I love, I want them away from all this.

He doesn't reply, so I say. "I can't talk about it in court if I think—I can't . . ."

"You couldn't talk about it at home either."

"No."

He turns then, his face wide open, his eyes large and hurt. "Why didn't you tell me!" He makes a restless movement of a few paces, then back again. "Instead, you go to a virtual stranger, a man you hardly know, just because he works in security, a man you know so poorly that he goes and does this and now you're involved, you're going to be on trial with him. Sitting in a, in a"—his voice breaks with frustration—"in a *dock* with him? You risked that, rather than tell *me*?"

"I didn't know he was going to kill him. I had no idea."

"That doesn't explain why you went to him, not me."

And it comes to me now that the truth is even worse than the lie I cannot tell. I have been saying to myself that I didn't tell Guy about Craddock because I was having an affair, but now I know that I wouldn't have told Guy anyway. I wouldn't have told him because I was ashamed and I wouldn't have told him because too much was at stake, our home, our happiness, our children. Worst of all—and here is the real truth of it—I knew that my affection for Guy might not survive an unsympathetic reaction. If he had said, for instance, "Why did you go up to his office?" I would never have forgiven him. It would have finished us, not immediately, but two, three, four years afterward. It would have corroded us beyond repair.

I have to say something, so I give my husband a partial reason for not confiding in him, a true one, but one that is no more than a small percentage of the truth. "I didn't want it . . ." I can think of no other word, ". . . tainting you."

"*Tainting?*" He turns, his voice incredulous.

"I know, I just . . ." I have half turned to face him. I lift my hands helplessly and drop them in my lap. "I just wanted to keep it away from you, that's all, away from our home, away from the children . . ." He gives a scornful huff, only partly convinced.

"I want you to go away, abroad, until the trial's over. I'm going to say the same to Carrie at the weekend, she can ask Adam, it'll be better coming from her. I thought maybe even a holiday, maybe—"

"I'm not leaving the country."

"Well, maybe for them at least, if they'll agree to go. Maybe Sath and

Carrie would take Adam away, but it would be better if it was all four of you. I just want you all away from it, is that so difficult to understand?"

He looks at me. His voice is more gentle. "Even if it means it's more likely you'll be convicted?"

I look back and my voice is gentle too. "I won't be convicted. I'm innocent."

16

And so it begins; it begins on a Monday morning, and as I sit in the back of the van that takes me from Holloway Prison to the Old Bailey, as it chunters and bumps, stops and sways, through the London rush hour, what I feel, mostly, is an acute awareness of the ordinariness of everything—to everyone around me, I mean. For the people dealing with me, it is just the beginning of another working week.

Two guards from Holloway have come along for the ride, but there are no other prisoners going to the Central Criminal Court that morn-·ing so I have the bench along one side to myself. The interior of the van smells of disinfectant, that pungent brand used in public lavatories, with a thick-sweet layer of vanilla on top, a scent so strong it makes me nauseated. The driver of the van brakes sharply at every red light or junction and guns the engine when we move off. I begin to sweat— traveling sideways isn't helping. Around halfway through our journey, one of the guards on the bench opposite me notices my effortful breathing and, without speaking, uses her foot to push a plastic bucket across the floor of the van toward me. I turn my head away.

The high windows in the van admit little light, but as we drive through the streets of London I glimpse patches of sky through the one-way glass. A little drizzle runs down a windowpane. Outside this van, office workers will be striding and weaving, some with genuine haste, others hurrying from habit. Someone will step in a puddle and curse. Someone else will pause to buy a coffee, clutching his Styrofoam cup as he strides off, and yet another person, or the same person, will step out into the road, to be woken by the angry yet indifferent blare of a taxi horn. The irritations of a Monday morning commute have never seemed more seductive to me. Will any of those people even glance at this van as it passes in the street, wonder whom it might contain?

Eventually, the van drives down a ramp. We descend into gloom, halt. I am cuffed where I sit, on the bench, before I am allowed to rise and clamber down the steps lowered from the back of the van, one guard ahead of me and another behind. As my eyes adjust, I see we have parked in a cavernous holding bay, on a metal turning circle. I am taken into the bowels of the building.

Whatever grandeur the Central Criminal Court of the Old Bailey may possess does not descend to the area where prisoners are kept. There is a checking-in desk, similar to the one in police stations, where I am given an orange plastic bib with a number on it. I am to wear the orange plastic bib at all times except when I go up to court, so whichever guard is on duty can see at a glance which court I am to be served up to. As I pull it over my head, I reflect that I haven't worn something like this since primary school. The guard behind the desk is an older black man with white hair and thick glasses sitting on the very end of his nose. He chats to me as he writes on his clipboard, his manner warm and welcoming. He is used to dealing with people in distress. "We will do your search in a minute, darlin' . . . ," he says. I smile at being called darlin'. He will call me darlin' every day for the next three weeks. "Now, a lot of people manage to hide their tobacco even during the search but I have to tell you if there is any smoking I will smell it straightaway and it is strictly forbidden down here, okay?"

"I don't smoke," I say.

"Good," he replies, with an approving smile over his glasses, like a head teacher. He gives me a mock-stern look. "It is *very* bad for you."

"Are you here all the time?" I ask. What I mean is, will you be looking after me? Can I rely on you?

He nods his head. "All the time, I'm here, from seven in the morning till eight o'clock at night. I get here before you all start arriving and I'm here until the last one goes."

When the formalities of my admission are completed, I am led down a low-ceilinged corridor. It is painted a creamy-yellow color, like weak custard, the texture of rough brick visible beneath the emulsion. A sign says, THIS IS A RED DESIGNATED AREA, with the word "red" in a red circle. Another sign says, YOU ARE NOW IN THE DETENTION OF SERCO . . . I don't have time to read it all as we pass but note the phrase at the end: ALL CRIMINAL ACTS WILL BE REPORTED TO THE POLICE. This strikes me as faintly comic but the twist of amusement I feel is tinged with hysteria. "It's hot down here," I say to the woman walking me down the corridor. I can feel my breath start to quicken. No natural light, the narrow walls, low ceiling, how do they work here, day in day out?

She is a wide-hipped white woman in her fifties who walks with a slow sway, her breathing harsh. Emphysema, I think. "You should be here when it's really hot," she says, breathing out through her mouth. She stops at the open door to a cell. "We have defendants wandering around with no clothes on. Don't want to go into court looking all sweaty, do you?" Unlike the man at the desk, this guard does not feel sorry for us, I surmise.

As I step into the cell, my heart constricts. It is a tiny, airless, windowless box. The walls are painted yellow and the floor blue in an attempt at cheeriness, but it is bare but for the concrete bench-seat at the end with wooden slats on top. I am underground, with no natural light or ventilation, wearing a plastic bib, in an area that will become stiflingly hot.

The door slams shut behind me. I sit on the wooden bench with my toes turned in toward each other, hands planted on knees, breathing in through my nostrils and out through my mouth, trying to stay calm.

My trial barrister, Robert, comes to see me later. I have been waiting less than an hour but it feels like days. *I must get a grip,* I tell myself over and over. *I will be sitting here day after day, every lunch break, every morning and afternoon, every time there is a delay. This is so much worse than the prison. I have to be able to do it. I can't do it.*

I can't do it.

It is the same nonempathetic woman guard who comes to get me. She leads me to a consultation room identical to the cell I have just left. It has a table screwed firmly to a metal frame and metal chairs that are part of the same frame. This, I guess, is to prevent prisoners from lifting up their chairs and either smashing them against the walls or breaking them over their barrister's head.

Robert is already wearing his gown and wig. As he sits down uncomfortably on the bolted metal seat, the gown slips from one shoulder. It remains there for the rest of our discussion and I have to resist a maternal desire to reach out a hand and hitch it up. Later, I notice that when he is on his feet in court, he allows his cloak to slip down his shoulder quite frequently. I come to regard it as an affectation on his part, a semiconscious attempt to make himself appear rumpled in an endearing, avuncular kind of way. *Don't underestimate Robert*, Jaspreet has said to me. *He may seem a little disorganized but it's a ploy. He's a very sharp operator.*

He has a huge file, which he dumps on the table between us. "Slight bit of bad news this morning," he begins, and I look at him. "They are arranging wheelchair access for the father." He goes on to explain that George Craddock's father will be attending the trial throughout, accompanied by his police family liaison officer—up to four of the victim's close family are allowed in court. The only one coming for "our victim," as Robert calls him, is his father, who is in the early stages of multiple sclerosis. Robert goes on to say that he doesn't believe the man is wheelchair-bound the whole time but thinks the FLO has dropped hints that having him sitting in a wheelchair in the corner of the court throughout the trial, in the full view of the jury, will strengthen the chances of a conviction. "On the other hand," he says, "it's the sort of thing you can bring up at appeal, elements of the trial you feel might have been prejudicial. There's always a silver lining to every problem." I like Robert a great deal, on the basis of my brief acquaintance with him, so am a little taken aback at the cynicism of this discussion but I find myself nodding too. *We haven't even started yet, and I'm beginning to think like them.* There is another thought that comes to me, although I try and squash it as soon as it arises: we haven't even started, and he's mentioned grounds for appeal.

He starts taking me through the likely timetable for the day, the swearing in of the jury, the prosecution's opening statement. He doesn't believe there will be any pauses for legal arguments on the first day, but they will crop up soon enough, and for those the jury will be sent outside and everything will slow right down and he hopes I understand why all that will be necessary. During this conversation, I am as calm and logical as I have ever been, but my claustrophobia does not abate. Get me out of here, I want to say to him, *please*.

After our consultation is over, Robert stands and excuses himself. He has to rush off to his room, check his paperwork is in order, breathe a bit, I expect. He shakes my hand before he goes, placing his other hand reassuringly over mine and looking into my eyes. He has heavy white eyebrows over a gaze of a surprisingly pale blue. I feel a little weepy and have to give him a bright, confident grin by way of disguise. He leaves; the guard comes; I am returned to my cell.

And then, after another wait that seems to stretch for days, comes the moment when my cell door is opened and it is not the same guard as before but two dock officers who stand before me, a woman and a man, both in smart white shirts. They smile at me. The woman says, "All right, then, up we go!" And I wonder what would happen if I became hysterical, refused to leave my cell. What if I fell on the floor, foaming at the mouth and screaming? The man's smile is purposeful and joyless. He looks at me as if he is assessing—swiftly and unemotionally— whether or not I am going to give them any trouble. We return briefly to the reception desk, where I remove my plastic bib. It is put back in a cubbyhole with the right number on it behind the desk, like the old-fashioned cubbyholes where hotels keep keys.

The dock officers fall into place, one in front of me, one behind, and we take a few steps back down the narrow, custard-colored corridor. They stop at a door just opposite my cell and open it to reveal a short flight of concrete stairs. It is only as we reach the top of the stairs and the officer in front opens another door that I realize, with a jolt of shock, we are about to enter the court. I had imagined some sort of transition walk, endless corridors to progress along, a chance to compose myself, but no, the court and dock awaiting me are right above my cell, just up a short flight of concrete steps.

As I step through the door, I see the courtroom, a high-ceilinged, wood-paneled room, brightly lit and full of people. Robert and his junior are already in place—both turn and acknowledge me with a nod. The junior is a young woman called Claire whom I have heard about but not met. She has a broad smile and a lot of freckles. The defense teams are clustered, talking in hushed tones. There are two lawyers from the Crown Prosecution Service sitting on the row of benches behind the barristers and on the row behind them, DI Cleveland. The atmosphere is that of a small railway station, full of chat and bustle and anticipation, aglow with a harsh yellow light. The officers and I enter directly into the dock, which is surrounded by high panels of toughened glass and has a long row of pull-down seats with green cloth covers.

Later, there are many things I observe about the geography of the cells and the courtroom. I never quite get over how close to the court the cells are—on several occasions during my trial, the cries of other prisoners downstairs are clearly audible in Courtroom Number Eight. The door the judge will enter from and exit through is on the same side as our door, across the court, and I work out that the judges' chambers—I imagine plush carpets, large oak desks, monogrammed silver ice buckets—are directly above our cells, the world of wigs directly above the humid underworld to which I now belong. While the judges lunch together at a large oval table, I think, served by clerks of the court (all those men), I am eating my airplane meal in a concrete box directly beneath them.

All this I think only later, much later in the trial, when there is plenty of time for reflection during the many bureaucratic and legal delays that, I come to appreciate, are part of the process. But as I enter the dock for the first time, there is no time to think these thoughts, for although the light and the bustle of the people are what strike me first, I see immediately that, already seated between your own two dock officers—there is you.

My dear, I think. *How you are changed.* Even though I allow myself to stare at you only briefly, I take in everything about you and, despite our predicament, it breaks my heart. You have shrunk—physically shrunk in each direction, even though I am standing and you are seated that's how it seems. How can being on remand have made you smaller? Your suit jacket—that same expensive gray suit that I stroked in the Crypt Chapel beneath the Palace of Westminster—seems to hang off your shoulders. Your cheeks are hollow—even though you are clean-shaven for court, there is a tinge of gray to your skin, as though stubble would suit you better. Your hair is combed neatly, a little flat, and I notice that it is thinning on top. Was it always thinning, or is it just that I notice it now because you seem so vulnerable? Your large dark eyes, the eyes that stared at me in the early days of our affair, those eyes now have a vacant look, as though you are looking at me and not see-ing me. Our gazes meet for a moment, but there is nothing there.

I sit down in the dock, one of your dock officers and one of mine between us. It must be an act, I think. He knows there can be no visi-ble connection between us; it would damage us both. But the vacancy in your glance is terrible. Where are you?

You have been held in the Category A cells, a different area from me. They brought you up first. Your name is first on the indictment, so you will do everything first during our trial. Even now I am seated, I can't resist trying to glance past the officer for another look at you. Last time I saw you, you were sitting in the passenger seat of my car as we pulled up at South Harrow Tube station. I would give so much just for half an hour alone with you before this all begins, not to talk about anything related to our separate defenses, just to be able to look into your eyes, touch your face.

That suit—the same, expensive dark gray suit you wore that day in the Houses of Parliament, when you took me down to the chapel in the crypt. You knelt at my feet afterward as you slipped on and zipped up my boot. I am back there for a moment and think how what we did together would seem so sordid if it were related to this court and yet it was so innocent. We hurt no one by that act.

All the same, thank God none of that is going to come out in this trial, I think then. The hot shame I feel is not for the act itself but for the way the act would be presented within the context of the charge now leveled at us, the way it would be used to blacken and damn us. How the prosecution would love that information—but they don't have it, I know that much, because of the law of disclosure. You will have seen the disclosure documents too, the ones where the case against us is outlined. I wonder if that is why you wore that gray suit for the first day of our trial. I wonder if you are signaling to me our triumph in that respect. No one knows about us and no one will. All we have to do is keep our nerve.

I look at the barristers to distract myself from you, and that is when it happens, a momentary confusion on my part, the significance of which will become clear to me only later. I see the prosecution barrister and she is exactly as I was warned she might be, a young woman, midthirties, small and immaculate, auburn haired, steely eyed. *But she's sitting in the wrong place*, I think, with a small inward frown. The layout of the court has been explained to me. Why is she sitting at the table next to Robert's, to the right of him? I glance across the court, then I realize. The prosecution barrister is not the young, immaculate woman. The prosecutor is a woman the same age as myself, large in her black robes, bespectacled, a school-matron type. She is sitting in the correct place, on the left-hand side of the court. Her junior is a young man who is rocking back in his chair.

The young, precise woman with the auburn fringe is not, as I first thought, counsel for the prosecution. She is part of the defense—not my defense, of course. The young woman is representing you.

The door to the bench opens and the usher enters, a woman with dark curls, a robe but no wig. She rattles through her lines, "All rise. All ye who have business here today gather near . . ." Her voice becomes a mumble, rising again with ". . . God save the Queen." She holds open the door for the judge and, all at once, everyone is on their feet: the defense barristers break their cluster and hurry to stand in their places, the young man who is the prosecution's junior stops tilting his chair and jumps up. The woman dock officer to my left nudges me with her elbow even though I am already rising. This collective act of deference does more than anything that morning to underline the seriousness of my position, to tell me I am helpless before authority in a way I haven't been since I was a child.

It is my first glimpse of the judge. He is short, with an expressionless, crumply face. He doesn't so much walk to his chair as process, with the air of a man upon whom responsibility sits rather lightly, a man who was gratified but unsurprised when power was conferred upon him. He turns and acknowledges the court. The barristers ranged in front of him, the lawyers and police officers, all bow, then sit. He glances toward the dock and I give an awkward little bending motion, then sit down as well.

The jury panel is called in. They enter through a door on the left and stand in a huddle beneath the public gallery, which is still empty. They look out of place, this ordinary group of men and women, in their outside coats and with their bags and rucksacks. The clerk calls out names, one by one, and I watch each juror as he or she makes his or her way across the court. Everyone in the court is watching them, each of us making our own calculation as to their possible disposition. Does the bald young man with the earring, who reddens as he walks but keeps his head up, seem like a bit of a hard nut, someone who has maybe been in a fight or two himself and might admire a man's ability to defend himself? Is the gray-haired woman who looks like a social worker likely to be predisposed to a defense of diminished responsibility? That older white man with a military bearing, he looks like he might think women are naturally devious—but the opposite could be true, of course. He might also be possessed of an anachronistic sense of chivalry that believes women to be innately less capable of violence.

Once all twelve are in place, there is a deal of shuffling and coughing as they settle. Most of them do not look over at us, seemingly aware that everyone else in the court is staring at them. They all seem, to a man and woman, terribly embarrassed to be here.

Then comes the swearing in. Silence in court is demanded as each stands and takes the oath. All but five of them swear by Almighty God. Of the remaining five, two swear by Allah and one other by the Guru Granth Sahib. Only two take the secular oath.

The judge makes his opening remarks, about how the jury must come to their conclusion only on the evidence they hear in this court. He concentrates in particular on the evils of researching our case on the Internet. They are warned about Facebook, Twitter, and all other social-networking sites, and such references in the mouth of a man wearing a horsehair wig sound so intrinsically comic that one or two of the jurors smile. Then the judge looks at the papers in front of him, leans forward, and says to his clerk, politely, "I don't appear to have a batting order . . ."

The clerk turns and stands and points at a piece of paper to his left. "It's right there, My Lord."

"Ah, many thanks."

The prosecuting barrister is on her feet already, the matronly woman, large and slow she seems, but serious, trustworthy. I would trust her. The judge has given her the nod. She looks at the jury, then says politely, "Ladies and gentlemen, I appear for the Crown in this case . . ." Her voice is quite quiet, with a soft Scottish burr. Her tone is downbeat, no obvious theatrics or righteous anger, merely a sorrowful acknowledgment of the sad necessity of her—of all of us—being there.

"On a Saturday afternoon in October of last year, a man was making a cup of tea in his kitchen." The whole court is silent. "Living alone, divorced some years ago, he didn't have much to do at the weekends. He had filled his teapot and was placing two biscuits on a plate when the phone rang. It was his widowed father, calling from the West Midlands."

At this point, the door to the public gallery opens—the public are being let in a little late. Everyone glances up as the security guard admits the small crowd of people who inch in self-consciously. Immediately, I see Susannah. She gives me a wan smile. Two young men follow in behind her with an older man, law students and their lecturer, I guess, and then about half a dozen people whom I guess to be curious members of the public.

The barrister has paused only briefly. "His father was called Raymond," she continues, and we all return our attention to her. "Raymond was a retired Methodist lay preacher, and the only person in his life with whom the man still had close and fond contact. The man answered the call and asked his father in detail how he was. His father was—is— in the early stages of multiple sclerosis, partially disabled. After ten minutes or so, the man mentioned to his father that he had a pot of tea brewing and his father replied that he should pour his tea before it became too strong, or to use his vernacular, 'too stewed.'"

The prosecutor pauses at this point, looks down at her notes, picks up the water glass in front of her, and takes a small, neat sip. Then she looks at her notes again before continuing, not as if she is reminding herself of something but as if she is reminding the rest of us of the seriousness of the story she is telling. I am to observe her doing this often during the trial and quickly come to regard it much as I regard Robert's gown slipping from one shoulder, as an affectation, a carefully cultivated physical tic. She looks up again.

"The man ended the conversation," she resumes, "by saying that he would have his cup of tea and then call his father right back. His father replied that he was going out to the corner shop shortly but if he missed him, he would try him again later. The man told his father to take care as his father was unsteady on his feet. He was concerned about his father stumbling on the curb."

At this point, she pauses again, but only slightly. She doesn't want to come over as melodramatic. "It was the last conversation that man was to have with his father. It was, in fact, the last conversation that man was to have with anyone." A small cough. "Anyone, that is, apart from the person who was about to kill him."

I have been so lulled by her tone, by her storytelling capacities, that it is only at this point that it comes to me, forcefully, that we are under way. There is no X or Y anymore, no personal mythologies or mysteries: there is only evidence. The trial of *Regina v. Mark Liam Costley and Yvonne Carmichael* has begun.

17

When counsel for the prosecution, Mrs. Price, began her opening statement, her tone was low, sorrowful, as if she really didn't want to be there,
performing her sad duty. But as she outlines the facts of our case, her
voice becomes stronger and she stands up a little straighter, as if the
truth is making her tall and able, as if even she, measured as she is,
cannot help but feel indignation at the temerity of our not guilty pleas.

"Ladies and gentlemen," she says in conclusion, and looks at the
jury directly. "You will hear defenses being offered in this court. You
will hear the first defendant in this case claim that he should be found
not guilty on the grounds of diminished responsibility, that he was not
responsible for what he did that afternoon, because he has a . . ." She
gives the smallest of pauses, just enough to let a tiny amount of incre-
dulity in through the gap. "A *personality disorder.* You will also hear a
defense submitted on the part of the second defendant, that she is"—
that tiny pause again—"*entirely innocent,* that she knew nothing of the
first defendant's intentions when she drove him, and his bag contain-
ing a change of clothing, up to the doorstep of a man who had viciously
assaulted her. You will hear her claim that she had *no idea* what might
be going on as she sat waiting in the car outside that property, waiting
an inordinate amount of time, you might think, for someone to whom
she was just giving a lift. You will be told that she had *no thought whatsoever* that something might be amiss when he took so long to return,
having changed his clothes and footwear but having neglected to
change his socks, the socks that transferred blood to the mat in the

footwell of her car." A long pause this time, for those tiny notes of in-
credulity to find each other in the ether of the courtroom, bind together
like atoms, form more than the sum of their parts. She lowers her voice
a notch. "The prosecution case, ladies and gentlemen, is that this
is"—she raises it again—"*nonsense*. The prosecution case is that this
was a joint enterprise murder, jointly discussed and agreed between
the two parties, that they planned it, quite coldly, in advance, that one
would do the deed and the other drive the getaway car, all the better to
facilitate their escape, that each was in full knowledge of the other
party's behavior, and that each is therefore as guilty as the other."

After this rhetorical flourish, she pauses and looks down at her desk,
where she also has one of the huge white plastic folders, the lever arch
sort, the same as the ones the jury and we in the dock have, along with
two other large landscape-style folders with plastic binding along the
left-hand side. These are Exhibits One, Two, and Three. She moves
the folders around on her desk, unnecessary shuffling, I think, to indicate that now, at last, we are getting down to business.

"Exhibit One, ladies and gentlemen. This is what I shall be referring
to as the map bundle. May I invite you to turn to the first page?"

In the folder is a series of maps. The first of them is small scale: it
shows the location of Craddock's flat in South Harrow and then the
locations of your house and mine—each with a straight line leading to
a wide margin that gives our addresses: you live in Twickenham, me in
Uxbridge. Subsequent maps are larger in scale and show the exact
location of Craddock's flat in his street. Some of the maps have small
rectangular pictures from CCTV footage to one side, joined by another
straight line.

The prosecution counsel takes the court through these maps, one
by one, explaining in detail how long it would take to walk between
the locations, how long to drive, the exact locality of Tube stops and
bus services, the location and names of nearby shops. "Smoke and
mirrors," Robert will later say to me, dismissively. "The prosecution
have to produce lots of facts. Juries all watch TV. They expect facts,
hard facts, so the prosecution gives them lots of them even when they
are not remotely relevant."

Once this is done, Mrs. Price lowers the register of her voice a note or two and says to the jury, "Ladies and gentlemen, I invite you now to turn to the second folder, Exhibit Two, the one I shall be referring to as the graphics bundle." We are about to realize why she has slowed down slightly, become more low-key, demure even. "I have to ask you to resist the temptation to flick through these graphics as I wish to explain each one in turn."

The first graphic is a diagram of a flesh-colored body, the upper torso, naked and bald, like a tailor's dummy. As I turn the page to it, I notice from the corner of my eye that you are not opening your folder like I am. You are staring straight ahead.

"I must now take you through the injuries sustained by Mr. Craddock on that Saturday afternoon, ladies and gentlemen, injuries sustained, I shall be demonstrating, only a matter of minutes after he concluded that last phone call to his disabled father, and at the hands of the man you see sitting in the dock, with the encouragement and collusion of the woman sitting beside him."

Marked on the flesh-colored body of the diagram in front of me is a series of bruises that have been drawn or Photoshopped onto it, startlingly exact and lifelike nonetheless. There are bruises to the upper body that look wide and diffuse, grayish in tone. There is a livid red mark on the forehead, a purplish bruise on the cheek. The lips are lacerated, the nose clearly flattened and broken. There is a strong red mark across the neck.

On subsequent pages, there are pictures of just the head, one in profile, that shows an ear badly lacerated with a part of the lobe detached.

Looking down at the graphics, turning the pages one by one, Mrs. Price lists the injuries sustained by George Craddock. On his torso was a series of bruises consistent with his having been stamped on while lying prone on the floor—imprints from the soles of trainers are clearly marked. His skull was fractured—cause of death was a swelling to the brain. His nose was broken. His lips and his right ear both had substantial lacerations. Four of his front teeth had been smashed.

After she has listed these injuries, there is a silence in the courtroom. I sit in the dock, staring straight ahead, just as you are. Whatever excitement has been engendered by the start of our trial, the ritual of the swearing in, the melodrama of the prosecution's opening statement, all that is stilled now by this: a man has died horribly.

"I would like now to call the first witness, Dr. Nathan Witherfield." The usher exits the court.

Dr. Witherfield is perkier than you would expect a Home Office pathologist to be. He is tall, with beaky features, a bright voice, and an eager demeanor. He reads the oath loudly and confidently. He declines the offer to sit down. His job is merely to verify what prosecuting counsel has just told us, the nature of the injuries sustained. As an expert witness, he is allowed to speculate, to give his opinion, in a way other witnesses are not, but his opinion appears to be no more than stating the obvious.

"Is your name Dr. Nathan Witherfield?"

"Yes it is."

"And are you . . . ?" Through a series of questions, his credentials are established. It is only then that he is invited to turn to the jury bundle, the large white lever arch file.

Mrs. Price addresses the jury: "If I can invite you to open it at the same time, and I have to ask you to turn to the photographs behind divider four, page twelve, and I must ask you again to resist the temptation to flick ahead through the pictures: it's important that I explain to you what you are seeing as you see it."

Clicking sounds fill the court as everyone flicks the metal levers on their large white files and then, as we all turn the pages, there is a great wafting, as if a flock of giant birds is flying around, gulls perhaps. For a few moments, it drowns the drone of the ineffective air-conditioning. The prosecution counsel allows us all to settle and consider the photographs. Like your graphics folder, your jury bundle remains closed.

"Ladies and gentlemen, I apologize in advance if any of you find this part of the evidence distressing. In most of the photos, the victim's face has been blacked out, in order to avoid the more alarming elements of his injuries."

These are not graphics. These are color photographs of George Craddock in his flat, lying on his back, most of his body in the sitting room but his head close to the kitchenette. His face has been blacked out to allow him some dignity in death, but his T-shirt and jeans are clearly visible, one leg of the jeans rucked up to reveal a white calf, and on both feet, gray socks, leather slippers. Around him is the place where he lived. Behind his body, the opening to a kitchenette: smart white units with wooden handles, a fridge-freezer, and gas stove. Other pictures we see later will show us a brown leather sofa with African-style print cushions in brown and orange; photographs on the wall of wildlife, a leopard on the prowl, a soaring eagle; a large white towel left on the seat of a modern dining chair, papers and books scattered across a glass-topped dining table with a cereal bowl and mug and spoon still sitting at the other end. Behind the dining table are alcoves of books. It is quite a smart bachelor flat, a brave attempt to make a rental property in a run-down area look desirable. It works, to a certain extent—plenty of people in London live a lot worse. But something troubles me about this glimpse at Craddock's life and eventually I get it: it's the cereal bowl. Craddock was a respectable, educated man, a lecturer with books on his shelves, but the cereal bowl still sitting on his dining table in the afternoon hints at self-neglect, I think.

The prosecution counsel invites us to alternate between the graphics bundle and the photographs in the jury bundle in order to go through Craddock's injuries in more detail. When she gets to the neck injury, she says to the pathologist, "And can you tell me, Dr. Witherfield, what kind of force would have been needed to cause this level of injury to the neck area here?"

"Yes," says the eager pathologist, "it would have to be blunt trauma injury of some force, consistent with stamping while the victim was in a supine position, faceup that is, on the floor."

"And how can you tell the force would have been considerable?"

"Well, the bruising, of course. And his voice box was shattered. In order to sustain that level of injury, I would say that the victim was immobile on the floor, and that the person applying the force would perhaps have been jumping as he, or she, stamped on him."

It is an electrifying sound, hardly describable in words. A kind of *aaargh* but high-pitched and involuntary, breathy with effort, almost a gargle. Everybody's head swivels to where Craddock's father is sitting in his wheelchair in the far corner of the court, nearest the door. The judge glances fiercely. The people sitting in the public gallery lean forward—they can hear a strange noise but not see who is making it. The rest of us stare. The police officer sitting next to Craddock's father has her hand on his arm and is leaning right into him, very close, speaking softly, attempting to calm him, but his cry goes on and on, so much so that I think for a moment he is verbally disabled as well as wheelchair-bound and this is his only form of speech. Then he shouts, "George! George, my boy! Georgie!" and I glance at the judge, who is frowning, but DI Cleveland is on his feet and shouldering his way over. He and the other officers surround Craddock's father, turn him in his wheelchair, pushing him from the court, but his cry can be heard fading out into the hall as he goes.

The court breaks for lunch not long after. The clerk calls, "All rise!" and we rise as the judge processes out. The barristers lean back in their seats, stretch their arms. The police officers form a cluster by the door, talking quietly. The family liaison officer has come back into court without Craddock's father and is shaking her head as she talks to the other officers. The dock officer next to me touches my elbow and I turn to go down to the cells without looking back at you.

Back in my concrete coffin with its yellow and blue paint, they bring me lunch: gray meatballs sitting in a puddle of inert brown gravy. I pick at a few grains of rice that are on the side. I take a small bite from a triangle of white bread with margarine smeared on it, then I gag, and the shred of bread comes up again immediately, like a small piece of leather I'm unable to digest. I swallow it down, take a sip of water from the plastic cup, then I put the tray of food on the bench next to me, lean back against the concrete wall, and close my eyes, the strangled cry of George Craddock's father filling my head, the reality of your actions forming a picture in front of me that seems so obscene, so unlike what I know of you, that I can scarcely comprehend it, even as my imagination contorts your handsome face into a mask of hatred and rage.

After lunch, your barrister, young Ms. Bonnard, gets to her feet to cross-examine the pathologist. Here is a quirk of the system that I find odd—this is the first we will hear of any defense, the questioning of a witness, but unlike the prosecution, there is no opening statement at this point—that will come later—so as Ms. Bonnard gets to her feet, we have no idea what her line of argument is, the point of her questions.

The point of her questions remains obscure to me. She asks the pathologist to estimate how long it would take death to occur due to the blunt trauma injury Craddock received. Then she raises some technical points about swelling to the brain, establishes that although he can estimate, in fact the margin is quite wide. She establishes that it is impossible to say precisely which of the blows to the head that Craddock received would have caused the swelling to the brain—he also had an injury to the back of his head that would have occurred when he fell against the floor.

If, as I think, she is trying to imply that his death might have been accidental, then at this stage my frank opinion is that she is clutching at straws—the severity of his injuries makes clear it was a concerted attack.

Craddock's father is back in court, still in his wheelchair, the family liaison officer next to him. Robert, my barrister, tells me later that the judge would have complained to the police that any further interventions by the father could prejudice the trial, and that if he does not keep quiet, he will be excluded from the court. He will remain impassive from that point, but his presence is a potent one.

Eventually, Ms. Bonnard says, "Thank you, Dr. Witherfield, if you would remain where you are for a moment." She turns to the judge, giving a slight bow. "No further questions, My Lord." She sits.

Robert stands. "My Lord, I have no questions for this witness." He sits again.

The judge turns to Dr. Witherfield. "Thank you, Doctor. You're free to go. May I please remind you not to discuss this case or the evidence you have given with anyone?"

The doctor nods efficiently and descends the steps.

Some of the jury are looking at Robert. They are giving him slightly quizzical glances, the like of which will be repeated in his direction several times during the prosecution case. I can see them wondering why he had no questions for Dr. Witherfield. I might have wondered myself had Robert not explained his strategy to me beforehand. "We will keep our powder dry," he said. "We let the other defense team lead, draw the fire, so to speak. It will only emphasize that Mr. Costley is the perpetrator here, not you. So we won't be questioning the pathologist or any of the prosecution's witnesses. You were an innocent bystander, so why should we need to question them? We will cement that in the jury's mind by *not* cross-questioning." The only witness Robert will be calling during my entire case is me.

18

The second day of our trial also consists of forensics. This is not the way I had anticipated it: I had imagined the prosecution would have concentrated first on presenting our motives, blackening our characters, building up all the while to our horrid act. But no, on the second day, we get the blood splatter expert.

I am able to be more detached today. Already, on day two, I am ceasing to see Craddock as a person: he is an exhibit. I don't think this is just because of my hatred of him: it is to do with the reductive process his life and death have undergone. This is what happens when we are dead. We become a series of facts. Only now and then do I catch a glimpse of the reality of Craddock, and it is always in an unexpected detail. In the graphics bundle, there are two sketches of a full-length tailor's-dummy-style figure, side by side on facing pages. One is you, dressed in the clothing that was discovered in a plastic bag dumped in a park bin two miles from your house. It is the navy blue jogging bottoms, the first pair, and gray T-shirt you were wearing when I picked you up at the Tube station that day. Most of the blood was on the dark jogging bottoms, not visible with the naked eye, but marked on the sketch with a line to a box describing them. There are some spots of blood on the gray T-shirt, and these are marked in graphics, but there is also an expanded photograph of the T-shirt with the spots ringed in pen. They are a brownish salmon color, but clearly visible.

The other full-body graphic is of Craddock. He was wearing a light brown shirt and the blood on it is more clearly visible—his own blood, the blood that would have poured from his nose after it was broken. When this graphic is discussed with the blood splatter expert, it is noted that a button is missing, that there is no way of knowing when this button became detached from the shirt, but as there is a small bloodstain clearly visible around the buttonhole, that would suggest it happened prior to the assault upon him. This chimes for me with the cereal bowl left on the dining table all day. Craddock lived alone, divorced. He bought designer shirts but couldn't be bothered to sew the buttons back on, even though he didn't have much to do in the evenings, I imagine: mark students' papers, watch television, masturbate to the porn he accessed regularly on his computer.

Once more, your barrister, the cool Ms. Bonnard, rises up to cross-examine the expert witness. The argument this time is about the difference between blood and dilute blood. Dilute blood is blood that has become intermixed with another fluid, water, say, or urine. It doesn't matter whether it's a bucketful or a single drop, it still counts as dilute. There is some debate about whether Craddock emptied his bladder during the attack. The blood splatter expert is presented with the relevant page of the pathologist's report that says his bladder was empty but is unable to confirm whether that would have occurred during the attack or whether the victim had urinated just before the assault. Again, Ms. Bonnard's argument is obscure to me. As far as I can tell, her purpose is to highlight that Craddock's bloodstained clothing was not tested for the presence of urine when perhaps it should have been, and there is also some business about whether a smear of blood found on the floor was dilute or not. It is clear that Ms. Bonnard will let no prosecution witness go unchallenged—there is to be no piece of evidence from the prosecution case that is to be left without a question mark hanging over it.

And again, when my barrister gets to his feet, it is merely to turn to the judge, bow politely, and say, "My Lord, I have no questions for this witness." Again, the jury glances at Robert questioningly. This time, one or two of them glance at me.

After the experts are done, there is a row of witnesses that I think of as the amateurs. Together, they take up the rest of the second day and the whole of the third. It seems to me that their main purpose is to ensure that the prosecution case is not presented too quickly. There is only one witness to Craddock's actions earlier in the day—the man at the grocery store. Craddock went in there that morning to buy *The Guardian* and *The Sun*, a liter carton of milk, a pack of Marlboro Light cigarettes, a tube of Werther's Originals, and a packet of salami. He paid with a twenty-pound note. He was given the items in a blue-and-white-striped plastic bag. He put the change directly into his pocket rather than a wallet. There is CCTV footage of him at the counter. I glance down when this is shown to the court, on the two television-size screens either side, one on the wall, the other suspended just below the public gallery. Even now, even after all this, the thought of seeing him as a moving, living human being fills me with revulsion and I am returned briefly to what he did: his face in mine, the students with their bin liners moving around the empty events hall, my face pressed against the cab's interior on the way home, the smile he gave me through the window of the hairdressing salon.

The questioning is very detailed, once again. "And how would you describe the manner in which he said this?" the off-license man is asked by the prosecution counsel at one point. The statement in question is: "And a pack of Marlboro Lights." All that is established by this examination is that George Craddock appeared completely normal that day, not anxious or frightened in any way, and that as far as anyone could tell, no one was following him.

Some witnesses are dispatched with what seems to be discourteous haste. A neighbor of Craddock's who observed my car driving down the road is asked, "When you say the car was driving slowly, do you mean very slowly?"

The neighbor is an elderly white woman who has dressed up for the occasion in a smart navy suit. Her hand trembles as she reads the oath, enough to make the card flutter. She glances at the dock as she enters and again as she leaves, but during her evidence, she looks firmly ahead.

"Er, I would say very slowly, yes, as if they were looking for something—"

Ms. Bonnard is on her feet immediately. "My Lord, this witness is not here to speculate about the thoughts of the people inside the car in question."

The judge inclines his head. "Mrs. Morton, you will kindly keep your answers to the specifics about which you are asked."

"Oh, yes, sir," Mrs. Morton says, trembling.

"So, very slowly then?" repeats Mrs. Price.

"Yes, very slowly I would say."

Even Ms. Bonnard has no further questions for this witness, and Robert, of course, has none.

When the judge tells Mrs. Morton she is free to go, she looks crest-fallen, as if she has failed an audition.

On the fourth day of our trial, the morning is taken up with legal arguments—it is a debate about the admissibility of hearsay and bad character evidence and has something to do with the witnesses that the prosecution wishes to call about you, your past life. Now that we are moving on to you, that will lead, inevitably, to me—and to what Crad-dock did. It is all about to get much harder.

The jury is not called until the afternoon, during which there is another event that plunges the court back to reality, sucks us down into the vortex of it, as events dotted throughout the trial will do every now and then, often when I least expect it. I am tired at this point, although not as tired as I will be later. I'm not sleeping well in prison: no one sleeps well in prison unless they are given a pill that knocks them out cold.

The public gallery is almost empty for once—the incident with your wife has yet to occur, there are no students that day, and Susannah hasn't made it this afternoon. There are two people sitting at one end who I think might be distant relations of Craddock, and the two retired people who have come most days at the end of the gallery nearest the door.

The woman who discovered Craddock's body is in the witness box. She was his landlady. She identifies herself as Mrs. Asuntha Jayasuriya, the managing director of Petal Property Services. She owns seventeen

rental properties in the area. It was only chance that the body was discovered so quickly—we might have had a week, ten days maybe, before
someone at the university reported that he had not shown up for work
and the police went round. We were unlucky. Craddock was in arrears
with his rent. Mrs. Jayasuriya's staff had written to him several times
but received no reply, so she had decided to turn up unexpectedly on a
Saturday afternoon. She wouldn't normally do that, but Craddock had
been a long-standing tenant who hadn't been in arrears before, so she
wanted to know if there was a problem, and she was in the area anyway. She let herself into the building and walked up the stairs to the
first-floor flat, hoping to surprise him, although it was she who was
about to get the surprise. She had her nephew with her but instructed
him to wait for her in the hall. There was no answer when she knocked
on the door of Flat B, but she could hear voices from the radio, which
made her suspicious that Craddock was in but just not answering, so
she knocked loudly, called out, "I'm coming in now, Mr. Craddock!"
and let herself in with her key. Once inside, she didn't even have time
to call out his name again. The door opened straight into the sitting
room and she saw the body immediately.

Mrs. Jayasuriya must be a lady of some self-possession as well as a
successful businesswoman because she did not scream or shout for her
nephew to come. She stayed standing exactly where she was and dialed
the emergency services from her mobile phone. She remains rigid in
the witness box while the tape of the call is played to the court. There
is no trace of hysteria or even shock in her voice.

"Emergency services, which service do you require?"

"Police, please, and an ambulance, but it's too late, I think. I think
he's dead."

"Who is dead, please?"

"A man. The man who rents my flat. I'm here at the flat and he's
lying on the floor. There's blood here. He's dead. The address is . . ."
Mrs. Jayasuriya gives the address with full postcode.

"Right, they are on their way, and what is your name please?"

"My name is Mrs. Asuntha Jayasuriya. That's *j, a, y* . . ." She spells
her name slowly.

"And how do you know he's dead?"

"It's obvious."

Then, on the tape, there is a small commotion as the nephew enters and can be heard calling, "Auntie! Auntie!"

Mrs. Jayasuriya snaps back at him in a language I don't recognize. It sounds as though she is telling him to stay back.

This would not necessarily be a shocking moment—Mrs. Jayasuriya is measured and pragmatic—but there is still something about it that silences the court, deadens even the small foot shuffles or turning of papers that characterize much of the other evidence. It is the wormhole effect. We are there. We are listening, and picturing, and present, and George Craddock is lying on the floor in front of us, his feet toward us and his head just into the kitchenette, and there is blood, and the alarmed calling of the nephew in the background, and then, beyond that, the incongruously urbane tones of a presenter on BBC Radio 4.

The jury are not called on Friday. The legal arguments about hearsay evidence continue. You and I are there, in the dock, as usual, listening to it all. At one point, you lean forward in your seat and place your forearms flat on the small shelf in front of you, resting your chin on your arms and staring straight ahead. I cannot tell if you are bored or unusually intent.

I cannot imagine your experience of all this so far. The Category A holding area here is probably very similar to the one I am in, but your prison experience will be very different, I suspect. And you have been there for so long now. Have you acclimatized? Are the privations of it routine? Are you frightened? You look so changed, so other, from how I remember you, from the brief glimpses I have been allowed, and it comes to me that the heady, early days of our affair now seem like things that happened in a film. I cannot believe we had sex in the Houses of Parliament. I can scarcely believe that we ever had sex at all. That acute feeling, the giddiness of it, as if I had plunged my face into a bouquet of lilies, their scent so blissful it would make me feel faint— that was what it was like. Was it happiness? Was that all it was? Or was it a kind of addiction, to the story, to the drama of what we were doing? If it was a film, we were the stars.

I have no visitors over the weekend. Susannah offered to come, but she was giving up enough time to attend the trial so I told her she mustn't. I made up a story about needing to spend the weekend not thinking about the trial, but in fact I wanted her to have a break.

There was no break for me, nor would there be. In the queue to get breakfast, a large woman called Letitia bumps into me with her meaty upper arm and shoves her face in mine and says, "Rich bitch, how's the trial going?" Rich bitch is what they call me in here. Everyone is called something.

Letitia is not making a polite or friendly inquiry. I turn my head away, and Letitia, who has thin, gray-blond hair and a nose that has been broken several times and the glint of genuine psychosis in her eyes, puts a fat forefinger beneath my plastic tray and neatly flips it up from the counter and over me. Hot tea sears through my T-shirt and baked beans splat against my trousers and the guard in the corner calls out wearily, "Letitia! Here *now*, please!"

A very young, very pretty black girl in front of me hands me a thin paper napkin from the pile on the counter and says casually, "That fucking dyke's out of order."

During Association Hour, Letitia sits in the corner of the room and glares at me while the television high up on the wall blares advertisements and the new drug addict on our wing stands facing the wall and slowly bangs her head against it. "Oi, Muppet!" shouts Letitia at the drug addict. "You'll give yourself a fucking headache!" Then she returns to glaring at me. I ignore her. I'm annoyed she's still been allowed Association after this morning's episode. Her aggression doesn't frighten me, though—after a week of processes, it comes as a relief.

On Monday, the prosecution starts on you—on us.

The first witness is a police officer. Her name is Detective Sergeant Amelia Johns. She is a trim woman with short red hair, pale skin, and a small, almost featureless face. After taking the oath, she adjusts her police tunic and smooths her skirt before sitting in the drop-down seat.

Mrs. Price is already on her feet. "Thank you, Officer," she says. "You are a detective sergeant in the Metropolitan Police. Can I just establish how long you've been a police officer for?"

"I've been a police officer for seventeen years," DS Johns replies, looking at the jury.

"And you were initially based in the borough of Waltham Forest, is that right?"

"Yes, that is correct."

"But you moved to the borough of Westminster, is that true?"

"Yes, that's correct, seven years ago. I was seconded to the security team for the Estate of the Palace of Westminster and its immediate environs."

"And would you just explain to our jury how that security team works, it's a slightly unusual situation, isn't it?"

DS Johns gives a slight smile and says, "Well, yes, it surprises some people the way it works. Security at the Houses of Parliament isn't actually run by the Metropolitan Police, it's run by the estate staff. The Metropolitan police officers there all fall under the control of the estate."

"So if I understand correctly, officers who work there are actually more like private security guards?"

DS Johns gives her smile again. "Yes, that's one way of putting it."

"Could you give us a concrete example of how this works?"

"Well, the police staff patrol, do crime reports, but for instance, if a crime was being committed in the House of Commons, in theory, no officer would have the right to enter the chamber unless he or she was asked to do so by either the sergeant at arms or one of her representatives."

Mrs. Price affects surprise. "So let's say, one member of Parliament turned and began to strangle another . . ." She turns to the jury with a wry look. "Something we all hope would never happen, I am sure, but let's say it did. In theory, the officers on duty would have no right to intervene unless they were summoned to do so by the estate staff?"

"That is correct."

"And the estate staff, what sort of people are they?"

She pauses. "Well, a lot of them are ex-army, there's quite a variety, in fact."

"Any ex–police officers?"

"Yes, a few."

Mrs. Price pauses. "And the man we have in the dock here, Mr. Costley. He was one such member of the estate staff, wasn't he?"

Something odd happens to DS Johns's face. It closes. The small smile she has been giving, what one would imagine to be her natural demeanor, vanishes. Her features are more arranged, as it were. I feel, even before she speaks, that her answers are about to become more careful. "Yes, he was a member of the estate security staff."

"He had been a police officer for eleven years, a detective sergeant such as yourself, then he left the Metropolitan Police and was employed by the estate."

"I'm not aware of exactly how long Mark was a police officer for."

"Very well, of course, but would you explain to me what his role within the estate was?"

"He was a security adviser."

"In what capacity did he work?"

I am watching DS Johns very carefully, her neat, guarded face, and I feel certain that something occurred between you and her when you worked at the Houses of Parliament. She has not looked over at you or me, not once.

"Mr. Costley was employed by the estate as an adviser. I mean, to the police officer in charge of events planning . . ." She pauses, as if this practical information is for some reason difficult to recall. "It was his job to, well, ensure compliance. Health and safety regulations, about events, to checking up on the duty log, supervising the shifts of the CCTV monitoring crews, and so on." I wonder how much she knows about what you really do.

"So, he was a sort of bureaucrat, then? Or someone important?"

A minute pause. "Well, all those jobs are important for the proper running of the estate. Behind everything the public sees there is a huge amount of bureaucracy."

"What I'm getting at is, if something went wrong, say, an incident, would he be the man running down a corridor or the man filling in the form about it afterward?"

"He would be the man filling in a form."

Mrs. Price has stopped speaking. She folds her arms and looks down at her table for what, to me, seems an inordinate amount of time. During this long moment, I notice, out of the corner of my eye, that you have leaned forward in your seat and dropped your head a little.

Eventually, Mrs. Price looks up. "Detective Sergeant, I would now like you to tell the jury about what occurred between you and Mr. Costley just before you applied to transfer to your current post in the drugs and firearms unit at Barking & Dagenham." She looks at the DS and gently prompts, "Please, if you would."

"Yes, of course," says DS Johns. "I made a complaint to the estate about behavior by a group of men but in particular Mr. Costley, a complaint to the estate's Human Resources Department."

"Would you please explain to the court what that complaint was."

"Inappropriate behavior, I mean, on several occasions. I had been in the Monitoring Office, that's the set of suites where we monitor all the CCTV cameras on the estate, divided into areas. They would watch the cameras and award marks to females according to their sexual attractiveness."

Mrs. Price has her back to me but I can imagine her expression being one of mock surprise. Then she says, somewhat cautiously, "Of course, reprehensible as this behavior is, some might say it is no more than what happens in many men in male-dominated environments—security guards in shopping centers, let's say."

"Mr. Costley's behavior went a little farther than that."

"Really, would you care to explain?"

"One of the estate staff, a young woman, complained to me that he would watch the CCTV cameras monitoring the visitors' entrance to Portcullis House, and that if he found a female visitor attractive, he would go down to the entrance and follow her."

At this, several members of the jury glance over at you. I am careful to look straight ahead.

"And did this staff member report to you what he would do after that?"

Ms. Bonnard is on her feet, but before she can say anything the judge gives a weary sigh and raises his hand from where it has been resting on the table, saying, "Ms. Bonnard, in anticipation of your objections, I believe we had a whole day of debate last week . . ."

"My Lord, I believe the question just asked this witness goes beyond—"

"As Mrs. Price is about to explain the necessity for the question, I trust, I will allow it. You will have your turn during cross-examination."

"My Lord." Ms. Bonnard gives a short, peremptory bow, and sits.

Mrs. Price bows to My Lord and then turns back to DS Johns. "As we were saying, DS Johns, could you please explain what you were told happened after Mr. Costley had spotted a female visitor on the security cameras that he found attractive and had followed her around the estate?"

"He would return to the CCTV Monitoring Center and say that he had followed her, he would comment on her figure, what she was doing, and so on."

"And did you yourself observe him saying this?"

"No, it was reported to me, but I once came across him going through the visitor log and cross-referencing it with the security clearance files."

"This would be quite a normal activity for a man in his job, would it not?"

"He had Google-imaged the woman concerned. On his computer screen, there were about twenty or thirty small pictures of her. He closed the screen as I came into the room, but his desk was opposite the door and I saw it quite clearly. He left the room and I saw the log with her name on it on his desk."

I think of the pictures of me that come up on Google—when you're in academia, you end up with quite a few, most of them very unflattering. Sometimes students take pictures during talks or lectures; they post them, they tweet, sometimes there is video. There is no such thing as privacy the minute you stand up in front of other people. It might only be two people, but before you know it, the whole world will be able to see how you didn't brush your hair properly that day.

"And when was this incident?"

"About three months before Mr. Costley was arrested for the offense he is currently on trial for."

I stare at DS Johns.

"And without wishing to identify her, can you say anything about the woman concerned?"

"She was an immigration officer who was visiting to discuss staff vetting."

It goes through me like a kind of sad shock. Of course. It wasn't me you were Google-imaging that day DS Johns is discussing. It was my potential replacement. I was in bits at the time. You were doing your best to be supportive, but you were already looking around elsewhere.

The questioning of DS Johns continues but I have the picture. You have been established as a predator, as someone whose behavior is worryingly underhanded.

When Ms. Bonnard gets to her feet for the cross-examination, she does so very slowly, with narrowed eyes. Am I imagining it, or does a shiver of anticipation go through the court, as if it was feeding time at the zoo?

"DS Johns," Ms. Bonnard begins, softly. "Thank you for coming here today, for taking time out of your duties."

DS Johns looks slightly disconcerted. Was that a question or not?

"I won't be detaining you long, I promise." Ms. Bonnard smiles at her. "Perhaps you can explain something to me. I understand that the young woman who made this complaint to you—about Mr. Costley watching female visitors on the CCTV, that is—I understand that the reason she is not in court herself today is that she is traveling abroad. Vietnam, I believe?"

"I think it's Thailand."

"Oh." Ms. Bonnard affects surprise. "Thailand, I've got that wrong, then. Are you in touch with her?"

"No, no . . . we weren't friends, it's just, it's just I heard she was going to Thailand. Before, I mean, before the trial."

"Well, we shall make do just fine with you, I'm sure. Why did this young woman come to you when she was concerned about Mr. Costley's behavior? Why not make the complaint herself, directly to Human Resources, I mean?"

"She was new in her job, she felt a bit intimidated by the men in the office. She came to me because—"

"That isn't the real reason, is it, DS Johns?" Ms. Bonnard is looking down as she makes this incendiary statement, and even though I later have cause to hate this young woman, I cannot help but admire her style, the way she lobs that contradiction over in such a casual manner, as if she is so confident of her ground she hardly needs to bother to put DS Johns in her place.

DS Johns falters for only a fraction of a second but it is unmistakable. "No, I, yes it was, I believe it was."

"The reason she made the complaint directly to you was that she knew you had had a short-lived relationship with Mr. Costley and that it had ended acrimoniously and as such you would be more than ready to hear ill of him, wouldn't you?"

"That's completely untrue." DS Johns glares at the jury.

"Which bit, that you had been in a relationship or that it was over?"

"A relationship. We weren't, that's not how I would describe it at all. He had propositioned me."

"You went for drinks after work with him on, I believe, three—or was it four?—occasions."

"It was a few times, once or twice."

"Was it once, or twice?"

"Twice maybe."

"Oh, really, my information is, it was three times. Would you like me to furnish you with the dates? On the last of these occasions, April of last year, you and he had intimate contact in a well-known Westminster drinking hole, a pub called the Bull & Keg."

DS Johns's pale face is set hard. "Firstly, the first occasion was with a group of people. So I would call it twice. Secondly, that contact you are referring to was initiated by him and I told him to stop."

"Immediately?"

"I'm sorry?"

"Immediately. Did you ask Mr. Costley to stop immediately?"

"No, not immediately."

Ms. Bonnard's voice becomes soft. "After around an hour, DS Johns, you and he left the pub together and walked to the Tube, where you parted amicably enough for a brief embrace."

DS Johns draws a breath. "It, it made me uncomfortable. We had had a few drinks together, and on our third drink, he had his hand on my knee beneath the table for some time."

"It didn't stay there, though, did it?"

"No . . ."

"DS Johns . . ." Ms. Bonnard affects a slightly weary air. "I have no wish to embarrass you in the courtroom so I suggest you allow me to explain to the jury. On that occasion you and Mr. Costley had been drinking together since around six p.m. He had his hand on your knee beneath the table—you were being surreptitious because a group of other colleagues were also in the pub—and at some point, he moved his hand upward beneath your skirt, pushed his fingers through your tights and into your knickers, where he proceeded to, I believe the appropriate colloquialism is, finger you. You did not prevent him from doing so, or object in any way. In other words, you and he had intimate sexual contact, did you not? Which in many people's eyes constitutes a relationship?"

And something happens at this point. Detective Sergeant Johns changes in front of our eyes. She stops being a professional, a police officer giving evidence in court, and becomes a person whose sex life we are all speculating about, seen through the prism of our own views on these matters. I am quite certain that the men in the court, her fellow officers seated at the back, the male jury members, perhaps even the judge, are now imagining her in her skirt, her legs parted. They are imagining what sort of knickers she was wearing at the time. I, of course, am doing the dates in my head and feeling slightly nauseated by the realization that you were fingering DS Johns two or three weeks after we met. At least two of the women jury members are looking openly shocked. They would never let a man do that, therefore DS Johns must be someone completely unlike them. Another woman, an older woman, has narrowed her eyes sympathetically. I am sure that what she is sympathizing with is DS Johns's public humiliation. Either way, each of us, according to our own prejudices, is reducing DS Johns to some kind of symbol of how we feel about that kind of thing. She has now become defined by that act, or the fact that she failed to prevent that act.

"I told him later that I didn't like it, the next day at work."

"You told him later, not at the time?"

"Yes, that's right." DS Johns is breathing slowly and carefully and appears to have recovered a little of her composure. "I told him the next day at work that I wasn't interested. After that, he became unfriendly and hostile. He made it clear he was giving me the cold shoulder. In meetings he would address other people and not me. He would get tea for other staff members and not me."

"And so, when your junior colleague came to you and complained about Mr. Costley, you were only too happy to take her complaint to Human Resources?"

"Yes," DS Johns replies firmly.

Ms. Bonnard pauses to let the firmness of her answer ring in the air before saying quietly, "No further questions for this witness, My Lord."

Yet again, Robert gets to his feet, gives his slight bow, and says, "I have no questions for this witness, My Lord."

The judge looks at Mrs. Price and she stands. Her voice is gentle, maternal.

"DS Johns, I won't detain you long. Can I just ask, after Mr. Costley began this program of giving you the cold shoulder following your rejection of his advances, did you upbraid him, or raise it with him at all?"

"I tried to talk to him. When we were alone in the office, one afternoon, I tried to say that we should put it behind us."

"And what was his response?"

"He told me I was paranoid."

Mrs. Price says nothing at this point, merely waits for a moment—to allow us, I think, to register the unfairness of the accusation. "Thank you, DS Johns."

The judge leans forward and tells DS Johns that her ordeal is over.

We all watch DS Johns leave the court, the aura of what we know about her hanging about her like a perfume. I watch her go, observing that she seems small and neat, and young.

Mrs. Price has remained on her feet. She looks up at the public gallery, coughs, and says, "My Lord, our next witness is Witness G."

"Yes, thank you, I'm aware of that," the judge says. "I suggest we break for lunch."

You are just a man, Mark Costley. What did I expect? Did I really think that you chose me because I was special? I am feeling so weary and sad at the small betrayal you committed against me by chasing DS Johns that I fail to note—of course—the much greater betrayal you have just committed against her, fail to realize that, at some time, you must have discussed her in some detail with your cool young barrister with the straight auburn hair.

19

When we return to the dock after lunch, a heavy velvet curtain has been pulled across the front part of the court, the part that leads from the entrance to the witness box. There is a long, thin rail in the ceiling to allow this. Witness G can now enter the court, give his evidence, and leave unseen by us in the dock or anyone in the public gallery, although the jury will still be able to see him. I make a stab at guessing what he looks like, of course, from the timbre of his voice as he takes the oath. I imagine him to be similar to the older male jury member, the white man with the military bearing, a tougher, more weather-beaten version perhaps. I think of him as well over six foot, with neat gray hair. I imagine him standing in front of a mirror with one of those very fine-toothed combs, the sort of comb my father used to use but that you don't see much anymore. *I could be quite wrong, though,* I think: Witness G could be small and ginger and weaselly—just one of the many things I will never be sure about.

He reads the oath in a loud, clear voice and declines to sit when the judge invites him to. When Mrs. Price gets on her feet for the examination-in-chief, she almost gives a small bow before she begins.

"Witness G, thank you for coming to court. Now, by way of explanation to the court as to why you have special measures, would you please explain what your job is?"

From the way his voice carries, I am guessing Witness G is facing the jury full on. "My title is Chief Training Operative."

"You work for MI5, our security services?"

"Yes, that is correct."

The jury are all staring in the direction of the witness box, intent and impressed.

"And can you explain what a chief training operative is or does?"

"Yes, certainly. My job is to oversee the very rigorous testing that we put all potential operatives through, both physical and psychological."

"Can you explain why the psychological element of the testing process is important?" Mrs. Price is coasting at this point.

"Certainly, yes." He clears his throat, in order to impart his expertise all the more efficiently. "One of the most important skills security operatives need to have is the ability to disguise their true profession from their friends and family. Some say they are civil servants, others working for import or export companies, academic careers, a job with the European Union. It's imperative that our operatives have the ability to handle this deceit over an extended period, otherwise they might put themselves, their families, and the service at risk."

"It must cause them some difficulties, sometimes, not even being able to tell their own husband or wife what they do?"

"Yes, that is correct."

Because I can't see Witness G, I watch the jury. I want to see the looks on their faces when the full truth about what you do is revealed. I wonder whether the thrust of Ms. Bonnard's case will be that you were traumatized by your work, if that will be the nature of the diminished responsibility plea.

The jury's interest is piqued. Here is what they were hoping for when they were selected for jury service: a good story.

"So how do you go about finding out whether or not any given individual is suited for a lifetime of deceit?"

Witness G gives a brief pause—I imagine a small, ironic smile. "Well, of course, the exact methods we use are confidential . . ."

There is a tinge of impatience in Mrs. Price's voice, even though Witness G is her witness. My guess is, she is not a woman who enjoys being patronized. "Yes, yes, I understand, but could you just give the court some idea."

"We subject potential candidates to a very thorough procedure extending over several months. There are psychological questionnaires and interviews. Then we put them in a situation within a company where they have to maintain a completely fake name, personal history, identity, over an extended period of time. Some people working in that company will be part of our training staff but the potential operative won't know which. Those people's job is to test the operatives' ability to maintain their cover story."

"It sounds to me," Mrs. Price says slowly, choosing her words with care, "as though this procedure is an invitation to become paranoid. It must be very difficult to know the truth about yourself at the end of it. Isn't it an invitation to fantasists?"

By now, I know that a good barrister never asks a question without being sure of the answer the witness will give.

"Absolutely not," Witness G says firmly. "The opposite, in fact. A fantasist who was unable to distinguish between truth and fiction would be a liability to himself and to the service. One of my most important responsibilities is to weed out the fantasists. In a situation of stress, they would be unreliable."

The jury members are agog, staring at Witness G. I feel a little more skeptical myself. How do you tell a genuine fantasist from someone who is just very good at deceit? Could any psychological process "weed out" a true fantasist? Surely the boundary between the two must be very blurry and, if it isn't before an individual enters the service, it certainly would be after he had been in it for a few years.

"Thank you, that's very illuminating," Mrs. Price says. "I want to turn now to the matter before this court, in particular to your contact with Mr. Mark Costley. Now, we are going a few years back here so you may refer to your notes if you need to." She pauses. Witness G must have brought a notebook or folder into court with him.

"Just after he joined the estate staff, Mr. Costley applied to join the security services, did he not?

"That is correct."

I glance at the jury again and feel a small thrill of childish satisfaction: *I already know something you are about to find out.* "Would I be right in saying that you were in charge of reviewing his application to join the service after the first round of psychological testing, the questionnaire, the interview, and so on?"

"Yes, that is correct."

"And can you tell me what conclusion you came to?"

"Yes. It was decided that Mr. Costley was not a suitable candidate to proceed to the next stage of training."

What I feel then is not so much shock as bafflement—my first reaction is to wonder if this is some sort of sophisticated double bluff. I cannot help myself from glancing sideways at you. You are staring straight ahead, your face impassive. All those hints you dropped me? The different phones? The safe house? When my momentary bafflement passes, what I feel is cold, just cold. You're not a spy; the spies didn't want you. Why did you lie to me, or not lie to me exactly, but allow me to think you were so much more enigmatic than you were? Didn't you think that sex in the Crypt Chapel while Parliament was in session was strange and exciting enough? I would have been thrilled and disturbed by that if you had worked for the Palace of Westminster catering department. It wasn't about your *job*. Why did you feel the need to seduce me with a lie? But you didn't lie, of course, not outright. You simply kept yourself mysterious enough to encourage me to make up my own story.

"And why was that?" Mrs. Price is asking Witness G.

"It became apparent during the testing that Mr. Costley had some degree of difficulty with the boundaries between truth and fiction. In short, that when invited to stick to a cover story, he came to believe it himself. This is exactly what I was saying earlier about a fantasist, the difference between someone who can maintain a lie over an extended period and someone who actually convinces himself it is the truth."

"What you are describing sounds close to a personality disorder, isn't it?"

"I would say not," Witness G replies. "I would say that—"

Ms. Bonnard is on her feet immediately. "My Lord, this witness is *not* a trained psychologist. He is not qualified to answer that question."

The judge merely looks over his glasses at Mrs. Price. She apologizes readily, her point already made. "I beg your pardon, I'll rephrase the question. Witness G, would it be fair to say that Mr. Costley exhibited behavior during his assessment that suggested he had difficulties distinguishing the boundaries between truth and fiction?"

"That is correct."

"And was your concern about his inability to distinguish boundaries sufficient for you to reject him as a suitable candidate, despite the fact that he had already passed the physical assessment and was extremely keen, as far as you could tell, to join the service?"

"Yes, that is correct. We don't accept candidates lightly but we don't reject them lightly either. Mr. Costley's enthusiasm was not in doubt and I am sure he was doing a very able job in his position with Houses of Parliament security, but in my opinion, he was an unsuitable candidate for us."

Up until now, Mrs. Price seems to have been supporting the idea of you as mentally unstable, but, of course, she was merely building that idea up in order to knock it down. "But . . . am I correct in understanding that, despite his unsuitability for the security services, you did not feel enough concern about his mental stability to report him to his line manager at the House of Commons?"

"I didn't consider him actively unstable, no."

"Can we be quite clear about this? Mr. Costley was, after all, partially responsible for ensuring the smooth running of the democratic processes of this country. You didn't feel any twinge of anxiety after you assessed him, about his fitness to continue in his current post?"

"No, as I've already said, not at all."

Mrs. Price chooses to labor the point. "So although you felt he might have difficulties distinguishing between fact and fiction, you were happy enough with his mental state to allow him to continue working in a bureaucratic but nonetheless highly sensitive role involving the safety and security of our elected members of Parliament, in a building which must be on a constant state of high security alert?"

Witness G lets his voice ring. "Yes, that is correct."

Ms. Bonnard is almost twitching as she rises for the cross-examination. After her interjection during the examination-in-chief, it is obvious what tack she will take. She keeps Witness G waiting for the briefest of moments while she adjusts her wig very slightly and tucks a lock of hair back underneath it. This is very finely judged. She can show him no obvious courtesy or disrespect, but she wants to make it clear that, unlike others in the court, she is not overly impressed by him. When she looks in his direction, I can see as she turns her head that she gives him a slow, warm smile.

She begins by taking Witness G back over his rejection of you. When she has done this, she adds, "And this was, wasn't it, you have said as much already, solely because of your concerns over his psychological state?"

He concedes the point readily enough. "Solely because of those concerns, yes."

For a few minutes, Ms. Bonnard takes him round and around, prodding him all the while for a bit more detail about his anxieties concerning your mental state. She is only asking him to repeat himself but is hoping, I think, that the more Witness G's concerns are repeated, the deeper they will lodge in the jury's mind. Eventually, she sits, Robert declines the opportunity to question Witness G on my behalf, and the judge looks to Mrs. Price. It comes as no surprise to anyone when she gets to her feet again.

"Witness G," she begins, slowly, reasonably. "Now, we already know I'm not allowed to use your name for obvious reasons," she says, "and I appreciate there is a limit on the information you can give the court about yourself, but can you just tell us a little about your background?"

"Certainly," he replies. "I am able to say that I spent a period of time in the armed forces, in operations that involved overseas travel, before moving to being based domestically. I am coming toward the end of my service now. I have been in charge of training and assessing at my current level for a period of eight years."

"You're not a psychiatrist, are you?"

"No. I have obviously received extensive training in—"

"But you're not a trained psychiatrist in the medical sense, you don't have a doctorate of any sort?"

"No, that is correct."

"You're not a member of the British Institute of Psychology or any other of the accredited organizations?"

"No, I'm not."

"What I mean is, and I hope you'll forgive me as this isn't a criticism, the only psychological training you have had is relevant to whether a man or a woman can lie to his or her family or work colleagues, whether he or she could maintain the deceit. In short, what I'm getting at is, you would not consider yourself, nor are you, qualified to pronounce on whether or not Mr. Costley has any sort of personality disorder as recognized by the legal diagnostic guides available to this court."

There is the briefest of silences from the witness box. "It is true that I do not have any of the qualifications you have mentioned."

"Thank you." Mrs. Price looks at the judge. "No further questions, My Lord."

The judge turns to Witness G. "Thank you, you are free to go. I am obliged to give you the warning that I give every witness about not discussing this case with anybody."

We all listen in silence as Witness G descends the few wooden steps from the witness box—his tread sounds heavy to me, yes, over six foot, as I thought. I imagine him out in the corridor at the Old Bailey, walking casually down the wide stone staircase, exiting onto the street, and the people who pass him merely thinking, if they think of him at all, that he is a police officer or a solicitor or businessman. What does that kind of job make you if not a fantasist—a robot? Isn't it to your credit, Mark Costley, that they didn't want you? You never lied to me, not outright. It is human nature to let people think we are something more glamorous than we are. I let you believe that I am one of the nation's top geneticists, when actually I am a moderately successful scientist who is now coasting on past research, doing the odd bit of examining or consultancy. I haven't been at the coalface for years.

That night, for the first time since the trial began, I dream about it. I don't dream about the arid courtroom or about you, there is no graphic nightmare about Craddock's murder, no visions of a bloodied corpse pursuing me with outstretched arms. Instead, I dream about a place in the Old Bailey that I have never been.

Earlier that day, we had started late because one of the jurors was stuck on a delayed train. The message had been relayed to us just before we were taken up, so the dock officers turned around to return me to the cell, and as we took the few steps down the corridor, the elderly black man with white hair behind the counter called out, "Ask her if she wants a hot drink."

I called out in reply, "I'd love a cup of tea," although I didn't want one really. Waiting for it would pass time; drinking it, pass a little more.

"Sit her by the kitchen area," he said to the dock officers, and to my surprise and delight, I was not returned to my cell but taken and sat down outside the small, functional room where our meals are heated in a microwave. One of the dock officers left, but the other perched on a table across from the doorway to keep an eye on me. It wasn't procedure for me to be allowed to sit here, clearly, but they had decided I wasn't the type to make a mad dash into the kitchen in search of a knife, although there was nothing but plastic cutlery in there anyway. The nice Caribbean man walked past into the kitchen and emerged with two cups of tea in plastic mugs. He put one down in front of me and I lifted it and took a sip. It was pleasingly hot. He sat on the chair next to me and I got the feeling that if it had been appropriate, he would have said something like, "What's a nice lady like you doing in a place like this?" Instead, he said, "You're a educated woman." He pronounced it *heducated, a heducated woman.* That was what my Fenland grandparents did, my mother's parents whom I lost touch with after her death, add *h*'s in front of a lot of words that began with vowels. "Have you ever had the tour?"

I wasn't sure what he meant, but then I realized he was talking about the building, the Old Bailey, the historic side rather than the modern bit we are in, the old courtrooms that always appear in the television dramas. I shook my head.

He shook his head in response, as if he was saddened and sorry that I hadn't. "You know, they do tours of the old bits. You should do it sometime. Lots of people do." As I took a sip of the hot tea from the plastic mug, I lowered my head to hide a small smile at the thought that, when my trial is over, I might want to come back here for a day trip, for fun.

He shook his head again. "Very hinteresting, I tell you, so much history in this place." He makes a slurping noise as he drinks from his own cup, sieving the tea through air in order to cool it. "The old court-rooms here, they are so small, you can understand why they needed new ones."

And then he told me about Dead Man's Walk.

And that night, I dream about Dead Man's Walk, and in my dream, I am able to picture it exactly, just from his description, even though I have never been there. It is at the back of the building in an alleyway that is now disused. The Old Bailey has a lot of disused parts, I learn—there is even a bit of Roman wall somewhere. Dead Man's Walk has existed for centuries and presumably it was once made of stone. The nice Caribbean security man told me that nowadays—he can't believe it, but it's true—it's covered in white rectangular tiles, like the inside of a public lavatory. You stand at the beginning, he said . . .

In my dream, I stand at the beginning of Dead Man's Walk. Before me is a series of archways, each one successively smaller than the other. I walk toward them. The first archway with its white tiles is only just tall enough for me to walk through without bending and so narrow that my shoulders skim it. The next archway is lower and narrower still, then the next, and the next . . . until I am having to crouch and slip sideways through smaller and smaller arches . . . but however small and low the arches get, I am able to slip through, which is horrible, because they never end . . .

The nice guard told me that the idea of the smaller and smaller arches was that as condemned prisoners walked to the gallows at the end of the alleyway, they tended to panic—"Can you blame them, the gallows at the end of it?"—and the smaller and smaller spaces were to give them less and less room to escape. But the logic of this seems bizarre, or perhaps just sadistic, for what is more likely to make a con-demned man panic as he walks to his death than the arches closing in on him, more and more, getting smaller and smaller, with the knowl-edge that the final arch will be a coffin.

There is no coffin in my dream, no gallows, no baying crowd. There is only one arch after another, and each one I squeeze through, I find it impossible to believe that I will be able to get through another, smaller one, but each time I do. It never ends. That's all there is to my dream, a series of sensations as I squeeze through each smaller and smaller arch, no blood or violence but a pressing, mounting sense of horror with each successively smaller arch. I wake from the dream with my chest heaving, sweat plastering my hair across my face, to find I am in a cell, in prison.

20

The jury may not know it, but I know because Robert has told me—and you, Mark Costley, must know it too. The prosecution witnesses so far have been largely immaterial: the only one that matters is their expert psychologist, and the only fact that matters is whether or not you are suffering from a personality disorder that means you can avail yourself of the defense of diminished responsibility. The jury still has its collective head full of 999 calls and debates about dilute blood, so I imagine they feel no real sense of anticipation over the delay that occurs the day after my dream. The prosecution expert witness, a psychiatrist called Dr. Sanderson, has to interview you in prison and do a psychological assessment. All it means to the jury is they get a day off.

It is a Wednesday morning. When I left Holloway Prison that morning, it was overcast, but within ten minutes of being inside the Old Bailey, I have lost all sense of what the weather or the world might be doing outside. It could be brilliant hot sunshine or a blizzard out there in the normal world, but the climate is always the same in here: every day electric lit, muggy, close. It strikes me as I climb the concrete steps from the cell area up to the court that I am not so much experiencing this trial as embedded in it. Already, the routine is so known, so intimate to me, that my pretrial days seem lost in the distant past. I can scarcely believe that once upon a time I had a home, a husband, a career, and grown-up children who weren't in touch as much as I would have liked them to be. The normal business of making coffee and toast in my kitchen seems like a distant dream. I try to picture the physical comforts of home as I mount those concrete steps, the deep pile of the dark green carpet on our stairs, the smooth wood of the oak banister beneath my hand. Walking up the stairs in my own home . . .

You are in the dock already. The police officers are on their feet talking softly to each other—DI Cleveland is standing by his chair, hitching his trousers, bending slightly and smiling at something one of his junior colleagues has said. He folds his arms a lot when he's standing, I've noticed that, holding them high up, as if his size means he feels a little clumsy unless his arms are safely tucked away. Mrs. Price's junior, the young man who swings in his chair, is offering Robert a Murray Mint from the large packet he is taking round the legal teams.

I can't see Ms. Bonnard, though, and that is unusual. Normally she is all ready, waiting for proceedings to commence with an air of diligent impatience. After a few minutes, she bustles in, clutching a file of papers to her chest, ignores the others, and crosses the court to where her own junior sits, another young man. They have a quick, urgent conversation, then leave the court together. After a few minutes more, she is back. Following behind her are a man and woman I later discover to be the defense psychological experts. Unlike other witnesses, they are allowed to sit in the court while the prosecution psychologist gives his evidence—it will be their job to contradict it later. They seat themselves behind defense counsel, in the same row as the lawyers from the Crown Prosecution Service. While we wait for the judge, Ms. Bonnard keeps turning back and whispering to them.

The door to the judge's chambers opens. "All rise," calls the usher as the judge processes in, and we do, oh, we do.

The judge gives his customary nod, we all bow and sit, and the usher is already heading out of the court to fetch the jury when Ms. Bonnard gets to her feet. "My Lord," she says, just a little bit too loudly. The usher pauses halfway across the court. The judge frowns over his glasses. Everyone looks at this young woman who has seemed so poised and confident so far. She has her back to me, but from the way her elbows protrude I can see that she is grasping the lapels of her cloak with both hands. She clears her throat; she has a plea of some sort to make. The judge looks at her and gives her his normal indulgent smile, but it has a slightly fixed quality—something is coming that he won't like.

"My Lord," she says, "before the jury is brought in, I'm sorry to say that we may have a further delay and it's difficult for me to tell the court exactly how long that delay might be."

The judge glances conspicuously at the clock just beneath the rail along the front of the public gallery.

"I'm afraid the problem is, My Lord, Dr. Sanderson's report. You see, it would appear that the printer in the building here is, after all, not working. This means that although I received the report by e-mail at seven a.m. this morning, I was already on my way here and I have, as yet, only had the opportunity to read it on my phone while on the train and as your Lordship knows it is twenty-eight pages long . . ."

She dries to a halt. The judge merely stares at her.

"My Lord, I really do feel that I will not be providing my client with full and adequate representation unless I have had the opportunity to read the report in detail, in hard copy, annotate it where necessary and discuss it with him. There are parts of the report that we find contentious and some, indeed, which go to the very heart of our defense. I would not be suggesting any further delay were it not a matter of the utmost importance."

The judge sighs. "Is it really not possible to provide Ms. Bonnard with a photocopy?" He looks around the courtroom with a tight little smile, as if this question is addressed to anyone who might happen to have a copy, including the usher and those in the public gallery, and he really cannot understand why *someone* cannot help him out. I feel an inappropriate but reflexive desire to raise my hand, like the teacher's pet that I am, even though I don't, of course, have a copy of the report either. Nor does Robert.

"My Lord, I understand there is another printer in the other room and it may be possible to get it printed but I will have to reread it in its entirety. I do appreciate that this is a most annoying delay and had I received the report before I left the house this morning I would of course have printed it out at home and digested it in hard copy during my journey."

The judge leans forward. "My understanding was that the report was e-mailed to everybody by midnight last night?" The smile is getting tighter and tighter.

"That may be the case, My Lord, but my Internet connection went down overnight and I was unable to access my e-mail until I was on the train."

The judge sighs again, purses his lips. I suddenly see how bad tempered he might be on a Sunday at home when the roast potatoes are ready before the lamb joint. He looks at the clock again. "I will call a recess until eleven a.m. Will that give you sufficient time, Ms. Bonnard?"

She bows her head briefly. "Thank you, My Lord, it will certainly give me sufficient time to print out and scan the report as quickly as possible. I may, however, need additional time to consult with my client."

Robert has his face turned to one side and his arm is resting across the back of his chair. I see him frown.

"How much time?" The judge pronounces the monosyllables slowly.

"My Lord, I would respectfully suggest that it might perhaps be best if the jury were released until after lunch, two p.m."

The judge stares at her briefly, then says to the air in front of him, "Jury please . . ."

Robert glances back at me, still frowning. The usher goes outside and fetches the jury in. As they cross the court to their seats, a young man in the back of the procession pauses to open his rucksack and the judge says, with a tinge of impatience, "Do please take your seat, sir, I can promise you it will not be for long."

They sit, and the judge says, "Ladies and gentlemen, a legal matter has arisen that requires some time to resolve. As I have already told you, it is your job here to judge the evidence, it is mine to judge matters of law. What this means, in effect, is that you get a break and I do not."

The jury all break into relieved smiles at the realization that the judge has, quite unexpectedly, made a joke.

"As a result, we will not now require your attendance until after the lunch break. You are free to go until two p.m."

That is it. They are ushered out. I wonder that the judge does not apologize for their unnecessary journeys that morning but suppose that might undermine his authority. Jokes may be dispensed from on high; apologies may not.

"Be upstanding in court," the usher barks.

We all rise, bow to the judge as he departs.

Ms. Bonnard turns to you, my codefendant, where you stand in the dock and says, "I'm coming down to see you straightaway." I'm a little confused. Wasn't getting the report printed the immediate problem? Your defense team gather papers and folders and leave the court in a flurry.

DI Cleveland turns back to look at his colleagues by the door and raises his eyebrows, then wanders over to the prosecution table. Mrs. Price turns to him as he approaches and raises her hands. "They're playing for time," she says. Then, lowering her voice only slightly, she adds, "Internet connection my arse."

Robert is still sitting with one arm along the chair, his expression thoughtful. Beside him, his junior sits in her chair, silent.

Dr. Sanderson fills me with fear the minute he enters the court. He has a heavy face, like a bulldog, and fluffy gray hair. He seems deeply unimpressed to be there, although I presume he is being paid. He stands in the dock and Mrs. Price takes him through his psychological assessment of you, during which, in summary, he asserts that there is no chance whatsoever that you are suffering from a personality disorder. He cites your good behavior while you are on remand, your lack of a previous psychiatric history, and solid work record. Most damning of all, he asserts that you are what he calls "an unreliable historian," and as evidence of that, he cites the calculated way you have pursued your interest in extramarital sex. In other words, you are a liar. You are not mad, or disturbed, or suffering from post-traumatic stress disorder or a borderline or antisocial personality disorder. You're just a liar.

Ms. Bonnard does what she can. She attempts to deal with Dr. Sanderson in the same way she dealt with the other prosecution witnesses: she goes on the attack. She asks him for his track record in giving evidence and establishes that he is almost always on the prosecution side. She quotes a report he wrote for the Home Office titled "Criminal Defenses and Malingering." She gets him to describe how malingering is a technical term for the way criminals try to avoid responsibility for their crimes by pretending to be psychologically disturbed and how some of them can research their disorders quite carefully.

"You often think people are malingering, don't you?" she asks him.

He looks at her coldly, the bulldog man, unrattled, and says, "I think they are malingering when there is no evidence they are suffering from a serious psychiatric disorder and are merely pretending they do in order to get off." He looks over at the jury after he says this in a way that suggests he would roll his eyes at them if he thought he could get away with it.

Ms. Bonnard then pulls out the final weapon in her arsenal. She asks Dr. Sanderson to comment on a case in which he gave evidence for the prosecution of a woman who had stabbed her stepfather after years of sexual abuse. "Your evidence, as I understand it, was that this woman was not suffering from post-traumatic stress disorder?"

"That is correct," he replies. "In my opinion, she was not."

"You are skeptical as to whether post-traumatic stress disorder actually exists," states Ms. Bonnard, looking down as she always does when she lobs in one of her killer statements.

Dr. Sanderson does not budge one inch. "It is not my job to be skeptical or otherwise. It is my job to make a diagnostic assessment according to the law."

Now I know why Ms. Bonnard played for time after reading Dr. Sanderson's psychological assessment of you. It is devastating for your case. Dr. Sanderson combines his cynicism with just enough moderation to avoid appearing harsh. I think he is a hateful person, without one shred of human empathy, the sort of person who, a few years ago, would have said that sexual abuse itself didn't exist except in the mind of the victim—but I have to concede that he means every word he says. He loves his job and is good at it. He is perfectly sincere.

When Robert comes to see me at the end of the day, I can tell he is unhappy. "Although our defense doesn't rely on Mr. Costley's innocence, obviously we would like him to be found not guilty because then you are automatically not guilty too."

"How do you think Ms. Bonnard did against the psychologist?" I ask, although I know the answer.

Robert frowns. His gown is still hanging off one shoulder and his wig is minutely askew; he looks tired. "Let's just say, she's handling things a little differently from how I would handle them." He sniffs derisively. "I normally have a slightly better working relationship with the other defense team in multiple-defendant cases. It's in our interests to work together, after all."

We both sit in silence for a minute or two, alone together in the small consulting room. Tomorrow, it will be my turn.

The prosecution case against me is straightforward. They rubbish their own victim. They present George Craddock as a monster. They do not attempt to discredit or diminish the story of his assault against me, in the way a defense would have done were it Craddock in the dock: they do the opposite. The worse they make him look, the more motive it gives me. They have evidence from the police computer expert about the pornographic websites Craddock visited. The ex-wife is unavailable—they have been unable to track her down in America—so they bring in her sister to give evidence about the Craddock marriage and the allegations made of domestic abuse. I didn't know you could bring bad character evidence against a dead victim, but apparently you can. You can do anything in this trial, I am beginning to think, because this is an upside-down trial. It is like the large mirror in the café where you and I met Kevin. It is through the looking glass. Everything that should count for me is against me.

Kevin himself is the next prosecution witness against me, and he gives convincing evidence about how I was measured and articulate during our discussion but how he still sensed, beneath my controlled exterior, a great deal of distress about what had happened to me. Kevin is a good witness, as likable in court as I found him in the café, a sympathetic man whose job it is to help women: he couldn't be worse for me. Up-side down, wrong way round: during Kevin's evidence, I come the closest I come during the whole trial to wanting to put my hands over my eyes and scream.

Kevin's speculation about the nature of the relationship between you and me is not something that is raised by Mrs. Price. It has been ruled inadmissible. There are only two people who are allowed to be asked about the nature of our relationship: you and me.

The taxi driver who drove me home after that night is a prosecu-tion witness too. They traced him from the receipt he gave me, which they found among my papers when they searched my house. He comes over well, too, strong London accent, a little bumbling but heartfelt, a nice man.

"What did you observe between the defendant and the victim in this case?" Mrs. Price asks him. By defendant, she means me. By victim, she means Craddock.

Robert gets to his feet. It is the first time in the trial he has raised an objection and several people on the jury look at him, surprised. "My Lord, this witness is being asked to give his opinion—"

My Lord raises his hand to interrupt Robert midsentence, pauses for a moment's reflection, then says, "I think this witness is being asked what he observed. Mrs. Price, you will ensure that your questions do not stray from that, won't you?"

"Of course, My Lord."

"Then you may proceed."

Robert sits. It is his first interjection, and he has been slapped down. I think how anything that makes him look weak must surely make our whole case look weak.

"Well, like I said to my wife that night, I was a bit concerned," the taxi driver continues, carefully, a little self-importantly, glancing from counsel to the jury and back again. "It was my last job that night, I live out in west London myself so was quite pleased to get it and thought I'd knock off a bit early and get myself home and my wife was waiting up and I said, I think this woman I took home was in a bad way, in the corner of the cab like. Dunno what was going on but she didn't look good."

The upside-down evidence is eventually concluded—and here is where the case against me falters. Without proof of the nature of our relationship, the suggestion that I urged you to kill Craddock sounds implausible. Other than making it clear that what he did to me was very bad, there is little the prosecution can do. I wonder if they know this, in their heart of hearts. I wonder if Mrs. Price is thinking, *Oh, well, as long as we get him, that's good enough. We will do our best to get her but it's not looking very good.* I wonder, not for the first time, about her degree of emotional investment in what is going on here. How much do these people care?

It is Friday afternoon. The jury are still settling back in their seats, still doing the small shuffling motion most of us do as we sit down, when junior counsel for the prosecution rises. Mrs. Price stays in her seat for this bit. Clearly, the junior barristers have to be given something to do. "My Lord, we have some submissions . . ." The young man of the Murray Mints reads out a paramedic's statement—the paramedic himself has not been called as a witness as he is in hospital having his appendix out. But his statement will suffice and the judge is directed to it. "This is in My Lord's bundle page two one three . . ." *My Lord's bundle*: it sounds like a baby wrapped in a blanket. There is a pause while My Lord flicks through his bundle. I don't really understand the relevance of the absent paramedic's evidence, but later Robert explains to me that it concerns the amount of clearing up that was done after Craddock was killed. This is important because your defense is going to be diminished responsibility. The more thorough you were in your clear-up, the more organized, then the more responsible—or sane—you appear to be. The details that follow still seem excessive to me. The prosecution has already demonstrated that you knew what you were doing. But we still get to hear about how both paramedics placed surgical gloves over their boots before entering the property. Normally, they would wait for protective suits and boots to arrive in order to preserve the evidence—the 999 call had stated a dead body, after all—but because of the length of time they were taking to arrive, the decision was taken to enter the property anyway in case resuscitation was required for any persons who might be on the property. This seems to me yet another example of where information is given in order to protect someone from criticism later, rather than because it has any relevance to our case. Mr. Murray Mint continues to stand in for the paramedic: "When I entered the property, I proceeded immediately into the kitchen, where I found an unknown male lying on his back with his head toward the fridge-freezer. I noticed a large pool of blood beneath the head . . ." We are back to the beginning again: the body. Again and again, the body is what we circle around—not the man, the body. The body is always there, like a corpse in a horror movie that appears wherever the main character looks; the bedroom, the kitchen, the sitting room, in his office at work, sitting in his car. This body does not follow us in that way—it is a real body, it stays in one place—but all the same, none of us can get away from it. The callow boy is still reading out the paramedic's statement, about the scene-of-crime officers arriving, then, eventually, the police doctor, ". . . and at eighteen hundred hours, life was pronounced extinct."

Extinct. Gone for good. Not just absent, not just away for a bit—extinct, never to return.

The word "extinct" is still hanging in the air when junior counsel says, "And just one more submission, My Lord," and drops a small depth charge into the already murky waters of what the jury know about you. "In 2005, Mark Costley pleaded guilty to the charge of common assault."

The jury members look surprised, and a little baffled. They feel this is relevant information and, of course, want more detail. They have not been privy to the legal arguments over the admission of bad character evidence, during which it emerged that you were found guilty of assault after getting into a fight with a man outside a pub. The man had insulted your wife, apparently. The jury is not allowed to hear the details of the case because Ms. Bonnard has argued that it might prejudice the jury.

I am still watching the jury's reaction to this information as Mrs. Price stands. I only just catch her saying quietly, "My Lord, that concludes the case for the Crown."

The prosecution has wrapped up so quietly and undramatically that I look around the court to see if anyone else is as surprised as I am. I can't help feeling there should have been some grand conclusion, but that will come later, in the closing statements. That is when I can expect the flourishes, if indeed there will be any.

The jurors all look a little surprised as well. The judge turns to them and says that, as it is nearly 3:00 p.m. on a Friday, he sees no reason to ask the defense to open at this point. He reminds them that they are to discuss the case with no one over the weekend. They are free to go until 10:15 on Monday morning. The prosecution case against us has taken two weeks. As it turns out, the defense will be a lot quicker.

One by one, the jury members get down from the jury box and file out in front of us. We all watch them go, off to their normal lives.

There is a collective exhalation in the court. The prosecution and defense barristers turn to each other. The woman from the CPS closes her file with a sigh. The judge turns to Robert and asks if he will be making a submission and Robert says yes, he will have it on the judge's desk by midnight.

Robert turns to me and says, "I'll be down in a few minutes, okay?"

I rise from my seat with a sense of anticlimax. I don't know what I expected from the conclusion of the prosecution case, but it was something more than this. Perhaps it is because I expected the paramedic's statement to lead somewhere and it didn't. Perhaps it is because I have not yet taken the stand. Is it arrogance or desperation on my part that makes me eager to do so?

When Robert comes down to the cell, he has the air of a man who is a little demob happy, perhaps because it is a Friday afternoon. He has brought his junior with him, Claire, and they cram together on the tiny table in the consulting room while I sit opposite and Robert tells me that that evening he will have a submission with the judge that the case against me should be dismissed. The only effective prosecution witness the Crown has brought against me was Kevin, he says, but although his testimony may have offered the jury a motive for my involvement, it was far from proven—and what, of course, was key to that, although Robert does not say it openly, was that he was not allowed to speculate about the nature of my relationship with you. Despite everything I have learned about you recently, I want to say to you: *You were right, keeping quiet about us, that is what is keeping me safe.*

As Robert and Claire get up to leave, I look at them. I want to delay them, although they are eager to go. When they are gone, there will be nothing for me to do except sit and wait in my cell until I am returned to prison. They, and all the other professionals in that courtroom, get to have a weekend away from this, to return to the outside world, normal life, weather, the News at Ten, a restaurant they think overpriced or a bottle of wine not as good as it should be. These things and much else besides await Robert and Claire and all the other professionals involved in our case but not me or you—or Craddock's father.

My question is genuine, all the same. "How is it looking for Mark?"

At this, they pause, exchange glances. Claire opens her mouth to answer but Robert cuts across her. "Well, all I can say is, if I was his barrister, I would not be advising a defense of diminished responsibility. You saw yourself, Ms. Bonnard couldn't shake Dr. Sanderson. She'd better have a damn good psychologist on her side, that's all I can say. She must have something up her sleeve. Costley's held down a responsible job for years, has a family, no serious psychiatric history. I was surprised that was what they were going for, under the circumstances. Of course, we are all obliged to take instruction from our client and I've not been privy to their conversations, so . . ." He presses his lips together, tips his head a little.

I ask them the question I asked Jas in the pizza parlor. "Why didn't he go for self-defense?"

Again, Robert and Claire exchange the briefest of glances. Then Claire says gently, "The forensic evidence would have made that defense quite difficult."

I don't know how to feel after they have gone. Perhaps, on Monday, because of Robert's submission, the case against me will be dismissed and I will be free to go. It all seems so sudden. I haven't even taken the stand. No evidence has been presented in my defense but then the evidence against me seems so tenuous too. It is halftime. The managers are in with their teams, giving them a pep talk, reviewing the game so far and telling them what needs to happen in the second half. For me, it's looking quite good; for you, quite bad. I'm worried for you, of course I am. But the tantalizing and terrifying thought that on Monday I could be going home is what fills my head, like a cloud, like a migraine headache. I can't think any other thought. I should have remembered Jas's story, at that point, the story he told about the experiment on the chimpanzee. If I had remembered that, my love, I would not have managed that bleak, small, foolish smile when Robert and Claire shook my hand as they left the consultation room on that Friday afternoon.

21

On Monday, the second half of the trial begins. All weekend, I have allowed myself to hope.

The Monday morning journey feels like an ordinary commute by now. I don't feel sick in the van anymore. I chat to the prison officers who accompany me. When we arrive, the elderly Caribbean guard at the Old Bailey greets me with a smile, and when I say, "How was your weekend, Thomas?" he replies, "Beautiful!"

Up in court, the public gallery has opened and Susannah is there, and as I take my seat I give her a hopeful thumbs-up. She returns it with a wan smile. Robert comes over from his table and says, "Now, don't get your hopes up." But even so, it is only later, when we are all in position but before the jury is allowed in, at the point where the judge says, "I am not minded to allow . . ." that I realize I have been lying to myself for the whole of the prosecution case. For that whole two weeks, I have been saying, they have no case against me. And all weekend I have been saying to myself, *Of course the judge will dismiss the case, not because motions to dismiss are often successful—they rarely are— but because* you *know they should, they will.* How does the mind divide so neatly? I've never understood it: there is too much about human psychology that is gray or ambiguous. How do people operate on two levels, going about their normal lives while the rest of it is falling apart? You don't need to be an adulterer to know about that. You only need to be someone who still has to go to work in the morning when her child is sick or in trouble—and that must be true of a huge proportion of the human race. "How are you?" the receptionist at the Beaufort asked me brightly the day after my son had been diagnosed with bipolar disorder. "Fine!" I chirruped in reply.

When the case against you is dismissed, or when you're found not guilty, you don't even go back down to the cells for them to do some paperwork. They just let you out, straightaway. There's a door in the dock that opens into the body of the court and you just walk through it and out into the corridor and down the stairs and right out onto the street.

I wonder what you are thinking, as I sit there in the dock—but you remain silent and impassive as you have done throughout. Surely you would have been pleased to see me set free, despite the seriousness of your own predicament? And then a sobering thought occurs to me: *Is this a question that I even need to ask?*

I am so swaddled in disappointment that I hardly notice the business of the court continuing. Of course. The defense cases can proceed apace now, beginning with yours. It takes effort to lift my head and look around, but I say to myself, *You must stay alert. You will be on the stand before you know it.*

The judge has finished rearranging some papers in front of him, looks up and around the court, beams at us all, and says, "So then, are we ready for the jury?"

Ms. Bonnard begins by calling some witnesses who will counter the poor impression of you given by DS Amelia Johns and Witness G, and your boss at the Houses of Parliament, a colleague from your days as a cop. It strikes me that your counsel is in a difficult position here. She wants to humanize you, and she wants the jury to start liking you a bit more, but she also wants to present you as psychologically disturbed enough to avail yourself of the defense of diminished responsibility. It's a tricky one.

The only witness that matters, though, is her psychologist. *She better have a damn good one.*

As it turns out, Ms. Bonnard has two. I have no idea how much choice barristers get when they choose psychologists to give evidence in their cases—presumably there is a register, presumably they have their favorites. But Ms. Bonnard has chosen a couple of wild cards—a young man who looks scarcely old enough to be on work experience and a woman like herself. I wonder if she thought the jury would be more favorable to her youthful, eager psychologists than to the prosecution's heavyweight and unpleasant Dr. Sanderson. It works for me. I like them both. They were the two people who were sitting behind Ms. Bonnard while Dr. Sanderson gave his evidence. I noticed them taking notes.

Although they are a team, it is only the young woman who takes the stand. She is called Dr. Ruth Sadiq and has neat dark hair and pale skin, very fine hands, I notice from across the court as she reads the secular oath—I am reminded of what Laurence said about how we receive information. She has also interviewed you in prison and presents a much more sympathetic portrait than Dr. Sanderson. Yes, she would agree with Dr. Sanderson that you are an "unreliable historian," but that is characteristic of people with psychological problems who hold down high-pressure jobs and family life: it could be viewed as a coping strategy. It turns out that Dr. Sadiq is a specialist in high-functioning patients with disorders. Personality disorders are often diagnosed in people who have chaotic lifestyles, she says—drug addicts or alcoholics, homeless people—the kind of people much more usually seen in the dock. Antisocial personality disorder is often twinned with those conditions, for instance. But very intelligent people with good support systems are able to come up with coping mechanisms that ameliorate their disorders—for instance, in the case of borderline personality disorder, a calm environment, the patient being surrounded by people who behave in a consistent way, means that the patient is able to pick up clues on appropriate behavior from those around him. Dr. Sadiq is soft-spoken—the judge has to ask her to speak up twice—and has none of the rhetorical certainty or sneering of Dr. Sanderson. I can feel the jury warming to her. My hopes rise.

"So you are saying, if I am correct," Ms. Bonnard prompts, "that the unstable behavior usually associated with borderline personality disorder is sometimes not apparent in people who have strong support structures."

"Yes, that is correct. I believe it manifests itself in other ways."

"Would you care to describe those ways to the jury?"

"Well, in its developed forms, borderline personality disorder can lead to what we call dissociation—that is, these people dissociate from real life and start to create their own self-sustaining narratives, almost as if they believe they are watching themselves in a film, if you like, a little drama around themselves, which they are the center of and in which they feel safe. This, I believe, would also fit the criteria of a narcissistic personality disorder."

Ms. Bonnard affects an air of pleased surprise. "So," she says, "people in a dissociative state, as a result of either borderline or narcissistic personality disorder or a combination of the two, could be using their own made-up stories about themselves in order to cope with daily life and hide their disorder from those around them?"

"Precisely, yes. If they create their own story about themselves, then they remain in control. As I said, safe."

"To other people they might just seem, well, a bit of a fantasist?"

Dr. Sadiq gives a smile and says, "Well, that's not a very technical term, but yes, I believe fantasist is what such people might be called, when actually they have a serious undiagnosed psychological disorder and are using a sophisticated coping strategy in order to manage everyday life."

It all sounds plausible to me, and it fits with your idea of yourself, your need to pretend that you were more glamorous and exciting than you were, the risky sex . . . the stories we tell ourselves about ourselves, the way we pick and choose our evidence. Trying to look at this coldly, to remove the element of self-interest in this theory, I am still convinced.

Ms. Bonnard gives Dr. Sadiq a warm smile and says, "Thank you, Doctor. Please remain where you are."

Mrs. Price gets to her feet for the cross-examination. She has none of the feline poise of Ms. Bonnard—that frightening slowness and precision. You do not get the feeling, as she rises, that her cross-examinations are spectacles. As she is nearer to the witness box than Ms. Bonnard, she doesn't have to turn her head and so I rarely catch sight of the expression on her face, but from the set of her shoulders I am guessing she still has that slightly weary air, as if her point of view is so patently correct that she can hardly be bothered with cross-examining at all.

"Dr. Sadiq," she says, looking down and up again. "Your *theory*, that people with high-functioning personality disorders can develop coping strategies that protect their lifestyles from becoming chaotic, that they can hide these very serious disorders for many years from friends, family, workmates, doctors, and so on . . . It formed the basis of your PhD thesis, I believe? The one you took at Kingston University. Is that correct?"

Dr. Sadiq is still composed, soft-spoken. "Yes, that's right."

Mrs. Price looks up and says simply, "It's your pet theory, isn't it?"

And then Dr. Sadiq gets it very badly wrong. She says nothing. She looks over at Ms. Bonnard, as if hoping for instruction, but all Ms. Bonnard can do is stare at her encouragingly. It is a big mistake. It makes her seem like a star pupil who is looking for the right answer. She glances at the judge and the jury but none of them are going to help her out either. She looks at the dock and I want to lean forward and say, go on, forget the self-deprecation, just be firm in your opinion, be unequivocal. It's 60 percent how you look, 30 percent how you sound, and only 10 percent what you actually say. That 30 percent is yours for the taking.

Dr. Sadiq says, "Well, yes, you could call it that, it's a theory I believe in. I do believe it is a good one, though, I think it explains a lot."

"But Dr. Sadiq, forgive me," Mrs. Price says patiently. "What I'm driving at is, the theory of high-functioning personality disorders that you expound in your PhD thesis, it is countered by most of the recognized psychological diagnostic tools used in criminal cases, isn't it? For instance, the *Diagnostic and Statistical Manual of Mental Disorders*?"

Again, that self-sabotaging pause. "Well, yes, but—"

"And what about the *International Classification of Diseases*?"

"Well . . . ," falters Dr. Sadiq.

After that, it's a blood sport. Mrs. Price lists—one after the other— the manuals, the papers, the works by authors with impressive CVs. My heart is in my boots. I know all about citations. I know how the whole point of presenting a new theory is to anticipate the countercitations from those who will disagree with you and to have, up your sleeve, a list of counter-countercitations. I could have told them that. They should have me up there. This is a nice young woman, intelligent, competent, with a perfectly decent theory—but she is entirely lacking the aggression that will allow her to present her theory as fact. The objectionable Dr. Sanderson is wiping the floor with her without even being in the room, just by the force of his certainty.

It is not quite lunchtime by the time Dr. Sadiq is allowed off the stand. If the judge had insisted at that point, as he had every right to do, that Ms. Bonnard continue with her case, then perhaps none of what followed would have happened. There would have been no time. Ms. Bonnard would have announced there and then that you were not taking the stand—the judge would have issued the statutory warning that the Crown would be allowed to draw a negative inference from your refusal to do so—and it is even possible that Robert would have opened his case there and then and that he would have called his only witness—me—immediately.

As it is, the judge looks at the clock hanging beneath the public gallery, in that obvious way that he often does. He smiles at Ms. Bonnard, perhaps even feeling a little sorry for her, and says, "I think now might be a suitable juncture to adjourn."

Ms. Bonnard is only too happy to agree. After we have all risen and the judge has left, I watch her carefully from behind. She sinks back down into her chair and leans forward a little. I can't see the expression on her face but I think she must know she's losing.

And then, from the corner of my eye, I see you leaning forward, lifting a hand, and giving a sharp *tap-tap* on the bulletproof glass. Heads in the courtroom turn and I look at you too, and it comes to me in a wave that you have been so still, so silent so far, that I have almost forgotten you are in the dock with me. The truth is, the man sitting a few feet away from me, the man who never moves or gives anything away by gesture or expression, he has seemed so unlike you throughout this whole process that I have almost entirely detached your fate from mine. Mark Costley, the thin figure in the dock, is so unlike X, the lover who pressed his open mouth against mine.

Ms. Bonnard lifts her head and turns, gives you a weary smile.

The dock officer sitting next to me rises and touches my elbow, and without looking at you again, I turn to leave the dock and return to my cell.

Ms. Bonnard seems to have recovered when she returns from lunch, which is odd, because things are looking bad for her and she has no-where else to go. "My Lord," she says, when we are all in position again and she is on her feet. "I will be offering no further witnesses."

As Robert gets to his feet, he looks over at Ms. Bonnard and I see him give her one straight, slightly questioning look, but she has her head down over her papers and does not return his gaze.

The judge smiles at Robert, as if he is relieved at last to have a fellow chap in front of him. Robert gives a slight bow and says, "My Lord, we are planning to call only one witness in our case, Yvonne Carmichael."

I rise.

As I stand, so do my dock officers, and we file past you and your dock officers—there is plenty of room in front of the seat but, even so, I would have to move only a little to one side to brush your knees as I pass. You stay immobile, staring straight ahead. The dock officer in front of me descends the three short steps to where there is a door in the side of the dock that allows us all out and into the courtroom. As I cross the courtroom to the witness box, walking past the ends of the rows of desks where the police officers, lawyers, and barristers are seated, I know that everyone is watching me but none more closely than the jury. I glance over at them at one point. I keep my head high. *You know what*, I think, and I wonder if it shows in my glance: *I've had enough.* I've had enough of being told what to do and how to look and how to sound. I am innocent. I didn't kill anyone. And I have nothing to fear from these wooden procedures or the cops or the paperwork or Letitia in the breakfast queue or any of them. I've had enough of being afraid. I'm not even frightened of the jury. Maybe they should be frightened of me.

The members of the jury are riveted. They are watching me with the same sort of starstruck horror they might feel if they had been visiting a zoo and a jaguar had casually stepped through the bars of its cage and strolled among them. I'm so glad that I'm finally getting a chance to get out of the dock. Guess what, defendants in murder trials are human too. I read the oath loudly and firmly, hand the card back to the usher, and then look up and around the court, as if surveying it for the first time.

The witness box is a very different vantage point from the dock. You are raised up so that everyone can see you but with the pleasing side effect that you can look down on them. I know this room so well by now: the quality of the light, the hum of the air-conditioning—I feel no fear. I sit on the drop-down seat behind me, and as Robert stands, he gives me a fond look, half a smile at one corner of his mouth, a friendly twinkle in his eyes. The doubts I have had about the way he is conducting my defense melt away. I can rely on him.

"Is your name Yvonne Carmichael?" he asks me.

Instinctively, I copy the professional witnesses—the police officers and pathologists. I am not one of the others, the accidental witnesses, I am a professional too. I look directly at the jury. "Yes, that is correct."

"Mrs. Carmichael, can you tell us what you do for a living?"

"I'm a geneticist."

22

Robert doesn't spend too much time with my career, merely establishing where I work, how long I have been doing it. He touches briefly on my lengthy and stable marriage, my two grown-up children, the fact that my husband, like myself, is a respected scientist. I don't like talking about Guy and Adam and Carrie—I can hear my voice dropping a register—but I know Robert has to do it in order to create the picture of me as Mrs. Utterly Normal. It's easy enough for him to do. I am. After a while, we get to the bit of my job that people are most readily impressed by, although it was actually one of the least taxing things I have ever done: my giving evidence at the House of Commons Select Committees. Again, Robert does not need to spend long on this, merely enough to establish my credibility, and by the time he has finished, I believe myself incapable of the things I know I have done, let alone the thing I am accused of that I didn't do.

"And it was on the last of these occasions that you met the man in the dock, Mr. Mark Costley?"

"Yes, that is correct."

Robert stands up a little straighter, folds his arms, says casually, "Can you tell me your impressions of him?"

"Yes," I say. "I liked him. We got talking in a corridor. He clearly knew his way around the Houses of Parliament, he gave me a guided tour, the Great Hall of Westminster." A tiny pause. "The Crypt Chapel. He knew a lot about the history and the way things were run. He seemed very competent."

I look across the courtroom and get what I have been waiting for since our trial began: you are looking at me. Your gaze is soft. I dare not look at you for more than a second. As my gaze shifts, I catch sight of the expression on DI Cleveland's face—he is sitting two rows behind the prosecution bench, directly in line with where you are seated. DI Cleveland is looking at me too and his gaze is not soft. He is thinking, *You fucked him and I know it, I just couldn't prove it.*

"You became friends?" Robert asks.

"Yes, we met for coffee a few times."

"Just friends," Robert states, and I nod. Without waiting for a fuller answer, he goes on, "I believe Mr. Costley wanted your advice."

"Yes," I say. "His nephew was considering a career in science. We talked about it."

Robert pauses at that point, a telltale pause, slow and deliberate, one that everyone in the court registers. "Mrs. Carmichael, we now have to discuss the events that have led, indirectly, to you being here, in a position it is safe to say you would never have imagined yourself to ever be in." He pauses again. He leans forward and says, "Would you like me to request that the public gallery is cleared?"

Robert has warned me that he will ask this question and has told me to say yes, but the strange thing is, even though I am entirely prepared, my cheeks feel hot with the humiliation to come and the quietness in my voice is perfectly genuine as I say, "Yes, yes, please, if that is possible."

It is Robert's gentleness, that is what makes me cry. It is when he prods me, in his modulated tones, with all the questions that the jury might themselves ask. "Some people," he says gently, "will find it hard to understand that you couldn't even tell your own husband about this horrible, vicious attack . . ."

My eyes well with tears—I can feel my face tense and wobble with the effort of staying composed. Still, I am able to look at the jury at this point and want them to understand, not just for myself. "I know that anyone this hasn't happened to would have difficulty with that, and before this happened to me, I would have thought that way too. But actually, your husband is the last person you want to tell. If I had told my husband it would have been in my home. I would have brought it into my home. And in two years' time, we might have been sitting at our kitchen table talking about how he felt about the fact that I had been attacked, but it didn't happen to him, it happened to *me* . . ." And suddenly, I crack, and sob, and realize how angry I am. What the hell was Guy doing in Newcastle? Why wasn't he at that party? Come to think of it, why weren't you? All the people who claim they love me, my family, all my friends, where the hell were they that night?

When I look up, one of the jury, the Chinese woman, has tears running down her face too.

It takes some time for my hot, angry tears to stop. Robert pauses between questions, but gradually it becomes apparent to everyone, and to me, that I am unraveled. Even the lightest of questions—what did I do the weekend after the assault?—provokes a fresh flood of tears from me, and although I am surprised and humiliated by my inability to control myself, part of me feels a great wash of relief: to talk about it at last, to tell the truth, to acknowledge my fury and hurt—I step outside myself and observe myself doing this, being honest. How can anyone doubt me now?

Robert looks at the clock, glances at the judge, and asks me one last question. "Mrs. Carmichael, when you went to Mr. Costley and asked his advice, did you have any thought in your head of vengeance against Mr. Craddock for what he had done?"

I shake my head, sob, clutch the tissue in my fingers like a child, wipe beneath my eyes, look at Robert, shake my head again, sob again.

"Just to be clear," Robert says softly. "Did you wish George Craddock physical harm, did you urge or exhort Mr. Mark Costley to kill George Craddock?"

I can only shake my head while I sob.

Robert looks down for a moment, waits for a while, then turns to the judge and says, "My Lord . . ."

"Yes," says the judge. I look at him and he has a slightly disdainful expression. I guess him to be the kind of man who cannot cope when a woman cries in front of him, who feels filled with helplessness and irritation, like Henry Higgins in *My Fair Lady*. Why can't a woman be more like a man?

"May I suggest, in view of the hour and in view of the very obvious distress of my witness . . ."

"Yes, I think so," the judge readily agrees. He looks around the court. "We will adjourn until tomorrow morning. Jury, may we have you here at ten a.m. sharp?"

The jury gather their bags. None of them look at me as they descend from the box and walk swiftly across the court. It seems odd that I have to sit here, watching them go. I can't help thinking that they will be sleeping on the image of me, wounded and human, sobbing with sincerity in the witness box.

When they have gone, Robert steps out from behind his row of tables, lifting his hand to the dock officer who is waiting to escort me back to the dock. He comes over and places his hands together, knitting the fingers, lifting the fist he has made, and giving a small shake of congratulations.

"Well done," he says softly, seriously. "You did really well."

I reply with a small smile and it is only then that it comes to me how completely drained I am, and a wave of missing Guy and my children and my home comes over me. I have managed to keep that at bay so well up until now, not to think of them, so other and extraordinary has this experience been, but it comes to me now, crashing over me in slow motion—if I don't get to walk out of this court soon, go back to my normal life, then I will die.

That night, for the first time since my incarceration, I sleep well on my thin mattress in my cell in Holloway Prison.

The next day, I am escorted again into the witness box, dry-eyed and collected now, wearing a crisp white shirt, hoping that the worst of my examination is over and braced for the cross-examination by the prosecution—but I can't imagine a plausible line of attack for them.

They can't try to blacken me by expressing doubt about the assault as they want Craddock to be a monster. They can ask about my relationship with you, I suppose, but they have no evidence either way. What can they do?

Robert is brisk in the remainder of his questions—he knows the jury has had a whole night to dwell on that image of me from yesterday, distressed and weeping. He knows they will probably be relieved to see me calm this morning, willing me to remain so. They are on my side. He does not return to the assault or its aftermath, choosing instead to concentrate on the events of that Saturday afternoon, how I picked you up at the Tube, drove you to the street, our conversation before and afterward—how you refused to tell me what had happened. He finishes with the question, "Mrs. Carmichael, did you, at any stage of this event, either before or during that drive to George Craddock's house, urge Mr. Mark Costley to kill or harm the man who had assaulted you?"

"No."

"Did you have any inkling that Mark Costley might be about to kill or harm George Craddock?"

"No. None at all, no."

When Ms. Bonnard gets to her feet, do I feel a twinge of unease? No, I don't think so. The moment has not yet begun to build. At that point, in fact, the moment is unimaginable.

"Mrs. Carmichael," she begins. "We all saw how difficult you found yesterday, here in court, and obviously I've no wish to distress you further, but I would like to ask you a few more questions about the night you claim you were attacked by the victim in this case."

That word, "claim," goes through me as neatly and as smoothly as if she had slipped a very fine needle into my stomach. How do I disclaim that word? I am not *claiming* anything. It happened. I stare at her.

Ms. Bonnard stares back. "There's just a few details that I would like to clarify with you, if that's all right?"

"Yes, of course."

"So, earlier in that day, you were working at home, is that correct?"

"Yes."

"You got into your party dress, and you took the Tube into town, is that correct?"

"Yes, that's correct."

"And you walked straight from the Tube to the university building where the party was due to take place—I believe it is called the Dawson Complex?"

"Yes, that's right."

"And you were at the party with Mr. Craddock for some hours, drinking with him, before you went with him up to his secluded office on the fifth floor, an area of the building that you both knew to be empty at that time of night?"

"He said he needed to get some papers, from his office."

"Yes, you mentioned that yesterday, Mrs. Carmichael." Ms. Bonnard's tone is bafflingly neutral. "I just want to establish, at the party, when you were drinking and smoking with Mr. Craddock, you were for a time seated together outside, in a small courtyard at the back of the building?"

"Yes."

"And, during this period, when you were seated together on a low wall, can you recall placing your hand on Mr. Craddock's knee?"

"No, I can't."

"Can you recall him placing his hand on your knee?"

I think for a moment, and I'm not playing for time. "He may have done, yes, he did, I think, just above my knee, to steady me."

"Can you be more specific?"

"We were laughing about something, some joke someone else had made. There were other people with us at that point, they had pulled chairs over and were seated opposite us. One of them said something funny and I spluttered my drink. I think I spilled some, I was unsteady, I put my hand on his knee to steady myself."

"You put your hand on his knee?"

"Or he did, on mine, or both. I'm really not sure. It might be both."

"So you were both in open physical contact during this conversation?"

"Well, yes, but it was just—"

"You were flirting, weren't you?"

"Well, I wouldn't call it that, we were talking, joking, I suppose, there were a lot of other people—"

"Mrs. Carmichael, I don't really wish to get into a detailed discussion of the definition of flirting, but if I were to tell you that people at that party noticed you two together, that wouldn't surprise you, would it?"

"No, I suppose not." Did I flirt with George Craddock that night? It's entirely possible. But there's flirting and there's flirting. There is social flirting, the kind of flirting we all do, all the time, with colleagues, with the man in the queue behind us as we renew our Oyster card, with the waiter who brings our iced water. Then there is flirting with intent. There is what you and I did walking down the corridors of the Houses of Parliament. The two are unmistakably different. Surely anyone understands that?

"Mrs. Carmichael, did you, or did you not, tell George Craddock that you were promiscuous?"

"Absolutely not!" I feel a flush of triumph that she is asking something so absurd.

She lifts an immaculate eyebrow. "Really? You seem very certain."

"Yes, of course I'm certain."

"What would you say if I were to tell you that I can produce a witness who observed you doing just that?"

"They are mistaken. Everyone at that party was drunk. It was that sort of party."

She gives a small pause, during which she arches her back almost imperceptibly, and then says in a low voice, "I'm not talking about the party, Mrs. Carmichael."

"Then I have no idea what you are talking about."

She gives a sigh, looks down at her papers, leans forward with her elbow on her box of papers, pauses again. I stay silent and wait.

"Do you recall," she says slowly, "the occasion that you spent a week with George Craddock? It was nine months before he was killed."

"You mean when I went to the university to do my external examining, for the students to present their work?"

"Yes, that's exactly what I mean," she fires back quickly, as if she has caught me out in some obscure debating point.

"Yes, yes, I do. I spent every morning that week assessing students along with him and another lecturer. I had lunch with them both on the Friday. We were in complete agreement, it was just a professional—"

"You remember? That's good . . ." She gives another long pause, a sniff, looks down, then up. "Then you might also remember telling George Craddock in front of a witness that you were promiscuous."

"No." I am shaking my head.

"Did you, or did you not, describe yourself as, and I quote from a witness statement, which I'm happy to read in its entirety, as 'cheap and easy, that's me'?"

"Oh." The penny has dropped. "That's so ridiculous! I was talking about coffee. In the atrium."

"Did you use the phrase 'I like to pretend I'm classy but in fact I'm really easy'?"

"Yes, but I was talking about the coffee machine."

"Mrs. Carmichael, I'm not asking you for the context that surrounded that comment. I'm sure you were bantering away on all manner of subjects with Mr. Craddock, but please answer the question yes or no: 'cheap and easy,' did you use that exact phrase? Yes or no?"

"That's so stupid."

"Yes or no?"

"It's ridiculous, you're giving the—"

"Yes or no?"

"I'm trying to—"

"Yes or no!"

"Not in the way you mean!" This last response is a cry on my part. I cannot help myself. I cannot believe this is happening.

Having goaded me until I cried out, the young barrister gives up, glances first at the judge and then the jury as if to say, see? I've done my best. You get the picture. Now I know why they always appoint young women barristers to defend rapists, just as Laurence said—poor Laurence, who had a knife held to his throat in our kitchen for doing no more than bandying the truth around a little too lightly, as if he was spinning coins on the table. Now I know what I would have faced had I attempted to go the legal route and take Craddock to court, if I didn't already—and I know that I am facing only a fraction of it. I am on trial for murder, but if I was standing here as a victim of a sexual assault I would have been on trial in just the same way. *I'm glad*, I think, and I think it viciously and unequivocally, *I'm glad you beat him to death. He deserved everything he got.* And I know, as I think this, that my face is a mixture of fury and venom but no more than a fraction of the fury and the venom that I feel.

It goes on. Eventually, we break for lunch.

At lunchtime, Robert comes to see me in my cell. To my surprise, he doesn't seem unduly concerned about what Ms. Bonnard is up to, seems to think it is rather ham-fisted, in fact. "She's making a clumsy attempt to paint you as some sort of scarlet woman, but we've already established you are anything but."

"Why is she doing it?"

Robert shrugs. "She's clutching at straws. She thinks the worse she makes you look the better Costley will look."

The examination-in-chief went so well, Robert says, that he's not worried about what Ms. Bonnard is trying to do, or what the prosecution may do in their turn. Whatever they make me look like has no relevance to whether or not Mr. Costley has a personality disorder. He understands it's distressing for me but I shouldn't be unduly concerned about it—he could object but, actually, he thinks it's better to let her go on and make herself look unpleasant and vindictive, and it's drawing the prosecution's fire. If they were planning on taking the same angle, they will look repetitive. "You came over as a fine upstanding citizen yesterday," Robert says, and it is easy to believe his vision of me; it is so soothing. It is possible that, at that particular moment, I myself had forgotten the truth.

After lunch, I am taken up to the dock in the usual way, stand when the judge comes in, then am released into the court through the side door in the dock. I don't look over at the jury when I walk across the court this time, although everybody watches me, as before. The public gallery is open again now and I don't even glance up at them. I don't feel frightened of Ms. Bonnard at that particular point.

"Mrs. Carmichael," Ms. Bonnard begins. Her tone is completely neutral, just like yesterday—I wonder if I am in for more of the same, the horrible, insinuating questions. Instead, she begins with, "Just for a bit of background, and I'll hope you'll forgive me, you were quite a high-flier at university, weren't you? Took a first, I believe?"

I remember what I have been told, to direct my answers at the jury. "Yes, that is correct."

She spends some time, then, on my education, my marriage, my hobbies. After the way she went for me this morning, I can see the bafflement on the jury's faces and, eventually, the judge's expression takes on a slightly hangdog look. He frowns slightly when Ms. Bonnard begins on my marriage.

"You met your husband at university . . ."

"Yes."

After a while, the judge leans forward and clears his throat, and Ms. Bonnard says, "I'm sorry, My Lord, just one more question and then it would be the right juncture to take a short break. Mrs. Carmichael, would you describe your marriage as a happy marriage?"

"Yes, very happy."

"No trial separations, huge rows, wild affairs?" She smiles at me.

"No."

"Thank you, Mrs. Carmichael, that will do for now. We will continue after the break."

The judge turns to the jury and says, "Members of the jury, I would suggest no more than ten minutes." They rise and begin to file out. The judge says, "Ms. Bonnard . . ." and Ms. Bonnard rises to her feet, gives a bow, and asks permission to approach the bench.

DI Cleveland leans back in his chair, puffing out his chest, lifting his arms above his head, then lowering them slowly. Craddock's father is motionless in his wheelchair. The family liaison officer is talking to him quietly, but he shows no sign of response. I look over at you, but you are sitting in your chair with your head tipped back and your eyes closed. *It's nearly over now . . .* I think. As far as I can tell, everything will ride on the closing statements.

The break takes longer than anticipated. The judge comes in and the usher goes to fetch the jury, then comes back with the message that one of them is still using the bathroom facilities. The usher delivers this message with the air of someone who is expecting to be boiled in oil as a result. From the expression on the judge's face, it seems as though he might, indeed, boil the usher in oil, but that is nothing compared to what he will do to the hapless jury member upon the panel's return. The judge lets his forearm drop to his table with a noise, whips off his glasses, and says, "I would like my jury back in court *now . . .*" The usher bows again, exits. DI Cleveland is standing by the prosecution table while all this is going on, talking quietly to Mrs. Price, and the judge turns to him and snarls, "Officer, please! Your place!" and bulky DI Cleveland snaps ramrod straight, like a toy soldier, flushes with embarrassment, bows, and returns to his seat, even though half the other people in the court are still wandering around unseated.

I have remained in the witness box throughout the break and am beginning to feel that was a mistake. How much longer can this take? A wave of weariness settles over me.

This time, Ms. Bonnard gets to her feet very slowly, and I feel something, some small shred of anxiety. I glance at Robert, but he is still looking down at his papers.

"I would like to take you back a bit, in your career," Ms. Bonnard says, "I hope you will bear with me." At that point, the middle-aged black man wearing a pink shirt and sitting on the far right of the jury box yawns broadly. I register how tired everyone seems to be, not just me. It's the close air in the courtroom, I think, that doesn't help. The air-conditioning seems to produce an irritating hum without having any noticeable effect.

"Can you just remind the court," she continues, "when was it you first attended a committee hearing at the Houses of Parliament? How long ago now?"

"Four years ago," I reply.

"That was a House of Commons Select Committee on—"

"No," I say, "actually, it was a Standing Committee at the House of Lords. Standing Committees don't exist anymore, but at the time the House of Lords had four of them, each covering a different area of public life." I covered all this ground with Robert yesterday, but I continue. "I was appearing before the Standing Committee on Science to give evidence on developments in computer sequencing in genome mapping." I wonder if Ms. Bonnard is trying to make me look careerist, in the way that television dramas always present a woman's work ambitions as somehow pathological.

"But you used to work full-time at the Beaufort Institute, didn't you?"

My darling, it took me far longer than it should have done to realize that what she was homing in on was not the ambitious nature of my career but its geography.

"Can you just tell the court where the Beaufort Institute is located?"

"It's in Charles II Street."

"That's parallel with Pall Mall, I believe. It runs down to St. James's Square Gardens?"

"Yes."

"There are quite a lot of institutes round there, aren't there? Institutes, private clubs, research libraries . . ." She glances at the jury and gives a small smile, "Corridors of power, that sort of stuff."

"I'm not . . . I . . ."

"Forgive me, how long was it you worked for the Beaufort Institute?"

I hear a note of irritation creeping into my voice. It's because I'm tired. "I still do. But full-time, eight years."

"Ah, yes, I'm sorry, you've said that already. And during those eight years, you commuted every day, bus and Tube?"

"Tube mostly, yes."

"You walked from Piccadilly?"

"Piccadilly Tube, usually, yes."

"And lunch hours, coffee breaks, plenty of places to eat around there? Pubs after work, et cetera?"

At this, Mrs. Price sighs, her hand goes up. Given his annoyance at the delay at break time, I am surprised the judge hasn't intervened already, but he merely looks over his glasses at the young woman barrister and she raises the flat of her hand in response. "Forgive me, My Lord, I'm getting there, yes . . ."

She turns back to me and lowers her voice a tone or two. "So in total, you've been working in or visiting the Borough of Westminster for, what, around twelve years? Longer?"

"Longer, probably," I say, and it starts there. The moment builds, it swells and builds—a sense of unease located somewhere inside me, identifiable only as a slight clutching of my solar plexus.

"So," she says, and her voice becomes slow, "it would be fair to say that with all that commuting and walking from the Tube and lunch hours and so on, that you are very familiar with the area?"

It is building. My breath begins to deepen. I can feel that my chest is rising and falling, imperceptibly at first, but the more I try to control myself, the more obvious it becomes. The atmosphere inside the court tightens, everyone can sense it. The judge is staring at me. Am I imagining it, or has the jury member in the pink shirt on the periphery of my vision sat up a little straighter, leaned forward in his seat? All at once, I dare not look at the jury directly. I dare not look at you, sitting in the dock.

I nod, suddenly unable to speak. I know that in a few seconds, I will start to hyperventilate. I know this even though I have never done it before.

The barrister's voice is low and sinuous. "You're familiar with the shops, the cafés . . ." Sweat prickles the nape of my neck. My scalp is tightening. She pauses. She has noted my distress and wants me to know that I have guessed correctly: I know where she is going with this line of questioning, and she knows I know. "The small side streets . . ." She pauses again. "The back alleyways . . ."

And that is the moment. I glance at you, sitting in the dock, and you put your head in your hands.

I am hyperventilating openly now, breathing in great deep gulps. Poor Robert is staring at me, puzzled and alarmed. *There is something she hasn't told me.*

The prosecution team is staring at me too, Mrs. Price and her junior, the woman from the Crown Prosecution Service on the table behind them, and on yet another row of tables behind that; DI Cleveland and his team, Craddock's father and his FLO by the door. Everyone is fixed on me—apart from you. You are not looking at me anymore.

"You are familiar, aren't you?" says Ms. Bonnard in her satin, sinuous voice, "with a small back alleyway called Apple Tree Yard."

I close my eyes. Ms. Bonnard does not speak for a long time. When I remain silent too, she says, still softly, "Apple Tree Yard . . ." She pronounces the three words quite contemplatively, as if she is remembering having been there herself. She does this so that the words, the significance of the words, that is, will hang in the air of the courtroom, the recycled, air-conditioned air we have all been breathing for nearly three weeks. I open my eyes and look at her. She looks back. She wants everyone in the courtroom, but especially the jury, to know this is a significant moment. It is all unnecessary, because my deep breathing is signaling the significance more unequivocally than any theatrics from a barrister could do. *All smoke and mirrors, you know*: all of it, even the forensics. The barristers have to give the jury what they expect in order to get the result they want. Ms. Bonnard is giving the jury what they expect and more: a witness caught out on the stand. What more could they ask for?

The logical part of my brain, the cortex, is functioning well enough for these thoughts to slide through my head as I stare at her, even while the intuitive part, the amygdala, is so confused I don't know what to think or feel: my thoughts are like rats in a burning building, running along one wall after another.

"Apple Tree Yard," Ms. Bonnard continues, meeting my gaze, "is the alleyway in the Borough of Westminster, St. James's to be precise, where you had sex with your lover, Mark Costley, in a public street, quite quickly I imagine, during rush hour, standing up in a doorway, before you went on to a party where you got drunk and had sex with Mr. George Craddock in his office in the Dawson Complex, while your students cleared up from the party downstairs. The next day, you told Mr. Costley that you had had sex with George Craddock and claimed that he forced himself upon you. Sometime later, you complained again to Mark Costley, saying that George Craddock was bothering you. You asked him to sort him out. You drove Mr. Costley round to Mr. Craddock's house, in the full knowledge of what might happen. Mr. Costley, your lover, went in to confront Mr. Craddock, in a state of high tension, distressed by your story, and was taunted by Mr. Craddock by the fact that you had been perfectly willing, whereupon Mr. Costley struck him several times, leading to his death."

I am staring at Ms. Bonnard. Everyone else in the court is staring at me. Why doesn't Robert intervene? Why isn't he on his feet? He isn't on his feet because he is as astonished by this turn of events as anyone else. He is planning a strategy. Is he? Is that what he is doing? There is so much in what Ms. Bonnard has said that I want to deny, but it needs unpicking first. All I manage is a feeble, curiously thoughtful, "That isn't true . . ." but I still don't look at the jury.

"Mrs. Carmichael," Ms. Bonnard says. She doesn't look at me as she speaks, she looks straight ahead, as if she is musing to herself, inviting the jury to observe. Her voice is firm but not particularly accusatory. She is doing no more than stating simple fact. "Only yesterday, you were in the witness box, just as you are now, and, under oath, you told this court that you had a happy marriage, had never had an affair, and insisted that your relationship with Mr. Mark Costley was platonic. You've lied to your husband, you've lied to the police, and you've lied to this court." She pauses again, looks at me, mildly. "You're a liar, aren't you?"

"No . . . ," I say weakly.

"Do you want me to give examples of each of those people you have lied to? All over again? You had an affair with Mr. Mark Costley that you hid from your husband, from the police, and from this court. Sworn witness statements, the court records . . . ?" Her voice is slightly raised, with a note of outrage. "Do I really have to go through it again? You've *lied* to your husband, you've *lied* to the police and you've *lied* to this court!"

"*Yes*," I whisper. I will say anything to be allowed off this witness stand. I would even welcome being back in my concrete cell underground with its ludicrous bright yellow walls and bright blue floor, as long as they let me curl up on the wooden bench. I will do or say anything if only they will leave me alone.

"I'm sorry?" She cocks her head at me in query but she is looking at the jury.

"Yes."

She lets the syllable hang in the air, like a star, then she says quietly, "No further questions, My Lord," and sits down.

23

There will come a time, after all this, when I will think of apple blossom. I will lie in a hammock strung between the apple trees in my garden and stare up at the constellations of flowers, white against the black branches, and wonder whether once, in some preindustrial era, Apple Tree Yard really was a yard with apple trees in it, or whether it was just a street name plucked from the ether, as so many are.

That time is distant now. Now, I am still in the witness box facing hostile questioning from Mrs. Price, although thanks to the efforts of your defense barrister, Ms. Bonnard, there was very little work for the prosecution to do.

Robert did his best. As soon as his turn came, he asked for time to confer with his client before he proceeded—the request was denied. Hamstrung by his palpable ignorance of our relationship, he concentrated instead on Craddock, reestablished the violence of the assault, my fear in the face of his reappearance in my life—but my admission rang in the room the whole while, like a Christmas jingle in a department store. And inevitably, in light of what I had just conceded, the assault seemed less bad: I could see it on the jury's faces. The black man in the pink shirt stared at me, expressionless; the older man of military bearing pursed his lips; the Chinese woman looked openly shocked. For each of them, their view of me was changed by this new knowledge. My actions, and the actions that were done to me—they had replaced me. I am not what I did, I wanted to say to them, or what was done to me: but as far as other people are concerned, we are indeed the sum of our actions and the things that act upon us. It is all the evidence they have. Our interior lives may be wildly different from how we are perceived, but how can we expect other people to understand that? They cannot climb inside our skin, however intimate with us they may be.

I see myself reflected in the jury's eyes and it is like looking in a fairground mirror that bulges and stretches, distorting me almost but not entirely beyond recognition. Three decades of being the most respectable science professional or suburban mother count for nothing set against one fuck in a doorway.

The next day, it is time for the summing up. The prosecution goes first and Mrs. Price has quite an armory at her disposal. The forensics look very bad for you, and in her attempt to defend you from the barrage of science ranged against you, Ms. Bonnard has handed me to the Crown on a plate.

Ms. Bonnard's demolition of me continues in her summing up.

"Ladies and gentlemen, you were given to understand, at the beginning of this trial, that my client was going to plead not guilty to murder on the grounds of diminished responsibility, and that we would be advancing evidence to prove that he has a personality disorder. Ladies and gentlemen, it is still our contention that Mr. Costley does indeed suffer from a serious psychological disorder, but you no longer need to feel that has been proved here in court for you to acquit him. Let me explain . . ."

Since the revelation to the court of our affair, you are now pleading not guilty on the grounds of loss of control. The "identifying trigger" that Jas told me about is, in effect, me. Ms. Bonnard continues, "We shall never know the truth of what happened between George Craddock and Yvonne Carmichael that night, the night she had sex with both Mark Costley and him within the space of a few hours, the first in a doorway in Apple Tree Yard, the other in an office in a university building after a drunken party. George Craddock is dead and cannot explain or defend his actions, so we only have Yvonne Carmichael's word for it that the encounter was not consensual. But we can assume that an encounter of some sort or another took place, and that Yvonne Carmichael told her lover, my client, about it, and that she later claimed she was being pestered by George Craddock. So whose idea was it that they drive to Craddock's flat that day? I put it to you that it was Yvonne Carmichael's idea. Mark Costley's only thought that day was to protect the woman he loved . . ." She gives a long pause at this point. "And what evidence do you have, ladies and gentlemen, that Mark is the kind of man who would want to protect the woman he loved? Well . . ." She gives a bleak little smile. "You could adduce that from the way he kept their affair secret for so long, in order to protect her, going so far as to attempt to withhold it from this court, prepared to take the blame for what happened for as long as possible, until even he began to realize that he had to tell the truth."

I sit in the dock. And I listen to this story. And it comes to me that all you need for a story is a series of facts that can be strung together. A spider sometimes strings a thread from a bush to a fence post several feet away, quite implausibly, it often seems, but it's still a web.

"Who knows what sparked off the violence between those two men that afternoon? Who knows whether Mark Costley, overwrought and distressed and desperate to protect a woman he loved, a woman he thought to be in a situation of genuine threat from George Craddock—whether that is true or not we shall never know—who knows what state of anxiety he was in as he challenged George Craddock, and who knows how Craddock responded, taunting him, perhaps, with his lover's promiscuity, a taunt that Mark found unbearable in the light of what he believed to have happened . . ."

It was a brave attempt, I have to give her that, but there was no evidence to support the theory that Craddock provoked you, was there, my love? Loss of control was always going to be a thin defense. You should have stuck to dim rep.

Who knows? as Ms. Bonnard might say. I would like to know. Perhaps you will tell me one day. I have my own theory, and it goes like this. I don't think you knew you were really going to kill George Craddock that day. If you had been planning on killing him, you wouldn't have asked me to collect you at the Tube and drive you there—why have a potential witness? You wouldn't have wanted a witness to murder, but you did need a witness to heroism, to your own view of yourself as a man who would do the right thing. What happened that day was a joint enterprise, but not in the way the prosecution meant. You wanted the joint fantasy. You wanted me to see you as my avenging hero. You took the change of clothes along so that you could tell me later you had gone prepared, and then tell me that it hadn't proved necessary, because you had taught him a lesson. He wouldn't be bothering me again. You were quite prepared to do him harm, to frighten him, to break the law in doing so, but you had no intention of killing him. You knew how hard that would be to get away with. You are many things, but you are not a fool.

Did he taunt you, my love? Did he tell you that he had enjoyed it, what he did, and that I had too? It's hard to imagine Craddock being that defiant to your face. Perhaps he was fooled by your average build and casual dress. Perhaps he had no apprehension of danger. Or perhaps you attacked him to frighten him and would have done so whatever he had said to you.

But he fell, didn't he? He fell to the floor. And at some point, something happened, some rage took over. Whether he taunted you, or whether you were merely caught up in the adrenaline of what you were doing, at some point you did indeed lose control. He fell, or you knocked him over. He struck the back of his head on the edge of the countertop in the kitchenette. And once he was on the floor, you did not stop. You stamped on him. You beat and kicked him to death. It is possible it took only seconds.

At some point, you stopped. At some point, you bent down, to see what you had done.

I wonder what happened then, my love. I wonder what happened in your head as that man breathed his last, the fine spray of expirated blood dusting your cheek as you bent over him—despite the time you had to dispose of the clothes and clean yourself, his DNA was still discovered on your arrest. DNA gets everywhere. At some point, you must have stood up, looked down at him as he lay on the floor, and I imagine there might well have been a moment when your mind sheared in two, as surely as the nerve cells in your victim's brain were sheared, when part of you was still living in your own narrative, the one you created and controlled, and the other part of your brain was trying to absorb the hard reality of what you had just done. For here is the thing about death and you must have realized it then—its irreversibility. Here, at last, was the fantasy that could not be put back in a box when the rest of your life, real life, intruded. Here was a permanent disassociation, the disassociation of George Craddock from life itself. At some point in the moments that followed, you would have had to compute that you were no longer living in a drama of your own making. You had lost control of the drama. It had happened and you could not make it unhappen when you returned to your wife and children in the suburbs. You had killed someone.

I can only imagine what happened then, and I imagine you walking away from the body for a few steps, thinking it through, pushing both hands, bloodied hands, into the hair either side of your temple, that wiry brown hair with its touch of gray, then turning back and seeing yes, the body was still there. It really had happened. The paradox of a corpse: life is gone, fled, but what remains is immutably present, and the fleeing of the life within is what means that the body itself can never flee. All those horror stories where corpses get up and walk again or haunt their killers, they were right on the nose. When you want the corpse to go away, what you are really wanting is to reverse your act. If you could breathe life into your victim once more, then he would be able to rise, turn his back, depart. I envisage you walking in small circles around that flat, steadying your breathing, unable to steady your mind.

But there must have come a point—and my dear, I wonder how long it took—when the two sheared halves of your brain rejoined to face the new reality. You were once a cop, after all, so you are a man who has had professional training in how to think on his feet. I wonder if you did it consciously or subconsciously—I'm not sure it matters. Either way, perhaps after some minutes of walking in slow circles, you must have chosen your route out of there, out of the circles. Your preparations for all eventualities, the clothing, the shoes, all that meant that

you could not call 999 and report an accidental death. You were experienced enough, calm and rational enough, to know that. If it had not
been for the preparations you so carefully made for a fantasy murder,
you might have stood a much better chance of getting away with the
real one. You could have told them what really happened, confessed to
a fight in which a man had been accidentally killed, be distraught
about the whole thing. Anyone with any sense knows that, long term,
that would be the best way to avoid a murder charge. But everything
you had done up until then to feed your fantasies was exactly what
made reality look suspicious. So you gambled, with your freedom, and
mine. You were not thinking of me sitting outside in the car—you were
not thinking of me at all. You were thinking that if you called an
ambulance now, that would be it—but if you took the high-risk strategy
of fleeing, there was a chance, a very slender one, but a chance—if the
body was not discovered for a while, if the CCTV cameras between
that flat and the station were not working, as they often aren't . . .

At some point, maybe there was some satisfaction in your head. It
had finally happened. Your paranoid fantasies had come true. You were
not just a man bored with his job who had invented a more exciting
narrative—the narrative was a reality now. You had made it so. I imagine you would have swung into action quite efficiently. You would
have addressed the issue of forensic evidence, retracing your steps from
the moment you entered the flat, wiped any surfaces that needed wiping with a cloth you found in the kitchen, the one that smeared George
Craddock's dilute blood in a circle on the floor. You would have checked
carefully that nothing was left behind. You would have gone to the hallway mirror and wiped any traces of blood from your face or hair. Only
when these tasks were performed would you have stood behind the
entrance door to the flat and taken the spare trousers out of your Nike
holdall and put them on, changed your trainers. At this point, I imagine you to be in the grip of something close to euphoria.

The sight of me, sitting in the car, patiently waiting for you, was that
not enough? Was that not enough for the sobering reality of what you
had done, what you were risking on my behalf as well as your own
but without my permission? Was there no point at which you looked
at my face as you approached the car and felt some small twinge of

compunction? You forgot me, by which I mean you forgot me as a real person, with her own needs and desires, her own narrative. By then, I was no more than a bit part in your story. *Drive.*

Courtroom Number Eight, Central Criminal Court, Old Bailey, EC4, so clean and modern and efficient. But even in this sterile, wooden room, with the square fluorescent lights in the ceiling and the blanket of weariness cast over its habitués, even here, there is an unmistakable frisson as the jury returns to the room. I know, just as you know, how much is at stake for you and me, but it is only as we are all bid to rise that I am reminded by looking around at everyone else in the courtroom just how much is at stake for them too. Each victory or defeat counts for or against a counsel. Ms. Bonnard is compulsively clearing her throat. The judge has made his feelings known in the summing up, so his reputation within the business is at stake too—this is the only time in the whole trial, after all, that he is not the undisputed autocrat. The police officers know what result they want, of course, and DI Cleveland is adjusting his tie, flipping it beneath his jacket and shrugging his shoulders in a small movement, as if making himself neat will produce the right result. Even the jury, who are now entering from the same door as the judge—they have been held in a special room while they deliberate—even the all-powerful jury don't get to leave this court unscathed. In a few moments, at their say-so, a man and a woman will either walk free from the Old Bailey, to return to their families, their homes, their ordinary lives—or they will be taken away, to the underworld, another world, for many years to come. The members of the jury will have to live with that decision for the rest of their lives.

As I rise, I glance up at the public gallery, and it is only then that I see, sitting next to Susannah, my husband, Guy. He is staring at me, waiting for me to look up and see him. He is dressed in a pale blue shirt and a blazer, his thick straight hair clean and his face broad and open, looking at me as if drinking in the sight of me, trying to work out everything about how I am. It is too much. My knees begin to shake; my life, my real life, up there, a few feet away—I know he wants to support me but it is a torment. I try a smile, and he tries one back, but even he cannot prevent the fear from showing in his face. Susannah gives me a hopeful grin and Guy lifts a hand in a tiny wave of acknowledgment, a little apologetically I think, because he must know that his unexpected appearance will be making my head reel. "Sorry," he mouths. Later, he will tell me that he kept his promise to stay away from the trial, but he had made no such promise about staying away for the verdict. He came back from Morocco after a weekend with Carrie and Sath and Adam. He has been at our home the whole time. Susannah has been calling him with daily updates. He knows everything, as he stands there in the gallery and I stand in the dock, and we look at each other for a moment or two before we turn our heads to watch the jury file in.

I am standing. Miraculously, I am on my feet. It is miraculous because I cannot breathe. My chest is like a sack of rocks pressing against the rest of my body and I even have time to consider, briefly, if this might be what having a heart attack is like. I know it isn't, though. The onset of a heart attack is often accompanied—I was once told by a friend in cardiology—by an overwhelming sense of doom, a black descent into a world that feels unfamiliar but inevitable. My breathlessness isn't producing that result; on the contrary, it is sending me soaring—I am as light as air, for it has suddenly come to me: it is nearly over, thank God thank God . . . I am already imagining stumbling from the dock, walking through the court and out into the corridor. I am imagining running down the stairs to the exit, Susannah—and now Guy, yes, Guy—waiting for me in the street outside. I permit myself the images I have been avoiding for the whole of my trial: my kitchen, the shabby leather armchair by the double doors that lead out into the garden, where I often sit with a coffee—at this time of year it will be bathed in sun; Guy upstairs working, distracted and absent; my son sitting on the back step smoking on one of his rare visits home; my daughter cooking with her boyfriend in the kitchen—they like to cook for us when they visit. These are the separate but interlinked pictures that appear in my head, snapshots of my previous life, my domestic life, it is all so near to me now. When will the kids be back from Morocco? This weekend, they said, come what may.

But first, the verdict.

Relationships are about stories, not truth. Alone, as individuals, we each have our own personal mythologies, the stories we tell in order to make sense of ourselves to ourselves. That generally works fine as long as we stay sane and single, but the minute you enter an intimate relationship with another person there is an automatic dissonance between your story about yourself and his or her story about you.

I remember this from the trial. I remember how, when the matronly Mrs. Price rose to her feet to give her opening statement, she was so calm, so well prepared. She had her story, complete. She did not need even to clear her throat. She glanced at her feet briefly before she began, to indicate, I guessed, her humility before the truth she was about to outline for the court. It wasn't *her* story, her downward glance seemed to say, oh, no, it was what *really happened*. Whatever my feelings toward that woman and the processes she represented, I had sufficient detachment to observe and admire this: she had a hypothesis, just as I have hypotheses. Hers was tested by assertion, by trickery if you like, by the misplacement of evidence from context to create that smoke-and-mirrors effect, so I'm not sure that the scientific analogy really holds water, but it did make me think this much: as a scientist, I have told more stories than I ever realized, or admitted to. You, Mark Costley, were a fantasist, a person who could manage his normal life only as long as it was propped up by a series of self-flattering tales in which you were a spy or master seducer or avenging hero and who knows what else. Your stories had become so necessary they had claimed you, detached you from any sense of objective reality. And the end of all our stories was this: you and I went to prison.

24

The day after my mother died, I followed my father from room to room. I did not approach him, or try to touch him. I was not seeking physical comfort, merely his presence. My mother had discharged herself from the Community Residential Adult Mental Health Unit in Redhill. She had been doing well in the weeks running up to her death, but later there was an inquiry about why she had been allowed to leave when she was known to be at risk. She had walked until she found the railway line—the same line my father used to commute to work in London and the same line I myself would use in years to come. She found a place where the line was accessible by easing through a wire fence— she must have ducked her head to get between the wires—and a scramble down a steep bank. A witness saw her descend the bank by sitting on her backside with her knees raised and her feet flat against the soil, placing her hands either side of her body, letting herself down the bank slowly, as if she was afraid of falling. The driver of the train said at the inquest that although she was standing in the middle of the tracks, between the rails, she was facing away from the oncoming train, and he wondered if she did that because she didn't want her face to haunt him. I wasn't allowed to attend the inquest but I heard my father and aunt talking about it later, what the driver said, and how warm it had been in the coroner's court, when it was so cold outside.

My memories of my mother are still sharp, although there are only a few of them. I remember sitting at the kitchen table with her, doing cat's cradle—I must have been four or five at the time. We were doing it with rough green wool. She was holding her fingers up for me to weave the wool and I was singing some vague chant I had learned at school. We weren't very good at it, not as good as I was with my friends anyway—it was more a holey cobweb than a cradle. Her legs were bare, tucked neatly under the chair in which she was sitting. Her ankles were chunks of bone above her slippers.

The day after my mother died, I followed my father from room to room. When he got up from the kitchen table to go and sit in the sitting room, I trailed after him and sat down on the arm of the chair he was in. When he went upstairs, I followed him up there too, and when he went into the bathroom and locked the door, unable to face me I think, I sat down outside and leaned my back against the door, hugging my knees and waiting for him to come out.

It is spring, the year after our trial. I am at home. My son has put up a hammock in the garden, a long one made of tough blue plastic rope. He has hung it between the two apple trees. I spend a lot of time in the hammock, wrapped in a gray blanket that Guy found in the spare room. It is unseasonably warm for April. I lie wrapped in the blanket, swinging gently between the apple trees, looking at the postwinter sky.

I was released from Holloway two days ago. Adam has been living at home the whole time I have been in prison. He says he has had enough of the scene in Manchester but I'm not sure I believe him. I think he may have moved back home to be with Guy. I was worried that my release might drive him away again, but when they brought me home he took me out into the garden and showed me the hammock, and said, "It's so warm, we thought that, after everything . . . we thought you might like to be outside."

That night, the night of my release, there was no alcohol or celebration. Carrie arrived from Leeds and, as she had driven down, she came with a car boot full of fresh food. Everything she made for me that evening was fresh: four different salads, an arrangement of exotic fruit on a platter. We all sat round the kitchen table, more or less in silence, and they all watched me pick at the fruit with a fork.

Carrie could stay only one night, then she had to get back up north.

She and Sathnam are getting married in the summer. She has a lot to arrange.

Guy and Adam are looking after me. I see them exchange looks across me from time to time.

Sometimes, as I lie in the hammock, I can hear the phone ring inside the house. The back door to the kitchen has been left open, so I can hear the murmur of Guy's voice as he answers. "Yes, she's fine," I imagine him saying. "She's very thin, but she's fine."

Adam has been helping his father clear out the garage. He looks well, and wiry, in baggy combat trousers and a cutoff T-shirt, still with the stubble that suits him. I know that when I am well again, there is a danger I will drive him away, but I am not well. I lie in the hammock and stare at the sky.

It is just over two years since you and I first met. I was released from prison two days ago, after serving three months of a six-month sentence for perjury—I pleaded guilty at the first available opportunity and so received a relatively light sentence at my January trial. I am out on license. I am free, but not free. If I breach the terms of my license, I could be recalled at any time. You were found not guilty of murder but guilty of manslaughter. You were sentenced to fourteen years in prison. With the time you spent on remand and a reduction for good behavior, you could be out five or six years from now. I was found not guilty of murder or manslaughter and released from the dock but was arrested for perjury immediately afterward, in the corridor outside. There were three officers waiting for me as soon as I left Courtroom Number Eight. DI Cleveland followed me out and watched with his pale eyes.

It worked, partially, your betrayal of me. The scales tipped. My lying to the court made you seem less guilty; the bad things I had done made you seem less bad. You were found guilty of manslaughter but not guilty of murder, on the grounds of loss of control.

305

I lie in my hammock and I stare at the sky and I think about you, my lover, Mark Costley, an ex-policeman who worked in an administrative capacity in security at the Houses of Parliament, who liked outdoor sex and spinning dramatic stories because it made him feel less ordinary. The spies didn't want you, my love. If they had taken you, none of this would have happened.

My lover, Mark: who or what was he? A man for whom the normal story of life was just too normal, a man who sought thrills, mostly through sex but also through stories, only to find that each successive thrill was not enough? Just as George Craddock's pornography habit became more and more hard-core until it left him unable to make the distinction between the thoughts in his head and the real thing, so your need for an exciting story about yourself led to sexual adventures, to full-blown affairs, and then to violence. The trouble with stories is they are addictive.

Guy comes and stands on the back step. He sees me looking at him and smiles. He has a cup of tea in his hand. He raises it to his mouth, takes a sip, then lifts the cup in a gesture that means, *do you want one?* I shake my head, close my eyes so that he will go away. When I open them, he is still watching me, but then Adam appears at his elbow, holding up a sanding machine that we must have had for over twenty years. Guy and Adam exchange some joke about the sanding machine and go back into the house.

About an hour later, Adam emerges onto the back step, sits down without looking at me, and begins to roll a roll-up. I look up at the house to see that Guy is standing in an upstairs window, staring out into the garden. He is on his mobile phone. He is talking while gazing out at the middle distance but after a moment or so, his gaze drops, and he sees me looking up at him. Immediately, instinctively, he turns away, turns his back and walks away from the window so I can't watch him while he talks. I wonder whom he is talking to. I wonder if it's Rosa.

Later that day, Susannah comes round. She comes out into the garden. She is holding a disposable cardboard tray with four Styrofoam cups of coffee wedged into it, and a paper bag full of pastries. She stands for a minute, framed in our back doorway, her tall, slim figure motionless, and looks at me in the hammock as if she is trying to make a brief assessment before she approaches. Then she smiles, walks over, picking her way carefully across the grass in pale wedge sandals. She sits on the edge of the rockery a couple of feet away, puts down the tray, carefully extracts two of the cups, brings one over to me. "Hey you," she says, and bends to kiss me, holding the hot coffee out of harm's way, "I thought you'd maybe like a proper coffee." She puts the bag of pastries down on my stomach, where it remains untouched.

I wiggle my way up, awkwardly, in the hammock, so I can sip the coffee without pouring it over myself. Susannah returns to the rockery with her cup, where she can tip her face to the sun. We sit sipping our coffee in silence for a while. Then we talk for a bit, in a desultory fashion, about how I am and how she is, about what I might do in the coming weeks, about how I will have to take it easy for a while. At one point, she looks toward the house and says, "I thought Guy and Adam were coming out to join us." I don't reply.

Susannah, the friend I dared not hope for when I was growing up; I see her hesitate. She is struggling with something, pausing, wanting to say it with care. I wait, and eventually she starts quietly, "Every day, you know, every day at the end of court. It was always so terrible, leaving the public gallery and looking down at you, knowing you were going to be led away by those people, that you had no choice, that you were going back to prison. Every day I would go down the steps into the outside and it didn't matter if it was pouring with rain, I would breathe in deeply and I couldn't believe that I could just walk away and you couldn't. It was so strange. And I'd see that old couple sometimes, talking, the old bloke was the worst, going on about how, in his opinion, you were worse than he was. I nearly pushed the old bastard down the stairs . . ." Then she gives me an infinitely gentle look. "First thing I had to do, before I even got on the train, was ring Guy, every day, I had to ring him. He made me promise. Every day, I'd go and collect my phone from that café and then I would stand outside, even if it was raining, and turn it on immediately, and I wouldn't even check my messages or e-mails because I knew Guy would be waiting for my call. And every day I'd have to tell him everything. What did you look like? Were you holding up? Who had been in court that day and how had they done? Was your barrister doing a good job? How did I think it was going? I'd be walking down to the station, and I'd go past the bar where the cops were all drinking pints and I'd cross the road keeping one eye on the buses and taxis because that bit of the road was always really busy, and the whole time I'd be talking to Guy. Even if my train was due, I couldn't go into the station in case I lost the signal before I told him everything."

I don't reply. She looks down at Guy and Adam's coffees and I know she is worrying they are getting cold. It's unseasonably sunny for April but the air temperature is still chilly.

I wonder when it happened. What was the moment of your betrayal? It would have happened in the cells at the Old Bailey, I suppose, during one of the consultations that we both had with our respective barristers. You would have been impressed by that cool young woman, against your better judgment in some ways. Her obvious competence would have won you over. You would come to see her as your avenging angel, or good fairy, perhaps.

Perhaps it was quite early on, when you watched Ms. Bonnard plead for a delay after she had read Dr. Sanderson's report on her phone on the way to court that morning, perhaps that was when you realized how serious it was. Perhaps it was when you were in the cells, reading the report on yourself, the one in which he rubbished so effectively any diagnosis of a borderline personality disorder with elements of narcissistic personality disorder. I imagine that Ms. Bonnard came to see you after she had won that adjournment. I imagine that you watched the look on her face as she explained to you, gently, that this was likely to inhibit your defense of diminished responsibility, that the debate over diagnosis that would go on in the witness box would be—I am sure she used this word—"problematic." Us. They say it a lot, the barristers. "It's going to be problematic for us."

Perhaps you thought of it then, or perhaps it was when you were in the dock later, sitting only a few feet away from me, watching Dr. Sanderson on the stand, watching how the usually brilliant Ms. Bonnard failed to shake him an inch. Here is the strange thing: he came over as a horrible man, a man who had not one ounce of human kindness in him, but no one in that courtroom would have doubted his verdict on your sanity by the end of that cross-examination. How did you feel, listening to that, hearing your chances of a not guilty verdict drown beneath the weight of his certainty? It might have been even later, of course. It might have been not until you saw Dr. Sadiq falter on the stand, or heard the first of the authorities Mrs. Price quoted against her. How did you feel then? How hot does the metal floor of the cage have to get before the chimpanzee puts its baby down on that floor and stands on it?

At some point you made your decision, the decision that led your defense counsel to change the basis of your not guilty plea to loss of control. No counsel does something like that on a whim, you would have known that—the prosecution has a field day if the nature of the defense changes midtrial. Your counsel would have consented to perform this loop-the-loop only if new information came to light during a trial. She had to have a reason, so you gave her a reason. You looked at Ms. Bonnard as she sat across the table from you in the cells at the Old Bailey, and you gave her your best stare, the open, direct one, the honest one, the one that always made a small muscle in my stomach contract, and you said to her, "There's something I haven't told you."

April ends and with it the sunshine disappears. We are in for a rainy May. Adam and Guy have a discussion over breakfast one morning as to whether it's all right to leave the hammock up or whether they should bring it in. Guy says if it was made of real rope, they would have to dismantle it, but as it's plastic, it will be okay.

I move around the house like a ghost. I don't want to get better, to start to be in charge of my life again, in case it drives Adam away.

I spend a lot of time in my study, pretending that I am catching up with e-mails, reconnecting with my life. This is an adequate explanation.

Sometimes, I leave the study and go and stand on the landing and listen to Guy and Adam moving around the house, talking to each other. Sometimes Guy works and Adam strums his guitar in his old bedroom. Occasionally, one of them goes out, but they never leave the house at the same time. Once, when Adam has gone out for a bit, I sit on the top step of the landing and listen to Guy downstairs, lumbering around like a big wounded bear and all at once his loneliness down there seems unbearable. I can't stand the thought that he might be hurt, and hiding his hurt until I am well again, so I go downstairs, but when I get downstairs, he is in the kitchen and suddenly I don't want to go in, so I go and sit, uselessly, in the sitting room, and after a while he comes in with a mug of tea and puts it in front of me. Then he ambles out of the room with a demeanor that someone who didn't know him would imagine to be casual. He has perfected this air of slow, methodical busyness around small domestic tasks. I want to call him back, to tell him to sit with me, so I can say, I want you to feel better, just don't speak. It's an unfair thing to say, so I don't say anything at all.

Guy believes that I fell out of love with him. He has tried, and failed, to apply his thinking during his own affair. He believes he was capable of loving Rosa while still loving me because he is a man—but as I am a woman and more sincere, I couldn't do it that way. So he has come to the conclusion that I could have done what I did with Mark Costley only if I didn't love him anymore. He is wrong. I have been more male about this than he could possibly imagine. His biological determinism on this issue is based partly on science and partly on chivalry, but he is wrong on both counts. His generosity of thinking toward me is causing him more pain than he need feel.

I did not fall out of love with him, not at any stage. I did not fall out of love with our lives here, in this house, with the world we had built around us. We built it for a reason. It suited us. It was where we were meant to be. I fell out of love with something more subtle and specific. I fell out of love with the way I had coped, over the years, with the hard work I had done, with the sacrifices I had made, with my ability to raise two children, in however compromised a fashion, while doing all the other things I did.

I had a sudden memory, while I sat on our sofa sipping the tea that

Guy had made me, of how when the children were small, I would have a kettle and coffee cup all ready in my study while I was doing their bedtime routine, would be singing a song to them while I splashed them in the bath and thinking about some technical issue of protein sequencing, so that the minute the kids were down I could go straight from kissing them good night to my desk. Carrie used to sleep for an hour each morning after breakfast when she was an infant, and in that hour, I would sit Adam in front of the television and write frantically or read research papers. Sometimes, I would catch myself in one of these phases and allow myself this thought, nothing more smug or extreme than this: *I can do this. Look at me, managing.* When the children were small, we would often go and visit Guy's mother for Sunday lunch. She died when the children were six and eight, but when they were infants, she liked to do a proper Sunday lunch for Guy and the rest of us and his two sisters, and every time he left the table to change a nappy, the three of them would practically break into the Hallelujah Chorus. Nobody praised me for all the combining I did, all the juggling. I never asked for praise. I took my own competence for granted as much as anyone else.

I wasn't vulnerable to you, to what I did with you, because I had fallen out of love with Guy. I was weary, and if I fell out of love with anything it was with that competence of mine. I fell out of love with myself.

I suppose there are two types of adulterers; the repeat types, and the one-offs. I fall into the latter category. I would never have had an affair if I hadn't met you. It was one of those one-in-a-million chance events, like happening to cross the road at the very minute that the white van comes round the corner and the driver is distracted by a phone call. For those of us who are one-off adulterers, it comes at a crucial time in our marriages and is, in fact, more about the marriage than the affair. Afterward, our shame and guilt are so deep, we can feel nothing but craven gratitude toward the spouse we have betrayed, for still being there.

You fall into the other type, I know that now, the serial adulterer.

Serial adulterers would have been unfaithful whomever they had married, although they may kid themselves otherwise. Their affairs are nothing to do with their marriages. They are something they need to do, because they can't bear life otherwise. On the face of it, the serial adulterers' way of operating may seem more reprehensible than mine, but in fact they are likely to be better at deceit and less likely to explode a perfectly decent marriage because of the thrills they experience elsewhere. Morally, there is no difference. I know that now.

I do not know anything about your marriage. I do not know how you conducted the ordinary part of your existence. My only guess is that you managed to lead a double life in the true sense of the phrase. At home, in Twickenham (of all places), you were, actually, ordinary. You and your wife watched television together and shared the housework. You occasionally had irritable words about whose turn it was to renew the tax disc on the car, just like me and Guy. And then there were the affairs, the almost back-to-back affairs. You could not have remained married were it not for the affairs, and the stability of your home life made the affairs possible—neither would exist without their inverse. Your life was bound to this exhausting game of Ping-Pong, back and forth, from one way of living to another. You had become so addicted to the adrenaline of this existence that you no longer knew how to live without it.

And after the imagined drama that made our daily lives bearable, we got a real drama, more of a drama than we could handle, and then we wanted our daily lives back, but they didn't exist anymore. We discovered that safety and security are commodities you can sell in return for excitement, but you can never buy them back.

I wonder what will happen when you are released from prison. Will you get your life back? I don't think so, somehow. Your wife didn't seem like the forgiving sort, and who could blame her? Will you contact me then? Will we meet? Will we be shocked at how middle-aged and ordinary we both are? I don't know. All I know is how Guy and I are managing now.

We love each other. I know that much.

———

Slowly, our lives return to normal. Guy goes back to lecturing. Adam stays with us but says he is going to look for somewhere to rent. He's thinking of moving to Crouch End. He's got a friend there who plays keyboards. Crouch End is a lot nearer than Manchester. Crouch End I can live with. My probation officer, an Irishwoman in her midsixties, encourages me to get out of the house a bit more. She says I am doing the right thing, taking it slowly, but it's time to start looking forward. Have I considered what job I might do now? No, I have not considered that. I wonder if one of the local cafés or shops might take me.

About a month after I was released from prison, I found myself alone for the day and, without really thinking about it, decided to take a Tube journey up to town. If I had thought it through, I wouldn't have done it, but I knew that, sooner or later, I would find myself in the Borough of Westminster, and I didn't want it to be by accident. I wanted to go there on purpose, so that I wouldn't be ambushed. The Beaufort Institute, the Houses of Parliament, Embankment Gardens—I thought I would allow myself one visit there, to see if I could spot the ghosts of ourselves at that time, as if I might bump into us, walking arm in arm along the river or sitting in a café together with our knees pressed tight beneath the table. *Do it once*, I thought, *then let go*.

I didn't go straight there. I did other things first, as if I could fool myself my pilgrimage was accidental. I did some shopping at John Lewis and then drifted down Bond Street peering through the open doors of the empty designer shops, glancing at the few black items hung on sparse chrome rails, the occasional immaculate assistant standing very still—and then, I swear, hardly thinking about it at all, I kept wandering south and crossed Piccadilly not far from the Royal Academy, where I glanced across at the entrance and decided I didn't fancy the exhibition, and considered abandoning the whole idea of this trip and going straight to Piccadilly Circus Tube, but instead I walked down Church Place, for no reason other than that it is pedestrianized and I felt like getting away from the traffic.

And then I was there. I had tricked myself into being there. I was standing on Duke of York Street, halfway down, looking to the left. It had been alternately sunny and rainy all that week and the sky was a strange yellow and gray color, thick, dark rain clouds bunched together around the sun, the odd bright patch, as if anything could happen at any moment.

The first thing I saw as I approached was that the old blackened building on the corner was covered in scaffolding. Already, half the windows were broken from demolition works on the building next to it—it was clearly next for the ball and chain. The looming office block that used to be there, the one opposite the doorway, was gone already. The blank windows I gazed at while I wondered if anyone was looking out, the sheltering bulk of the thing—it was all just sky, that gray-and-yellow sky. Hoardings had been put up to protect the site and a large sign said in red capitals on a white background: DEMOLITION IN PROGRESS: KEEP OUT. Behind the hoardings, I could hear the roar of the works going on, the mechanical diggers and industrial hammers, the drills, the shouts of the men in hard hats. Then, as I stood there, gazing at the hoarding, I heard a vast grinding noise like an old train creaking into a small station and the arm of a huge yellow digger swung upward and heaved into view above the barrier, giant mouth aloft for a moment before it dived down with a crash. Even though the hoarding was between me and it, the monster, I backed away against the opposite wall.

They are knocking it down, my love, I thought as I stood there. Apple Tree Yard is almost gone. My undoing is undone; it is being dismantled, brick by brick.

I stood and listened to the destruction I could not see. Then I walked a little way down the street, looking for the doorway, the one where you left your DNA inside me. I couldn't work out which one it was. They all looked too shallow—and it was dark that evening, after all. The heat of that moment, the absorption—hard to believe it now, hard to believe I was capable of any of it. Everything looked different in the daylight, and behind me, behind the hoardings, the mechanical diggers, the hammers, and the grinders continued their work, loud and oblivious beneath that gray-and-yellow sky.

And here is my guilty secret, my love. Sometimes at night, I rise. I slip from the bedroom, and Guy turns in his sleep as I do but even if I wake him by leaving the room, he knows better than to rise and follow me. I come here, upstairs, to my study. I plug in the oil-filled radiator and turn on the computer, returned to us by the police after the trial. The small lights on the computer wink as the radiator begins to click and I am dry-eyed, clearheaded, as I open up the folder, *Admin*. There are folders within folders, and more folders still. And eventually I get to *Accountancy*, and, just to be sure, I scroll through each individual document, and sometimes open them all, one by one. I have done this a dozen, maybe twenty times now, and still I cannot stop myself from doing it, these nights. I am looking for something that isn't there. I am looking for the document *VATquery3*, which I began writing more than two years ago, on the night of our first encounter in the chapel in the crypt in the Houses of Parliament, where I recounted what we did beneath the barbecued saints and the drowned saints and the saints in every state of torture. The document doesn't exist anymore. It has been deleted, but not by me. The only person who could have deleted it is my husband. He must have come up here immediately after my arrest, perhaps even while police were in the house. And for him to do that, he must have already known of the file's existence. He was taking a risk in deleting it, protecting me. If he had been caught, that would have made him my accomplice.

I am looking for the file, even though I know it isn't there, but more than the file, I am looking for something else. I am looking for information that was never even on the computer in the first place. I am looking for a fact that would be knowable only if the relationship between a computer and the person operating it could be reversed, if the computer was a large eye watching the individual at the keyboard, recording his or her thoughts or actions. I am sitting, staring at a file that doesn't exist anymore and trying to guess whether or not Guy read it before he deleted it.

I don't write anything anymore. I know better. I scroll through my files until I tire of the task, then close the folder and the folder it is in and the folder that one is in too . . . tucking the documents away for the night as if I am turning out the lights in a school dormitory one by one. Then I lean back in the chair and pull my dressing gown tighter around me and let myself be lulled by the warmth of the oil-filled radiator and the emptiness of my thoughts. It is the small hours of the morning, and I am small in my chair, and a small but painful image comes into my head. It is us. We are lying, half-dressed, sated, in the Vauxhall flat I thought was a safe house but, in fact, turned out to belong to your wife's dead uncle and was waiting to be refurbished and let. We are lying on the bare mattress with the pale heap of the duvet with no cover on it at our feet. The light through the net curtains is tinged with gray but still illuminates too much; it shows every wrinkle and age spot—all the telltale signs of what I really am but at least that's true for you too. It is late September, and in anticipation of the hot October to come, today is surprisingly warm. The room is small and bare. We are lying facing each other, semiclothed, wrapped around each other, entwined. You have one arm across my waist and the other wrapped around my shoulders with the fingers twisted in my hair, holding the back of my head, so my face is pressed into your chest. You are asleep, I think, you've slept and woken and slept again. I am wide awake, breathing in the scent of you, skin, hair, a hint of sweat, the smells of our satedness. I need the loo. I wonder if I move very, very slowly, whether I will be able to unentwine myself without waking you—it's the hand in my hair that prevents that. I lie for a moment, enjoying the weight of your arm on my waist, its heaviness, determination, purpose. Even though my nose is pressed against your chest so close your hair is tickling my nostrils, I am able to smile to myself.

I know that you are not asleep anymore. I say softly into your chest, "Know what I really want . . . ?"

"Mmm . . . ?" you murmur.

"I want you to kill him," I say. "I want you to smash his face in."

You tighten your grip on me, without replying. I push myself in closer to you. After a while, your breathing becomes heavy again.

Eventually, after some time, even though your breathing is still deep and I don't want to wake you, I try, experimentally, to shift a little, to move my head down and slip your fingers from my hair. I tip my head back ever so slightly to look at your face as I move.

You don't even open your eyes. You frown slightly. The arm across my waist pulls me into you, tightens its grip, the hand in my hair moves its fingers, reasserts itself. "I don't think so . . . ," you murmur.

I smile to myself as we twine a little tighter. I am smiling at my folly, at yours. We both know that I could get up if I wanted to, that it is a game we play, this claiming you like to do, a game that flatters us both. For a few minutes more, we will pretend—I am yours and you are mine, and neither of us has any choice in that, and if we have no choice then we have no responsibility either. If we are the victims of our desires, our overwhelming desires, then none of this is our fault, is it? No one will get hurt. We are free from shame, from guilt. We are innocent.

ACKNOWLEDGMENTS

This book in its current form would not have been possible without the access I was allowed to a murder trial at the Central Criminal Court, Old Bailey, during the summer of 2011. I am greatly indebted to Judge Stephen Kramer for giving me special permission to sit in the well of the court, to Lorna Heger of the Crown Prosecution Service for applying for that permission on my behalf, and to Detective Sergeant Mark Whitham for introducing me to Lorna. I would also like to thank Detective Inspector Nick Mervin and all the officers on his Murder Investigation Team for the coffees and sandwiches and endless patience with my questions. Thanks are also due to Vincent Zdzitowiecki of Police Operations at the Palace of Westminster, to Dr. Sarah Burge of the Wellcome Trust Sanger Institute, to Dr. Ruth Lovering of University College London, and to Glenn Harris of 33 Bedford Row Chambers. I hope all of the above will forgive the moments in this novel when I have bent factual details to my own purpose—or plain got things wrong. Thanks are also due, as ever, to my agent, Antony Harwood, and my editor Sarah Savitt.

I am, yet again, deeply indebted to the Arts Council England for their support of this book.

A Note About the Author

Louise Doughty's novel *Whatever You Love* was short-listed for the Costa Book Award and long-listed for the Orange Prize for Fiction. Doughty is the author of several other novels and a book of nonfiction, *A Novel in a Year*, based on her hugely popular newspaper column. She also writes plays and journalism and broadcasts regularly for BBC Radio 4. She lives in London.